Oh, Gulliver!

Oh, Gulliver!

Mary Burton-Gulliver's Diary and Her Memoir of Gulliver's Travels

Part One
Mrs. Gulliver and the Secret of Size

by
Erga Netz

Tough Poets Press
Arlington, Massachusetts

Front cover photo by Ole Steen Hansen
Back cover photo by Ofir Abe

ISBN 979-8-218-14890-4

Tough Poets Press
Arlington, Massachusetts 02476
U.S.A.

www.toughpoets.com

Oh, Gulliver! is dedicated to the memory of
Izzy (Isidore) Abrahami, my brilliant friend and colleague.
We shared our lives and work for 25 years.
Izzy'le died on April 1st, 2013, and in his last years,
when work didn't come easy,
I could still lift up his spirits with each new chapter of
Oh, Gulliver!
Thank you, Izzy'le.

From left to right: Mrs. Mary Burton-Gulliver, Lemuel Gulliver, Betty and Johnny.
Artist: Thomas Morten, 1865

Contents

spied upon; he is making good progress learning Lilliputian, which he uses to beg for his freedom; the first conditions are set out.

trips; the Empress's lust turns into wrath, but Lemuel is blissfully unaware of all the plotting against him.

A Preface to the Preface

Subversive, rebellious, quirky—*Oh, Gulliver!* is all about intelligent fun.

Read it and you shall awaken happier.

Oh, Gulliver! is a series of four novels, telling us what really happened to Gulliver on his four voyages, all the delicious stories he secretly whispered to Mary, his wife, at night.

Mary wrote all those stories down, and candidly chronicled her own adventures. Realising that this was considered pornography, which would get Gulliver the death penalty, all the saucy details were omitted from the final *Gulliver's Travels* and Mary hid all those pages carefully in a secret drawer.

The story goes that, recently, these pages were discovered by a university professor of "Gender Studies in the 17th–18th centuries." This woman, who prefers to remain anonymous, translated Mary's memoir into current spoken English, added footnotes to explain the background of Mary's era, and gave the manuscript to me, believing for some reason that I'd be the right woman to unleash Mrs. Gulliver's secrets on the world.

I think she's right.

And I feel that now, more than ever, it is important to look at the world through Mrs. Gulliver's sensual and quirky perspective.

Check it out for yourself!

E.N.

The Preface

I too, come from a long tradition of dealing with problems by avoiding having to deal with them. And that is why I took up solitary hiking in Wales. It was my last attempt to save my marriage.

I always thought that a relationship, a love relationship, was a mysterious miracle when it happened, and my three years of marriage hadn't shed any new light on this mystery. It was complicated when we tried to talk about it, and not any better when we tried to pretend that we had no problems. Jealousy, impatience, vanity, vulnerability, overwhelming urges, and vengeance seemed to be ruling us, as we were drifting towards and away from each other. And it all escalated when we fell to discussing politics.

So, the option of going for a lonesome hike in the mountains didn't seem to be all that bad. I hoped that the distance, the absorbing physical activity, and the clear air might refresh my views on love and life. All the while, as I embarked on this journey into remote regions of my mind, I was trying hard not to contemplate what my husband might be doing while I was up on the mountains, and with whom.

It wasn't such a bad idea after all, thanks to the wondrous chance discovery of this astonishing manuscript, which I found while I was collecting campfire wood.

It was hidden in a drawer, masterfully camouflaged at the underside of a wobbling table which I spotted near an abandoned barn. As I was hacking this table into campfire logs, I discovered a concealed compartment and was startled to see that it contained hundreds of yellowed handwritten pages, dated from 1699, along with some newspaper clippings from that period, almost crumbling—of course—and even a few faded, crude, mind-boggling *erotic* drawings!

That was the end of my holiday. Instead of hiking I set my tent inside that abandoned barn and spent the rest of the summer mesmerized by those pages.

* * *

This 300-year-old manuscript was a gift from heaven, not because it so directly related to my PhD work and my professional life, but, strangely enough, because of its relevance to my private, marital life.

It took me some time to decipher what it was but, when I did, I was blown off my feet. What bizarre fate brought this unique manuscript to me? How did it know that I had dedicated my academic life to study the issues of gender in the 17th and 18th centuries!?

These pages were a genuine 18th-century diary, written between 1699 and 1748 by one Mrs. Lemuel Gulliver, *née* Mary Burton. Though she lived and wrote some 300 years ago, her impudence was as fresh as could be. I found myself blushing as I read her memoirs and, I must be frank about it: I was even occasionally aroused.

As I was reading Mary Burton-Gulliver's memoirs I was astonished, realizing that she was intending to publish them! Not because of the incidental sexual nature of it (other "pornographic" works have been published, banned, and clandestinely circulated for centuries before). No, I was surprised because, in her correspondence with the publisher, one Mr. Richard Sympson Junior, she insisted on using her own name: the name of a woman! This would have certainly been a first, since women simply didn't do that at the time.[1]

Well, she was a brave woman, that's for sure. Her feats would make Lara Croft[2] green with envy of her incredible adventures in Brobdingnag, the land of the giants. Reading in Mary's heroic memoir about all the obstacles she had to overcome 300 years ago left me dumbfounded and quite often even sceptical.

But it was all there, written clearly in plain English, full of details and facts that I could easily research and check.

And it all really happened!

Remarkably, this manuscript has more than just historical significance for us. Undeniably, what Mary wrote 300 years ago seems to be ever so relevant to our world today, not only her sly and witty observations regarding politics and society, but also her views on love and marriage.

I took the liberty to do some "translating" of Mary's text to contemporary English. I added notes[3] wherever I felt some explanation and background information about life in the late 17th, early 18th century might be needed. I hope the impatient reader will forgive me for this. Anyway, you can always skip these notes.

* * *

Of course, I was familiar with Jonathan Swift's *Gulliver's Travels*, but this manuscript, written by Mr. Gulliver's own wife, sheds new light and exposes shocking facts about the tame version which was published in England in 1726. That's why I took it upon myself to share Mary Burton-Gulliver's legacy with the world. It took me several years, a few maceanats,[4] and some residencies, to work on the manuscript, and after a good number of rejections from sceptical agents,[5] I am ever so grateful to Rick Schober and Tough Poets Press for recognizing the moral, humane, and financial values of *Oh, Gulliver!*

From now on, you can embark on the most bizarre adventures of Lemuel Gulliver, as the masterful pen of his wife, Mary Burton-Gulliver, reveals in uncensored detail.

I guess not many people know who these people—Lemuel and Mary Gulliver—were. Today our "Bread and Game" consist of reality television, Facebook, Twitter, YouTube, Instagram, TikTok, and the like, so hardly anyone cares for novels, let alone novels that were written 300 years ago.

You might recall *Gulliver's Travels* as the story you read when you were a child, about the giant among the tiny people of Lilliput—and you would be right.

Clever publishers realised that this portion of Gulliver's story befits toddlers' minds. But there is more, so much more, to Gulliver's adventures. So much so that even he censored himself when he first published the memoirs of his four amazing sea-voyages.

So, if you've never read the full *Gulliver's Travels*, let me enlighten you:

Lemuel and Mary got married in 1688 and lived in London's Old-Jewry until Lemuel Gulliver, a surgeon, encountered professional difficulties and therefore decided to go to sea, as a ship-surgeon.

He had some very fantastic voyages in the next twenty-five years (1690–1715), of which he wrote in his *Travels* book.

He tells about Lilliput, an island on which he was cast in 1699, where everything was one-twelfth the size of our world, but Egos and Eros were twelve times as inflated;

Brobdingnag (1702), where everything was twelve times as big as in our world, but vice, lust and corruption were just the same as ours: huge;

Laputa (1706), a flying island, hovering over Balnibarbi, both being communities of logic-defying scientists working in collaboration with mad rulers. Uncannily recognisable today, right? From Balnibarbi he continued to Luggnagg, where he met with celebrity ghosts and suicidal immortals;

and, finally, in 1710 his travels brought him to Houyhnhnms, a land inhabited by noble horses and savage humanoids.

Against all odds (and not least due to the mind-boggling courage of his loyal, loving wife) he always managed to return safely from all these dangerous voyages and, in 1726, he published his *Travels into several Remote Nations of the World, by Lemuel Gulliver, first a surgeon, and then a captain of several ships* (somehow neglecting to mention his wife's role in his rescue. Well, you know, men . . .) Following the commercial success of the book, it was republished eight years later, this time using the pseudonym of Jonathan Swift.

A colleague of mine, a Professor of History from Stanford University, pointed wisely to the syntax of Swift, who by now is considered one of the great stylists of the English language.

Gulliver, nowadays known as Swift, handles irony via syntax (said my colleague) with small inflections of the voice that carry the sense that you say X but what you do not understand is that your meaning is Y. But in his wife's writing, noted my colleague, this irony is mostly lacking, and this is once again something that puts the lady in a weak position vis-à-vis the voice of the husband. And indeed—I agree with my colleague—historically, Mary Burton-Gulliver was not the only woman to lag behind her husband. (This might explain the saying: "Behind every successful man there's a woman ogling for glory.")

Now that I discovered Mary's diary, I can confirm that Lemuel omitted many, many details of his adventures and quite often he twisted the truth.

In his defense I must add that he probably thought that in doing so he was protecting himself, his wife, and his children.

But judging by Mary's memoir, she was above and beyond fear.

Though she started out as a timid young woman, in the course of her turbulent life, she evolved to become an incredibly brave and resilient woman. She even dressed as a man in order to save her husband, facing horrid dangers and overcoming them all. No wonder Lemuel loved and adored her (at least until he became mad) and confided in her all the saucy details of his own adventures.[6] We're lucky today that he told his wife so much more than what he committed to paper, and we're so fortunate because she was brazen enough (or licentious enough) to write it all down.

And 300 years later, fate brought me to this precious manuscript, which I saved from a horrible fate of auto-da-fé!

There were some events, which Mary was not intending to publish, being the responsible person that she was, but I think that 300 years on, there's no danger that publishing the complete history and secrets of Mrs. Gulliver's would harm anyone. I myself feel no scruples sharing this story with 21st-century readers. In 300 years, people haven't changed a bit. We all share the same wishes, dreams and desires. The ever-expanding means of sharing information only make us realise how similar we are to each other.

Hopefully this realisation will sink in deep enough so that politicians will not be able to divide and rule us anymore. Hopefully, greed will stop ruling the rich when they come to the same conclusion: One We Are.

Notably, Mary Burton-Gulliver had that same inkling 300 years ago. I have much admiration not only for her observations, but also for the way she weaved together her memories and diary entries. She made a clever mix of times, which allows for a clear reading of her story. She was also so wise as to tell her husband's memories exactly as he told them to her, without any interference on her part. (At first I was mind-boggled by her open-mindedness, but then it opened my mind, too. And if you can open up to it too, it will un-boggle you as well.)

Well, if any story is worthwhile reading in the 21st century, it must be this revealing, candid and uncensored retelling of Gulliver's travels, 300 years on.

Sit back, hold tight, and enjoy the ride!

Lemuel Gulliver, from the frontispiece of the first edition of *Gulliver's Travels*, printed for Benj. Motte, at the Middle Temple-Gate, in Fleet Street. It was drawn by his wife, Mary Burton-Gulliver, since, by that time, Gulliver was so mad, he wouldn't allow anyone else to see him. Note that she was about 50 years old when she discovered her drawing talents![7]

My Dear Mr. Richard Sympson Junior,

Your visit last week touched me deeply.[8] I apologize again for refusing to see you at first, but after you saw the conditions in which I live, an old, sick, and lonely woman, I hope you understood and forgave me.

I also hope you recovered from your bad fall and that you haven't broken any limb when you slipped in my yard.

My abode was not maintained for the last 33 years since my late husband (your father's cousin) retired to live with his horses. Ever since Mr. Gulliver died four years ago, his horses took to strolling dejectedly in the yard. I can see that they are inconsolable to this day. They either do not mind trotting in their own excrement or, despite being as intelligent as Mr. Gulliver took them to be, they are still incapable of collecting their own shit.[9]

I sure mind all this dirt, but I cannot keep up, all alone, with the pace of their metabolism.

I reassure you, good sir, that I was not offended by the smell of your clothes after your fall, and I am glad you came with your private Landau, so you need not have suffered peoples' disdain upon your return.

And finally, I am truly sorry I could not oblige your request for more of my late husband's memoirs. I appreciate you taking over your father's publishing trade, and I am sure you will fare well, even without another voyage story of Gulliver's.

The reason for my refusal is that, sadly, he did not travel anywhere after he moved in with his horses, and he didn't write a single word since. All those years he preferred conversing with his horses and, in fact, he almost entirely forgot his English.

Truth be told, I must confess that it was I who actually wrote the last chapter of his book. Your father entreated me to do so, to enable the publication of *Gulliver's Travels*. My poor Lemuel never knew it, and probably would not have cared, as he only valued the opinion of his horses. To be on the safe side, I did make sure the horses would not chance to see the books. As much as I doubted Gulliver's claim that they were intelligent beasts, I took no risks. I had more than enough of his wrath—and never enough of his love.

But enough about me.

Coming back to your predicament: You told me that you must have another best-seller, or your publishing house will be bankrupt . . .

So, YES, I *can* save you!

I can now offer you something even better than another travel story of my husband's!

Yes, indeed!

I have resolved to let you publish *the whole truth* about Mr. Gulliver's voyages, including each and every intimate detail, which he only shared with me!

More than that, I wish to make known the whole truth, all the facts and details concerning my own contribution to saving the Lilliputians. And I want the world to know that it was I who saved Mr. Gulliver from his giant foes!

Forgive my insolence, but I am fed up with this discrimination and I do think that we women should fight for our rights; we should be recognised as equals, at long last![10]

So, this is what I can offer you:

After Mr. Gulliver passed away, I began collecting all my notes and diaries, which I started writing when I was 27 years of age. It was indeed a mammoth mission, reading and re-writing this profusion of pages I accumulated over 49 years . . . I embarked on this to distract myself from my pains, both the physical and the emotional. Reminding myself of my youthful, brave, and lustful past helped me forget my lonely, timid, repulsive present. Strange: even though I did not speak with my husband for almost 20 years, to this day I still miss his silence.[11] I guess I always nurtured the silly hope that his love for those horses would exhaust itself and he would come back to me. Being the hopeless optimist that I am, I now look forward to our reunion in the afterlife. Unlike him, I am quite confident that there will be no horses there. Perhaps Lemuel will have outgrown this strange attraction for the equine; perhaps he will find my soul appealing again . . .

Reading my memories diverted me from my grief. It almost felt as if I was re-living my long and adventurous life. A year ago I started toying with the idea of actually publishing this as a book, and commenced re-writing and filling-in the gaps to make the story clear. And just as I am about done, lo and behold, you come to visit me, unexpectedly, asking for more of Gulliver's travels!

I see it as an omen, the fact that you appear now when I have resolved to publish the story of my life.

Mr. Gulliver started writing the memoirs of his incredible travels already in 1702, as soon as he returned from his voyage to Lilliput. Being the honest man that he was, he was ready to publish the whole truth. But I urged him to omit all the details about his intimate experiences. He understood my concerns, and we swore to each other never to reveal the full nature of what happened to him there and, later on, what has come to pass—for both of us—in subsequent travels.

But I must confess: I could not resist writing all those stories, secretly, already then . . .

In the long days and even longer nights, when Mr. Gulliver went back to sea, I simply could not help it. I craved him so much. Against my good judgment (as I thought then) I wrote in my diary all that which my husband told me, all that which has happened to us. It gave me solace and, indeed much pleasure during those lonely nights. Today I am ever so pleased that I have written it all down, for now I can present all these collected tales to you!

When you read my story of what has really happened to Gulliver, you will surely agree that, 23 years ago, when your father published *Gulliver's Travels*, it was still impossible to include in it all the stories, which I now offer you to print. Back then we had our safety and reputations to consider, for the sake of our children.

But now that both Johnny and Betty have gone to the New

World, this worry is gone as well. I doubt if they will ever know about it. Surely, they cannot be harmed by the publication of my book, even if my name is on it.[12]

As I was preparing this manuscript for print during the past year, I saw fit to add a number of chapters in which I described the political, religious, and social backgrounds of Mr. Gulliver's intimate adventures in the various lands upon which his fate cast him. Even though these chapters are not of an explicit nature, I feel that this addition is important for the modern reader of 1750, to better understand Mr. Gulliver's predicaments and motives. My husband was one of a handful of Europeans who could testify to the facts of life 50 years ago in those remote regions. I believe no human has visited these parts of the world since. I am very much aware of the political and social implications for which I am now responsible and I can assure you, good Sir, that having committed all of Mr. Gulliver's stories to memory, I chronicled them as accurately as humanly possible. Concerning Brobdingnag, I can testify for myself, as I was fortunate enough to be there and to come back alive, with my beloved husband.

The added chapters on daily life in those remote regions might also help to get the book in its entirety past the scrutiny of the Court's Censor. These are all respectable and acceptable tales, which I carefully inserted among stories of a more licentious nature.

Come to think of it, I do not see why we should fear the Court's fury anymore. After all, the future is now: we live in a modern world, almost halfway through the 18th century. Since the first publication of *Gulliver's Travels*, the world has changed completely. While back in 1702 Lemuel and I feared trial and imprisonment if we published his story with all its delicious details, today books such as *Girls' School*[13] are published here in England, and Mr. John Cleland is making a fortune with his *Memoirs of a Woman of Pleasure* while suffering no legal consequences.[14]

You, as the publisher of my book, stand to gain a lot of money. As for me, I simply need this income. That is why I insist on an advance payment,[15] and on having my name clearly printed on the cover of the book. I do not fear the publicity; in our parish, they think my old age is the reason for my infantility. I am lucky not to be suspected of witchcraft. People cannot understand why I remained loyal to poor Mr. Gulliver all those years when all he cared for was his two horses. After our children packed their families and disappeared on the other side of the ocean, I hardly exchanged a word with any of our neighbours. I think they were sure Mr. Gulliver's disease was contagious and that I got it too. I cannot blame them: nobody understood why I refused to sell the horses when Mr. Gulliver passed away. I know the vicious tongues are sure that I, too, have a special liaison with them. And they think I am mad! Now it is too late to sell the horses, anyway. They are too old for the butcher.

Yes, I readily admit: I do have financial considerations when I offer you, dear Sir, to publish the full and uncensored stories of my late husband's travels. The meager allowance I have of Mr. Gulliver's estate is dwindling; my children are gone and their letters (and money) are far between. I cannot deny my needs. I recognise that as a lonely, old, and ailing woman, my sole protection is in money. That is why I propose that you print on the cover of my book the following text:

> "I beseech you, dear Reader,
> to Recommend my little book to your Friends
> and NOT to Lend it to them!"

You might wonder at the ease with which I break the oath that Mr. Gulliver and I took never to tell these intimate stories. But, as you will eventually understand and agree, I may now feel released from these solemn vows of ours.

It was not plain cowardice that dictated our secrecy. I too was gullible at youth, but Mr. Gulliver had always remained susceptible to what people might think of him (and not only here in England, but also wherever he traveled in the world: in *Lilliput, Brobdingnag,*

Laputa, Japan, and *Houyhnhnms*). He always tried to do the right thing. He believed in authorities; he loved both his Kings, James II and then William the III, even though they loathed each other. Everyone knew that their insurmountable differences made them mortal enemies, but Mr. Gulliver loved and respected them equally, arguing that "all Kings were appointed by our Lord, the same Lord, for us to obey, and for His own mysterious reasons."[16]

I think that this was his downfall: his persistence not to learn anything from his experiences. I must admit that I found his childishness endearing, and from the vantage point of my advanced age, I can share with you my observation that we, feeble women, find it safer to rely upon our own resilience, rather than to depend on our spouses' mental prowess. No offense, dear Sir, but like all men, Mr. Gulliver was very stubborn. I cannot convey to you all the sufferings I endured while tending to him during his last years of lunacy. He was a changed man and he treated me abominably. Though he is dead for four years now, I still shudder when I remember how he abused me during the last years of his life. So I feel no moral obligation towards the creature he had become following his last trip to Houyhnhnms.

For example, it is with horror and pain that I recall how in one of his bursts of rage against me, when his mind fell victim to hallucinations and lies, he screamed and cursed me, claiming that I too was a despicable *Yahoo.*[17] On another incident, his malice towards Master Bates, who was his tutor and patron when Gulliver learned the medical trade, took the better of him. Master Bates, who beseeched my father to marry me to Gulliver; Master Bates, the man I alternatingly thanked and cursed all those years, for beseeching my father to marry me to Gulliver . . . On that incident of lunacy, when I tried to calm Gulliver with my words and deeds of love, Gulliver reciprocated with screams: "You're just like Master Bates," yelled my poor, crazy husband. "He masturbates all the people he can get his right hand on, while he uses his left hand on himself!"

I was shocked, too.

Yes, in the course of 57 years of marriage, I witnessed my husband's metamorphosis from a gentle, loving man, to a raving lunatic. I cannot help but love the good man for whom I long, but I abhor the monster he turned out to be.

Therefore, as I was collecting my diaries and assembling this book, I found it so difficult to re-write the story of my life, taking into account all the hindsight, which by now I have acquired. So, dear Sir, when you read this manuscript, you will be joining my journey of outgrowing the blind innocence I still possessed when I first applied ink to these pages, being 27 years of age. Just as I did, you too will gradually learn all that which I know now.

I trust that you, as perhaps the last living relative of my late husband, will undertake to publish my book. Your father, may he rest in peace, benefited much from publishing *Gulliver's Travels* and I am confident that you will gain as much, and perhaps even more, by publishing my own memoirs.

Yours Sincerely,

Mary Burton-Gulliver
Redriff, Tuesday, October 28th, 1749

Mary Burton's Diary and Her Memoir of Gulliver's Travels

Part One
Mrs. Gulliver and the Secret of Size

Chapter One

THE SAD LIFE OF THE MARRIED-WIDOWS-OF-THE-SEA;
HOW THE AUTHOR PASSES HER DAYS WHILE HER HUSBAND IS
AT SEA; THE REASONS SHE DECIDED TO WRITE A DIARY.
(Wapping, Wednesday, May 6th, 1699)

Being married is fine, but being married to a ship-surgeon hardly feels like being married at all. We last saw our Papa[18] two days ago, as we were waving our good-byes at port. The *Antelope* was carrying him away from us, and we were all in tears. As I was hugging my sobbing children, I couldn't help shed tears as well. Will we ever see him again? Will my poor children still have their father when they grow older?

I sometimes lament the misfortunes of my children, having a father who is in love with the sea and with adventure more than he loves his family. But, on the other hand, I am fortunate to have my two surviving children to comfort me and to fill up my days with cherished duties. I might consider myself lucky not to be heavy with child every year like my neighbours, the shopkeepers' wives. But, on the other hand, while my man is at sea for the next two years or so, I have no one with whom to share my bed.[19]

I am a dexterous worker and my chores are quickly done. What better way to fill up my lonely hours than to write the story of my life? Not that there is much to tell but, perhaps, if I will start writing, something exciting, surprising, titillating, shaking might happen to me.

Chapter Two

THE AUTHOR GIVES SOME ACCOUNT OF HERSELF AND FAMILY;
HER YOUNGER YEARS, LEARNING SECRETLY TO READ AND WRITE;
HER AFFECTION FOR THE OLD TESTAMENT AND HER SECRET
PLEASURES WHILE READING SOLOMON'S SONG OF SONGS;
THE AUTHOR IS GETTING MARRIED.
(Wapping, Thursday, May 7th, 1699)

My father, Edmund Burton, was a rather successful hosier[20] in Newgate Street. His success was mostly due to his close friend, the famous surgeon Master James Bates. I was his second daughter (of my father, not of Master Bates). Apart from Stella, my eldest sister, and myself, all six sisters of mine died before they reached their first year. My father had no sons, a fact that deeply grieved him, and for which he resented and blamed my poor mother all her life, and even after her death in childbirth.[21] It was a daughter again. The poor baby was born dead, and our mother died shortly after, too. Perhaps of shame.[22]

Stella and I were not allowed to study further than the writing of our names, but our mother still remembered her grandmother's stories about the time of Queen Elizabeth I,[23] when all girls were allowed to study (if their fathers so wished). My mother learned reading and writing from her own mother—secretly—and she passed these secrets on to us. I was faster than my sister in learning to read, and that, I think, was the core reason for the resentment my sister always felt towards me. I guess my bragging did not help either. Our mother taught us to read the Bible whilst making us pledge never to reveal this to our father. It is possible that Stella became so religious because of her difficulties in reading.

The three of us were much amused whenever our father would

pompously recite King James I's famous saying: "To make women learned and foxes tame, has the same effect: to make them more cunning."

We knew full well how right he was!

Having learned to read the Bible, I soon got to the best part of it, which I read over and over again, well hidden from sight. The Song of Songs of Solomon gave me many secret pleasures. Reading verses such as: "I rose up to open to my beloved; and my hands flowed myrrh, and my fingers sweet smelling myrrh, upon the handles of the lock"[24] always caused my slit to get wet, and as I sneaked my hand down to my still locked treasure, I read on: "I charge you, O daughters of Jerusalem, if ye find my beloved, that ye tell him, that I sick with love. His head the most fine gold, his locks bushy, black as a raven." My fingers would caress my own raven-black bush, as I tried to breathe quietly, and I read on: "Where is thy beloved gone, O thou fairest among women? Where is thy beloved turned aside? That we may seek him with thee. My beloved is gone down into his garden, to the beds of spices, to feed in the gardens, and to gather lilies." I imagined how King Solomon would go down on me, to my own garden of spices, to feast and feed in it, and my happiness was complete.[25]

In this pleasant (and secret) way I spent my tender years at my father's home, helping in his business, sorting out wool and knitting dexterously, alongside my mother and sister. We were all quite good at it and thanks to my father's close friendship with Master Bates we never lacked clientele, as Master Bates would commend to his patients to buy their foot garments only from my father. The famous surgeon and my father were childhood mates and kept their friendship throughout their lives, even though my father was but a simple hosier. My father would always say that "Master Bates is our benefactor." He spoke about Master Bates with much affection and admiration, so we were always perplexed why our father never wanted us to meet our benefactor. Up until my wedding day, I never set eyes on this good man!

My mother died a few months before my wedding. Stella was already married, and a mother herself, and my father was keen to have me off his hands as quickly as he only could. I felt the same. Hosiery has never been my passion.

I remember that fine day when my father told me that I was to wed a sea-surgeon. I had mixed feelings about marrying a sea-farer, but then I heard that my future husband was called Lemuel Gulliver. I was to wed a man called Lemuel![26] All my fantasies were to materialise! It was too good to be true, I thought. And then my father told me that, upon advice of Master Bates, Lemuel was to quit the seas, establish a surgeon-shop on land, and marry me!

I was lucky (so I gullibly thought) that Stella, my elder sister, was already married (to Mr. Owen Lavender Jr., my father's apprentice. My father wanted to keep the business within the family[27]). Had Gulliver been back from the Levant three years before, my father would have given my elder sister to him!

I did manage to sneak a peek at my future husband when he came to negotiate the dowry[28] with my father and, oh, was I happy to see that he was indeed a handsome man! Not yet 30 years of age, he showed no sign of the Plague[29] and looked quite healthy. You may say what you wish about the dangers of sea-voyage, but you must admit that it tans the men magnificently, tones their muscles, and lands them a confident, manly posture. I was smitten. My mother would have been so proud and happy for me, marrying a surgeon! I was enamored, pleased and hopeful that my husband's respectable profession would guarantee long and healthy life for my children and me. (Stella, by the way, still is healthy and happy, living in our childhood house in Newgate Street, with her Owen Lavender Jr. and their eight surviving children. More than I can say about my poor self.)

But back in 1688, when we first met, Lemuel was indeed a ravishing man, 27 years of age, while I was a fresh maiden of sixteen.[30] The age difference did not really bother me, seeing that Master Bates blessed our union.

Later, Lemuel told me that, when he was a seventeen-year-old bound apprentice to Master Bates, he was immediately liked by the entire household including, of course, Master Bates himself. Lemuel was ever the polite, gentle, and obliging type. I did not have an inkling, of course, what life had in store for me, so I was much pleased to be the chosen one for Master Lemuel Gulliver, and by no one other than the good Master Bates.

Stella was already giving suck to her first baby and heavy with her second, so she was in a position to tell me all about marital life. Still, I was hoping that my marriage would be more Biblical than hers and, yes, was I ever looking forward to my first night with Lemuel, my own King Solomon!

Chapter Three

THE AUTHOR'S FIRST HAPPY YEARS AS A MARRIED WOMAN;
HOW SHE LEARNED TO LOVE AND TRUST HER HUSBAND;
HER HUSBAND LEARNS TO LOVE AND TRUST HER, TOO,
WHEN SHE GIVES HIM A SON.
(Redriff, Wednesday, November 6th, 1748)[31]

Chapter Four

I dreamt about Lemuel. It has been so long since I last saw him in my dreams. In the beginning, I dreamt about him so often. In my dreams, he always loved me. I miss him awfully. And tonight, Lemuel appeared again, begging me not to forget him. I dreamt that I was crying and woke up sobbing bitterly. With trembling hands I reached for the tinderbox,[32] lit up the candle and fetched my notebook. Suddenly I was overcome with the conviction that only if I resumed writing about him would Lemuel survive the sea and come back to us.

Oh, I know it is a silly, childish notion, but what do I care. Usually, if I cannot fall asleep, I read my Bible for a while, arouse and dive into my ocean of joys. But tonight, as if I am possessed, I feel I must write about my love, my Lemuel, or else . . . Yet, I am aware how preposterous this idea is. Well, anyway, no one will ever read these words, so now, feeling so vulnerable and lonely, I just give in to this superstition, this figment of my fragile mind.

Usually I am a strong woman. In all these years that Lemuel was sailing away, I discovered I was even stronger than I ever thought I was. So, very soon after I started writing my memoir I felt embarrassed about it: what do I have to tell? My life is a series of happenings which happen to all the women I know. Like all wives of sea-farers, I live the life of a "married-widow." Of the fourteen years of my marriage, I spent a total of no more than five years with my husband. The rest of the time he was away at sea. Whenever he came back—and this miracle did happen twice—I beseeched him to stay with us and try to recover his surgery trade, but he would not comply. The sea and far, strange lands attracted him in a mysterious way. That was the real reason we removed from the Old-Jewry[33] to Wapping. Lemuel said he hoped to get business among the sailors, but I think he just wanted to be near the sea, and close to seamen.

"Indeed," I told him, "what business could you expect from sailors? Those who return are healthy enough not to have died of scurvy, and those who died at sea do not need you anymore."

He did not heed my words. We hardly had any income and, rather than remove back to the Old-Jewry and back to profitable land-diseases, Lemuel was determined to go back to sea. He said it was out of financial considerations that he was leaving us. He figured that Johnny, Betty and I could live on the God's pennies,[34] and if his voyage would be successful, he would return a very rich man.

If, if, if.

It was a good plan but, like so many other good plans, it did not work out. Now we do not even have a grave to visit. My poor Lemuel's remains are somewhere at the bottom of the ocean.

We gave up all hope of ever seeing any of the *Antelope* crew two years ago. I swallowed my pride, put on the badge, and the three of us commenced surviving on the little pension I got from the Almshouse.[35] I am a very good sock mender, and thus I supplement our meagre needs. But I would happily starve if this would bring him back. Oh, I miss him so much! I do not think any woman has ever loved her man as much as I loved my Lemuel. When I close my eyes, I can still revive his warm embrace and I swoon from his masculine scent just as I did fourteen years ago, on our virgin night . . .

My man was an honest surgeon. He worked hard. Well, whenever work was coming. He was a good father, not just providing for his babies, but also educating them. We decided early on that we would teach all our children to read and write, though we realized we would have to keep it a secret in the parish. We were a good team,

Lemuel and I, caring for our children during the day and loving each other at night.

It took some time for me to trust him. I loved him too much and was so fearful of losing his love. I could not bear seeing him talking to our neighbour women, I was so jealous. But, of course, I did not say a word to him, I was much too proud. Was I ever surprised when one night—we were but a few months married then—Lemuel, regaining his breath after his sweet joy, whispered in my ear: "Will you always love me, Swifty?"

"Of course I will, BigJon."[36] I said. "How else?"

"I am older than you are. Soon I will be too old, you know, for this."

(It amused me how ashamed he was to speak about lovemaking, while I liked to talk about it so much! But he did approve of my whispered passages from the Bible while we were making love. He saw it as a mark of my modesty.)

"I cannot believe you will ever be too old for this," I laughed, gently stroking his limp Jon. "But, even if, what then?"

"Well," he sighed and bit on my earlobe, "you might be wanting for another man. This would kill me. Please tell me that you will never want another man. Please, Swifty, please, will you promise me? Just say it, will you please, Mary? Say it!"

I was perplexed. I thought: not so long ago I was secretly in love with King Solomon. Now I am a fool for Lemuel. How in God's name can I predict what will happen in the future?

Lemuel seemed to guess my thoughts. "No matter," he said. "Just say it, Love-pie. Let me hear you tell me that you will never leave me . . ."[37]

"Why, of course," I said. "Of course I will always love you!"

And at that instance I suddenly realized something that mystified me to no extent: as easily as I could say that I will always love my Lemuel, I could also tell myself that he will always love me! The future is a mystery in any case, so I might as well live now as if the future will be just as I want it to be!

This was quite a revelation to me, and it instantly eased my mind. I understood that, in order to trust my husband, I must first trust myself. If I were to believe that he will always love me, I must first decide that I will always love him. From that moment on, whenever I saw my Lemuel laughing with any of our neighbour women, I did not conclude that he loved me any less. I could see that each time he succeeded in making a woman smile at him, my darling Lemuel felt so much manlier. As childish as it may seem, proud, grown-up men still need the confirmation of their humbled wives that badly.

In many ways, I was much stronger than he ever was. Well, much good it does me now, knowing that. Now, alone, when I have my two surviving children to raise and protect, I feel as weak and lost as I felt when he was so adamant on going back to sea, for the third time since we got married.

And for the last . . .

I am too sad and too tired to write on. Tomorrow. I will not neglect my Lemuel any more.

Chapter Five

THE LOSS OF HER CHILDREN DUE TO THE CURSE OF THE SEA,
WHICH THE WITCH COULD NOT LIFT; HER HUSBAND'S
STUBBORNNESS AND HER RESIGNATION TO THE STATUS A
MARRIED-WIDOW; HER CLOSE FRIENDSHIP WITH HER NEIGHBOUR.
(Wapping, Thursday, April 13th, 1702)

I was heavy with our fifth child and, oh, so happy to have my Lemuel by my side! After he came back from the second voyage he took after our marriage, a voyage to the West Indies, we spent three blissful years in each other's arms, with our two surviving children. We were delighted with the impending arrival of a fifth baby. True, Lemuel was struggling to find work as a surgeon, and was stubbornly refusing to join my father's hosiery business, but we compensated for his daily frustrations by nightly celebrations.

I did not see it coming when, without a warning, he announced that he had gotten a post as a sea surgeon on board the *Antelope*, which was due to set sail in a fortnight! I nearly fainted. Our baby was due any day then, and I was aching and terrified of the looming birthing. I beseeched Lemuel to stay with me, to stay with us, and he, crying with me, said, "Swifty, remember what you told me nine years ago, after Master Bates died? You said I was too good a surgeon. You commended me for not imitating the bad practice of too many among my brethren." (Indeed, he could not cheat, my poor Lemuel.) "You said, 'Too bad Master Bates died. He could have recommended you to some ship, like he recommended you to the *Swallow* before we got married.' You encouraged me to go to the West Indies and to the East Indies. 'You like the sea, you like to travel.' That is what you said."

"Yes, I said all that and more," I cried. "I even hoped you would get from the sea some addition to your fortune. But you know, back then I did not know about the curse which is set upon our little family!"

* * *

Even the overwhelming evidence of the curse did not convince him, though it was plain to see. With each voyage he took, another little soul was added to my list of sorrows: James died before he learned to say "Papa," while his father was sailing to the East Indies, and Emma died before she learned to say "Mama," while Lemuel was in the West Indies.

"Look at Betty, our sweet baby," I said. "We are blessed to have her still, grace the fate that your voyage to the West Indies did not prove to be very fortunate. You grew weary of the sea, and intended to stay at home with your wife and family. I was content to remove from the Old-Jewry, where my sister lived but a few minutes' walk away, to Fetter-lane and then even to Wapping, an hour's walk away from my sister, as long as I could have you with me, and as long as I could ascertain the health of our children. Lo and behold, little Betty is now three years old! She says 'Papa' to you, she dotes on you. Have you the heart to desert her now? And me, and Johnny? And the little soul which now grows in my belly? Do you not want to see your new child?"

I am confident that this is what saved our Betty from certain death. Lemuel stayed with us for three blessed years after our Betty was born. But he did not even wait to christen the little soul I named George. Our fifth baby was born two months after his father set sail on board the *Antelope* and, as I despairingly expected, little George did not survive the winter of 1700. The whole while I was carrying this infant inside of me, I was terrified and desperate. Lemuel did not stop lamenting the looming End of the World, which was due on January 1st, 1700. I reminded him of all the previous Ends of the World,[38] but this did not ease his panic. In fact, he was angry with me for not realizing the extent of the danger we were facing! I thought he might be possessed, or under a curse. I do not know it still. But I am sure there was a curse set on my dead babies . . .

It is a horrid curse. Our first boy, Johnny, who is now thirteen, was born one year after our wedding, when Lemuel was a successful surgeon in London, alongside Master Bates. Our second child, James (named after our benefactor, Master James Bates), died in 1692, a few months after Lemuel closed his practice and went to sea aboard the *Stork*. Three years later my Lemuel came back from that voyage, promised to stay, and a few weeks later he was on board the *Fortuna*. Emma was born prematurely five months later, and died at birth.

Betty, our fourth, is the sure proof that evil powers are mercilessly toying with us. She was born soon after we moved from Fetter-Lane to Wapping, three years before Lemuel took to sea, this time never to come back.

Back in Fetter-Lane I had a neighbour, Mrs. Mary-Jane, who was an excellent witch and a handsome lass. Though she passed her youth, her past beauty was plain to see. Mrs. Mary-Jane knew exactly what I should do to keep my man at home. I did it, and it worked. Of course it worked. Mrs. Mary-Jane was a Head Girl in Hogwarts School of Witchcraft and Wizardry. Not many people know that such a school exists, or that those witches and wizards call us "Mucus," but I know, for Mrs. Mary-Jane told me quite a lot about it. I think she fancied me. I was truly bewitched by her. But, then again, she might have put a spell on me.

She gave me clear instructions when to come to her and what to bring along with me. She handed me her vile pipe to smoke and, next thing I knew, I woke up on her bed. It seemed as if night had already fallen because it was so dark. But then I realized that my skirt was covering my face. Pulling it down I felt Mrs. Mary-Jane's arm heavy on my naked belly. Why would my skirt be up on my face, exposing me thus? How much time had gone by, and what had transpired? Mrs. Mary-Jane seemed to be fast asleep, but her fingers were moving, as if of their own accord, circling my belly button.

She was breathing heavily, and her hair, always neatly kept, was now totally dishevelled, as if it had life of its own. I was still drowsy, and though I trusted her to perform miracles with her witchcraft, her Medusa-like hair terrified me. I tried to roll gently away, but Mrs. Mary-Jane, with her magical powers, was instantly awake.

While chanting incantations, she arranged her hair and then gave me a jar bearing the face of Cardinal Roberto Bellarmino[39] and told me to urinate into it. Mrs. Mary-Jane went on chanting while she added Lemuel's nail clippings, hair and some pins, and we both buried it upside-down in her garden.[40] Two weeks later I dug for it, as she instructed me, and when it was not there—just as she predicted—I knew that the magic would work. And, indeed, Betty's birth went smoothly, Lemuel was working as a surgeon at our home in Wapping, and for those blissful three years I was as happy as could be.

I love Betty dearly, for I am afraid she is my last offspring. The witch instructed me that we would have to repeat the magic as soon as I will be heavy with child again, but Lemuel left hastily, before I could collect the necessary ingredients.

It is now two years since our fifth baby, tiny, helpless George died, and the last we heard of Lemuel was eighteen months ago, when Captain Prichard came back home. The sole survivor of the *Antelope*, Captain Prichard told me about the storm that drove the ship off course; about the illness of the men, which my husband could not cure; and about the wind that drove the ill-manned ship on the rock, which split the ship. Captain Prichard told me that, as he was busy with seven of the crew to let down a boat, he did see my Lemuel, along with five of the crew, let down the other boat. That was the last he knew . . .

I cried and cried, and in the days that followed, I took up every excuse to go visit my friend Vanessa, Captain Prichard's wife. Whenever I could, I asked him to tell me again and again about my Love's last moments. And each time he told it to me, I hoped his tale would end differently.

I could not indulge in those stories for too long. Captain Prichard went back to sea; my heartbroken, frightened children needed me more than I needed my grief. Daily chores took over, and Vanessa, sweet Vanessa, my best friend Vanessa, as soon as her husband took back to sea, came to comfort me, as only a loving woman knew how.

We first met on the pier, three years ago, when the *Antelope* took both our husbands away on that fateful voyage. My Lemuel was one of that 32-man crew. Vanessa's husband, Captain Prichard was the only one to come back.

It was a Monday, that fateful May 4th, 1699. The *Antelope* was to sail a day earlier, for the saying goes "Sunday sail, never fail." But for delays in stocking the ship, it only set sail the next day. Silly me: I was so glad to have Lemuel with me for one more night. Had they sailed on Sunday, surely everything would have been different.[41]

But three years ago, on the pier, my three-year-old Betty was crying bitterly in my arms, and my ten-year-old, brave Johnny promised to take care of us, "Until Papa will be back" he said, the poor orphan!

As we walked down the pier, alongside other desolate women, the married-widows-of-the-sea, each with her own crying brood, I noticed her. At first I thought she was a sailor's daughter, since she had no child on her arms. She seemed very young and, indeed, very pretty. She saw my Betty crying and came to her.

"Come, come," she said, "your father will be back home in a couple of years, I promise you!"

My shy, little Betty hid her face in my neck and stopped crying. I smiled to this strange, lovely woman and heard Johnny's voice: "What is your name?"

"Oh, stop it, Johnny," I said, embarrassed.

"Why, let him. I am Vanessa. Vanessa Prichard. And you are Johnny, I presume. So nice to make your acquaintance!"

And that is how we became best of friends.

Vanessa's marriage was not a happy one. She loathed her husband the Captain, who was so much her senior in years. She was glad he was at sea and, unlike me, did not watch for news of her husband's fate. When the months went by and there was no word from the *Antelope*, Vanessa actually grew cheerful, while I did not know where to take my worries. One night, after we made love, Vanessa sighed, "Oh, I wish the *Antelope* would sink, along with our husbands. Then we could stay like this, my love, forever, you and I!"

Well, the *Antelope* did sink along with my Lemuel and all her men—sparing only Vanessa's husband. Such are the bitter, cruel jokes that life plays on us.

I do hope to find a good man, and not a seaman, so that my children will have a father that will care for and protect them. Though I am quite old, already thirty years of age, I am still good-looking (so Vanessa often tells me). Five births have not left much of a mark on my body. My skin is smooth, my breasts are silky and I so much yearn for the touch of a strong man, bringing to our bed the scents of his hard day's work . . .

Until this man will materialise from the mists of my imagination, until I find the right father for my children, I resign to the fate of the widow, protecting my honour and that of my children as best I can. I only pray[42]

Chapter Six

HER HUSBAND SUDDENLY RETURNS FROM HIS SOUTH SEA
VOYAGE; THEIR LOVE REKINDLED; HE WRITES HIS STORY
AND IS CONVINCED BY HIS WIFE TO KEEP THE SECRETS.
(Wapping, Tuesday, April 28th, 1702)

I finally got to write again, tonight, after two weeks of, oh, so much thrill and excitement! I am still swooning from all these events. Little did I know three years ago, when I wrote that something interesting might happen to me should I start a diary, how true this will turn out to be!

Where to begin? Well, two weeks ago, as I was sitting and writing, suddenly my Betty came running home, crying that a strange man was trying to grab her!

I rushed out of the house, ready to tear this man's eyes out of his skull, when that strange man turned out to be my dear, dear Lemuel!

My poor love was thin and dishevelled, but his eyes, his loving eyes pierced my heart all over again. Laughing and crying, I fell on his shoulders. He, hugging me tenderly, so tenderly, cried as well, and Betty joined in with the crying, not knowing what came over me. My son, Johnny, just came back from grammar school, and the clever boy recognised his father right away! It was indeed a fine reunion. Was it three long years since we last waved goodbye? As if by magic, the miserable days and the long, lonely nights evaporated, as if they never existed. And as I laid the table for my family, my whole family, Lemuel swore solemnly never to go back to sea.

And I do believe him. Yes. This time I do, in truth!

The word was out that Mr. Gulliver was back, and many a neighbour came by to congratulate us on his safe return. They all asked him about his rescue, but he would not tell a thing, claiming he was too tired and spent. But was he ever so thrilled to learn that Captain Prichard did survive that fateful storm! When the *Antelope* was lost, my Lemuel told me, he lamented the loss of all the men, confident that only he survived that ordeal.

My cheeks ached from my laughing and smiling, as I watched Mr. Gulliver talking with the guests. But my lips were aching to be alone with him after those three long years of solitude.

At long last the visitors did leave, jeering good-heartedly. Johnny and Betty were fast asleep and Lemuel and I sat there with the kitchen table between us, too happy and too weak to stir.

Lemuel stretched his arm across the table, touched my fingertips ever so lightly, and I felt my body melting. His fingers continued up my arm. I shut my eyes, savouring the waves of sweetness that his touch sent through me. I breathed deeply and inhaled the long-lost scent of my man, my love. His weather-beaten lips pressed onto the surrendering softness of mine. I could taste the sea in his kisses and, for a passing instant, I felt that I loved that sea. I loved everything that ever touched, smelled and saw my husband during those three years of longing. Suddenly, Lemuel was on his knees, his face buried in my lap, crying silently.

"Mary, oh, my Swifty, you are the greatest woman I have known for a long, too long time."

I almost cried of happiness and pride. I was thrilled to grasp that no woman has ever touched him the way I do.

Yes. I knew about the lewd women that sailors ravished at every port, but I also knew that the base lovemaking of those women could never equal the tender loving, which Lemuel and I were sharing. I grew to accept Lemuel's joys with those women. Certainly, when I knew that my Lemuel was safely covering his BigJon with that new invention, the "condum,"[43] to protect me from those women's diseases.

My trust in Lemuel knew no bounds. That night, when our bodies shared their secrets, when Lemuel's BigJon was pounding at my wet shores, coming to port in my warm, soft harbour, I felt we both escaped the clutches of death. We were alive. Oh, so much alive.

Once over, Lemuel collapsed on top of me, made a quick and apologetic move to roll off me, but I hugged him with all my might. I did not want him to get away from my tight embrace. I wanted to keep him next to me, inside of me, forever. Lemuel murmured something that sounded like "Hekina Degul" (but I was not sure) and I whispered in my lover's ear, "Was this indeed your first time since our parting, three years ago?" to which my good man replied, "Swifty, lovepie, my lust, my ever-joy. You are the fountain of my pleasures, the mother of my children; to you I can confide everything. I know you are a good and clever woman. My story is incredible, but I do have the evidence to prove it. I will tell you all, in good time."

Slowly, lovingly, he pulled himself out of me, and I was engulfed by the scent of our lovemaking, filling, I sensed, the whole room, the whole universe.

I presently came out of this reverie, for Lemuel was back beside me, placing some wondrous toys on my bare, ticklish belly. But my laughter soon turned to horrible fright; those toys were moving! Walking, and actually sniffing at my belly, even—I thought—chewing at my hair, way down there! I could hardly suppress my scream—I did not want Johnny and Betty to wake up—but I was terrified. I shrugged these terrifying creatures off of my belly and rolled off our bed as my laughing husband scooped the lot in his palms. Brining his hands nearer my eyes, I saw them: five miniature cows, two bulls, four ewes and two rams!

"How did you perform this magic?" I blathered. Mingled with my fears of Lemuel's new, supernatural powers was the recognition of the usefulness of such an incantation for general transport, commerce and for our personal prosperity!

But Lemuel laughed and commenced to tell me the fantastic story of his voyage to Lilliput, the island where everything was twelve times smaller than our own world. It has been two weeks ago when he started sharing with me these amazing tales, and still, each night, he amazes me after we make love with more and more incredible yet true stories. He did have some astonishing adventures there, many pleasurable experiences, but, oh, the dangers he faced!

I am still sorry he did not bring with him any Lilliputian human. Would that not be an astonishing spectacle? Lemuel told me that actually, one of them, a good friend of his, bearing the strange name of Reldresal, did implore Lemuel to take him along, but my dear, considerate man decided against it, fearing that Reldresal would be very lonesome here, and it would be difficult to protect him from the dangers of our world. My clever Lemuel thought that the English gentry would love to gaze at the Lilliputian creatures and would be willing to pay handsomely for it, and he did not want to expose his dear Lilliputian friend, Reldresal, to such a circus fate.

Lemuel's little Menagerie is indeed a source of marvel to our neighbours and a marvellous source of income for us. Lemuel travels up and down the county, showing his Lilliputian herd to anyone who is ready to part with a penny for a peep. Happily for us, many are such peepers!

Lemuel told me that many a man wanted to know from whence the herd had arrived, and some even offered him huge sums to lead an expedition back to Lilliput, but my Lemuel was loyal to his former hosts (despite the many wrongs that some of them did him!) and he kept the whereabouts of Lilliput a secret.

While Lemuel travels to earn our bread, I spend my days with the children alone again. But at least I have the happiness of Lemuel's sharing my bed at night. Each night he tells me more about his extraordinary voyage to Lilliput, and even teaches me some Lilliputian. It is of great value to us, when we want to converse freely without the children understanding us.

Chapter Seven

AFTER A PERIOD OF MARVELOUS SUCCESSES SHOWING THE
LILLIPUTIAN HERD FOR MANY A PENNY, GULLIVER IS ATTACKED
BY A VILLAIN WHO STABS HIM AND BEATS HIM UP, TRYING TO
STEAL THE MENAGERIE; "OUT OF THE STRONG CAME FORTH
SWEETNESS,"[44] AND LEMUEL DECIDES TO CHANGE THE COURSE
OF HIS LIFE AND EMBARK ON A NEW CAREER.
(Wapping, Thursday, May 11th, 1702)

My fears came true. I told Lemuel to keep his peeping business for the safe boroughs nearby our home, but his ambition took the better of him.

"You see, my Love," he said, "with our treasure here, of five little cows, two bulls, four ewes and two rams, we will soon be invited to Court! Our Royal Highness, Queen Anne herself will marvel at my Lilliputian herd! And with White Spot being pregnant, can you imagine what will happen?"

Our Johnny gave this name White Spot to the prettiest cow, which was stark black, with a single white spot on her forehead. Betty, who caressed and cradled her, as if she was her own baby, wanted to call her Anne, because she seemed so regal. But Lemuel, trembling with indignation and rage, would spank her if she had not come running to hide behind my skirts. Dear Johnny settled the dispute: "We will call her White Spot."

Indeed, White Spot was pretty, and very soon we witnessed some Lilliputian bullfights on her account. It was Lemuel who figured out that they were fighting with each other in order to conquer White Spot. As soon as Betty would pick her up to caress and cradle her, the fighting would subside. Lemuel, with his sharp sense of business, devised a plan of charging the public to watch the fights, and even raise bets, but Johnny remarked that the bulls might kill each other in the process, and thus the venture was put to rest.

But suddenly, the bulls did not seem to be as excited when White Spot was nearby, and presently we found out why: her growing belly gave her away. Were we ever so excited! At first Lemuel lamented that he did not sell tickets for the coupling (God knows when this coupling transpired!) but he was soon full of plans for a public calving. And in order to attract as much public as possible for the miniature birth-spectacle, and in the hope to even be invited to perform the feat in Court (for Lemuel was certain that Our Queen Anne would not want to miss the event) Lemuel started travelling with his menagerie to further boroughs—to my chagrin.

Yes, I was worried. Though I knew that every borough of London was infested by crime of all sorts, and you did not have to travel far to fall victim, I somehow felt safer near home. Well, I am but a woman.

My Gulliver laughed at my fears and took to the roads, and ten days ago he came back home, beaten, stabbed, nearly dead—but he managed to save his Lilliputian herd.

I nearly died myself when I saw him stumbling home. He was smiling triumphantly, and raising high the transport box, perhaps to ease my worries, but I only had eyes for his bleeding and his miserable limping!

He could not tell who the villain was. It was in stark daylight when the stagecoach in which Lemuel was traveling was stopped by a lone highwayman. The other gentlemen were quick to relieve themselves of their purses and goods, except for my Gulliver, who would not give up his box. He nearly died when the bandit stabbed him and was only saved by the approach of a coach of another person of quality, with a good retinue of servants belonging to it. The wicked outlaw galloped away and disappeared as quickly as he arrived.

Traveling back home, Lemuel's companions were nursing his wounds as best they could, while scolding him: "You brainless fool, we were robbed betwixt sun and sun, therefore the county must pay our losses again!" Whereupon my Lemuel let them have a peek, for free, at his Lilliputian herd, and they kept silent in owe for the rest of the trip.

"I had to fight for my property," claimed Lemuel as I admonished him, too, for being so foolish as to risk his life in this manner. "Our herd is priceless," said Lemuel, "and the County could never pay its loss, even if I was robbed in daylight on the highway for which the County vouches to be safe!"

Lemuel recovers well from his wounds and he no longer limps, but his herd suffered lethal blows when the box was violently shaken between the hands of Lemuel and the villain. After White Spot perished while calving prematurely, the rest of the menagerie languished and died, one by one, betwixt sun and sun.

In tears, Johnny and Betty buried the lot in our backyard. Lemuel was too heart-broken to attend in the ceremony. I was crying as I saw the little coffins, which Johnny so cleverly built for each beast, being lowered into the grave. I did insist that one communal grave would suffice, rather than turning our backyard into a graveyard.

I was crying because I was already envisioning my Lemuel taking back to sea now that his source of income died. But last week my Lemuel told me, to my delight, that he has had enough of the sea! He decided to stay with us at home, forever, and to publish the story of his last, final voyage! He was fantasizing how he would present the first volume to Our Queen Anne. With tears of happiness, I agreed with him that telling about his sea voyages and the creatures he thus met might prove to be an even more prosperous proposition than actually showing them around. (And definitely, a better venture than venturing back to sea!)

Given the recent commercial successes of other voyage stories, I am confident that my Lemuel's voyage is much more wonderful than any voyage that was ever put to print, including Sir More's *Utopia*,[45] Sir Bacon's *The New Atlantis*[46] and, more recently, Captain Archibald Wolfhang's *Travels to the Very East*![47]

I plan to read all these books now, while my Love, my Lemuel, sits at the windowsill to commence his memoirs. What a fine, educated couple we make!

Each evening, after I put our children to bed, I read the pages over which Lemuel laboured during the day. And then we make love.

Last night I told Lemuel that he should burn all the pages where he wrote about his adventure with the Lilliputian Lovers, and that he must not mention the full extent of his relations with Reldresal, the Principal Secretary, or with the Lilliputian Empress, and all the rest of it.[48]

At first my dear Lemuel could not grasp my meaning. Having been to sea for so long, in close proximity with such a different culture, he could not fathom the lethal consequences of his publishing his story in full. But finally he agreed, so I expect to read tonight only the memories, which are fit to print, and fit to Our Queen Anne's eyes.[49]

Chapter Eight

Eight days ago, my wretched husband took back to sea, just two months after his miraculous return from Lilliput and his solemn promise to stay with us forever. I am desolate. Two months ago, when he was suddenly back from his voyage, back from the dead, I was so thrilled that our family was re-united, I was sure of prosperity and happiness for my children and myself, I was looking forward to bearing more children . . .

But eight days ago, at the port, as we were waving again our good-byes to Lemuel, my heart was sinking with heavy forebodings. I pressed the little hands of my two surviving children, sensing deep down that my wish for more offspring was doomed. I have little hope of ever seeing my Love again, the sea being so treacherous . . .

At least I am relieved he did not accept Captain John Biddel's sly proposal, to travel back to Lilliput and steal Lilliputian people for show![50]

The Captain came by an evening, two weeks gone, riding his mare from his Deptford home. First, he professed to be mourning along with us the loss of Mr. Gulliver's Lilliputian herd. But then Biddel implored my Lemuel to join him on a lucrative voyage back to Lilliput, to conquer it for the glory of Queen Anne and the prosperity of the conquerors.

"In a normal slave ship" said Biddel "we can pack a few hundred Negros, and we make excellent profit with this merchandize, even if some items expire en route. Imagine how much more money we will make, squeezing into my *Explorer* thousands of those Lilliputians!"[51]

When Lemuel pointed out that the Lilliputians could not slave as well as Negros, Biddel was not discouraged.

"We will sell them for Show! They will make a fortune for their owners in fairs all over the Continent! And in America! Can you imagine this? We will be richer than the King and Queen of England!"

I was in the back yard, transplanting our cabbage, but I could hear all this exchange and Lemuel's reply: "This is sacrilege! No mortal should ever aspire to top his Better, or to enslave his Lesser!"

I must admit, I was proud of my man, and stepped in, intending to plant a kiss on his lips, when I saw Biddel pulling out his pistol. "Perhaps this will convince you?!" he said.

I rushed between my love and the muzzle. "Gro debul i drurr!" I called out to Lemuel, "Advontus gro! Borach pesso gro!"[52]

Biddel was scared out of his wits. He looked at me, terrified, certain that I was mad. Of course, he did not grasp that I was talking Lilliputian. But I could not care less. Biddel's hands fell limp and I was ever so proud of my Lemuel when he threw that Biddel out of our house, pistol and all, calling after him, "Curse on you, Captain Biddel! I will make sure never to set foot on a ship you master! In fact, I will never set foot on ANY ship at ALL!"

And then he deserted me, eight days ago. I'm left to fend for my family all on my own.

As I write this, I am suddenly struck by the thought that perhaps Lemuel did go to sea in order to save us and the Lilliputians, to make sure Biddel cannot force him to set sail and look for Lilliput. Perhaps he took to the sea in order that Biddel will not try to harm us, so he could bend Lemuel to fulfil his sickly whim.

I love my Lemuel all the more for his tender care of the Lilliputians, despite the many wrongs they did unto him. In a true Christian spirit, he was always loyal to them.

But I must be more cheerful. Ships do return ashore every day, laden with riches and brave crew. Indeed, the saying goes that more people die on the streets of London by careless carriage drivers than at sea.

My Lemuel WILL come back. I am sure. And no matter what strange land he would come to, no matter how lonesome he would be, even if he would be relieving his Manly needs with other women or men, he would always be careful to keep me from those women's diseases, for I safely packed his condum, as usual, in his inner, secret fob.[53] And if I should be so lucky to see his loving face again, to feel his warm, strong body pressed onto mine, and his manhood safely perched inside of me, I know he will tell me all about his adventures with other women. Or men, as he did during the past blessed two months, telling me all about his funny, scary, delicious adventures in Lilliput. Oh, Gulliver! your words were ever the fuel of our tender, happy, lustful nights!

But now I am left with just the memories, and as comforting and as pleasurable as they might be, they are no substitute for my Lemuel, my dear, lost again Lemuel.

No.

He will be back!

The last days passed by as if in a heavy haze. I went automatically through the motions of taking care of my little children, but I felt hollow inside.

In the past I used to spend many pleasurable days with my best friend Vanessa, as we were baking our families' bread together or brewing beer, curing bacon, salting the meat, or making pickles, jellies, and preserves; making our candles and soap; spinning wool and linen.[54] We used to make merry together, laughing, talking, telling secrets to each other, and making love. I miss her badly; she still lives in Wapping, while we are here in Redriff.[55]

I have only myself to blame for this separation. I was foolish enough to think that Lemuel would be happy and eager to hear about my lovemaking with Vanessa. After all, he told me all about his lovers, and Reldresal, and the Empress of Lilliput, and all the while, I did not feel the least tinge of jealousy! Why men cannot be more like women?

I thought that, just as much as I was happy to hear of his happiness, he would be happy to hear of mine! I could not foresee the disaster, when he asked me, for the thousandth time, "Swifty," he asked me, "will you always love me?"

"Of course, BigJon." I laughed for the thousandth time.

"You will never take another lover, you promise me, right?"

I was silent. My cheek resting on the dark curls of his manly chest, I thought about Vanessa.

"Will you promise me, Lovepie? Please?"

"There will never be another man," I laughed, "but there is another woman!"

And I told him all about Vanessa.

Lemuel was enraged. He threw a tantrum and forbade me ever to talk to her again. I was flabbergasted. I said, "But why? She is but a woman! And besides, I do not mind your lovemaking adventures. Why do you mind mine?"

"But it is different!" he bawled. "Oh, woman, do you not see the difference?!"

"How is it different?" I truly did not understand.

At that moment Betty ran into our room, crying, "Mommy, why is Daddy angry?"

Lemuel did not even look at her, but concluded in Lilliputian, "Li lon ina i hekdebul. Li Quinbus. Ina Ranfu. Li i Hurgo!"[56]

He stormed out of the house and came back two days later, and without as much as looking me in the eye, he told me that he sold his manuscript *Voyage to Lilliput* to his uncle, Richard Sympson, and with the advance of six hundred pounds[57] he bought a good home in Redriff.

I gasped, and he began packing our belongings. I cried as I was obeying his barked commands to go ahead and help him pack. I cried all the way to Redriff, hugging Johnny and Betty. The poor souls had not even had time to say good-bye to their friends.

I glanced outside the coach as it rolled down the street and saw Vanessa rushing from her home and standing helplessly in the middle of the road, hesitatingly waving her handkerchief.

Only when we reached our new home did Lemuel's spirits rise. He even helped me off the coach and I felt such a relief when our bodies touched and, for a brief instance, Lemuel's face was squeezed onto my breasts.

Back on firm ground he hugged me, at long last, and I felt his eager manhood through his breeches. I got instantly wet. That much we loved each other.

It is indeed a better home. A stone house with a chimney and even sash windows. "We are safe here," he said. "Here we will have a room all for ourselves," thus he whispered in my ear, and I melted. "We will sleep in the kitchen. It is big and warm, you will see. Here I will finish writing my Lilliput travel memoir for Sympson, and we will be together all the time!"

It was a wonderful prospect, and I fell for it.

We settled in this fine, cozy home, and had a few weeks of bliss in it. But now I know that Lemuel's sole purpose in moving us here was to take me away from Vanessa. Well, I forgive him; I understand that, in a strange way he did it out of his love for me, desperately fearful of losing me.

Or maybe he tried to get us as far away from Biddel as possible?

That is why I was ever so enraged when he told me he was going back to sea, just two months after his miraculous return from Lilliput!

"And what think you of your children? What of our love?"

"I think well, Mary. Johnny and Betty are ever so dear to me, and I love you as much as any man can ever love a woman. But you broke my heart, woman. I tried, I honestly did, but I can no longer kiss you, without thinking that you would rather be making love to that woman, Mrs. Prichard."

"This is not true," I cried. "I . . . I . . . I never had sexual relations with that woman, Mrs. Prichard. Well, not the way you and I do, at least! She was just a very, very, very good friend. And now you leave me, and I do not even have her friendship . . ." I sobbed bitterly. "I missed you so . . ."

"Well, you better go back to reading the Bible, while I am away. Perhaps I will feel better about it all when I will have returned."

And he was gone.

My sole moments of relief from my sorrows are late at night as I lay in bed listening to my children's innocent breaths and remembering Lemuel's love and his fantastic adventures in Lilliput. In the dark of night my hands explore my lonely body, and I think about my love Lemuel and about my best friend Vanessa. And as I retell myself the stories my Lemuel told me, I sometimes imagine that my hands belong to Lemuel. Other times, that they belong to Vanessa. And sometimes, that my fingers are tiny Lilliputians. Thus, I make tender love with my imagination. Only in the dark of night my sadness subsides for a while, when I lay in bed alone, but satisfied—at least for a while.

Perhaps I will just go ahead and do all that which I forbade Lemuel to do.

I will write down Lemuel's adventures that are too dangerous to publish.

This will be my communion with my husband. And I will keep these pages safely hidden away, in the secret drawer of this table.

Tomorrow. I will start tomorrow. I anticipate these pages to be my sole happiness in the remaining days of my poor, desolate life.

Oh, Gulliver, will I ever see you again?

Chapter Nine

GULLIVER IS CAPTURED BY THE LILLIPUTIANS; WHAT REALLY
HAPPENED TO HIM WHILE HE WAS TIED TO THE GROUND ON THE
SHORES OF LILLIPUT; HIS FIRST ENCOUNTER WITH LILLIPUTIAN
DIGNITARIES AND HIS FIRST LILLIPUTIAN DINNER, FOREBODING AN
EVENTUAL CONSUMPTION OF ALL LILLIPUTIAN PRODUCE.
(Redriff, Thursday, June 29th, 1702)

It is quite late but, then again, the sun sets late at this time of the year.
I sit at Lemuel's spot by the window, mimicking his writing.

His uncle Sympson sent me a letter, telling me how he liked
Lemuel's recounting of his voyage to Lilliput, and that he is waiting
for Lemuel's return to prepare it for print. I was alarmed: if Lemuel—God forbid—never comes back, will I have to give back the
advance Mr. Sympson gave him? Or will Mr. Sympson ever relent to
a woman—me—preparing the book for print?

What will become of us?

I soon resolved to brush off all these worries and persist in my
confidence that Lemuel will be back. I feel that as long as I keep
writing the true tale of his voyage to Lilliput, I keep him alive, wherever he is now. I had to laugh betwixt myself, imagining how I will
secretly show Lemuel these pages when he will be back . . .

So, here is how it all started:

* * *

It was three years ago, in the beginning of November 1699, when
Lemuel's ship was wrecked and he was cast to swim as fortune dictated him, pushed forward by wind and tide. When he finally got on
shore, he was so tired and spent, he just collapsed and fell into the

deepest sleep he has ever had.

When he woke up, he did not feel at all refreshed. He found that his arms and legs were strongly fastened on each side to the ground. His hair, which was long and thick, was tied down in the same manner. He could only look upwards. The sun began to grow hot, and the light offended his eyes. First, he thought he was dreaming, but the pain, when he tried to raise his head, convinced him it was all really happening to him.

Then he heard small voices, and in a little time felt something alive moving up his left leg. This creature or creatures were busy with the front flap of his breeches, as far as he could tell, for suddenly he felt the cool wind on that part of his body, and tingling, gentle squeezing of his tender flesh down there.

The sensation was both pleasant and disturbing, because he felt a growing urge to release his urine. He felt as if his yard[58] was pushed and shoved at its base, while tiny pressures were applied to his bollocks.[59] All the while he heard shrill voices crying out in unison, something that sounded like "Hekina degul."[60] As much as he felt uncomfortable laying on his back, unable to move, the sensations on his yard, the nature of which he could not fathom, gave him a growing pleasure, and with this growing pleasure, his yard was growing too.

At first there was silence and then he heard again the high-pitched shouts "Hekina Degul, Hekina Degul!" and to his great disappointment, he felt the little creatures quickly roll off his body, and as his yard was no longer touched in this manner, it gradually got soft again. Upon which moment, he sensed the little creatures rush on his body again, fold over his front flap, and cover him back up.

He was in the utmost astonishment and fright and roared very loudly. As he roared, he sensed the creatures running away.

All in panic, Lemuel was struggling to get loose, and he managed to break the strings and wrench out the pegs that fastened his left arm to the ground, and at the same time, with a violent pull which gave him much pain, he loosened a little the strings that tied down his hair on the left side, so that he was just able to turn his head about two inches to the right.

And then he saw those creatures. They looked like ordinary human beings, even dressed like us, only they were littler. Much littler!

If they had not been running so fast, he could have held five or seven of them in his palm and squeezed them to death. But the creatures ran off a second time before he could seize them. And then there was a great shout in a very shrill accent, and after it ceased, he heard one of the creatures cry aloud, "Tolgo Phonac!"[61] and in an instant he felt more than hundred arrows discharged on his left hand, which hurt him like so many needles.

He was groaning with frustration and pain and, then, as he was striving again to get loose, they discharged another volley larger than the first, and some of them attempted with spears to stick him in the sides but, by good luck, he had on him a buff jerkin,[62] which they could not pierce.

Lemuel told me that he was then resigned to just lie till night when he would easily be able to free himself under the cover of darkness and run away. But it did not look like he would be left alone; from the increasing noise, he realised that more and more of those little people were gathering around him.

About four yards from him, over against his right ear, he heard a knocking for over an hour, like people at work. When turning his head that way, very slowly, and as much as the pegs and strings would permit him, he saw a small stage erected about a foot and a half from the ground, with a ladder to mount it.

Two small creatures, one clad in red and the other in green, one bobbling on rather high heels, the other on flat shoes, were signalling to each other for quite a long time to climb the ladder first. Eventually, they both relented and squeezed, and shoulder-to-shoulder they mounted the ladder as one. From whence these Hurgos,[63] occasionally cutting each other short, gave Lemuel a long speech, of which he understood not one syllable. Though they seemed to address Lemuel, numerous of the small people were gathering at the foot of the stage, eagerly listening to these speeches.

Lemuel thought, though, that he understood very well the meaning of these speeches. As small as these persons were, and standing on that little stage, they were quite near his face and he could hear and see them easily.

One of the speakers, the one dressed in green and wearing low heels, seemed to lace his speech with many threats, while the other little person, dressed in red and masterfully balancing himself on fantastically high heeled shoes, was mostly cajoling and seemed to make many promises, to which the little listeners on the ground were nodding complacently, while the green person was giving every sign of his disaffection.

When the little Hurgos finished talking, all the little creatures turned towards Lemuel, clearly expecting him to reply.

So Lemuel, in his best, humblest and politest English, spoke shortly.

It seemed as if he was successful in expressing his urgently pressing needs in signs and sounds, for the Hurgos were immediately calling out to the people, "Peplom selan! Bosan gue empos!"[64] And Lemuel saw that they were all running frantically away from him in all directions.

With much relief and with his free hand, he opened his front flap and released his water.[65]

Overcoming his urge to drench them all (fearing another volley of arrows), he aimed carefully so as not to hit any of those little creatures. With a satisfied sigh he closed his flap and was now ready to eat and drink.[66]

Being almost famished with hunger, having not eaten a morsel for some hours before he left the ship, he found the demands of nature so strong upon him, that he could not forbear showing his impatience (perhaps against the strict rules of decency) by putting his finger frequently on his mouth, to signify that he wanted food.

The Hurgos seemed to understand him very well, but still not to agree with one another. After some lengthy hushed debate, the green one seemed to relent and they both descended from the stage.

Later Lemuel learned that Flimnap, the red-clad high-heeled little person, who was the High Treasurer, was trying to convince the green person on flat heels, Skyresh Bolgolam, who was the High Admiral of the Realm, to kill Lemuel on the spot, as he was laying there, tied to the ground and defenseless.

Flimnap, being responsible for all the Emperor's possessions and in charge of maintaining and increasing them, feared that Gulliver's appetite would surely drain the Emperor's treasury. He reasoned that the best way to preserve Lilliputian's wealth (meaning the Emperor's, of course) was to get rid of this Man-Mountain, before he lapped Lilliput up.

Luckily for my Lemuel, Bolgolam reasoned that, as much as he would like to see the Man-Mountain dead, and as much as his fingers itched to shoot the first poisoned arrow himself, the stench of so large a carcass might produce a plague in Lilliput and would probably spread through the whole Kingdom.

Bolgolam was asking, his fist near Flimnap's nose, "Where can you bury this abominable creature? The earth underneath us is not deep enough! You will be dropping—if you ever tried digging that far—the whole of Lilliput into eternal space! No, we should maintain him. This Man-Mountain might turn out to be useful for us. I mean, for Our Emperor, of course."

And thus the command was given to apply several ladders to Lemuel's sides, on which over a hundred of the inhabitants mounted, and walked towards Lemuel's mouth, laden with baskets full of meat.

There were shoulders, legs and loins, shaped like those of mutton, and very well dressed, but smaller than the wings of a lark.[67] Lemuel ate them by two or three at a mouthful, and took three loaves of bread at a time, about the bigness of musket bullets.

The little people supplied him as fast as they could, showing a thousand marks of wonder and astonishment at his bulk and appetite.

Then Lemuel made another sign that he wanted to drink. They found by his eating that a small quantity would not suffice him, and being a most ingenious people, they slung up with great dexterity one of their largest hogsheads, then rolled it toward his hand, and beat out the top. Lemuel drank it off at a draught, which he might well have done, for it hardly held half a pint, and tasted (so he told me, three years later) like a small wine of burgundy—but much more delicious. They brought him a second hogshead, which he drank in the same manner, and then made signs for more, but they had none to give him.

It is not true to say that in the course of his two-year stay in Lilliput, he was a burden on the Emperor, having eaten and drank as much as he did, for my Lemuel's excrement was eventually put to very good use: fertilising the Lilliputian lands. Lemuel told me, proudly, that the crops were growing far taller, faster and in much larger quantities than before his arrival. In fact, Lemuel produced so much waste that he was sure it would still be in use for hundreds of years to come. He cleverly computed that this would alter the Lilliputians completely, as their future generations would become bigger, too. And, indeed, already in the second year in which Lemuel put his waste to good use, the Lilliputian newborns were five percent bigger than those who were born the year before Lemuel's metabolism started enriching Lilliput (causing their mothers much more agony at birth, I might add). Lemuel told me that he thinks that by the year 2000 (when the world is anyway bound to end again) the Lilliputians will be slightly smaller than us, hardly to be recognized as Lilliputians at all.

Chapter Ten

UNDER THE COMMAND OF BOLGOLAM AND FLIMNAP, LEMUEL
IS TRANSPORTED TO HIS PRISON-TEMPLE; NATURE'S CALL IS
NOT APPRECIATED BY THE LILLIPUTIAN RIFF-RAFF, AND THE
EMPEROR PUNISHES THEM BY HANDING THEM OVER TO LEMUEL;
BENEVOLENTLY, LEMUEL SPARES THEIR LIVES, BUT THIS IS NOT
ENOUGH TO SECURE HIS FREEDOM; HIS FIRST IMPRESSION OF
THE LILLIPUTIAN LANDSCAPE.
(Redriff, Monday, July 3rd, 1702)

Lemuel was transported to Mildendo, the capital city of Lilliput, after he was raised by pulleys and ropes and laid on top of a specially and hastily built wagon, to which he was chained again.

Bolgolam was commanding the troops while Flimnap supplied materials and horses. They were orchestrating the labor of hundreds of Lilliputians and as many horses to pull this heavy wagon across the plain from the beach to the metropolis. But Lemuel was not aware of any of this because he was fast asleep; Flimnap gave orders to infuse his drink with soporiferous medicine, which totally knocked him out.

It took them two days to reach the outskirts of Mildendo, to the abode which was assigned to Lemuel. This building used to be an ancient Temple, esteemed to be the largest in the whole kingdom, but having been polluted some years before by an unnatural murder, was, according to the zeal of those people, looked on as profane, and therefore had been applied to common use.

(When Lemuel told me this, I asked him what was the difference between natural and unnatural murder, and he explained to me that the Lilliputians considered murder to be natural when it was commissioned by the Emperor, and unnatural when it was the idea of any other person. The first is praised as a wise and necessary political act, while the person who commits an unnatural murder is condemned by the Emperor to death, which would then be considered a natural murder).

Luckily for Lemuel, the pollution of that ancient temple coincided with his arrival and the Emperor decided to imprison him there. All the ornaments and furniture were carried away, to be used secularly by the Empress.

There was much debate about the form of Lemuel's imprisonment (as he was later informed) since all Lilliputian prisons were mere iron cages, in which orange-clad prisoners would be held, awaiting justice to be done them (sometimes for years). But as there was no cage big enough to hold Gulliver, and surely no way of sewing him the proper orange attire, the compromise was reached to shackle him to the temple.

When Lemuel mastered the Lilliputian language well enough to follow the street gossip, he overheard the bitter comment that "In Lilliput, the bigger you are, the more likely you are to get a better treatment, and the bigger criminal you are, the better the treatment." There was no denying it: the temple was much better than an iron cage!

The great gate to the north was about four feet high and almost two feet wide, so Lemuel could bend and squeeze himself in through it. On each side of the gate was a small window not above six inches from the ground. Into one of those windows the Emperor's smiths conveyed fifty-one chains, like those that hang to a lady's watch in Europe, and almost as large, and they were all locked to my poor Lemuel's left leg, with thirty-six padlocks.

These chains were about two yards long and gave him not only the liberty of walking backwards and forwards in a semicircle but, being fixed within four inches of the gate, allowed him to creep in and lie at his full length inside his temple.

Lemuel used this very limited freedom of movement very civilly and sociably, intending to gain his freedom soon, by convincing the Lilliputians that he was harmless. Therefore, even though he was hard pressed to discharge himself, seeing that there were so many Lilliputians all around the Prison-Temple (and being by nature a very shy person), Lemuel decided to get inside and discharge his body of that uneasy load in the privacy of his Prison-Temple.

This done, and the stench quite hard to bear, he hurried back out, only to face hundreds of excited Lilliputians, pressing onto the Temple's windows and retreating in awe. Some of the Lilliputians became quite enraged (Lemuel's actions quite offended their remaining religious feelings as regards the former temple) and six of them even shot arrows at Lemuel, which he cleverly avoided.

The commotion was so loud that soon the Emperor himself arrived, galloping hard and followed by numerous advisors. When the Emperor guided his horse nearer to Lemuel, the horse was so alarmed that he reared up on his hind feet and nearly toppled the Emperor. But the Emperor, being an excellent horseman, kept his seat until his attendants ran in, and held the bridle while the Emperor had time to dismount.

The green and red Hurgos, Bolgolam and Flimnap, rushed toward the Emperor (whose magnificent dress, by the way, consisted of numerous colours). Flimnap, bobbing on his high heels, was not as fast as flat-shoed Bolgolam, who was quicker to reach the Emperor and to bow deeply, all the while talking excitedly. He seemed to be informing the Emperor about recent events, while trying to contradict Flimnap's version. All the while, the emperor observed Lemuel all around with great admiration, yet from a safe distance.

Lemuel bowed deeply, just as he saw the Hurgos do, and, again using his finest body language and the most polite words he could find in English, explained what he did inside the temple, and why.

The Emperor pretended to understand every word, and he ordered the capture of the insolents that shot arrows at my Lemuel. He commanded that they would be delivered bound to Lemuel's hands. A number of soldiers pushed the criminals forwards with the butt-ends of their pikes into Lemuel's reach and, obediently, he took them all in his right hand, put five of them into his coat-pocket; and as to the sixth, Lemuel was toying with the idea to eat him alive, but the poor man squalled terribly and shat in his pants, which disgusted Lemuel so much, that in revulsion he placed all six back on the ground, to everybody's relief.

As a token of appreciation, and as punishment to the insolents, the Emperor gave them orders to clear Lemuel's pile of excrement from the Prison-Temple (and spread it on the Emperor's fields) so that Lemuel was able to sleep on a clean floor that night.

The news of Lemuel's arrival spread quickly through the Kingdom, and it brought prodigious numbers of the rich, the idle, and plain curious people to see him. It was getting rather crowded and the Emperor, fearing that the villages would soon be emptied, with no one working in His Royal fields, was quick to provide several proclamations and orders of state against this inconvenience.

He directed that those who had already beheld Lemuel should return home, and not presume to come within fifty yards of his Prison-Temple without license from court, whereby the secretaries of state would get considerable fees.

So, for now, Lemuel was left alone.

And as he stood there, chained to his Prison-Temple, he could not help admiring the view. The sun was setting behind Mildendo, the metropolis of Lilliput, painting its towers and domes deep, lush pink. In front of him, and on his right hand side, fields of miniature zea maize, triticum aestivum and cannabacea[68] were stretching as far as he could see.

The fields were intermingled with woods, and the tallest trees, as he could judge, appeared to be seven foot high. He turned around and, leaning on the roof of his Prison-Temple, he saw the ocean in the distance. He saw the traces of the crude wagon which the Lilliputians built to transport him from whence they found him on the beach and noticed the wide curve they took around a bump in the ground, which must have seemed to the Lilliputians as an insurmountable mountain, about one and a half feet tall.

This Lilliputian "mountain" was indeed barren at the top, and Lemuel thought it must have once been a volcano, but with its mouth gaping wide and deep, it seemed dormant enough. Lemuel saw water flowing from the volcano's slope, forming a little river that flowed into the ocean.

Sighing deeply, and determined to gain his freedom soon, Lemuel bent down and crept into his Prison-Temple. Despite the cumbersome 51 chains and 36 padlocks, he fell asleep immediately.

Chapter Eleven

THE AUTHOR SHARES HER WORRIES WITH THE READER;
LEMUEL'S FIRST MORNING IN HIS PRISON-TEMPLE;
HE DISCOVERS THAT HE IS BEING SPIED UPON; HE IS MAKING
GOOD PROGRESS LEARNING LILLIPUTIAN, WHICH HE USES TO
BEG FOR HIS FREEDOM; THE FIRST CONDITIONS ARE SET OUT.
(Redriff, Tuesday, September 12th, 1702)

With the fast approach of winter, my old fears are reviving. Can I provide for my children as befits the orphans of a ship-surgeon?

What am I thinking?

There is no evidence that Lemuel is dead!

Anyway, Johnny will have to start working soon. He is a strong lad, and big for a thirteen-year-old. But my Betty needs looking after. And what about the child in my belly . . .? Oh, I hope the curse is lifted, and that my baby will survive. I hope it will be a boy, not only because he will be able to provide for me when I am old, but also because he will be a constant reminder for me of my lost Lemuel, my Love lost.

But for now, all I have is the worries for my children, for my growing fatherless family. At least I have the memories of my nights with Lemuel and the stories he whispered in my ear at night, while hugging and caressing me.

These memories give me the power to live on and the hope against hope that our family will reunite in due course. Lemuel left us but three months ago and there was word that the *Adventure* has reached the Cape of Good Hope on its way to Surat.

I believe with all my being that Lemuel is well.

He will come back to us in good time, having had a prosperous, eventless voyage—unlike his last one, when he was cast ashore in Lilliput:

* * *

On his first morning in his Prison-Temple, when Lemuel crept out, he was alarmed to see hundreds of Lilliputians surrounding the place. The Emperor gave specific orders that no Lilliputian was allowed to come near enough to Lemuel to be trampled on, so, from a safe distance, they all looked at him excitedly and expectantly.

Lemuel told me that he was so much hard pressed to give water that he resolved to walk as far as his chains would allow him, round the Prison-Temple, where he was relieved to see no Lilliputian was to be seen.

The volcano area seemed vacant enough, though more and more stalkers were rushing in that direction. But as soon as Lemuel opened his front flap, he was relieved to see how that act alone sufficed to scatter them all away.

Sighing with relief, Lemuel eased himself by giving water to his heart's content, aiming carefully over the volcano, into the little river, which flowed into the ocean.

As soon as he turned around and came back to the entrance of his Prison-Temple, he noticed some little people running towards a couple of Hurgos who were both sitting at a tiny table in front of his Prison-Temple, dressed in exquisite red attire.

Lemuel recognised one of them as Flimnap, the red-clad Lilliputian who addressed him from the stage three days before, while he was still tied to the ground.

Some little people were talking excitedly to Flimnap, who immediately wrote something using an almost invisible quill on a tiny, stamp-size parchment. As Lemuel sat, leaning on the temple's wall, he saw the man rolling the parchment and rising from his chair. Bobbing confidently on his pair of very high heeled shoes, he approached Lemuel, bowed deeply, and said:

"Clumglum Flimnap, dehul hekino. Hekina lang mar o clum slum Mildendo." (Meaning: "Minister Flimnap, at your service. Please be good to give this to my knight at the City Gate.")

Of course, Lemuel did not understand a word of this at the time.

To his astonishment, Minister Flimnap then handed him the minuscule rolled parchment, and indicated to pass it on, waving his hands to the left in the direction of Mildendo, the metropolis.

When Lemuel got up and looked in that direction, he noticed a little knight mounted on a little horse, standing at the gates of the city, looking expectantly at him. The knight at the gate probably had an amazingly good eye-sight, for he seemed to spot the parchment that Lemuel was carefully holding between his thumb and index finger, and he began waving frantically, gesticulating to Lemuel to hand the parchment over to him.

And, indeed, when Lemuel bent over the fields that spread between his Prison-Temple and the city gates, and handed the parchment to the Lilliputian knight, the parchment was snatched away from between his fingers. The knight tucked it under his arm and galloped on his little horse with all his might into town, in the direction of the Palace some yards away.

Lemuel followed the knight's slow progress for a while, and it suddenly dawned on him: these people were spying on him! They reported each and every move of his to the Emperor and they had the audacity to use him as a messenger, to deliver those reports even faster!

Lemuel kept gazing at the knight, amazed at the Lilliputian's insolence, until he felt some irritating stabs at his right leg. Looking down, he saw a couple of Lilliputian soldiers pointing spears at his ankle, tagging, and retrieving as fast as they could. Minister Flimnap, standing at a safe distance too, was waving and signalling to Lemuel to sit down again.

Obediently, he did.

What else could he do?

The Minister thanked him officially and pointing at the other red-clad little man he said, "Loclum Reldresal, dehul hekino" (General Reldresal, at your service.)

While Minister Flimnap, clearly very relieved, was busy collecting his items and getting ready to leave, the General, who seemed to have no fear at all, came ever so near Lemuel and, pointing at himself, said, "Li Reldresal!" and pointing at Lemuel he asked very clearly, "Ina?"

Lemuel understood this quite well. In fact, in all the travel books he ever read, there have always been such dialogues of introductions. So, he willingly replied, "Li Gulliver! Ina Reldresal!"

All the little people around were cheering in astonishment and Reldresal, obviously proud of himself, addressed the crowd. "Gro Gulliver! Gro Quinbus Flestrin!" (He's Gulliver! He's a Man-Mountain!) And they all laughed good heartedly, including Gulliver, who did not want to appear any different than any of them.

And thus, the Lilliputian lesson progressed, with Reldresal pointing at things around them and telling Gulliver their names.

Lemuel was a quick pupil and adamant to learn how to express his desire to get his liberty. He gave many signs to that effect, pointing at his chained leg, bowing deeply and even waving his hands as a bird, which did not make the impression he was hoping for.

As he waved his hands, the hem of his coat was swaying wildly and the wind blew Reldresal's papers away, as well as many a hat. The soldiers collected the papers promptly, people ran after their hats, and General Reldresal's answer was, as Lemuel could apprehend it, that Lemuel's freedom must be a work of time, not to be thought on without the advice of His Majesty's Council, and first he must "lumos kelmin pesso desmar lon emposo;" that is, "swear a peace with Him and His Kingdom."

However, General Reldresal made it clear that Lemuel should be used with all kindness and, using simple words in Lilliputian, which Lemuel was swift to learn, combining many gestures and hand-signals, he managed to convey to Lemuel that in good time he would acquire, by his patience and discreet behaviour, the high opinion of His Royal Highness and His subjects.

The first sign of such obedience, Lemuel guessed from General Reldresal's speech and gestures, was to let certain officers search

Gulliver. This Lemuel could clearly fathom: they surely suspected that he might carry about him weapons, which would be dangerous things, judging by the bulk of so prodigious a person.

Lemuel said, partly in his newly acquired Lilliputian, and partly in signs, that he was ready to strip himself and turn up his pockets before any Officer of the Crown. He knew that his condum was safely tucked away in his secret fob.

Chapter Twelve

THE AUTHOR RECEIVES A LETTER FROM HER HUSBAND,
AND HER HOPES TO HAVE A HEALTHY BABY ARE REVIVED;
SHE CONTINUES TO WRITE THE STORY OF GULLIVER,
HOW HE IS BEING SEARCHED AND HIS WEAPONS CONFISCATED;
LEMUEL SUCCEEDS TO CONCEAL SOME PRECIOUS COMMODITIES;
A WAR IS ALMOST DECLARED AGAINST HIM, WHICH HE
GOOD-NATUREDLY AVERTS.
(Redriff, Wednesday, February 3rd, 1703)

What a good omen! this morning Captain Richard Branson brought me a letter from my Love, my Lemuel!

Captain Branson's ship, the *Virgin* docked safely in Redriff, after having landed at the Cape of Good Hope for water, on its way back from Surat. There he met my Lemuel, who asked him to bring me this letter. Oh, he loves me so, my dear husband. He loves me still!

[A note from the copy editor: here was inserted the actual letter from Lemuel to Mary, which reads as follows:]

My dearest Mary

Four and twenty hours once we took sail I already miss your Kiss, My dearest Mary, My Mary. The power of your kiss is like a sacred Chalice.

We had a very prosperous Gale till we arrived at the Cape of Good Hope, where we landed for fresh Water, but discovering a Leak we unshipped our Goods and shall winter here; for the Captain fell sick of an Ague.

I have a consolation in the certainty that I shall see you, My dear wife, and my children in a few months! Thank God I shall Kiss your Lips! All of them! The dearest pleasures in the universe!

Ever yours, affectionately, my dearest, L.G.

So the *Adventure* has arrived safely at the harbour of the Cape of Good Hope, sometime last Autumn! Soon winter will be over and he will continue his prosperous journey. If my calculations are correct, he is due back home in one year or so.

Well, I am relieved that at least for now he is safe at port. While he tends to the ague of Captain John Nicholas, I am sure he is also relishing the ladies of the Cape and I am confident he is using his condum regularly.

I feel so relieved!

It means that their journey might take a little longer than expected, but I will wait for my Lemuel. If it takes forever, I will wait for him. Oh, and this is such a good omen, for I am heavy with child . . . This must surely be a sign that the curse is repelled, and my baby will survive . . . ?

With renewed vigour, I continue to tell the story of my husband, what happened to him three years back, during his last voyage, when he was stranded in Lilliput:

That same day my Lemuel was forced to be stripped of his possessions, but he was willing to do anything at that point to gain back his freedom.

General Reldresal summoned two of the soldiers to approach Gulliver, and politely introduced them as Clefrin Freloc and Marsi Freloc. (Lemuel figured that Freloc means Officer of the Crown. They didn't look like brothers.) They obeyed the General with much apprehension, though they need not have feared. My gentle Lemuel took up the two clerks in his hand, put them first into his coat-pockets, and then into every other pocket about him, except for his secret fob where I always packed his condum.

The Frelocs, Clefrin and Marsi, screamed their findings from high up to General Reldresal, who listened carefully and, sitting at his desk, composed a lengthy description of Lemuel's possessions.

By good chance, the whole box marked "Quinbus Flestrin" (meaning "Man Mountain" as they called my Lemuel) survived the Great Fire and Lemuel got hold of it in a clandestine way. Back home, using a magnifying glass, he translated it to me, and we delighted in it to no extent!)

The List read:

"One great piece of coarse cloth, large enough to be a foot-cloth for His Majesty's chief room of state"—that was Lemuel's handkerchief.

"A huge silver chest, with a cover of the same metal, containing some sort of dust, which set both officers a sneezing for several times together"—That is how they described Lemuel's snuff box.

"A prodigious number of white thin substances folded one over another, about the bigness of three men, tied with a strong cable, and marked with black figures, probably writings, every letter almost half as large as the palm of our hands"—that was Lemuel's journal-book.

"A sort of engine, from the back of which were extended twenty long poles, resembling the fence before His Majesty's Court"—That was the description of Lemuel's comb.

"A hollow pillar of iron, about the length of a man, fastened to a strong piece of timber, larger than the pillar; and upon one side of the pillar were huge pieces of iron sticking out, cut into strange figures"—That was Lemuel's pistol. He had two of them upon him.

"Several round flat pieces of white and red metal, of different bulk, with profiles of unknown Lilliputians, in real size"—These were a few crowns and copper farthings bearing the images of William and Mary.[69]

"Two black pillars irregularly shaped, larger than any Lilliputian. Within each of these is enclosed a prodigious plate of steel"—These were Lemuel's knives: his shaving knife and his meat knife.

"A great silver chain, with a wonderful kind of engine at the bottom"—This was Lemuel's timepiece and they mistakenly understood it to be his God, since he tried to explain to them in his awkward Lilliputian, the meaning of Time and its monetary Value.[70]

"A net almost large enough for a fisherman, but contrived to open and shut like a purse, containing several massy pieces of yellow metal, bearing the same real-size images of those two unknown Lilliputians, which, if they be real gold, must be of immense value"—Yes, that was Lemuel's purse, where he kept his guineas.

"A girdle about the Quinbus Flestrin's (Man-Mountain's) waist, made of the hide of some prodigious animal, from which, on the left side, hung a sword of the length of five men"—that was Lemuel's scimitar and scabbard.[71]

"A bag or pouch, divided into two cells, each cell capable of holding three of His Majesty's subjects. In one of these cells were several globes, or balls, of a most ponderous metal, about the bigness of our heads, and required a strong hand to lift them; the other cell contained a heap of certain black grains, but of no great bulk or weight, for we could hold about fifty of them in the palms of our hands"—these were Lemuel's bullets and gunpowder.

The list thus compiled, Lemuel landed Clefrin and Marsi carefully back to earth. He was debating with himself, should he reveal to his captors his private pocket, which escaped their search, wherein there was a pair of spectacles (which he sometimes used for the weakness of his eyes), a pocket perspective[72], and some other little conveniences, which, being of no consequence to the emperor, he did not think himself bound by honour to declare. Lemuel apprehended they might be lost or spoiled if he ventured them out of his possession, so he resolved to cheat his captors just this once.

General Reldresal made the Frelocs sign the document ceremoniously. They all gaped at Lemuel, and he read their minds: He was expected to sign the document as well, according to Protocol. But how could such a simple act be achieved, seeing that Lemuel's thumb was as big as the whole parchment? (Naturally, they assumed that a beast like Lemuel would be illiterate and would need to sign by putting its thumb in ink and on paper. At that time, they were still deeply prejudiced against my Lemuel and only later did they learn of his many virtues!)

Almost imperceptibly for Lemuel, General Reldresal shrugged his shoulders, rolled up the parchment, handed it to Lemuel and signalled him to deliver it as before. Still wishing to make a good impression, Lemuel meekly obliged, but as he was standing there, watching the slow progress of the rider towards the Palace, he could not help resenting the way he was used by those Lilliputians.

As he sat back dejectedly, General Reldresal thanked him again, and continued to teach Lemuel the Lilliputian language.

The lesson was soon interrupted by the sound of an advancing army, accompanied by a loud march, played on trumpets and drums. Gulliver wanted to get on his feet to see what it was all about, but General Reldresal waved his hands so vigorously that the message was clear:

"Sit!"

The Emperor himself soon appeared from around the Temple's wall, clad in colourful robes and reining in his horse. The Emperor glanced at Gulliver, turned around and gave a majestic sign, upon which Gulliver heard the march resume, and the sounds of feet and clamour were soon translated into a snaking line of armed soldiers and mounted knights, led by a Lilliputian which Lemuel remembered from three days past. It was the one dressed in magnificent green, the Admiral of the Realm, Skyresh Bolgolam (as Lemuel came to know his name later).

Admiral Bolgolam ordered the troops to surround my Lemuel and to draw their arms.

At first Lemuel feared that this was an execution, but he soon understood (his Lilliputian being already quite advanced) that under the threat of these thousands of poised arrows, he was expected to hand over the items on the list, which an aid to the Emperor was now reading aloud.

He was ordered by Admiral Bolgolam to slowly withdraw his scimitar from its scabbard, and the Emperor commanded two of his officers to examine it. They ran their fingers along its edge and came to the conclusion that they did not know what would be the purpose of such a dull instrument.

General Reldresal instructed Lemuel to give a demonstration of the use of this equipment, and Lemuel stood up and obediently mimicked slaying and hacking an invisible enemy.

Enthusiastically, General Reldresal explained to the Emperor (as Lemuel could surmise) that this weapon's strategy was to blind the enemy, by reflecting the sun's rays into their eyes. Many officers were quite impressed by this innovation, but Admiral Bolgolam pointed out, to the great shame of General Reldresal, that on a cloudy day this weapon would be useless.

Lemuel's pistol did not make much more impression on the Lilliputians, though they did appreciate the distant noise it made when Lemuel fired a shot in the air.

His watch was a subject of wonderment, seeing that it was some sort of Deity, but Shumclum, the Lilliputian High Priest (dressed in ominous black) dismissed it by saying that it was repeating its message—whatever those ticking noises were conveying—too often.

Shumclum was waving a heavy book and proclaiming that there is no mention of this God in the Holy Blundecral,[73] so anyone who would listen to this incessant ticking is bound to go to Hell. For fear of brainwashing and conversion to the Ticking God, Lemuel's watch was hastily whisked away by two of the tallest yeomen of the guards, who bore it on a pole upon their shoulders, as draymen in England do a barrel of ale. But not before they were ordered to stuff their ears with some invisible matter.

Finally, as advised by the Admiral, the Emperor took possession of Lemuel's scimitar and the two pistols, to prevent him from using them against any of his people.

Then the Emperor turned to his troops, still standing with their arrows poised ominously at Lemuel, and screaming at the top of his tiny lungs, the Emperor was delivering a furious speech along these lines: "Men, you are now facing the greatest danger that ever faced our glorious Lilliput! And if anyone says that Lilliputians want out of a war, not wanting to fight, you should answer that this is a crock of bullshit. Lilliputians love to fight, traditionally. All real Lilliputians love the sting and clash of battle. The mightier our enemy, the mightier our might!"

The soldiers cheered and a few arrows were shot in the air, celebrating this mighty speech. When the cheers subsided, the Emperor commenced, "This Quinbus Flestrin sitting in front of you can be tamed. And by all that is dear to us, you shall tame him!

"Only two percent of you right here today would die if a major battle ensues. But death must not be feared! Death, in time, comes to all men!

"Advance and may Our God be with you!"[74]

He then jumped carefully on his horse and safely departed from the maybe-soon-to-be-battlefield, with Shumclum the High Priest and other close advisers quickly close behind him.

Admiral Bolgolam raised his sword and screamed, "You heard our Dear Emperor! You will defend Him to the last! Let no Quinbus Flestrin, let no Man-Mountain scare the shit out of you! Go on, march!"

And with that the march was resumed and the numerous little soldiers commenced stepping to the beat, as menacingly as they ever could, circling Lemuel and marching on, until they all disappeared back into the metropolis.

As the soldiers were marching on and out of sight, Lemuel grasped that this elaborate military exercise, parading the soldiers and horses in a close proximity to him, was his opportunity to prove that he was tame enough to be set free, and he waved good-naturedly to the departing troops, and saluted them with much respect.

But still, he was not released.

Chapter Thirteen

THE AUTHOR'S SISTER COMES FOR A VISIT; WITH REVIVED
SPIRITS THE AUTHOR CONTINUES TO TELL ABOUT GULLIVER'S
FATE IN LILLIPUT AND HIS ATTEMPTS TO PROVE HIS DOCILITY;
HE CLEVERLY ENTERTAINS THE ROYAL HOUSE, BUT FALLS
IN LOVE WITH THE EMPRESS; HIS ORDEAL OF SHAME TURNS
TO GLORY, BUT FREEDOM STILL ELUDES HIM.
(Redriff, Wednesday, February 17th, 1703)

Good tidings keep rolling in! My dear sister, Stella, came on a visit, chaperoned[75] by James, her fifteen-year-old lad. What a man he has become!

Because of Lemuel's wild wanderings, not only in the wide world, but also here in London, I did not get to see Stella and her family for many a year. The boy I remembered suckling on his mother's breast, whilst she was jolting me with tales from her married life on the eve of my own wedding, that baby is now such a handsome young man!

Stella left her eldest daughter, fourteen-year-old Nancy, in charge of the maids and her nine younger siblings. She and James took the public coach—and here they were!

When we were done crying and laughing, we cuddled around the fireplace, all five of us, each hugging a steaming cup o' tea.

Stella said she decided to come now, before the winter will turn rough again. My clever Johnny pointed out that we had so much violent rain this summer, and Stella was much impressed when he wisely predicted that it would seriously affect subsequent harvest.

Yes, we discussed the weather—not that it helps any—and remembered the famous fog of November Twenty-Ninth, 1699. Even Betty remembered three years past, how dense was the fog. So much so, that we could not see a yard ahead. Also in Newgate Street, told us Stella and James, nobody dared go outside and the city lay in deathly silence. We could laugh about it now and had quite some merry a time the whole evening. But when the children fell asleep in the big bed, Stella asked me, much worried and vexed, if there might have been a letter, or any other sign of life from Mr. Gulliver.

Was I ever so happy to show her his letter! Was she ever so quizzed about his sweet, loving line: "Thank God I shall Kiss your Lips! All of them!" Of course, I did not explain it to her. I shrugged my shoulders and silently blessed my marital luck. (Stella told me that Mr. Owen Lavender Jr. never kisses her, but insists on mounting her nightly. She says she is exasperated with giving birth, punctually, every autumn, but I do not believe her. I think she just says it for my sake.)

Stella was relieved to learn that Mr. Gulliver is just being delayed and in good time will be back, who knows, perhaps even in time to see the birth of the child that grows in my belly.

"But if he is delayed," she beseeched me, "do send Johnny with a line to the Penny Post[76] and I will come! We can bear this expenditure!" She laughed again, but good-heartedly.

Mr. Lavender Jr. is well off, since the hosiery trade my father struggled to erect, with the help of his good friend Master Bates, is flourishing. But Stella is not bragging about her good fortune. Come to think of it, her parting words still echo in my head: "Dear sister," she said, "cheer up! You have your two surviving children and the assurance of restful nights, while I—I cannot complain, I have the maids watching my brood, but come each month, I wrack my brain to find another reason to let Mr. Lavender Jr. sleep alone." She looked at her bulging belly and concluded wistfully, "I am not so good at it."[77]

Strange how we always long for that which we do not have, whilst those who have that which we want long for that which they do not possess, but we do.

Ah! Life in Lilliput was no different, according to Lemuel's stories:

* * *

Though his living conditions were relatively good (he even got a bed made especially for him, consisting of six hundred Lilliputian beds put together), and food and drink were readily supplied to him, Lemuel was anxious to be free and extremely curious to see the whole of Lilliput.

He did get to see many of the inhabitants, though, since, as the news of his arrival spread through the Empire, it brought prodigious numbers of rich, idle or plain curious little people to see him. So much so that (later he learned) the Emperor gave orders that the watching of "Quinbus Flestrin" will only be allowed for half a day per person, against a fee (called, in short, the QuinTax," which was used to cover Gulliver's upkeep, and that of the Emperor's).

So, of course, he was not released.

During each of his daily audiences with General Reldresal, who was appointed to keep watch on the Man Mountain and to teach him the Lilliputian language, history, culture and manners, Gulliver was entreating the General to beg the Emperor to grant him his freedom.

General Reldresal's answer was, as always, that this must be a work of time, not to be thought on without the advice of His Majesty's council, based on the reports they will get from their undercover spies.

Lemuel wondered if any of those undercover spies were women. He noticed that he had a great effect on the Lilliputian female species. They seemed to be drawn to him by some invisible force. Lemuel could not fathom what was this force of attraction, but I, being of the female species too, know how attracted we are to the scent of a healthy, hard-working male.[78] My prodigious Lemuel's aphrodisiac must have been a powerful magnet.

He was very proud to tell me that the very first female Lilliputian he actually touched was none other than the Empress.

It was right after my clever man built a little stage, using his handkerchief and some local trees, for the Emperor's army to practice military maneuvers.

(Lemuel wrote about this in detail in his book, so I need not repeat all those boring technical details.)

The entertainment pleased the Emperor so much that He convinced His Empress to let Lemuel hoist Her up, close chair[79] and all, so She could join the Emperor up there.

When Lemuel picked up the Empress' close chair, he distinctly felt Her breasts, bursting out of Her deep cleavage, brushing lightly at his forefinger. And when they exchanged glances, the Empress' cheeks got all red and She licked her lips. Luckily no one saw that, as it happened about a yard off the ground.

Lemuel told me that he was immediately smitten with love to the Empress, because She reminded him of me. The thought of me and of our children so far away, helpless, and desolate, unknowing of what has become of him, tormented Lemuel to no end. He told me that his heart lost a beat the first time he held his eyes on the Empress, with Her raven long hair and Her pert, almost naked breasts (for the fashion among the Lilliputian nobility was such that women's breasts were considered to be their best jewels, for all to admire. By penalty of death all women whose jewelry has withered were forbidden to expose themselves). Some older Lilliputian women were covered head to toe in what looked like a blue sac, with but a slit that revealed their eyes. Lemuel could not tell how old those women were, or if they were women at all. At night they all looked like tiny ghosts, rushing silently across the plains.

That little incident, when his finger brushed against the Empress' breasts while She licked her lips, gave my Lemuel some hope that, if Her Grace would grace him, he might soon be released from the chains with which he was still constrained.

While the troops were marching to and fro on the little handkerchief-stage, Lemuel was trying to catch the Empress' glance, hoping to make another good impression on Her.

It was a rather warm day, and my ever-inventive Lemuel suggested to his teacher, General Reldresal (who was always nearby), that he might make himself useful to their Royal Highnesses by gently waving on them a tree, which he might easily uproot for that purpose. The General presented the offer to the Emperor, and the Empress entreated Her Husband to allow Gulliver to ease their Royal Heat. The Emperor agreed, on condition that Gulliver would plant the tree back again when the Royal Couple would no longer need the wind.

Carefully scanning the nearby trees, Lemuel chose the one that best fitted the mission, pulled it out of the ground and gave it a good shake to get rid of the earth and rubble (this he did stretching his arm as far as he could over the crowd and above an uninhabited land). As he leaned his elbow closer to the Royal Seats, and commenced waving the tree behind them, he could not help overhearing Their conversation: "Darling," said the Empress, "I have a marvellous idea: Let us have this Man-Mountain stand with his legs wide apart and We will ride our carriage right between his legs!"

"Oh dear, oh dear," said the Emperor, "that would pose too great a risk to Your health. In fact, I think the wind is far too strong now. You better get in your close chair and back to the palace, and right now!"

Lemuel did not dare suggest that he stop waving the tree, in fear that his eavesdropping would be revealed, so he obediently clasped the close chair under the close watch of the Emperor, and lowered the Empress back to the ground. His only consolation was that She seemed to be as dejected as he was when She left with Her Ladies in Waiting back to Mildendo.

As soon as they were far enough, the Emperor snapped for Skyresh Bolgolam, the Admiral of the Realm, "We contrived a new drill to tame our Man-Mountain and harden the hearts of Our Soldiers!" he announced. "Summon Our Army, right away!"

Promptly, Lemuel was ordered to stand like Colossus,[80] with his legs asunder, as far as the chains permitted him, and the Emperor gave the command to his troops to march underneath.

Lemuel, who was indeed ever the shy and private person, was

quite flabbergasted when he could clearly see some of the young officers glancing up as they passed between his legs.

Seeing what they saw (for his breeches were in quite ill condition), they had much opportunity for laughter and admiration.

My poor Lemuel was at first sure that they were laughing at his shrunk yard and tight bollocks (the cold wind having that effect, you know) and therefore was quite relieved that the Empress was far and away. But as his thoughts wondered in that direction, he suddenly heard many gasps from the Lilliputians marching between his legs and he apprehended that the mere thought of the woman he craved, resulted in the resizing of his yard to new measures, which planted fear and envy into the soul of each and every soldier who happened to be between his legs at that moment.

Admiral Bolgolam gave a sign to the Army Conductor, who immediately increased the beat and, almost running, the rest of the troops rushed underneath Lemuel, who was relieved to have this form of torture and humiliation over and done with.

And still he remained chained to the Prison-Temple, with no liberty in sight.

But that same evening the Emperor sent general Reldresal with an important message to be delivered privately to Lemuel.

Chapter Fourteen

LEMUEL GAINS HIS FIRST FRIEND IN COURT; HE GETS
ADVICE ON SEEKING ASYLUM; HE IS SERVICED BY
THE LOVERS AND RETURNS THE LADIES' LOVE.
(Redriff, Thursday, February 18th, 1703)

"Quinbus Flestrin (Man-Mountain)" General Reldresal said, "our most High Emperor of Lilliput, the delight and terror of the universe, etc., etc., wishes me to speak with you as a friend."

To which my Lemuel gave his humble thanks and appreciation, though he already knew that Reldresal wanted to be friends with him, of his own accord. Unlike all other dignitaries who would come to visit Lemuel (most of them just out of curiosity) Reldresal insisted from the start not to stand at a safe distance on the upper circle, eye-to-eye with Lemuel, but to stand on Lemuel's palm or knee.

And so, sitting on his bed, leaning on the wall, his arms hugging his bent legs (one of which was still chained to his Prison-Temple), Lemuel was listening closely to Reldresal, who was marching as he was speaking, back and forth on Lemuel's knee, sometimes jumping from one knee to the other. (Reldresal was renown in Lilliput for his agility.)

Lemuel was assured of Reldresal's loyalty when Reldresal was urging him to seek official Asylum at Lilliput. "You should start the process as soon as possible," was Reldresal's advise. "If you have an Asylum Status here, in time you will be entitled for a Residence Permit, and later a Citizenship, and later—who knows—you might even rise high up in Court!"

"I always had political aspirations." confided Lemuel, "I have a vision and a dream. Yes, I can! My party could really change the world!"

"I am afraid," coughed Reldresal politely, "that becoming the head of a party—any party—is out of the question. You should have been born on Lilliputian soil to merit such high post."

Still, the prospect of rising high up in Court was also quite appealing to my Lemuel. He was very flattered by Reldresal's confidence in him and, from what he could see of Lilliput, walking as far as his chains would allow him, he liked this little quaint land. If he could not get back to England, he might as well try to make it, almost to the top, right here!

If he could make it there, he could make it anywhere.

But there was more.

As Lemuel lowered General Reldresal back to the ground, the General coughed again. "Oh yes. The Emperor knows full well how difficult it must be for you, away from your home and family."

Lemuel shed a tear, which the General was quick to wipe off his bold, bared head.

"In our Empire, we use the services of Lovers, for men who are without a family or away on the road. Seeing as we do that your needs and possibly your abilities are far greater than ours, the Emperor will provide you with six Lovers, tonight."

At first Lemuel tried to convince the General that the mere idea was preposterous, but to no avail. General Reldresal just thought my Lemuel a prude and, laughingly, he jumped on his Lilliputian horse and galloped away.

As night fell and it became dark, Lemuel became aware that he had no place to hide. Still chained to his Prison-Temple, all he could do was hope that the Lovers would not be hurt emotionally, when he would reject them, or physically, when they would insist on servicing him.

As nothing happened and nobody came, he decided to go to sleep, hoping that the General had come to his senses, after all.

Lying on his coarse bed, fast asleep, he was suddenly woken up by soft whispers in his ear: "Quinbus Flestrin, hugru Festo" (meaning: "Man-Mountain, you are really great.")

And they continued in soft Lilliputian: "You are worthy of love. We all love you!" He opened his eyes, but in the pitch dark, he could not see anybody. As the sweet voices persisted, he could make out that there were six of them, whispering somewhere nearby.

"Where are you," he whispered back, "let me see you!"

At that he heard some giggles, and immediately six little lamps were lit. In this dim light he saw six Lilliputian women of various ages, from 20 to 60, and various sizes from 5 to 7 inches, dressed sombrely in black, sitting on little stools near his head.

"What is it," he gasped, "what are you doing here?"

"We are your Lovers," answered the one who seemed to be the oldest and most respected. "The General sent for us, to love and comfort you."

"It is all paid for in advance by the Emperor. Worry not," added another one.

"So, what is it that you do?" asked Lemuel, somewhat amused.

"We tell you that we love you, of course," they all said, bursting into laughter. "Everybody knows that!"

"Well, I am from another place, as you can tell," said Lemuel. "Please excuse my ignorance."

Upon which they proceeded to explain to him that the Lilliputian men are prone to be lonesome when they travel away from home, and even when at home if their spouses do not show them enough love. Which is why many moons ago, a profession has evolved of "Lovers." women whose occupation it was to give men love, affection and, when needed, admiration.

"And what about sex?" asked Lemuel, bewildered.

"Oh, sex," said the Lovers. "This, each man is bound by our holy Blundecral and the holy matrimony contract to give his wife, at least four times a week."

"Oh," said Lemuel, "and if not?"

"He is stoned to death, of course," said the Lovers, as a matter of fact, to Lemuel's terrified astonishment.

"So, well, indeed, how do you go about your work, as Lovers?"

asked Lemuel, and the tiny women resumed whispering more loving, comforting and encouraging words in his ear, until Lemuel could not take it anymore and he burst into tears. While they were whispering gently, he could not help thinking about his poor, dear mother, who never had time to hug or caress him; about his childhood sweetheart, who died in the Plague; even about his children and his wife—and he felt that he was missing it all, oh, so bitterly. As the professional, warm voices played in his ear, he was overcome by emotions and, crying, crying bitterly, he was suddenly aware that he was all alone.

The Lovers were just closing the door behind them, the last one waving good-bye.

In a strange and inexplicable way, Lemuel did feel much better.

"But, wait a minute!" he called out and was much relieved to see the door open again.

"We were only paid for one session," apologised the eldest Lover.

"But the General will surely pay us tomorrow more, when we tell him . . .?" ventured the youngest.

"Oh well," said the oldest, "let us go back in."

But when they sat themselves again on their little stools and resumed their "We love you," Lemuel stopped them sharply.

"We were talking before about sex," he said. "How do unmarried men get by in this province?"

"They get married, of course," said the oldest.

"Or they are hired by married men, who cannot fulfil all their matrimonial duties, to have sex with their wives, of course," added the youngest.

"And if a woman wants to have sex more than four times a week?" ventured Lemuel cautiously.

"It is always a problem," sighed the Lovers and exchanged glances with each other.

"In fact," said the oldest, "many women among us are petitioning the Emperor to make the law five times a week."

"But it is very difficult. The rumour goes that the Emperor, who is also the Highest Priest, He himself cannot fulfil His obligations and He secretly hires men to take care of the Empress, and many a time she pays for extra, with her own money, too!"

"While we, the poor Lover women, can never afford it!"

"Could I be of any help at all?" asked Lemuel hopefully.

"Oh, so sorry," cried the Lovers as one, "we could not possibly afford you!"

"Why not?" Lemuel's heart sank.

"You are too big, much too big for us! We pay according to size, you see."

"Oh, that," said Lemuel, "What if I will not ask to be paid?"

"We could always exchange loving with sex," reasoned the youngest with the others.

And so the business was concluded, though Lemuel knew full well he could do without their loving and his crying. Yet, he was much intrigued to have sex with them.

The ladies then climbed onto his lap, and opening the flap of his breeches, gasped in delight at the size of his still soft manhood. As he watched them help each other to undress, Lemuel caressed his yard and soft bollocks, and felt the familiar sensation of heat and urgency, as it was growing big.

He figured that he would not need to use his condom, as no penetration was likely to occur.

The ladies held hands together and balanced themselves on his thighs, giggling in wonderment. In the soft candles' light, he noted that their skins were white and their bodies seemed to be very firm. He could not see any difference between them; no signs of age on their perfectly shaped bodies, heavy yet firm breasts and smooth bellies.[81]

Leaning back on his hands, Lemuel watched how the ladies formed a circle around his proud yard, stepping gently on his bollocks and belly with their naked little feet.

The sensation was overwhelming.

Never could he fathom that such a delicate touch would produce such a pleasurable effect! He shut his eyes and felt how six little warm bodies clung to his erect yard, rubbing their little breasts and warm limbs close to it.

The ladies seemed to enjoy themselves enormously, too, for he soon heard only heavy breathings. Hugging and caressing his yard, which was becoming harder and harder, one of the ladies collapsed suddenly and sat down with her legs wrapped around the base of it, writhing her tiny, wet seat of pleasure on a bulging vein. Arching her body, she was clutching at his bush, and this sent sharp sensations up Lemuel's spine. He felt her tiny slit warm and wet at the base of his yard and he felt a great urge to taste this wetness.

Gently, he scooped her off his belly and rolled her on her back, on the palm of his hand. She probably sensed his wish and lay there with her legs asunder, her arms above her head, grasping the tip of his finger for support. Delicately, Lemuel stuck out the tip of his tongue and licked her legs and wet womanhood. She squealed in delight and spread her legs still wider, pushing onto the tip of Lemuel's tongue.

The taste was exquisite, reminiscent of delicate mead.[82] As he explored her Lilliputian womanhood with the tip of his tongue, he felt the other five ladies rubbing their own wetness, bellies and bosoms against his ever erect yard, stretching their arms high up, trying to get to his crown.

Ever so carefully, with his other hand, he picked one of the ladies up and placed her astride the top of his yard, where she started whirling vigorously.

At that moment Lemuel was overcome with bliss and joy, and therefore he was not fast enough to remove the lady from up there, before the juicy fruit of their labours burst out in gushes, toppling over the lady, covering her with the thick-warm liquid.

Soon all those delighted ladies were covered top to bottom, rubbing each other's bodies with Lemuel's produce. The lady in his palm called out, "Let me down too, please, my good Man-Mountain!" and Lemuel watched in amazement how the six of them were rubbing each other excitedly.

"Was it as good for you?" asked Lemuel tenderly and was quite pleased to hear "Yes! But we are not done yet!" and the six of them rolled off him and positioned themselves on their backs, side by side on his bed, gesturing for him to advance with his tongue.

Lemuel then pushed aside his chains, turned on his knees and started toying with his tongue not only with the ladies' cavities, but also around their breasts, bellies and the back of their necks. They were laughing and turning in all directions, to better feel Lemuel's tongue all over their bodies. Then they asked him to put his hands on the floor, and each of them mounted a finger.

Rubbing against his fingers, feeling the hairs penetrating, one by one they all reached their desired heights, satisfied, spent and happy.

When they dismounted from his fingers and dressed up again, Lemuel sniffed at his fingers and treasured the delicate scent of six ladies' love.

Chapter Fifteen

THE AUTHOR CONTEMPLATES HER MISERABLE EXISTENCE,
AND THE COURSE OF HER BOOK; BOLGOLAM HAMMERS
LILLIPUTIAN HISTORY INTO GULLIVER, SPARING HIM
NO DETAILS AND NO THREATS, TRYING TO RECRUIT HIM
TO THE SLAMECKSANS, BOLGOLAM'S PARTY.
(Redriff, Wednesday, November 6th, 1748)

I must confess: I find this work, collecting my notes about my husband's secret tales and making a real book out of them, to be very rewarding.

As I read what my younger self wrote, forty-six years ago, I feel young again. I remember how I was sitting at this same table-of-secrets: night fell, my children were sound asleep and I—I was reminiscing Lemuel's stories, I was smiling as I was writing, and I retired to bed, caressing myself to sleep, being so inspired by my Lemuel's wild stories and my own delicious memories.

And now, well, at my seventy-sixth year, my ageing, aching body no longer gives me the pleasures it once did. I do not miss them as much as I had thought, when I was full of vigour, falling asleep well satisfied, almost every night.

No, these days my pleasures are in food and in thought.

I spend much time contemplating my supper, then preparing it, and while I eat it, I keep myself company by conjuring in my imagination all that which has happened in the fantastic lands I and my husband visited so many years ago.

As I read again and again the pages I secretly wrote in my youth, I see that they contain almost only the tales of Lemuel's intimate escapades, while the events that linked them are missing. If I want all this to be fit for print, I should add the missing links, the details of intrigues at Court and other bizarre events that my husband encountered in his voyages.

I now find new pleasures in conjuring up nearly-forgotten memories and weaving out this wondrous story, all my own. It is funny how I can now get just as excited from telling a good story as I did forty years ago, from Lemuel's nestling down in my garden.

I think I should also write about our first years together, and how we became best of friends and lovers. It would fit nicely after Chapter Two, I think. I still see it as a miracle, that people who are total strangers, somehow, suddenly, gradually, eventually, become one with each other. I will make a note of it now, and will get back to it later, maybe tomorrow.

For now, back to Lilliput:

* * *

"I know everything," were the ominous opening words of Admiral Skyresh Bolgolam, standing inside the Prison-Temple on the upper circle, eye to eye with Lemuel.

His green costume was shining in a manner that was very unpleasing. Lemuel could not help thinking of this jade Bolgolam as a tiny, yet dangerous dragon, about to breath fire onto Lemuel's face.

He was sitting on his 600 Lilliputian beds, very much aware of the fact that, even though he was bigger than Skyresh Bolgolam, he was still chained to his Prison-Temple, still at the mercy of this little man, whose single word could set thousands of poisoned arrows shooting right at him.

Dismally, Lemuel assumed that his night of passionate lovemaking with the Lovers might not have pleased the local authorities as much as it pleased those directly involved.

"It was not my fault" he mumbled.

"Be quiet when you listen to me and listen to me very carefully!" roared Bolgolam. For a tiny Lilliputian, he had a very deep, resonant voice.

"I know everything, and I will tell it all to you." Breathing heavily, he seemed to try to overcome some aversion. "I would never choose to do it myself, but I have direct orders from the Emperor. For some reason, He seems to like you. Be grateful. Be very grateful."

"Oh, I am, of course I am," Lemuel was quick to say, and quicker to regret speaking.

"Hush! I personally cannot stand you, and it is only for the glory of our Emperor and his Empire that I am here to tell you all you need to know about us. The Emperor, in His Eternal Wisdom, seems to think that you can be useful. Call me stupid, for I think He is wrong. If you repeat these words, you are dead."

"What words?" Lemuel was indeed baffled.

"Well said," said Bolgolam. "There might be hope for you yet."

"Oh," was all Lemuel could utter.

"Man-Mountain, we are at war!"

"Why? What did I do? Did they complain about me . . .?"

"Stop blabbering and hear me out, Man-Mountain," barked Bolgolam. "My time is short and precious. And my patience is even shorter."

Lemuel was about to say "sorry," but he was wise enough to sit still.

"You should know that we are mortified by two evils: within—the constant haggling, ogling, and squabbling of the Tramecksans for the favour of our Emperor, and without—the constant threats of our malicious neighbours, the Blefuscudians, to invade our peace-loving island and to conquer us all. Our enemies are plenty. Our time is pressing."

And to Lemuel's amazement, Bolgolam went on to unfold this incredible story:

It began upon the following occasion. Apparently, it was allowed on all hands, that the primitive way of breaking eggs, before the Lilliputians would eat them, was upon the larger end; but His Present Emperor's grandfather, while he was a boy, going to eat an egg, and breaking it according to the ancient practice, happened to cut one of his fingers.

The sight of his own blood was so offensive to the little boy that he started stammering, and from that day on could not pronounce the sound "S" as it used to be pronounced (a soft "Th") and was only able to pronounce it as a harsh "S."

Whereupon the Emperor, his father, published an edict, commanding all his subjects, be they Tramecksans (from the T-Party, those wearing high-heels) or Slamecksans (from the S-Party, wearing flat shoes[83]), upon great penalties, to break the smaller end of their eggs, and to pronounce the letter "S" no longer softly, but harshly.

Special undercover agents were dispatched to the streets, towns, and villages all over Lilliput, and whoever would go on saying "Thuch a pleathant day" for example, instead of "Such a pleasant day" would be srashed on the thpot.

Some Lilliputians, most of them from the T-Party, highly resented this law—as Lilliputian histories document—since they could not figure out the new spelling and pronunciations, and certainly did not like being srashed.

They formed a splinter party, named The Big-Endians and in the course of history raised six rebellions. Their battle cry was "To BE!" (Big Endians) and, if it was not for the monarch of the neighbouring island Blefuscu, who fermented the silly and dangerous notions of breaking the egg on the wrong side and of confusing the Lilliputian alphabet, the BE's would no longer be.

As it was, the monarch of Blefuscu supported the BE usurper and helped him kill His Present Emperor's great grandfather (the father of the boy who cut his finger on that fateful breakfast).

"My forefather, Skyresh Cholgolam, I am ever so proud to say, was a true member of the S-Party. When the BE usurper, aided by the Blefuscudian Monarch, took the throne, my father kept loyal to our True Emperor. Though he failed to save His Present Emperor's great grandfather's life, he did manage to save His son from the clutches of the BE's!"

Bolgolam laughed, and Lemuel shuddered. This sinister mirth was not boding any good.

What followed was a dark tale of dreadful BE rulers, conspiracies of the Blefuscudian Monarch and dormant terror cells all over Lilliput.

At some point, the Blefuscudian monarch no longer liked the BE usurper, and under the pretext of helping the Lilliputian rebels, the Blefuscudians invaded Lilliput!

The BE tyrant, unsuccessfully hiding in a hole, was betrayed and captured, his teeth knocked out, and was humiliated and finally hanged. And all because those BE's could not appreciate the wisdom of breaking an egg in the proper manner, at the smaller end!

"That was the moment for which my forefather Cholgolam was scheming. Now that the BE's were gone, he raised the flag of freedom to Lilliput and mobilised both the S-Party and the T-Party against the Blefuscudians.

"My forefather Cholgolam triumphantly presented to the overjoyed Lilliputians the lad who was in hiding (the one whose breakfast started it all). Both the T-Party followers and the S-Party followers were so happy to have a true descendant of the Lilliputian throne that they forgot—for a moment—their egg dithputes and united behind His Present Emperor's father."

Lemuel was hard pressed to understand it all and was dazed by all the strange names that were thrown at him. Silently, he reminded himself that the BE's are those who no longer exist, the red T-Party wear high heels, and the green S-Party wear low heels. He still did not remember who breaks the egg on which side, but he was hoping that by and by he would manage to decipher what Bolgolam was really aiming at.

"In one sweeping battle we rose to the occasion and threw the Blefuscudians' army into the sea. Unfortunately, they stole our battleships when they were thrown into the sea, and set sail to Blefuscu. This chapter in our otherwise glorious history gave us all a lesson: do not expect your enemies to drown peacefully! They will try to survive, at all costs . . ."

Bolgolam was catching his breath. He seemed to be reaching a painful moment in his narrative. Lemuel kept silent, fearing the worst.

"But this was not the end of our troubles," Bolgolam went on. "Unfortunately, there were, and still are, Lilliputians who, for some unfathomable reason, tend to side with the Blefuscudians.

"They are all from the despicable T-Party, of course, and are trying to revive the BE. (My spies tell me that they call themselves now EST: Envy Se T-party!) They stick to the wrong, wide side of the egg. They have secret meetings, where they break the eggs wrongly, and hopelessly confuse the 'S' with the 'Th'. Our Emperor has zero tolerance for those criminals. When they are caught, they are severely punished. Therefore, many prefer to go into exile. They flee for refuge to that loathsome empire, Blefuscu."

Bolgolam was clutching his fists and clenching his tiny teeth.

Lemuel could clearly feel the pain, as Bolgolam concluded his narrative with the computation that almost six thousand ESTians from the T-Party had, at several times, preferred to suffer death, rather than submit to break their eggs at the smaller end, or speak proper Lilliputian. The ESTians even went as far as declaring that their language is the true Lilliputian, while the real true Lilliputian, which Bolgolam was so proud to speak, is but a dialect.

One hundred-and-ninety-two people were killed trying to cross the channel, and about two-hundred were injured. Many hundred large volumes have been published upon this controversy, while the books of the Big-Endianth have long been forbidden, and the whole party rendered incapable, by law, of holding employments.

"That is so tragic," Lemuel could not refrain from uttering.

"Yes, it is. We should all be standing united as one, behind our beloved Emperor! His Royal Highness is secretly an S-Party supporter, I am sure of it. But still, many a Lilliputian seek for the truth elsewhere, though they will never find it, of course, over there. It is not there! I will make sure they see the light where the light shines truly! In the meanwhile, we are torn within, whilst our enemy plots to invade us. Again!"

Heaving and gasping, he added menacingly, "And that is where you step in, Man-Mountain!"

"Me?" said Gulliver, bewildered. "I have nothing to do with all of this. I do not belong here. I am just an innocent bystander, a castaway, hoping to find here asylum!"

"Are you crazy? Innocent or not, castaway you will be, if you stand by and not obey!" Roared Bolgolam, rising to the top of his tiny toes, while aiming to look down into Lemuel's eyes.

This sounded so frightening, and Bolgolam continued in this manner on and on, so that Lemuel had no time to ponder how precisely the Lilliputians would ever manage to cast him away.

"You are at the mercy of our good Emperor, and He is not too happy, having to carry your burden on His Royal shoulders. Do you know how many new taxes He must levy to maintain your sick appetite? Do you think He is happy when His citizens complain?

"I am the only one here who can make sure the Emperor will grant you freedom. But only when I know for certain that you are as good a Lilliputian as any of us good Lilliputians.

"At least we must be assured that you break your eggs correctly. I can overlook your poor pronunciation of our Lilliputian language. That is the only concession I am willing to make in your case. And it would help if you declared yourself to be an S, and join the S-Party."

And Bolgolam added portentously, "You can expect my next visit when you least expect it and think very carefully where you stand!"

At that Bolgolam left Lemuel sitting there, dejected and perplexed, wracking his mind how he would ever be able to see the difference between the small and the large end of those minuscule Lilliputian eggs.[84]

Chapter Sixteen

The author remembers her youth; Reldresal, too, explains Lilliputian politics in basic terms, recognising Lemuel's total lack of understanding in politics; the bloody history of Lilliputian parties; Lemuel is invited to join the T-Party.
(Redriff, Thursday, November 7th, 1748)

My moods swing like Betty's when she was a sixteen-year-old maiden. She was a handful, my daughter at that age. I do not blame her. I never did. It is not easy, blooming from a child into a woman. I remember Betty's tantrums and constant arguing. Was I the same when I was at that age? I am sure my mother would say "Yes."

Well, I am definitely as moody now.

Yesterday I was full of vigour and excitement, collecting my scribbles of almost fifty years past; so sure of myself and my writing ability, so excited to re-live those delicious moments of desire and contentment, so ridiculously fired by the certainty that I must, I must publish Lemuel's full story.

Today I am disheartened. My aches take the better of me. It is so hard to fly on the wings of memory and be again the woman I want to be, the woman I ever was, when my suffering body drags me down.

No, I do not know this woman, who is now writing my memoir in the candlelight, the woman whose old face I see when I glance at the reflection in the dark window.

She sits on my chair at this very table, the table that is almost as old as I am. The table squeaks, but the pains are mine to feel.

Oh, let the devil take me.

If I can only find the power to continue writing the story of Lemuel's travels, perchance I might forget again my old age and unrelenting pains. If these pages will ever make for a coherent book, I had better fill in all the missing information. I had better tell all the stories that I carelessly skipped fifty years gone, for the silly reason that they were not arousing enough.

I was a silly maiden, even when I was thirty years of age.

* * *

Lemuel was alarmed to realise that his presence in Lilliput rekindled old animosities at the Royal Court, and that so much of this animosity was now targeted at him.

His hopes that the Emperor was favouring him, as Reldresal was consistently assuring him, vanished completely after Bolgolam's visit. Gulliver was thoroughly perplexed as to where he was standing with the Emperor, since he heard contradicting versions from Reldresal and from Bolgolam. A worrying thought crept into Lemuel's mind: was it possible that the Emperor, the most powerful man in the world, as they all said, had no say in Court?

Lemuel could not foresee that, during his two-year stay in Lilliput, tensions among the various factions against his own person would be mounting so high, that finally he would be pressed to escape, in order to save his life.

But back then, still chained to his Prison-Temple, his only way of knowing what was happening in the outside world was from what his visitors were telling him. Luckily, his daily visitor, his Lilliputian teacher General Reldresal, was a kind person and, in the course of teaching him the Lilliputian language, he also gave him much hope for a speedy release.

Most of the lessons were conducted whilst Lemuel was lying on his belly, his face close to the General. Curious Lilliputians were coming and going all the while, females openly gawking at him, making it quite distracting for Lemuel to concentrate on Reldresal's lessons.

Still, Lemuel and the General became very close as time went by, indeed very close, and finally it was Reldresal's heroism that saved my Lemuel's life.

As much as Reldresal was trying to paint a rosy future for Lemuel in Lilliput, he could not hide from him the fact that Bolgolam was not his only enemy. There were more who voiced their concerns about the Man-Mountain's disastrous effect on Lilliput. In fact, the hostility towards the Man-Mountain started to spill on to the few who still dared to voice their support for him.

"And tomorrow the discussion about your fate is scheduled in Court." Reldresal was whispering this very softly, looking fearfully around, lest he was overheard.

"But," Lemuel whispered back, equally, if not more fearfully, "what are the chances, that . . ." He could not utter the horrifying thought that bothered him all along. "I have surely proved in this fortnight how docile I am, and even how useful I could be . . .?"

"It is more complicated than that," whispered Reldresal. "Let me give you a lesson in Lilliputian politics. Then I will not have to whisper all the time. You see," Reldresal continued in his normal tone, "until your arrival, all Affairs of States were conducted along very clear lines and affiliations, plainly marked and recognised by the height of our heels. And when you came—"

"The height of your Heels?!" Lemuel could not restrain from cutting into Reldresal's lecture. "I thought it was the eggs and the 'S' . . .?

"You have been misled," said Reldresal gloomily, "and I can tell by whom. Never mind." And he mumbled almost to himself, "I knew that Bolgolam would not wait too long before he would pounce."

The General shrugged his shoulders and continued his lecture. "You are so simple-minded, my dear Man-Mountain. The eggs and the 'S' are fake, just a cover-up story, something Lilliputian children can easily grasp and be swayed by. The truth is that our animosities run deeper than mere eggs and articulation. Lilliputian politics is a grave matter and it all boils down to our heels."

Again, Lemuel thought he did not hear Reldresal well. "Your heels? Heels!?"

Reldresal was nodding condescendingly but Lemuel insisted, "What do Heels got to do with Politics!?"

"I like your naïveté, Man-Mountain. It is very endearing. Indeed, sometimes you are just like a little child." Reldresal smiled benevolently. "Our high heels represent our high morals. But of course, you could not just grasp that, being the coarse creature which you are. Let me explain it to you from the beginning: As you can see, I am wearing high heels, because I belong to the T-Party, the Tramecksans.

"In Lilliputian, Tramecksans means something like 'The Heart Is On The Left Side, Where High Values Reside' (and we also tend to wear red-coloured clothes on official events, which, of course, represent the heart and the blood circulation).

"I am proud and happy to tell you that we are hugely favoured by 99% of the Lilliputians, while the S-Party, the Slamecksans, our political enemies so to speak, are only favoured by 1% of all Lilliputians.

"You know, Slamecksans, the full name of the S-Party, means in ancient Lilliputian 'Both Feet Firmly On The Ground And Lots Of Money In The Pockets.' They pathetically try to distinguish themselves from us, by wearing green clothes and low-heeled footwear. But, as I told you, they are only supported by 1% of our populace."

"So you, the T-Party, having the favour of 99% of all Lilliputians, must be controlling everything round here?" ventured Gulliver.

"Not at all," sighed Reldresal. "Sadly, this detested minority, the S's, are holding 99% of Lilliput's wealth."

"That is very confusing," said Lemuel. "How did that happen?"

General Reldresal looked about him and, noticing that a number of Lilliputians were listening curiously, he signalled Lemuel to enter his Prison-Temple for the continuation of the lesson.

Lemuel dragged his many chains and squeezed himself inside the stuffy space. He sat with his back leaning against the wall, placed his hand, palm up, on the ground and, after the General stepped onto it, raised him to his knee, onto which Reldresal jumped gracefully and resumed his speech. "You asked about the emergence of the 99% and this history, which is shrouded in secrecy. It started quite violently, though.

"Many moons[85] ago, there were a handful of Lilliputians who liked to fight each other. They called themselves Slammers. They were quite savage, and whoever killed the other, kept the other's clothes and weapons.

"Those who survived the fights amassed all those clothes and weapons, and got themselves quite a reputation for people you would not want to see, unless you were at a safe distance.

"With all this excess of clothes and weapons, they erected fashion shops and built small armies to defend their properties. The Slammers lured many of the terrified, helpless Lilliputians to join them, by promising them not to beat them, and even to give them some clothes.

"What else could the Slammers do, once they had those armies at their disposal, but to send them to fight with each other? The next step for the Slammer-Commanders was to develop war strategies, while standing on the hills and watching the bloodshed from a distance that gave them good, professional, perspective. The Slammers were recruiting young Lilliputians who knew not any better, to do the killing and pillaging for them, promising the poor youngsters a share of what they plundered for the Commanders. It was a small share, of course, and many of these lads got killed in the process of killing each other, so the Slammers did not have to part with much of the booty, and that is how they amassed their fortunes."

"That does not sound very fair," said Lemuel.

"Why not? They did their best at what they were best at."

"The way you put it," said Lemuel, "it sounds almost noble."

"It is," Reldresal reassured him. "If my forefathers were Slammers, I would not be wearing these high heels today and preaching high morals to you."

"Can you not just go and fight one of the Slammers and take over his wealth?"

"I wish it was that simple," sighed Reldresal, "but today that kind of fighting is no longer legal. We live in a just and peaceful world, in which we settle disputes by bribes in Court. Even the Slammers have agreed to stop fighting each other and that is why they are no longer called Slammers, but Slamecksans, or the S-party.

"Instead of those noble, ancient, savage fights on Lilliputian battlefields, we have modified and dignified our competitive urges into graceful games at Court, to honour and to please the Emperor. I hope, no, I am certain, that one day soon you will be invited to Court to observe our games." And Reldresal added modestly, "I will be delighted to demonstrate to you my humble superiority, when you see how your servant, representing the T-Party, is beating his S's opponents."

"The T-Party . . . How did the T-Party come into being?"

"We are descendants of the Trampled Lilliputians. We are proud to be the lucky survivors of all those skirmishes. In the course of history, we understood that our survival depends on our ability to hide away, or, when we are discovered, on our ability to appear big and terrifying. Hence the origin of our high heels.

"Many moons ago, the cleverer among the Trampled Lilliputians came to the conclusion that if we cannot have all these riches which the S's possess, at least we can enjoy some of it, by being as friendly as possible with those who possess them. That is how our forefathers came to establish the T-Party, and promised to represent unfailingly the rest of the 99% of all Lilliputians.

"Those 99% of all Lilliputians believed what we told them, that there is no room in Court for everybody, and therefore we should represent them there. They seem to be happy, thinking that we, the Tramecksans, do this loyally enough."

"You explain it extremely well, but it is still exceedingly confusing," acknowledged Lemuel. "So which party is actually controlling Lilliput?"

"It is hard to tell, and that is how it should be. You see, morally we are far superior to the S-Party, and we are far more favoured by the Emperor, too, because we jump higher and better than any S man." And to demonstrate the T's superiority, Reldresal leaped from Gulliver's left knee to the right one, and continued from there. "I can humbly confess, my dear Man-Mountain, that I, simple born and bred Reldresal, am a champion at Court-Jumping! That is how I got to this position, of Principal Secretary for Private Affairs."

"Quite impressive," said Gulliver, nevertheless careful not to move his legs too abruptly.

As Reldresal continued to demystify Lilliputian Court administration, Gulliver's admiration of the Emperor was increasing with every new piece of information. The Emperor demonstrated immense fairness in his power-distribution among his cabinet members. Though he himself was a descendent of one of the Lilliputians' greatest warriors, he seemed to have a place in his heart for all Lilliputians, no matter from what breed they came.

Supported for many generations by the Shumclum Clan of high priests, all the Emperors were considered, for moons immemorial, to be supported not only by all Lilliputians, but more importantly by Lilliputian deities.

There is irrefutable evidence and many predictions relating to the eternal superiority of the Emperors, in the Holly Blundecral,[86] which was dictated by the Gods to the first Shumclum, the same Gods that installed the Shumclum Clan as their representatives, according to the Shumclums protestations. Only the Shumclums were able to interpret and clarify to the Lilliputian masses, the seemingly contradicting messages written in the Holly Blundecral.

The Emperor, in his benevolence, gave the high-heeled, red-clad T-Party members far more seats in his Administration, more than he gave to the low-heeled, green S's, explaining that thus he is mirroring their popularity among the Lilliputians.

Each seat of the T-Party was representing a different aspect of Lilliputian's life, such as the Weather, the Wavelets, the Sun and almost every Star, while the minority S's were holding four seats in all: The Gifts to the Crown (as they called the Tax Enforcement Office[87]), The Maintenance of The Gifts to the Crown (as they called the Treasury[88]), The Ministry of Internal Peace (as they called the Police Force[89]), and the Ministry of External Peace (as they called the Army[90]).

Yet, the Emperor was careful not to let known which, if any, party he favoured. Being a shrewd statesman, as Reldresal was saying with much admiration, the Emperor kept on baffling everyone; he never favoured one colour in his attire, which was as colourful as the rainbow; inside his Palace he would wear low heels, but when he would be engaged in public speeches, he would wear the highest heels in the whole of Lilliput. At all other times, he would mix; he had a collection of 2,700 pairs of shoes, of both high and low heels, and he would always wear one high-heeled shoe and one low-heeled shoe, which gave him a hobble in his gait.

"So I am sure," Reldresal was now whispering comfortingly, "that the Emperor will relent and will give you your freedom, following the debate in Court tomorrow."

"I see what you mean," whispered Lemuel, though he could not quite follow how Reldresal came to this conclusion.

"But you, Dear Man-Mountain," said Reldresal triumphantly, "you are clearly a Tramecksans! With your freedom soon granted, you will tower above us all, no matter what heels you will be wearing. So, you are a natural T-Partier!"

"I am most honoured, my dear Reldresal," said Lemuel, and he meant it, I know. He was ever so pleased to be acknowledged and welcomed.

"You will remain loyal to the T-Party's cause, of course," warned Reldresal. "I have reasons to suspect that one of these days this detestable S-Party man, Admiral Skyresh Bolgolam, from the Ministry of External Peace, will try to make an S-Party member of you."

"Oh," coughed Lemuel, "I doubt that he will ever want me. He is quite nasty to me whenever he can be."

"Well, nothing is beneath his plotting, so I trust you will not fall for his menacing threats and false promises of fame and gain. Remember, those S's are favored by very few Lilliputians! If you go with us, the T-Party, you will be loved and admired by 99% of us!"

And with this appealing prospect, he requested that Lemuel would lower him back to earth. Eager to please, Lemuel let Reldresal hop from his knee to the palm of his hand, and he lowered his hand ever so slowly and carefully to the ground.

Reldresal jumped off Lemuel's palm, waved good-bye at the door, mounted his horse and disappeared, leaving Lemuel to contemplate the Lilliputian state of affairs and his own gloomy future, which was to be determined by unknown little people the following day.

Chapter Seventeen

Now I am puzzled, as I read the notes which I wrote more than forty-five years ago, by the question: How could Lemuel have known exactly what had transpired in Court, while he was still chained to his Prison-Temple?

Did he tell me all this or did I invent it all? And does it really matter, either way?

Perhaps Lemuel told me so much about Lilliput that I felt as if I had been there myself. When I wrote of his first voyage, I was still that naïve, simple woman, who never ventured further than fifteen miles from where she was born.

I drank thirstily his recounting until I felt as if I had been there myself.

Or is it my imagination, perhaps my longing to have been there myself?

Remembering something that has happened, or imagining something that might have happened, have the same exhilarating stimulation, so I find, on my mind and soul.

So this is exactly how I imagine what has happened in Lilliput, having heard Lemuel's stories:

* * *

The following day Lemuel had no official visitors. It felt strange, strolling around his Prison-Temple, hearing but the clinking of his chains and the bemused and bewildered cries of the newly arrived Lilliputians who came to gaze upon him.

The words of Bolgolam and Reldresal kept echoing in his mind, sending shivers of fear, intermingled with rays of hope, as Gulliver was contemplating his future.

It was a hot day in Lilliput, and his Prison-Temple was stuffy. He noticed that the gazers, having paid the due fee to see him from up close (outside the Prison-Temple gates, though), were following him as a shadow wherever he was dejectedly pacing.

After a while, he realised that they were, in fact, following his shadow, trying to stay under it, to keep cool. Lemuel felt his heart swell with kindly feelings towards these little people, so eager to see him, braving the distance, the heat, and the fee they had to pay.

And all for him!

He had never been a celebrity before. The only people that truly loved and adored him were we, his wife and children. And here he was, surrounded by hundreds of Lilliputian admirers, anxious to speak to him, to hear his broken Lilliputian, to be amused by his mistakes and to love him all the more for his genuine attempts to blend among them.

And all this while, about 500 feet away from this tranquil, friendly place, he knew that other Lilliputians were plotting his demise. Lemuel was almost sorry that Reldresal and Bolgolam confided in him so openly.

Would not a blissful obliviousness be much better than this wretched state of insistent worries?

He could only imagine what was going on at the Palace, and his imagination went wild. Under this heightened state of agitated fears and muted hopes, he could remember details very vividly, and when he finally reached our home in London and told me all he remembered, it was quite easy for me to piece together those tidbits.

Sweet Lemuel, his naïveté blinded him from deciphering what was really going on, by whom and upon whom. I guess women are indeed as cunning as foxes, and learning how to read at an early age, I soon learned to read between the lines just as well. Yet, I think women's greatest achievement to date is our ability to let our men believe that they are the wiser.[91]

So here is the accurate description of what I am sure happened in Court on that fateful day, when my Lemuel's life was spared (and not for the last time . . .).

On that day the top item on the agenda read: "*How do you solve a problem like Man-Mountain?*"

It surely was an exciting day at Court. Even the Empress was there!

Being the only woman ever allowed to attend Court meetings, she always waived this option and preferred to spend more quality time with her Ladies in Waiting.

But not this time.

Though she pretended otherwise, secretly, she craved my Lemuel. She could still feel the roughness of Gulliver's finger brushing against her soft, exposed breast. Ever since their chance meeting, a yard above ground, when they exchanged hot glances and one warm caress, the Empress was burning to feel more of Lemuel's fingers, on both her teats[92] and to progress even further.

She hated her position, which did not allow her the freedom to sneak into Lemuel's Prison-Temple at night (she very well knew that any other Lilliputian woman was free to do so, night in night out), and she hated Lemuel for his mere existence, for the unfulfilled, never to be fulfilled promise of requited desire, which he embodied.

The opportunity to be near him, if only while his fate was to be discussed, was tempting. She cancelled her chocolate-tasting event in town and accompanied her husband to Court.

The Lilliputian protocol dictates that whenever a discussion is announced, courtiers are expected to take their seats according to their expressed opinions.

This custom resulted in the T-Party members almost always and almost all, sitting on the left-hand side of the Emperor, colouring that side of the assembly red, and the S-people sitting at the right-hand side of the Emperor, which would become, on such occasions, all green.

Therefore, when the Emperor entered Court, accompanied by his Empress, everybody, but everybody, was in shock (except for the Empress, of course, who attended such a meeting for the very first time, and therefore had no expectations).

All the courtiers were shocked to see the Empress there, while the Emperor was baffled by the sight of the colour mix round him.

His courtiers were not seated according to old loyalties!

He saw high heels rubbing shoulders with low heels, left and right; red and green mingling as coats were flapping. The Emperor scanned the Assembly, but was not relieved when he spotted the black robes of Shumclum, the High Priest.

Usually, Shumclum was a reliable indication of where the majority of opinions lay, but today he sat right at the center, across from the Emperor's throne, with a blank look on his face.

The Emperor was glad a discussion would ensue, which would clarify for him where the winds were blowing, so that he could appear to be leading the people rather than to be drifting along.

What was made clear quite soon was that anti-Gulliverians were all sitting at the right, with Skyresh Bolgolam, the S-Party leader, Admiral of the Realm, prominently in the lead of the opinion-pull. Pro-Gulliverians sat on the left, looking up to Reldresal, who by then was accepted as the Man-Mountain authority.

As the discussions got heated, the Emperor pretended to fall asleep, and the Empress pretended to be slightly bored.

General Reldresal, being the one Lilliputian who had seen Lemuel daily, in the role of the Man-Mountain teacher and guide, was requested to give a full account of the prisoner's behaviour: "As I hope you all read in my written reports, our Man-Mountain is learning fast, he is friendly to the population, and he only eats once a day."

The blank faces round him were a clear indication that the

reports were never read.

"We all saw him, of course," said Bolgolam. "I doubt if there is a Lilliputian in His Highness' great realm who has not taken the trip to see the Beast."

"And more than once!" Flimnap, the Lord High Treasurer, rubbed his hands with evident glee. "At least he is useful on that account. The money keeps rolling in!"

"And he is very kind to all his visitors, no Lilliputian needs to fear him, though, I concede, he is bigger than any of us!" Reldresal was eager to add. "They do not stop coming, for a second and even a third peep!"

"Yes, and that brought about a large income, as my esteemed friend Flimnap, Lord High Treasurer justly pointed out, in the form of the newly formed Peeping-Tax!" came a cry from Bukluk, Chief of Pleasant Scents, a pro-Gulliverian on the left.

"I admit, the Peeping-Tax was another inspired idea of our Great Emperor, but is it enough?" mused Balmuff, the Grand Judiciary, another anti-Gulliverian. "Is there anything left of it for our Great Emperor, once he is fed and clothed? And what about us? Is there anything left for us?!"

Flimnap conceded glum and misery to the country, admitting that the costs of keeping the Man-Mountain would eventually ruin the kingdom. "So far it is manageable, but, holding the most important post of Your Lord High Treasurer," puffed Flimnap importantly, "I assure you, my Beloved Emperor and esteemed colleagues, that we cannot sustain the growth of this Man-Mountain.

"If we continue to fatten him, Your treasure, which I am bound by my High Post to count and re-count, will dwindle!"

Lalcon, the Chamberlain, also a T-Party member, but sitting on the other side of Bolgolam, stood up next. "His Great Big Highness, I am charged with Your wellbeing and peaceful sleep, and I foresee troubled nights if we attempt to keep Your Highness' lifestyle at court as it is, and to feed and clothe the Man-Mountain as we do now."

But General Reldresal was quick to jump to Gulliver's defence. "My Great Lord, His Royal Highness, Sunshine of Lilliput. I put it to You, that feeding our Man-Mountain is the greatest investment Your Highness could ever make! Your prisoner, Your Man-Mountain, produces the best fertiliser on a daily basis and in bottomless quantities!"

"Yes!" jumped in Crembo, the Chief of Numbers, a pro-Gulliverian, "and Your Royal Highnesses clearly see that, with these daily fertilisings, our economy will be booming as the crops will be rising! There will be more than enough for feeding and clothing Your prisoner!"

"But if there will be surplus of goods after feeding and clothing the Man-Mountain, prices would have to fall!" cried Flimnap.

"Taxes revenue will dwindle!" Mashmo (Lord of Rings and Belts), sitting right behind Flimnap, grasped the disastrous implications of falling prices.

But Limtoc, a Knight of the Finest Arts, clearly a pro-Gulliverian and perhaps even a pro-Lilliputian, was blind to these risks. "Your Highness might even be able to abolish some taxes, and with less taxes to pay, Your people will feel no need to work so much, they will have time on their hands to be creative, and to be ever so grateful to their Emperor!" concluded Limtoc in delight.

But many in the assembly responded in alarm to this forecast. "Taxes can never be abolished! What will become of our respected Assembly?!"

The noise was unbearable, and the Emperor could no longer pretend to be asleep. "Speak up, Shumclum, what do Our Gods tell you We should do?"

High Priest Shumclum, sitting right at the centre and facing the Emperor, rose to his feet and confessed to being confused. "On the one hand, there is evidence in our Blundecral that Mashmo, our esteemed Lord of His Highness' Rings and Belts, is right, when he says that to keep Your prisoner, Our Benevolent Emperor would be required to levy new taxes, which, if I am not mistaken, people might resent."

"And eventually might all revolt and refuse to pay!" called out Lalcon the Chamberlain.

"Yea, yea," sounded other anti-Gulliverians.

"But on the other hand?" The Emperor prompted him on, hoping that a resolution might come out of these weighings.

"Yes. Ehm, on the other hand." Shumclum was indeed confused. "If we do not feed and clothe this Man-Mountain (whom our highly esteemed friend here, Admiral Bolgolam, so cleverly captured), if we decide not to feed him, he might grow to be desperate and start consuming innocent Lilliputians. Some Lilliputians might resent this, too, and it would be quite difficult, even for me, to find a justification for this in our Holy Blundecral"

"Yea, yea," agreed the pro-Gulliverians on the left.

"I see where you are heading at," roared Bolgolam at Shumclum. "You do not like my Prisoner, do you?" And he jumped on his seat, waving his fist. "I said it before, and I will say it again! I reiterate that I still assert that we ought to abolish religion from affairs of state! There is no place in our Esteemed Assembly for pious hubbub!" And he turned mockingly to Shumclum, "You think I should not have captured him, do you?"

Shumclum was shaking his head, alarmed, and lost for words, he could only mumble, "My Lords, this is blasphemy. Surely, you do not . . ."

"Well, you better think again," Bolgolam cut him short, "if you are at all capable of independent thinking!" And he turned to the Emperor. "Your Highness, under my loyal command, and with Your Royal blessings, our army triumphed over the greatest danger that ever faced our greatest nation!"

"True, true," they all were eager to agree. The mighty Lilliputian army has always been above scrutiny.

"And under my command, we will annihilate him, if our benevolent Emperor so pleases!"

They all burst out clapping their hands enthusiastically and banging their heels, both the high and the low, on the wooden floor. The racket was shattering, and they all felt their patriotic spirits surging.

All, except for Reldresal.

He looked around in dismay and, when the noise subsided, he asked, "And how do you propose to annihilate Our Emperor's Man-Mountain?"

"Indeed, how?" Shumclum was glad somebody seemed to share his worries.

"Leave that detail to me," barked Bolgolam.

"I am with Bolgolam here. In my opinion," humbled Flimnap, "the Man-Mountain's diet would be very expensive and might cause a famine. If my esteemed colleague may indulge to make use of my advice, I am determined to starve him."

"But I, for one, apprehend his breaking loose!" heaved Mashmo in terror. "As His Highness' Lord of Rings and Belts, I have some understanding in chains, and I do fear that those 51 chains and 36 padlocks would not restrain a desperate, hungry Man-Mountain for much longer!"

"You are all amateurs!" muttered Bolgolam. "The professional course of action would be to shoot him in the face and hands with poisoned arrows, which would soon dispatch him."

A terrified silence fell on the Assembly, while all considered the audacious, yet professional move.

But Reldresal was less impressed. "Be good to consider, my esteemed colleague, that the stench of so large a carcass might produce a plague in the metropolis, and probably spread through the whole kingdom."

"This is no concern of mine," huffed Bolgolam. "Our good friend here, Chief of Pleasant Scents, Master Bukluk, is the one who is best equipped to deal with that. I can only assure you of a swift and definite dispatch of the gobbling Man-Mountain."

Some started clapping their hands, but seeing that many of the Assembly remained thoughtful, the clapping died out.

"There must be another way," pleaded Bukluk. "I mean, of course, I can easily deal with the stench. I, too, am a professional, but what about all the useful aspects of this Man-Mountain? Are we not overlooking here something vital?"

"My dear colleague," beamed Reldresal, "wisely spoken! We can make excellent use of his Highness' Man-Mountain, surely, beside his fertilising talents!"

Some feeble "Yea" was heard, but very feeble.

"I do not like this Man-Mountain any better than any of you here," Bolgolam picked up on the mood, "but if His Highness will order me to refrain from annihilating the Man-Mountain, I will highly recommend that we recruit him to our side, before our enemies get to know about his existence, and before they try to steal him from Your Royal Highness. When war ensues, we will need men like the Man-Mountain in our troops."

"Do you propose releasing him?" asked the Emperor shrewdly.

The Assembly gasped in unison. Bolgolam was the first to recover.

"Another brilliant idea from our beloved Emperor! That will be a winning stroke!"

Murmurs were heard all over. They were quick to grasp the new possibilities.

"He will be ever indebted to His Royal Highness and will be a perfect undercover spy," said Majes Nobd wistfully.

Up until that moment, he kept still, so when he suddenly spoke up in a creaky, seldom-used voice, everyone turned in alarm, and the Empress dropped her fan. Nobd was there in an instant, picked it up, and handed it to her gallantly.

"Who . . . who are you?" asked the Empress falteringly.

"Nobd, Majes Nobd, M'am, Head of Secret Intelligence, at your eternal service."

Clicking his high heels together he turned to the Assembly. "No one will ever suspect that we are using this huge Man-Mountain as an undercover spy. And he could spot things for us, from high above."

"No, he should be drafted to the Navy!" exclaimed Bolgolam. "Firstly, he is mine, I mean, Your Highness, that I led his capture, for You. Of course, he belongs to Your Highness, of course. But the Navy needs men like him, surely!"

"He will drown the whole fleet if he ever set foot on a ship!" roared the whole Assembly. They needed the good laugh. Tensions were mounting high.

"If I may put a word in," said Flimnap, "our great Emperor will make the best use of this Man-Mountain if the prisoner will be employed at the Treasury. Our Tax collectors are facing huge obstacles in their daily rounds. People seem to get smarter and smarter, hiding the fruit of their toil in the wiliest of ways. If the Man-Mountain would accompany them, people will be far too terrified to cheat on us."

"We are the luckiest Emperor in the whole Universe," beamed the Emperor. "We have such clever and resourceful Court!"

They all lowered their eyes modestly and the Emperor announced royally, "We give the command to release him!"

"But, His Highness," High Priest Shumclum was jumping in agitation, "His Highness surely recognises that the mere idea of a Man-Mountain in the midst of the great nation of Lilliput is demoralising to all Lilliputian men, seeing that he is that much bigger than we are!"

But Knight Limtoc, the pro-Gulliverian, answered immediately, "I do not see it as demoralising at all. As His Highness' property, we could get him to supplement our matrimonial duties, in exchange for his food and board! After all, let us all face it, the mere presence of the Man-Mountain in our midst by itself is a dangerous aphrodisiac to all Lilliputian women!"

And they all sneaked a quick glance at the Empress.

"Oh," she said, "as far as I am concerned, he should work for Us till he drops."

That seemed to be a good compromise, and committees were

sat, and budgets were allocated, to decide about the best ways of using Gulliver, and then of disposing of him.

Chapter Eighteen

THE AUTHOR TRIES TO FORGET HER LABOUR PAINS
AND WORRIES BY SCRIBING THE STORY OF HER HUSBAND'S
ADVENTURES IN LILLIPUT; LEMUEL PREVAILS TO WIN HIS
FREEDOM, THOUGH UNDER STRICT CONDITIONS;
HIS RELEASE CONTRACT; THE AUTHOR EXPLAINS GULLIVER'S
APPARENT MEEKNESS, DEBATES LEMUEL'S FATE.
(Redriff, Friday, March 5th 1703)

Betty was also born on the Sabbath.[93] This must be a good omen. I just sent Johnny to the Penny Post with a note to my sister Stella to come and attend the birthing. Of course, I can handle it on my own, and Mrs. Poppins[94] will soon come, along with all the neighbours, but Stella will never forgive me if I do not pretend to need her.

Yesterday I fell into exceedingly sharp travail in great extremity, but the pains are still bearable and far between, and writing has always helped me forget my worri[95]

I had to stop there to breathe. Might Stella and Johnny come when it is all over? As long as the baby lives, God willing, please, please, please.

Poor Betty. It is the first birthing she will attend, and she is already seven. She is a brave child and tries to hide her worries from me. Bless

H

e

r

Is it getting nearer? I remember, with George, God rest his soul, four years ago nearly, the child stayed in the birth for a good three days. The neighbours came and went, and Mrs. Poppins said that it was normal, not to worry. As a good Christian, she insisted I should embrace the spiritual rewards of my toil. "It might be your just punishment for the sins of Eve," she said, looking at all the neighbours that crowded the room, "and it might be a test of God. It is His rod that hits you. Should you pass the test, should you kiss the rod, God Almighty will certainly reward you."

And she hastened to add, "If not in this world, then in the next."

If I was not confined and in so much pain, and if it was not for all the eyewitnesses around my birthing-chair, and if I would not have cared for my children's reputation, I would have strangled her right there and then.

While my good neighbours nodded righteously, I silently cursed the rod of God, and that of Lemuel's.

I did not know it then, but I do know now, that while I was rolling in agony, due to Lemuel's rod and no one else's, my wretched husband was having the time of his life with the Lilliputian Lovers.

But even if I were not in such horrible pain, I would never discuss the will or justice of God with Mrs. Poppins. I sometimes wish I could find solace in Him, like all other women seem to do. But I cannot find it within me.

Mrs. Poppins was insistently praying while setting her tools and despite my pains (or maybe because of them?), I could not banish the thought that it was more than religious duty for her to praise the Lord in our ears. After all, she got her Certificate from the Bishop of London, and had to pay a good fee to renew it, with every visitation of his, did she not?[96] That was why she was so keen on presenting her Certificate, and telling me what was written there, even though I saw it already four years, seven years, ten years, and thirteen year ago, with each birth I gave.

She said, as she always did, that knowing her credentials would ease my pains and hasten the delivery. Groaning, I was silently praying that this time Mrs. Poppins would not need to perform a quick baptism of my baby.

Well, I only trust Mrs. Poppins because I told her once about Willughby's and she agreed with his views wholeheartedly.[97]

After the third night of that torture, four years ago, Mrs. Poppins said my baby did need help coming out and she insisted that everyone leave the room. I think they were all quite disappointed, except for my poor, tired little Johnny. The dear boy was so worried over me and could not endure the sight of my anguish.

Mrs. Poppins reclined the birthing-chair and covered my face with a cloth, so I could not quite see what she was doing.

Still, with all the agony I suffered, as I grasped the stool's handles with all my might, I could sense that she was inserting something into me[98] and the next thing I knew my belly felt hollow and the baby was in my arms.

His head was strangely elongated, and he was not breathing.

With the tips of my fingers, I tenderly touched the tiny heels and elbows that kicked me so vigorously just a few days before, and prayed that he would survive. Silently weeping, I envisioned him growing up to become a big lad, fighting and kicking. I imagined how he would be fighting out there in the big world, to protect us.

Well, it was not to be.

When Mrs. Poppins straightened herself from betwixt my legs, proudly presenting the placenta and ready to place it on my baby's head to ensure his good eyesight, she immediately noticed that something was wrong.

She grabbed my baby from my arms.

I was too fatigued to ask her if the baby would live. With all the pains I still endured, I was not sure if I myself would live to see daybreak. Tears welled up in my eyes, and I could vaguely see Mrs. Poppins rubbing my baby's head and breast with something. I remember the smell of garlic. Now that I think of it, she might not have been using it to ward off the demons, but to resuscitate my poor, dead baby.[99] Oh, I pray I shall not have to smell garlic during this labour!

I should not think of all that now. I am sure my baby is healthy and will survive! And me, too . . . the Gypsy foretold that I will have three children, and will live to see them all die in old age![100]

I better distract myself now. Perhaps it is time to start the fire and shut the windows.[101] I will get Betty to do that now. She has been doing all my bending over for the last month.

If only Lemuel was here, I could wish him my heartburns and back-aches . . .

Well, I will continue to write his story in Lilliput. I did not write for nearly three months now.

I console myself with Mrs. Poppins' conviction that the more difficult to carry the baby in the belly, the healthier it will be outside of it.

Oh, I should not think about the pains anymore.

I hear Betty coming back with the mugwort and saffron.[102]

That is better. This drink surely kills the pain and it even tastes nice, but I should not make another portion. It might put me to sleep, and I do crave it.[103]

Well, now. I left Lemuel's story after he was serviced by the Lovers.

My wretched lucky husband.

I know that if he were here now, the baby would surely survive.

No.

Think about something else. How Gulliver was released from his Prison-Temple and set free!

Yes, I will write about that now:

* * *

But first I must tell, shortly, that Lemuel was coaxed by Bolgolam and Reldresal, without them knowing of each other, to join their respective parties.

Bolgolam was dropping hints of threats and punishments, lest Gulliver would not join the S-Party (the Slamecksans), while Reldresal was cajoling him to join the T-Party (the Tramecksans,) promising honour and admiration.

Lemuel's pride was well catered for by these entreaties, but he also sensed, sensibly, that he should stay, as much as possible, above

Lilliputian politics. He did tell me that he was nursing hopes to eventually establish his own party: the L-Party. (No, not the "Lemuel party," but the "Liberal party!") Sadly, because of his hasty escape from Lilliput, he did not get to fulfil his political ambitions.

The morning after that decisive debate in which the T and S parties discussed his fate in Court, Lemuel, who had a hard time falling asleep, woke up from a nightmare: He was wading away from Lilliput in the shallow waters, wearing 600 Lilliputian high-heeled shoes on his right foot, and 600 Lilliputian low-heeled shoes on his left foot. He was surrounded by Lilliputian boats, each manned by a Bolgolam, and all those Bolgolams were screaming at him to go back. "Go back to your world! To your wife and children!"

When Lemuel jerked up in his Lilliputian bed (made indeed out of 600 Lilliputian beds), he was shocked to hear Bolgolam's screams, commanding him to step out.

In an instant, Lemuel remembered that the day before was the Big Day. Though he was not aware of the details of the Court discussions, he was acutely aware that his fate was at stake.

Tired and anxious, he hastily emerged from his Prison-Temple, and his heart sank when he saw the somber delegation that was facing him. It was headed by the feared Admiral Skyresh Bolgolam, the Admiral of the Realm. Bolgolam marched towards Lemuel on his low-heeled, green polished shoes, attended by two under-secretaries, and several other persons of lesser distinction (as Lemuel could surmise by their high heels).

Skyresh Bolgolam demanded that Gulliver kneel on the ground with his head bowed and his hands behind his back (which was the custom of keeping all chained prisoners, except that Lilliputian prisoners would also have their heads covered with a sack. Luckily, there was no sack large enough for my Lemuel's head).

Kneeling with his forehead on the ground, Lemuel feared that an execution was at hand.

His own.

He prayed silently for the salvation of his soul, and to meet us, his wife and children, soon in the afterlife. But as time passed and he felt no tiny blades on his neck, he gradually came to realise that the purpose of that posture was simply to disgrace him.

It worked.

As much as he was bigger than his tormentors, he could not help feeling humiliated in this position.

His chief concern was that Bolgolam would soon ask him where his affinity lay, with the T-Party or with the S-Men. Lemuel was wracking his brain all this while how to get out of this entanglement, but he could not come up with any polite or safe response to this dreaded question.

So, I could imagine his relief when he heard Bolgolam announcing that he had a special message from His Royal Highness to Gulliver. He unrolled a large scroll and commenced:

> "From the most mighty Emperor of Lilliput, delight and terror of the Universe, whose dominions extend five thousand Blustrugs to the extremities of the globe[104]; Monarch of all Monarchs, taller than the sons of Man; whose feet press down to the Centre, and whose head strikes against the sun: pleasant as spring, comfortable as summer, fruitful as autumn, dreadful as winter. Etc. etc."[105]

Here Bolgolam took a deep breath and demanded to know if Gulliver was all right, for Lemuel's shoulders were shaking violently and he was almost choking with laughter, which he was desperately trying to conceal.

"I am all right," sniveled Lemuel. "I humbly beg your pardon. I am so moved to know that the great Emperor could spare a few moments for my insignificant self. Pray, continue."

"Well," Bolgolam went on reading:

> "His most sublime Majesty proposes to the Man-Mountain, lately arrived to our Celestial Dominions, the following

Articles, which, by a solemn oath upon the Holly Blundecral and the portable Lullupiter Lapis, he shall be obliged to
perform, in return for his confined freedom."

Freedom!

Lemuel hastened to agree, ever so relieved.

A confined freedom sounded so much better than an execution.
He felt that he could live with a confined freedom, so long as he was
not killed.

And so Lemuel was requested to swear his oath, first in the manner of his own country (which, Gulliver told them, was by saying "I
Swear" while holding one's hand on one's chest, above one's heart
and the other hand, fingers crossed, behind one's back) and, afterwards, in the method prescribed by Lilliputian laws, which was to
place the Holy Blundecral and the portable Lullupiter Lapis on his
head, to place the middle finger of his right hand on the crown of his
head, above the Holy book, and his thumb on the tip of his right ear
and to hold his right foot in his left hand.[106]

This choreography was successfully performed, to the cheers of
Lilliputian onlookers, and only then could Lemuel hear the precise
articles on which he already swore, which were:

"First,
The Man-Mountain shall not depart from Our Dominions,
without Our License under Our Great Seal.

"Secondly,
He shall not presume to come into Our Metropolis, without
Our express Order; at which time the Inhabitants shall have
two hours warning to keep within their Doors.

"Thirdly,
The said Man-Mountain shall confine his walks to Our
principal high roads, and not offer to walk or lie down in a

meadow or field of Zea maize, Triticum aestivum or Cannabaceae.[107]

"Fourthly,
He will not take to the said roads under the influence of Glimigrim,[108] and he shall take the utmost care not to trample upon the bodies of any of Our obedient subjects, their horses or carriages, nor take any of Our said subjects into his hands, without their consent. If, on the other hand, the said Man-Mountain will wish to marry, he should do so with at least 12 Lilliputian virgins, but not more than 70. Needless to say, the said Man-Mountain should refrain from producing offspring. In any case, the Man-Mountain is obliged to assist all Lilliputian men in their Matrimonial duties, if they so wish, in return for food and board. To assist the Man-Mountain in maintaining nightly peace and order, We appoint him a Chamberlain, Little Lalcon, whose duty will be to hand out numbers and guarantee satisfaction to all.

"Fifth,
Every evening Our Principal Secretary of Private Affairs, General Reldresal, will come to the Liberty-Temple[109] to receive the said Man-Mountain's report of his conduct and contribution to the benefit of Our glorious Lilliput. If, as a result of this audience, Our Principal Secretary of Private Affairs, General Reldresal, requires extraordinary dispatch, the Man-Mountain shall be obliged to carry him in his pocket and return him back safe to Our Imperial Presence. Likewise, the Man-Mountain shall be obliged to carry Our Imperial Family wherever and whenever We so desire.

"Sixth,
He shall be Our ally against Our enemies in the island of

Blefuscu, and he shall do his utmost to destroy their fleet, which is now preparing to invade Us. Should the said Man-Mountain perish in the process, his inheritors will get a framed likeness of Us, as is Our custom with every fallen Lilliputian. We respect, remember and are truly grateful to Our heroes.

"Seventh,
The said Man-Mountain shall, at least once a day, or as nature permits, produce fertilisers for Our fields, to be gathered inside The Ancient Volcano next his Liberty-Temple and to be distributed throughout the land. At his times of leisure, the said Man-Mountain shall also be aiding and assisting Our workmen, in helping to raise certain great stones, towards covering the wall of the principal park, and other of Our royal buildings and fortifications.

"Eighth,
The said Man-Mountain shall, in two moons time, deliver to Us an exact survey of the circumference of our dominions by a computation of his own paces round the coast.

"Lastly,
That upon his solemn oath to observe all the above articles, the said Man-Mountain shall have a daily allowance of meat and drink sufficient for the support of 1,728 of our Subjects, with free access to Our Royal Person, and other marks of Our favour. In return, the said Man-Mountain solemnly swears to produce daily ten hogsheads of manure to be distributed all over Our Kingdom as We see fit.

"Given at our Belfaborac Palace at Mildendo, the twelfth Day of the Ninety-first Moon of our Reign."

The document thus read, Gulliver's chains were immediately unlocked, and he was at full liberty, confined as he was, only to the Articles above.

My Lemuel was loyal to his word, and though he was big and strong enough to easily crush the Lilliputians as soon as he was freed, he also realised that he could not get very far from the island, and surely could not get back home by swimming.

Gulliver was mightier than the Lilliputians, but the ocean was mightier than Gulliver. He might be big enough to destroy all the Lilliputians, but he depended on them for his survival. And as he realised that he needed the Lilliputians, he hoped he could make himself useful to them, too, at least until he would be saved. For he always nurtured the hope that somehow, and against all odds, some miracle would happen, and he would return home to us safely.

With these thoughts, Lemuel prostrated himself at Bolgolam's feet. Making sure that no Lilliputian was trapped underneath him, he humbly laid himself on the ground, his nose at the same height as Bolgolm's.

Curtly, Bolgolam commanded Lemuel to rise, but demanded that Lemuel be sitting down; and after many courteous expressions from Bolgolam's aides, Bolgolam concluded that he hoped the Man-Mountain should prove a useful servant, and well deserving of all the favours the Emperor had already conferred upon him, or might confer upon him in the future.

Yes, Lemuel's vanity was well catered for.

When he was in England, he could never have dreamt of being admitted to Court, let alone gaze at our King. While here in Lilliput, at that moment in time, Lemuel was as happy and proud as he could be: a free man, liked and protected by the Mighty Power, the Emperor of Lilliput!

His future seemed to be as good as it could ever be.

At least so long as he could avoid this Bolgolam creature.

Chapter Nineteen

THE AUTHOR'S LIFE AS A CONSTANT TRAGEDY; LOSING HER
LOVER AND HER BABY IN THE SPAN OF A FEW MONTHS;
TO PREVENT LOSING HER HUSBAND AS WELL, SHE RESUMES
TELLING HIS STORY; LEMUEL IS LIVING THE LIFE OF A FREE MAN;
HIS DAILY SERVICES TO THE EMPEROR OF LILLIPUT, AND HIS
NIGHTLY CONTRIBUTIONS TO LILLIPUTIAN'S DOMESTIC BLISS;
HIS OBSERVATIONS OF THE LILLIPUTIAN ISLAND AND ITS
INHABITANTS, AS HE FULFILLS THE ARTICLES OF HIS RELEASE.
(Redriff, Tuesday, May 1st, 1703)

Is my life doomed to roll from one tragedy to another?

When I try to count my blessings, they do not add up to much. In my thirty-one years, what did I achieve? Only two of my six babies still live—and who knows for how long . . .

My last baby, Rosalind, lived long enough to be baptised, which was a great consolation for Stella. I cannot believe we are sisters. With all the secret readings we both did, under the guidance of our dear mother, she did not learn anything about the people who populate our world.

I guess you cannot learn to read between the lines. This gift is probably something you either have, or not.

Stella reads the Bible literally, and whenever it does not make sense, she is asking the priest what she should think.

She speaks a lot with her priest.

Two months ago, when I lay dying—or so I thought—giving birth to Rosalind, Stella came like the tempest. "Push!" she urged me, "push!"

As if I did not know how to birth! She is so full of self-righteousness. In between the contractions she was assuring me that my conviction that Lemuel will be back is a dangerous folly.

Even Mrs. Poppins could not make her stop. And the worst was that the godsibb[110] neighbours agreed with her.

Stella insisted I accept my widowhood and return to our old father's house in Newgate Street, to live with her, with her Mr. Owen Lavender Jr. and their eleven children.

"Did you get another letter from Mr. Gulliver?" She demanded, "Push! It has been half a year now, and no word from him. Do you not realise what this means?"

I only knew it meant I was miserably unhappy. And longing for him.

He might be a rascal, and not my sister's cup of tea, but he is my husband—and my friend. He has his drawbacks, of course. Who has none? But he loved me.

No!

He loves me still, in his way. It is not yet a year since he took to sea on the *Adventure* and it is not yet time to despair!

It was not yet time to despair two months ago, when I was giving birth to Rosalind, God rest her soul, while Stella was urging me to give up all hope for him. I was in so much distress with that lengthy delivery that I was grateful to Mrs. Poppins for finally sending everybody out. I was not looking forward to another failed delivery with Mrs. Poppins' invention,[111] but I was glad for the peace from Stella's haranguing. My sister's fourteen babies seemed to have just popped out of her belly so, of course, she thinks I should be able to do that too. She only lost three children, and not in birth, while I lost four of my six, and none of these four survived a fortnight.[112]

I was too weak for the churching and I thought Rosalind was also doing poorly, but Stella insisted. After the baptism,[113] when I refused to pack and move, Stella stormed out of our home, swearing never to come back again.

I was crying for my Rosalind; the poor infant was shivering and blue. My sweet Johnny tried to cheer me up by reminding me that most of Stella's visits culminated with her promising never to be back again.

The clever lad.

I did laugh when he said, "And you know what, Mamma, the worst thing is that she never keeps her promises."

I am so blessed to have him and Betty. Well, these are my two blessings: my dear children!

And this morning I could still proclaim to have three of them.

Well, not children, but blessings.

This morning I was still hugging my love Vanessa, and now she is gone, too. It was too good to last for too long. She stepped back into my life when I needed her most, and was snatched out of my arms when I still need her so.

She ran away from home, my poor Vanessa, and came searching for me the day after we buried Rosalind.

I lost Vanessa nearly one year ago, when Lemuel, in a fit of rage and jealousy, tore our family away from Wapping, and me from her.[114] Vanessa told me that she was asking everywhere for us, and finally heard that we had moved to Redriff. She resolved to sell her home and buy another one, near us in Redriff, when her husband, Captain Prichard, whom everyone considered dead at sea, came suddenly back from a ruinous voyage, a ruined man.

He lost his ship and all his fortune to pirates and was lucky to save his skin. Vanessa was hoping that, being such a renowned seaman, he would get another position and would leave her again, but that did not transpire. Apparently, ship owners considered him bad luck.

Prichard, no longer called Captain, took to heavier drinking.

Soon he spotted that Vanessa's periods seemed to be constant (for she still tried to prevent making love to him by telling him that she was menstruating[115]) and one night, when overly drunk, he tried to rape her!

Luckily, said Vanessa, being so drunk he could not raise his tool, so he beat her instead with his fists.

My poor Vanessa, she was pleased to suffer his beating, as long as she did not have to suffer his prick inside of her!

But after some months of this treatment she could not bear it anymore and, under the pretext of going to see a surgeon for her wounds, she took the public coach and came to me.

We had a brief, glorious few weeks before Mr. Prichard discovered where she was, and came to claim her back.[116]

What have I got left? My only sister will not speak to me, and my late husband's five brothers and two sisters always thought I was not good enough for their surgeon brother.[117]

I loved two people, and I lost them twice.[118] My Lemuel is certainly dead at sea and Vanessa . . . We are probably doomed to be parted until her husband's death . . .[119] My goodness, what am I thinking? Heavens forbid I should wish for anyone's death.

But still.

I am a woman, and I need to be reminded of it every so often. I need to be loved, I want to love, I crave making love. Oh, I so much wish my Lemuel would be back soon. Sometimes I fantasise how it will happen.

Yes, every now and then I feel, with all my being, that it will happen. It might take another year before I will hug him again, but it will happen! Like a foolish girl, I believe that as long as I keep his memory alive, writing all his adventures in Lilliput, I will keep him alive, too, wherever he might be now.

Besides, it always lifts my spirits, writing down Lemuel's amazing story. So, back to the year 1701, when My Lemuel gained his freedom in Lilliput.

* * *

Up until his hasty and narrow escape from Lilliput, Lemuel enjoyed himself each night, satisfying at least three Lilliputian women at a time, as stipulated in the Fourth Article of his Release Contract.

He soon made friends with his Chamberlain, Little Lalcon, a neat young man who did not have much trouble keeping the nightly visits of the Lilliputian women in good order. The women were willing to accept Lalcon's authority, since he was reasonable and fair. He did not allow any group of women to stay more than 20 minutes with the Man-Mountain and sent them all back home promptly at midnight.

Lemuel was happy with this arrangement. At last, he could make love each and every night! Back home, in the months after our wedding and before I was heavy with my first baby, Johnny, there were days in which we romped morning, noon, and night.

But the Lilliputians, as Lemuel told me, were so much inclined, by motives of concupiscence, to be physically engaged with each other—as their law dictated: at least four times per week—that they had to find a solution to the problem of having too many children.

For this purpose, they created the Town Public Nurseries, where professional people took turns in watching over the babies until they were old enough to produce children themselves.[120]

And so, as Lemuel gained his freedom and he could travel all over Lilliput, his quality of life had much improved.

Every morning, when he needed to relieve himself, he strolled at his leisure out of his Liberty-Temple to his volcano, which he fondly nicknamed "Ajax,"[121] where he discharged himself for the glory and prosperity of Lilliput, and in accordance with the Seventh Article of his Release Agreement.

A new profession came into being, which was very highly respected and well paid, that of the Imperial Ex-Men, who would pan Lemuel's excrement as it flowed down the river from the volcano and distribute it all over the Empire.

The Emperor was, of course, the Owner of all Minerals in Lilliput, and as such Lemuel's product was deemed His sole property. But even the Emperor could not convince Lemuel to join in the ranks of the Imperial Ex-Men.

As much as Lemuel was best endowed to scoop the goods and distribute them about the Empire in the swiftest and most efficient fashion, he did not feel inclined to do so and finally came up with an excuse that was accepted by the Emperor, namely that relieving himself daily of such quantities of cargo was taxing enough, and therefore he should be allowed to spend the remains of the day in other employments for the Glory of the Emperor and His Great Empire.

He had two moons' time, according to the Eighth Article, to compile an exact survey of the circumference of the Lilliputian dominions by his own computation of his paces round the coast.

That was a mission which Lemuel was eager to fulfil, as he was very curious to study the land on which he was stranded.

Indeed, he was hoping to spot some human-sized ship on the horizon.

As he walked around the island, he could ascertain that the tallest trees were about seven feet high and the common size of the natives was somewhat under six inches high, with an exact proportion in all other animals, as well as plants and trees.

Lilliput being but a small island, it took him one day to ascertain that the island's circumference was about 12 miles, and its area is about 11.5 square miles.

That evening, when Principal Secretary of Private Affairs General Reldresal arrived for the daily report, Lemuel proudly informed him that the survey of Lilliput was done, and the Emperor could come at any time to hear it.

General Reldresal was surprised and a bit confused to hear that the Eighth Article was already fulfilled and mumbled that this information must be conveyed with all due ceremony to His Majesty in private, soon after court convenes at the capital, Mildendo. Reldresal explained that Lemuel should give an official address to the whole court, followed by a private audience with the Emperor.

His vanity thus catered for, Lemuel was anxious to visit the capital and was eager for his court address. He hoped that the Lilliputian protocol dictated that the Empress should grace the meeting, if only briefly.

The next morning, having fulfilled his daily obligations towards the Seventh Article, Lemuel commenced his vigilant walk to Mildendo.

The people had notice, by proclamation, of the royal invitation of the Man-Mountain to address the court at the Metropolis. Therefore, his progress was very slow, because he had to be careful not to trample on any of the numerous living creatures that crowded the footways, eager to see the Man-Mountain on the move. He was also careful not to trample on any of the fauna, fences, or buildings on his way.

At long last he reached the walls of Mildendo, which were two feet and a half high, and at least eleven inches broad, so that a coach and horses might be driven very safely round it. It was flanked with strong towers at ten feet distance.

Lemuel stepped over the great western gate, and passed very gently, and sideling, onto one of the two principal avenues. He walked with utmost circumspection to avoid treading on any stragglers who might remain in the streets, although the orders were very strict that all people should keep to their houses at their own peril. The garret-windows and tops of houses were so crowded with spectators that he thought in all his travels he had not seen a more populous place.

As he was cheered on by the masses, his heart swelled with pride and gratitude, and he waved to the multitudes magnanimously, in the same fashion he had often seen Charles II, James II, Mary II and William III do in England.

Gulliver had the privilege of viewing the Metropolis from the viewpoint of a bird, which was quite an unsettling experience for him. As he carefully walked in the avenue, his gaze hovering above the city, he estimated that Mildendo was capable of holding five hundred thousand souls. He noticed that the houses were from three to five stories, and the shops and markets seemed well provided.

The Emperor's Palace was at the centre of the city, where two great avenues met.

It was enclosed by a wall of two feet high, and twenty feet distant from the buildings.

His Majesty gave Lemuel permission to step over this wall, and the space being so wide between that and the palace that he could easily view it on every side.

The outward court was a square of forty feet and included two other courts: in the innermost were the royal apartments, which he was very desirous to see, hoping that the Empress would reveal herself to him.

Unfortunately, it was impossible for him to stride over the gates and adjoining buildings without doing infinite damage to the pile, though the walls were strongly built of hewn stone, and four inches thick.

Though the Emperor deemed that Gulliver's address to the court was of extreme urgency, this could only come to pass three days later.

It took Lemuel three whole days to cut down, with his knife, some of the largest trees in the Royal Park, of which he cleverly made two stools, each about three feet high, and strong enough to bear his weight so he could safely enter the Royal Inner Court.

Chapter Twenty

A LETTER FROM CAPTAIN BIDDEL AWAKENS FEARS AND
WORRIES; THE AUTHOR RECALLS GULLIVER'S RECEPTION
AT COURT; HE IS IMMEDIATELY SWEPT INTO COURT
INTRIGUES AND LANDS THE NEW OFFICE OF SHINBET,
HAVING TRIUMPHED OVER OTHER CANDIDATES.
(Redriff, Tuesday, June 15th, 1703)

I cannot believe it. This rascal, Biddel, sent me a letter.

Me!

As if he did not realise that it was because of me that Mr. Gulliver kicked him out of our house a year ago, when he wanted to recruit my husband on a kidnap voyage to Lilliput.[122]

I clearly remember his scared glances at me when Mr. Gulliver pushed him out the door. He thought I was out of my senses, because I spoke Lilliputian with my husband . . .! At the time we found it very droll, realising that he was convinced I was a mad woman. Lemuel and I had merry times, reliving that moment. I think it was one of the last times I spoke Lilliputian with Lemuel. One week later he was already on board the *Adventure*, heading to Surat.

Silly me, months later I was still hoping that if I practiced my Lilliputian aloud, it would bring Lemuel back to us. How could I have envisioned Betty's bitter tears when she ran home one day, beaming with happy expectations, only to discover that I was not talking to her father; that he was not back home yet? My heart shuddered when I tried to comfort her, and I vowed not to utter another word in Lilliputian until Lemuel would be back.

Silly, silly me.

Now I am sure that only if I keep this vow, my Lemuel will be back. Oh dear me. All those silly, gullible vows.

Again and again, I do everything I can to gain some control over my life, only to realise again and again how helpless I am in the face of . . . of . . . destiny?

Is life predestined? I cannot believe it is. By whom would it be?

Oh, I am so confused. I wish I could be so silly as to believe in God.

I feel that I would not be able to face all my hardships without the conviction that Lemuel does love me. But is it true? No word from him for so long. Still, when I cling on to the folly of his eternal love, I feel strong enough to move mountains.

Except this morning, when I held Biddel's letter in my shaking hands. I am engulfed by fears. They haunt me all these hours.

Would he be vengeful? Would he dare harm my kids?

Oh, Gulliver, why have you forsaken me? How could a weak, lone woman defend herself and her brood?

Biddel did not leave a return address. This loathsome man might appear at my doorstep any day now . . . Perhaps I should just start speaking Lilliputian to him, to scare him away? But then, what about my vow? And what if Betty will be home when he comes? It would break her poor heart again.

I hope my children face no risk from him. This wretched Biddel was cruel enough to want to kidnap Lilliputians and sell them here for show . . .

Despite all what Lemuel told me about the hardships and dangers he suffered in Lilliput, I still feel compassion for these little creatures. It was instilled in me by my Lemuel. He also told me about the fine treatments he got there.

Well, here is what he told me about his Royal reception at the Lilliputian court. Perchance writing all this might distract me from my fears of Biddel . . .

* * *

As soon as Lemuel finished constructing two stools from twelve of the tallest local trees, his impending visit to the palace in Mildendo was announced. The population was instructed again to stay indoors, and they all watched his prodigious progress toward the Royal Inner Court, carrying in both arms these humongous seats.

When Lemuel approached the Inner Court, he placed one stool outside of it and the other inside, and carefully stepped from one to the other, safely landing right in front of the palace, in front of the wide royal balcony.

The Royal Orchestra burst out in a magnanimous march. Holding his red high-heeled shoes in his hand, General Reldresal climbed ceremoniously onto Lemuel's left shoulder, to guide him through the protocol.

A Lilliputian woman came forward, cradling in her arms a tiny baby, which Lemuel could hardly see, and which she fearfully held up to Gulliver, to hold and kiss, as tradition dictates.

Fearful of dropping the infant, Lemuel held his palm next to the woman, while she, urged by the Emperor's soldiers' spikes and trembling all over, placed the bundle onto Lemuel's open, rather shaky palm. The baby did not seem to mind, and even shrieked in delight as it was lifted higher and higher, but when Lemuel's face and protruding lips came nearer, it shrilled fearfully and wet its swaddle[123] and Lemuel's hand.

"That will suffice," General Reldresal comforted Lemuel. "Just give it back to its mother. A little lōtium[124] never harmed anyone, certainly not a Man-Mountain."

The ceremony thus concluded, the wide doors of the balcony were opened by colourfully clad servants, and turquoise-robed Admiral Skyresh Bolgolam stepped onto the balcony, staring up into Gulliver's face.

Lemuel's heart sank.

"Know, Man-Mountain, that you are graced by His Grace, His Royal Highness, the Emperor of Lilliput, and the rest of the universe!

"Only by his pity on you, are you fortunate to breathe Lilliputian wholesome air, and to serve His Majesty!"

Lemuel bowed his head in deeply felt gratitude, following closely General Reldresal's whispered instructions, and the Admiral stepped back, revealing behind him the assembling Lilliputian Parliament.

"You are privileged to join His Royal Diversion and Office Nominating. For reasons which are beyond my humble perception, Our Good Emperor sees in you one of Us. As such you should put yourself forward for an office at court. I am sorry to say," added Bolgolam with spite.

Lemuel was nevertheless very touched, but also apprehensive.

General Reldresal assured him that the process was quite harmless.

"This diversion is only practiced by those persons who are candidates for great employments and high favor at court," explained General Reldresal, holding onto Gulliver's ear and whispering into it, while Lemuel strained to see what was going on inside the large hall across the balcony.

He was almost sure he could dimly see the Empress there.

Reldresal continued his explanations: "We are trained in this art from our youth, but do not worry, you do not have to be of noble birth or liberal education to take part in this competition.

"Everybody knows, for example, that Admiral Skyresh Bolgolam was the only Blefuscudian ever to seek refuge in Lilliput. Though he was born in Blefuscu, our Enemies' island, to a family of cannabaceae distributors, he has managed by patience, practice and a pathological lack of fear, to demonstrate fantastic political skills, rope walking, jumping and otherwise amusing Our Emperor, until he landed the most powerful office of the Admiralty of the Realm."

"Is the Empress . . ." Lemuel was going to ask if the Empress was there, too, but then he thought he heard the General saying something about walking on rope.

"Why would he need to walk on rope?"

"That is self-evident," said the General patiently. "You will soon see for yourself. It is great fun, too. You know, of course," he added modestly, "that I have the reputation of being the best at it."

"Oh . . . but why . . .?"

"The diversion today is for the new office of Secret Holding Information New Board Evaluation Technology."

"That is a long title," said Lemuel.

"You are quite right," said the General. "We call it shortly 'SHIN-BET'"

"A catchy name," approved Lemuel. "It sound ominous, too. Is the Empress also here?"

"Of course," said the General. "None of the ladies would want to miss this for the world. The Emperor tried to ban the presence of women in these auditions, since it seems to excite them to no extent, resulting in fresh demands to amend the Matrimony Laws. Unfortunately, this attempt resulted with the compromise to let the ladies sit at the front row. Their glee and heavy breathing are quite distracting, I must warn you."

Lemuel did not want to appear too much obsessed with the Empress, so he tried to change the subject: "And who are the candidates for this SHINBET office?"

"There are three candidates today. You can see them warming-up inside: Clefrin and Marsi, the Frelocs."

"Oh, I remember them," said Lemuel. "They are the ones who frisked me when I arrived. And who is the third candidate?"

"Why, it is you, of course," the General said. "Do not worry. The job is tailored for you. They stand no chance against you."

"But . . . but . . . what IS this office, anyway? I am very honoured, of course," he hastened to add, "but I am not sure I am up to the challenge. After all, I only just arrived . . ." In truth, he was afraid to make a fool of himself in front of the Empress.

"Do not worry," said the General. "You can always count on me. I will help you. We are friends." And to demonstrate his friendship, he gave a friendly punch to Lemuel's jaw, hitting a tooth.

"Ouch," said Lemuel. "Thanks. Do I have to jump?"

"No, heavens, no. It would be totally unfair for you to compete in jumping against any Lilliputian, even myself! You will see what Clefrin and Marsi do, and then it will be your turn."

Clefrin and Marsi stepped onto the balcony.

They were not wearing the khaki army uniforms which they wore while searching Lemuel. Marsi was dressed in red and wearing low-heeled shoes, while Clefrin was wearing green, and masterfully balancing himself on a pair of green high heels.

Walking to the balcony's edge, they stood on both sides of Lemuel's head, turned to the Emperor, who was sitting inside the big hall, and bowed deeply.

At last Lemuel could clearly see the Empress, in a magnificent brown dress that enhanced the beauty of her bare breasts.

Lemuel was irritated to note that one of the ladies seemed bent on blocking his view, desperately trying to position herself in Lemuel's line of vision. Later he learned that this was Lady Flimnap who, contrary to her husband, was resolute to gain Lemuel's favours.

"Our Dear Emperor," recited the Frelocs in unison, "we, as mortal as we are, salute you, and to prove this, we humbly petition to entertain His Majesty, with a dance on the rope."

"What?!" said Gulliver. "I think my Lilliputian is not that good. Did I understand right? Dancing on rope?!"

But he needed not wait for General Reldresal to answer.

The Emperor roared, "Permission granted!" and to the cheers of the court and wives, a contraption of sticks and tight rope was brought on to the balcony. It was a slender white thread, extended about two feet and six inches from the ground.

Clefrin and Marsi removed their upper coats and adjusted their wigs. They stepped in unison towards the rope, stood with their backs to each other, took three steps in opposing directions away from each other, and then, simultaneously, each put his right hand into his pocket and pulled it out, waving a bundle of cloth.

From the sound of it, Lemuel judged that it was full of coins.

This was apparently the sign for a number of dignitaries of the court to rush out to the balcony, some bobbing on high heels, but still quite fast. Five fought for a position in front of Clefrin and six were heaving in front of Marsi.

"Fine, Marsi, you may start, then!" announced the Emperor.

A hush enveloped the hall as Marsi pranced on his high heels towards the rope, flanked by his six aides who were whispering in his ears.

Lemuel could not quite hear what was said but he did think that he heard them whispering numbers. Marsi was nodding in agreement to each and every one of them and when they approached the rope, they grabbed Marsi's arms, three on each side, and hauled him onto the rope.

Wobbling violently, and holding onto the six hands for dear life, Marsi managed to take a couple of steps before he lost balance and fell into his six aides' arms.

"You see, there is nothing to it," said the General to Lemuel, as the public inside the hall clapped approvingly and Marsi and his team stepped aside, still negotiating numbers.

"It is quite beyond me," mumbled Lemuel. "How do you expect me to . . . to . . ."

"Oh, you will do better than both of them, I am sure," reassured him the General. "Clefrin will not manage to balance any more than Marsi."

But Clefrin seemed rather cheerful, and his five aides, also whispering numbers, were smirking self-assuredly as they hastened Clefrin onto the rope.

He too was not stable at first, but making good use of the five arms that were extended to him, managed to take three, four and then five steps . . . Crestfallen Marsi and his former aides walked into the hall while Clefrin was taking his sixth and seventh steps, and he almost reached the other side, but for the Empress, whose slender figure and blinding white breasts suddenly came into view.

She was so much taken by the excitement of the diversion that she stepped forward onto the balcony, with Lady Flimnap in tow.

This caused a great commotion among the aides and even

Clefrin was not impartial to this sight, and they all fell in a heap to the ground.

"Bravo!" exclaimed the Empress, and the General whispered into Lemuel's ear, "Her Highness wants you to win, you know."

"Really? Why? How . . . how come?" stammered Lemuel.

The sight of the Empress' cleavage and erect nipples had also distracted him from the rope entertainment, and the General's remark brought him painfully back to reality.

"No time to squander!" called General Reldresal. "It is your turn now. You can do it!"

"What . . . how . . . you do not expect me to . . ."

"Of course not," said the General. "You let your fingers do the walking," and with his tiny fingers he demonstrated to Lemuel what to do.

The whole court was by now on the balcony, but Lemuel had only eyes for the Empress.

Hesitatingly, he hovered with his right hand over the balcony.

A sigh of awe engulfed the crowd.

Lemuel made a fist and let his index and middle fingers stretch and reach the floor. Gratified by the Lilliputians approval, and urged on by General Reldresal, Lemuel's confidence was increasing.

He bent his fingers in a deep curtsy to the Emperor and the Empress, and when they both acknowledged his good manners with a royal, graceful nod, Lemuel walked his fingers towards the stretched rope.

He breathed deeply and took a careful aim, sprang his fingers onto the rope, and carefully walked them, step after careful step, from one end of the rope to the other.

A huge, happy roar arose, and Lemuel, ever the fool for recognition, turned his hand and walked his fingers all the way back!

They were all in rapture. The General was jumping up and down on Lemuel's shoulder, carefully holding onto Lemuel's earlobe, and screaming: "You did it! I knew it! I never doubted you, my dear Man-Mountain!"

"Thank you, Reldresal, thank you all!" Lemuel was now waving his triumphant hand. "I could not have done it without you!"

"I know," said the General. "And you can count on my support also when you head the SHINBET. Do not worry!"

"Oh, my Goodness," gasped Lemuel. "I totally forgot. How stupid of me to win this contest. What will become of me next . . .?"

Chapter Twenty-One

THE AUTHOR'S CHARACTER AND PERSON ARE CHALLENGED
BY FREAKISH EVENTS; SHE TRIUMPHS OVER THESE TRIALS
AND TRIBULATIONS, AGAIN, THANKS TO HER UNENDING
LOVE AND LOYALTY.
(Redriff, Wednesday, June 30th, 1703)

I am still shivering.[125] Luckily my children did not wake up from all the racket, and I did manage to fix up my dress when Betty called for me, crying.

She had a bad dream, she said.

She dreamt that little people were trying to steal me away from home.

I kissed her tears and promised her that no such thing will ever happen, but I was shocked to realise how much she obviously did hear, without being woken up!

It started just when I was about to turn to bed myself, when a gentle knock on the door deceived me to think that it was one of my neighbour women, missing a candle, or a flint. Instead, I saw this darkly clad, big man, aggressively pushing his way into my home, my sanctuary, my shelter, heaving a big box onto my kitchen table!

Stumbling back, I was reaching for a knife, but he was faster and stronger. He pulled me to him, covered my mouth—and nose![126] — with his big sweaty paw and whispered coarsely right into my ear. I still want to vomit when I remember his warm, stinking breath: "Stay put, nasty woman," he said. "Do you not remember me? I wrote to you that I would come by."

It was that abominable Captain Biddel!

I nodded vigorously, as much as I could, being short of breath and full of disgust, and he let me loose.

"I need your help here," he said to my utter surprise. "We can be partners, if you insist."

And he proceeded to tell me something, which I could not follow. I was trying to catch my breath. I was silently praying that my children would not make a sound. I was fighting with myself not to glance in the direction of that door, behind which was the bed I was sharing with them.

And while he was blabbering, I thought I was hallucinating, for I could clearly hear tiny voices conversing in Lilliputian, somewhere in my kitchen!

So, all I could think of saying was, "Mr. Gulliver is coming soon. You should talk to him."

"I asked around," he said. "I know your man is dead at sea. You need not lie to me. He is not coming back any time now."

And as he heaved himself onto my bench, he produced his flintlock pistol, gunpowder and bullets and placed them on my table.

The insult!

As if he thought I would cower away from it, as if he thought I would not dare, or would not know how to charge a pistol![127]

"He was a fool not to join me in my expedition, your man. Up until now, it was plain sailing. But, darn, I would not come to you if it was not for the fact that the merchandise refuse to collaborate."

"Did you . . ." I uttered, in total disbelief. "You did not . . ."

"Oh, yes, I did," he laughed coarsely. "I sailed back to where we picked up your man and started circling until we found the island of the little creatures. That was not so hard to do, and it only took us a couple of days. Catching the lot was also easy enough, though there were not that many living items left.

"It looked like they were butchering one another for quite some time before we arrived. Those little islands were in ruins.

"But we snatched what we saw and packed them as good we could. Most of the items survived the trip. But unlike Negros, who are intelligent enough to start slaving, these little idiots just stand there. Perhaps they are crying. I cannot tell."

"Of course they would!" I was almost crying myself. "Would you not shed a tear if you had lost your home and your country, violated by fearsome giants?"

"Frankly, my dear, I don't give a damn!" was Biddel's heartless response. "But you seem to care for them. That is good. I dare not whip them, for fear their value will drop. Anyway, I would not manage to do that in that box, and I am certain they would scatter away should I let them out of it for a good whip."

I was in total shock and my countenance was probably showing it, since he laughed again and said, "Oh, my, my. Obviously, we have a midgets-lover here. So kindly explain to them that which is in their own good!"

"What do you mean?" I mumbled, still at a loss.

"You speak their tongue. I know that well enough. I have a good ear for strange languages, and a good memory to boot. What they say to each other sounds to me just like what I heard you say to your silly man, a year gone."

I could not deny it, and he was threateningly reaching for his pistol. What is more, I must admit, I was eager and curious to see the Lilliputians he kept in that box!

"But . . ." I mumbled on, "what do you want me to say to them?"

"Oh, stupid woman," he said. "Is it not plain enough? I want them to perform! I want them to laugh and sing and jump and dance when folk have paid me to gaze at them!

"Kindly explain to them," he continued, mockingly, "that if they do, I will feed them and clothe them and might even give them a Sabbath[128] every now and then. But if they will not collaborate . . ." and he left that sentence hanging ominously in the air.

Well, it was a sore sight.

When he opened the box, I saw in what miserable conditions those poor Lilliputians had spent their sea voyage and land trip. Cramped into this hastily timbered little prison were 13 human creatures and about 30 flocks and herds.

The light that suddenly flooded them allowed me to see them

clearly, while they were helplessly frozen for a while. Three of the males seemed to be Hurgus, of a higher breed. Their clothing was shinier, and they seemed to be better fed. One of them was obviously a Tramecksan, judging by his red cloths. The others—three males and seven females—were huddled together in one corner of the box, near the animals. I could clearly hear them saying to each other, "Grosit quinbusit!"[129]

The Tramecksan was first to recover. He hushed them, brushed invisible dust from his red coat, and called out to me.

"Borach Lill, Flestrin! Hek lill san!"[130]

I was so glad to see them. My whole being was awash with warm feelings of gratitude. These people, who clearly had known my Lemuel, were to me a sudden gift from heaven. But I was careful to speak Lilliputian in a hushed voice, so as not to upset my little Betty should she happen to wake up: "Who are you, dear sir? Did you know my Husband?"

"What?"

"How . . .?"

They were all calling to each other at once. The Tramecksan silenced them again and called up to me:

"Big Mountain Woman, I am exceedingly honoured to acquaint myself. I am Treasurer Flimnap, or leastways I was the treasurer of our most beloved Emperor, back in our fatherland, Lilliput. Nowadays I am lamentably reduced to be the head of these gloomy innocent prisoners. And may I intrude on your privacy, Madam, to ask you who your highness is? And how did it transpire that you speak our tongue? I do not recall ever having the honour of your introduction . . ."

"Tell them, tell them," Biddel was urging me. "I do not have the whole night for this."

But I could not help laughing in joy: "They are so cute!"

"I know they are. That is why I think we could make a fortune, you and I, when we show them in fairs all over our great country!"

"What a horrid idea!" I said, horrified.

144

"Come, come, woman. What else would you do with them here? If they want to eat and clothe, they need to work, like any other breathing creature! Go ahead, tell them, or . . ."

And he started walking round my table, approaching me ever so ominously.

I slowly edged the other way, while speaking in Lilliputian to the little people inside that prison-box. They listened attentively, as they were turning round, following me.

"My most esteemed Treasurer Flimnap," I said. "This man here, Captain Biddel . . ." I pointed at him, and the Captain raised his hat and bowed his head. "Captain Biddel wants to take care of you, feed you and clothe you."

One of the two other Hurgus, a green-clad Slamecksan, was excitedly saying to the Tramecksan, Flimnap, "This Female-Mountain speaks Lilliputian! We surely can trust her, no?"

"Even if she is but a woman!" added the other Slamecksan.

Flimnap was glancing at the rest of them, the ten Lilliputians that constituted his folk, and seeing that they were agreeing with the Slamecksans, he pushed those two away and said, "I can attend to this, no doubt. I gave you my solemn word, all along, that I will shepherd you out of these dire straits and bring us all back safely to our beloved Lilliput. You shall see, we shall overcome!"

He turned back up to me and before I could say anything, he said, "I will pose no conditions to you, woman. Just let my people go!"

"What is he saying?" Biddel was now standing right behind me.

"He is humbly asking that you will set them free."

"Ha," said Biddel cunningly. "Tell him that if they behave, I will let them loose with a good corrody, to boot. I will establish for them their own Chatham Chest!"[131]

"Captain Biddel here says that he will, but first you have to do as he says."

They were whispering among themselves, and I could not follow what they were saying to each other, but I did gather that they were leaning towards assent and pressing Flimnap to strike a deal. He turned up to me and asked, "What is it, Woman-Mountain, that we are required to do?"

"He is asking what they should do," I told Biddel.

"Good job, woman!" Biddel was getting excited and pressed himself nearer to me.

I must admit, at that point, with my excitement to see the Lilliputians and speak once more the secret language I shared with my Lemuel, I did feel such happiness growing within me. For a moment I could even imagine that it was Lemuel, pressing himself behind me, and even though I knew it was Biddel's tool which I felt rousing, I did get wet . . .

He must have felt it, too, that Biddel, for he was breathing heavier. "Tell them that they should sing, you know, like this," and he burst with a pathetic demonstration of a song. Even the Lilliputians were now laughing.

Biddel's mood was rising. "They should dance!" and he turned around, flapping his arms clumsily. The Lilliputians were rolling with merriment on their prison's floor. I smiled, trying not to burst out in outright mock.

"Can they play music? Ask them, ask them!" urged me Biddel, again pressing himself behind me.

"Captain Biddel here is asking if you can play music," I said, smiling.

The Lilliputians were nodding eagerly. "That would be lovely, if the Captain would furnish us with materials, we could build our music instruments."

"They can," I told Biddel, and he responded enthusiastically, "Oh, tell them to sing us one of the songs of Lilliput!"

They were excitedly talking to each other and finally Flimnap turned up to me and said earnestly, "You should know, Woman-Mountain, that till now we wept, yea, we wept, when we remembered Lilliput. And now he that led us captive asks of us words of song. Our tormentor, Captain Biddel asks of us mirth. 'Sing me one of the songs of Lilliput." We will do that," said Flimnap, now turning to his flock: "We will build our harps anew, we will sing and be merry. But we shall never forget thee, O Lilliput! Let our right hands forget their cunning!"

He was a bit overdoing it, I thought, but the Lilliputians were nodding eagerly, and Flimnap carried on: "Let our tongues cleave to the roofs of our mouths, if we remember thee not, if we set not Mildendo above our chiefest joy!"

The Lilliputians were now clapping enthusiastically and Captain Biddel, who was visibly moved too, told me, "He is my kind of guy. I want to shake his hand. Tell him, tell him!"

Flimnap was eager for a private word and vowed not to run away when he would be let out of the prison to shake hands with Biddel. But he was clearly reluctant to be picked up by Biddel, so I stretched my hand and scooped the little fellow in my palm, ever so gently and slowly, for I knew, from Lemuel's stories, that a rapid ascent would be a shocking experience for such a little person. I slowly lowered him onto my kitchen table and let him loose.

Once he was out in the free world and out of earshot of his fellow Lilliputians, Flimnap bowed deeply to Biddel and said in a low voice, "We can be partners, my dear Captain Biddel. These people, as you saw, will do anything I tell them to do. But you must understand that they have to know who is the boss here. Me. You must build for me a special cabin. A real bed. I need new clothes. In red."

Captain Biddel laughed heartily when he heard my translation and stretched out his forefinger to Flimnap. They shook hand and finger in assent and winked at each other.

"Your word," said Flimnap, "is their command, as long as my word is your command. Are we understood?"

At this point the captain was so pleased with himself, with me, with Flimnap and with the whole world, that he just laughed even heartier. "This is fantastic. I can already see them dancing to my tune. I am ever indebted to you, my dear Mrs. Gulliver."

He pressed himself yet even nearer to me and whispered in my ear: "Tell him that they will also have to make love to each other, on some late night shows, for extra money. Tell him, tell him," he urged me and, in his excitement, planted a wet kiss on my neck which, despite my despising him, sent shivers of pleasure down my spine.

Before I could translate anything, Flimnap was screaming, "Did he say Gulliver?! Did he?!"

I mumbled in Lilliputian, as I was trying to push Biddel off me, "Yes, I am Mrs. Lemuel Gulliver. Surely, you remember my husband?"

"I remember him all too well!"

Flimnap was now screaming with all his little might, his face reddening, and his fists up in the air at us. Biddel was trying to undress me, bent on fulfilling his lust, and as I was desperately trying to squeeze out of his sweaty clasp, I could still see in the corner of my eye, on the other side of the box, inside their prison, the other Lilliputians huddling fearfully together, their good spirits deflated and gone.

"Gulliver?" I heard them saying to one another worriedly. "Did Flimnap say Gulliver?"

"If this woman is in," Flimnap turned to Biddel, ignoring me altogether, "the deal is off!" And he started walking away, towards the edge of the table.

As much as he was clearly bent on making love to me, Biddel was also keeping an eye on his merchandise. When he saw that Flimnap was heading away, Biddel let go of me and clasped the poor Lilliputian in his fist.

Unknowingly, Flimnap saved me from being raped.

"What is wrong with him?" Biddel asked me. "Where does he think he is going?"

Waving frantically his arms, Flimnap was screaming to Biddel, "Gulliver NO!" Somehow he did learn his first word in the English language. "NO Gulliver!" he went on and on.

Biddel looked puzzled. And suspicious. And confused.

"What has he got against you?"

"I have no idea," was all I could say, even though I started understanding that which was going on in that little head of Flimnap.

Biddel just nodded to Flimnap, repeating to him, "Alright, Gulliver no!" he shoved him back into that prison box, closed it, and turned to me. "You proved yourself to be a good partner. Now let us make love."

What was he thinking, the rogue!

This time I was saved by the little voice of my Betty, calling for me from the next room.

"Darn it," said Biddel. "Well, perhaps when I come to give you your share, we will be able to consummate our business union in bed, too."

He hastily locked the prison-box and was gone.

I fixed my hair and clothes and rushed to comfort Betty.

Now that she has fallen asleep again, I am too awake and nervous to go to sleep. I thought writing down that which has just transpired would calm me down, but I find that I am now even more anxious than before . . .

It cannot be that I fancy this horrid Biddel, surely. But it was such a good feeling to be treated as a woman again . . . Oh Gulliver, why have you forsaken me, and when will you be back? Will you ever make love to me again?

I am so nervous, even my handwriting, I see, is still shaky.

In the past, writing Lemuel's story always consoled me. Perhaps I should just keep on writing now the story of Lemuel in Lilliput. Perhaps I should write about the reasons why Flimnap hates me so, why he took so violently against Mr. Gulliver. It started, indeed, when Lemuel gained the post of Head of SHINBET.

It's nearly morning. I will do that tomorrow. Surely.

Chapter Twenty-Two

As good as her word, and resuming the tale of
her husband, the author reveals what has transpired
when Gulliver was transporting the Royal House
all over Lilliput; Lemuel proves to be useful to
the court; what Lemuel gains in those trips;
the Empress's lust turns into wrath, but Lemuel is
blissfully unaware of all the plotting against him.
(Redriff, Thursday, July 1st, 1703)

As it was, with the new title of Tall Commander of the SHINBET, Lemuel's duties seemed quite benign.

When he worriedly asked Reldresal what should he actually do as head of the SHINBET, Reldresal scratched his head and said, "Well, the key is in the title. How did it go, exactly?"

Lemuel scratched his head too. "I remember something about 'Secretly Holding something' . . ."

"Oh, yes," said Reldresal, "you are the head of the 'Secretly High Inquisitors Non Believers (of) Empirical Truths.'"

"Are you sure?" asked Lemuel.

"Actually, I am not. It might as well have been 'Specially Hidden Information Not Believed Especially True,' or 'Safely Hidden Information Noble Births (&) Erroneous Titles' or even 'Surveillance, Hiding, Inquisition, Nosiness, Evaluation (&) Truthfulness.' But, guessing as I do what sort of missions would be expected of you, your title is very likely 'Supremely High Intelligent Negotiator Between Enemy Territories.' That was it!"

Lemuel was troubled. "Does that mean I should go to war? I am not really the type. If this is the case, I will give up the honour altogether."

"Nothing to worry about," Reldresal hastened to comfort him. "I am quite confident your tasks are harmless. In fact, I vaguely remember that your title was 'Society Holding Information Not Befitting Emperor's Time.' Nothing to worry about."

Lemuel liked that explanation best, and as no one bothered to inform him of the specific tasks he should perform under this respectable title, and no one complained about the idleness of his department, Lemuel's missions were still constricted to the Articles of his Release Agreement.

He was quite happy to transport the Emperor and the royal house from one part of the island to another, when called for, since it gave him many opportunities to gaze at the Empress.

Sadly, he could not do much more than gazing at the Empress, even though he was convinced that she too would want him to do more. But due to protocol, stringent etiquette and the Emperor's jealousy, their relationship remained platonic.

Still, as long as neither Bolgolam nor Flimnap were part of the retinue, Lemuel derived much pleasure from these trips.

He would place the Royal Couple in his breast pocket, and from that vantage place they could survey the view and breathe the fresh air. The Empress insisted that one lady-in-waiting would always join them, and almost always she chose Lady Flimnap, as she was the oldest and, by all accounts, the ugliest.

This was probably the real reason why Flimnap, the Lord High Treasurer, often looked on Lemuel with a sour countenance. It was because of those royal flights all over Lilliput, in which the Empress shared a pocket with Lady Flimnap, that the treasurer took a fancy to be jealous of his wife, from the malice of some evil tongues.

Some courtiers whispered in Flimnap's ear that her grace, his wife, Lady Flimnap, had taken a violent affection for Mr. Gulliver.

They interpreted wrongly the fact that Lady Flimnap was always descending from Lemuel's pocket with trembling knees and heavy breathing, murmuring, "He is killing me. Killing me."

That is why Flimnap had always been my Lemuel's secret enemy, though he outwardly caressed him more than was usual to the moroseness of his nature.

Outwardly, Flimnap, as the High Lord Treasurer, kept on representing to the emperor "the low condition of His treasury; that He was forced to take up money at a great discount; that exchequer bills would not circulate under nine per cent below par; that Mr. Gulliver had cost His Majesty above a million and a half of sprugs (their greatest gold coin, about the bigness of a spangle[132]); and, upon the whole, that it would be advisable for the Emperor to take the first fair occasion of dismissing Mr. Gulliver."

Luckily, the Emperor was ever so pleased with Lemuel, and used any occasion to travel by means of Gulliver on state visits, rather than to take to the bumpy Lilliputian roads.

The rest of the retinue was stuffed into Lemuel's pants pockets, where they had to squeeze together without much legroom. For the cargo of horses and carriages, Lemuel flipped his coat tails and scooped them there, horses on the left side and carriages on the right.

As uncomfortable as those trips might have been for the Lilliputian aides and courtesans, they still preferred the "air travel" from place to place and were squabbling for whose turn was it to "fly with Gulliver," as the new term was quick to be coined.

The accumulated weight was indeed heavy for my Lemuel, but he was always a hard labourer and was glad to pilot the Royal House all over Lilliput since, thus, he got to know the local folks, and specifically the local females intimately during overnight trips.

He did prefer that the Lilliputian lust-stricken women would come to quench their concupiscence at his Liberty-Temple, since there he had a rather comfortable bed. But also, on the fields of Lilliput, under the blanket of pitch-black nights was he ever so happy to acquaint himself with new women.

As he could not consummate his love to the Empress, he resolved to sample all Lilliputian ladies instead, and he calculated that it would take him the span of five years to complete this mission.

(When he told me this upon his return, lamenting that his ambition was cut short since he had to escape from Lilliput after spending there but two and a half years, I eased his sorrow: I explained to him that young Lilliputian girls would mature into young Lilliputian women during those five years, and this unstoppable flow would not only continue in a perpetuum mobile,[133] but would also result in increasing numbers of people, of both sexes, that would not allow him ever to intimately know all Lilliputian women of the world. So: mission impossible.)

Lemuel nurtured his secret desire to sample the Empress all this time and was plotting endlessly towards this goal. It became such an obsession with him that, eventually, he was sure it was a mark of true love.

As naïve as he was in deciphering his own emotions, he was a seasoned man and could read women's subtle signs of courtship. He could tell when a woman fancied him, and that, in itself, aroused his desire instantaneously. When he was at home with me, I was ever the one to benefit, circumstantially, from my flirtatious neighbour women!

And indeed, the Empress' desire of Lemuel might have been as consuming as Lemuel's desire of her. But it did not transpire for them to be alone with each other. The Empress was either joining her husband in his expeditions to the country, when Lemuel would carry the whole Royal House and retinue upon his person, or the Empress would stay back in the palace, while Lemuel would have to carry the Emperor and His aides according to His royal wishes and whims.

Tragically, the Empress' frustration proved to be Lemuel's destruction. She was in a bind: while every other woman could openly make use of Lemuel's services—and for free!—she, being the Emperor's wife, could never do the same. Had anyone found out that the Emperor himself was not fulfilling his matrimonial duties, he would have lost all credibility and ruling power.

The financial consequences were such that she could not afford this disgrace.

Later, Lemuel found out that, as a result, she was plotting for a long while his humiliation and eventually his destruction. She was the one behind the idea of making Lemuel transport his own excrement all over Lilliput (which did not succeed) and, before then, it was she who inspired the Emperor to march his troops between Lemuel's spread legs (hoping that the spears would be held high enough to injure him!).

When all this did not succeed, she plotted to unleash my Lemuel on Blefuscu, the neighbouring island, with the hope that he would perish in the battle. And, finally, when all this did not work out and her secret fetish was almost exposed, she contrived his execution.

Ironically, when they did manage to consummate their lust, she wanted Lemuel to stay in Lilliput forever but, by then, it was too late. Her plotting was far more lethal than Bolgolam's or Flimnap's and it nearly killed my husband. But luckily, and thanks to Lemuel's dexterity, she did not triumph and he came back to me!

(Well, at least for a couple of months, and then he was gone again.)

Chapter Twenty-Three

CAPTAIN BIDDEL'S LILLIPUTIAN PEEP SHOW PERFORMS
AT SADLER'S WELLS, AND THE AUTHOR LEARNS ABOUT IT
FROM AN ADVERTISEMENT IN THE LONDON GAZETTE;
SHE RESOLVES TO TRY AND HELP THEM, BECAUSE OF THE
FINE WAY HER LEMUEL WAS RECEIVED BY THE LILLIPUTIAN
EMPEROR TWO AND HALF YEARS BEFORE; THE EMPEROR
TRUSTED LEMUEL AND CONFIDED TO HIM THE TRUE
HISTORY OF LILLIPUT AND ITS POLITICS.
(Redriff, Tuesday, July 10th, 1703)

Just as my clever Johnny predicted, Stella was back here on a visit, this time to coerce me into marriage.

"You know as well as I do," she said, "that Gulliver is dead at sea. How do you intend to survive? Soon his allowance will run out. Did you not have enough of the shame, wearing the badge and begging for alms?[134] No, my dear sister, it is either marriage for you or the spike.[135] So, your only salvation, and that of your children, is in marriage—and I will take care of that."

I was obstinate. I tried telling her that there was no tangible evidence of Lemuel's demise and, anyway, I vowed that I would wait for him. If it takes forever, I will wait for him!

"Come, come, sister," she said, condescending, "we do not need an official testimony. We will get a bann for marriage[136] and that will suffice."

She did not even bother responding to my vehement proclamation of my love for Lemuel! She just stormed out, claiming she was in a hurry, must be back home that same day. She is now an important merchant-woman, and aids her rich husband with his hosiery business, my sister does.

But before she left, she uttered a most ominous promise: "Get ready, Mary Burton, for you will come with me on my next business travel to Northhampton, where you are to meet your future husband!"

And gone she was, the impudent.

I was desolate. I still am. I was plotting how to liberate myself from this bond. I was even contemplating selling this home and moving with my innocent children somewhere where Stella would never find us. I was even conspiring to commit suicide, when my eye fell on the *London Gazette*,[137] which my sister left behind in her hurry.

An advertisement caught my eye. It read[138]:

Advertisements.

☞ A Guide to the Practical Physician: Shewing, from the most Approved Authors, both Ancient and Modern, the truest and safest way of Curing all Diseases. Lately Published in Latin by Theoph. Boner, M. D. And now Rendred into English With an Addition of many considerable Cases, Rules and Means of Cure, that were omitted by the aforesaid Author. To which is added an Appendix concerning the Office of a Physician, by the same Author. Printed for Thomas Flesher at the Angel and Crown in St. Pauls Church-yard.

A Very strange Group of Midgets, called ILLIPUTIANS, lately brought from the East-Indies, being the first that ever was in England, is daily to be seen at Sadler's Wells Illington Road from Nine a Clock in the Morning till Eight at Night.

ALL Persons born in the County of Northampton are desired to take Notice, That there will be held a County Feast on the 13th day of November next, at Merchant-Taylors-Hall, for the promoting of Mutual Society and Charity: Tickets for that purpose are to be had at the Places following; Mr. John Cannons at the Queens Head Tavern in Great Queen-street, Mr. Henry Lamb next to the Goat-Tavern in West-Smithfield, Mr. Tho Cannon at the White-Hart Tavern at Pye-Corner end, Mr Benjamin Alsop at the Bible in the Poultry, at Jonathan's Coffee-House in Exchange-Alley, at Mr. John Harris's Coffee-house in Love-lane in Aldermanbury. Mr Rich. Coale Cheesmonger under

"A very strange group of Midgets, called ILLIPUTIANS, lately brought from the East-Indies, being the first that ever was in England, is daily to be seen at Sadler's Wells on Islington Road, from nine a Clock in the Morning till Eight at Night."

Sadler's Wells![139]

That is just a short walk from my sister's house in Newgate Street!

I resolved to pay her a visit and try to convince her that my poor health requires that I partake of the waters. She will do anything to get me married again, so I am sure to spend enough time at the Wells to accidentally run into that Biddel. Perhaps then I will be able to convince this creature to treat his "ILLIPUTIANS" somewhat better than forcing them to perform from nine a Clock in the Morning till Eight at Night.

I shudder to think what feats my Lilliputian friends are forced to perform after Eight at Night . . .

This is so distressing.

And to think that it is all my Lemuel's fault, for revealing the mere existence of Lilliput to Captain Biddel.

And my Lemuel was used by the Emperor so majestically.

True, the Empress' lust was almost my Lemuel's destruction, but all in all, these poor Lilliputians-in-exile do not deserve the fate they now suffer from Biddel.

I tenderly remember what Lemuel told me about his meeting with the Emperor:

* * *

"Welcome, Man-Mountain" said the Emperor, as he opened the large doors to the balcony and stepped outside. "I gave orders that we shall be alone, but please, come nearer, so that I can whisper directly into your ear."

Lemuel's heart swelled with pride. A private, intimate audience with the Emperor!

That morning, when General Reldresal came galloping to summon Lemuel to court as soon as possible, my Lemuel was weary of the prospect of another transport mission across Lilliput. He had not been to his Liberty-Temple for quite some time, having flown the Royal House in his pockets for so many days and nights.

Therefore, when Reldresal told him that instead of a transport mission, he was to have a private audience with His Highness, Gulliver took quite eagerly the few steps from his Liberty-Palace to Mildendo, with Reldresal and his horse in his pockets (to save the poor guy the half-hour gallop he otherwise would have had to take).

Upon the Emperor's request for more privacy, Gulliver, most willingly, dragged his stool nearer to the palace wall. He leaned his cheek on the balustrade so that his ear was strategically positioned at the edge of the balcony. As he did so, he noticed a shadow within the room behind the Emperor.

"You met my wife, Her Royal Highness, I recall," said the Emperor dryly. "She is the only witness to this meeting. I hope you do not mind."

Do not mind!

Lemuel was so excited he was already perspiring. He took out his handkerchief to wipe off his brow and noticed that the Empress, stepping a bit nearer, swooned and needed to lean on a chair. Lemuel was certain that his heart and the Empress' were beating to the same, ancient wild beat.

"Excellent," said the Emperor. "Do cover us with this foot-cloth. One can never be too careful."

Lemuel placed the handkerchief on his head and secured its other tip over the open doors across the balcony. Under the cover of the handkerchief, the Emperor proceeded. "Go ahead, tell me all about your first mission. I commanded that you explore Our shores and deduce Our size."

Lemuel commenced to whisper the data on the size and circumference of His Emperor's empire but, as he was progressing with his learned report, he was quite hurt when the Emperor was whispering into Lemuel's ear, slyly and insistently, "Are you sure? Perhaps you should go out and check it again?"

After Lemuel's resolute whispered protestations and proclamations that he was a qualified surveyor, having occasioned to practice this profession in the course of his numerous voyages, the Emperor relented, and changed the subject. "During your survey, Man-Mountain, did you see anything suspicious?"

"No," Lemuel whispered back. "It is the usual landscape, only smaller than what I am used to."

"Stop bragging," whispered the Emperor sharply. "Your size is of no consequence here. You are Our subject and, as such, you are at Our Royal mercy!"

"True, I humbly beg Your pardon, Your Majesty," whispered Lemuel.

"We forgive you," whispered the Emperor magnanimously and proceeded. "Did you see people hiding? Crossing by boats to our enemy's shores at night?"

Lemuel was baffled. "If they were hiding, how could I have seen them? And I conducted my survey during the day, of course."

"Darling . . ." He suddenly heard the Empress' voice, and his heart leaped to his throat.

"Yes, woman?" The Emperor turned to her, and Lemuel's heart sank back; she was not addressing him.

"It does not matter now, darling," the Empress whispered to the Emperor. "Let us move on with The Plan!"

"Do not push me, woman," snapped the Emperor in a harsh whisper. "All in good time!"

He turned back to Lemuel and whispered on. "What you are about to hear, is top secret. If you ever repeat this to anyone, I will deny it all, of course, and will execute you for slandering your monarch. Understood?"

As dreadful as this sounded, Lemuel was very curious to know what the Emperor's Top Secret might be, and he nodded his consent.

"That is not enough," snapped the Emperor "Do it properly!"

"Darling . . ." It was the Empress, again. "Everyone will see! Make him swear with his fingers, under the carpet."

"You have reason, woman," grumbled the Emperor. "Go ahead, Man-Mountain, do as you are told! Swear as you do in your own country, and then do the Lilliputian oath. Hurry up. We do not have much time."

Lemuel started by crossing his fingers and saying, "I swear," and continued in the Lilliputian tradition,[140] all the while keeping his handkerchief over his head, covering both the Emperor and the Empress.

"That will do," said the Emperor, though he could not mask his awe. "Now listen carefully, for I will say this only once. It is a long and tedious story."

And he commenced to unravel the complex Lilliputian politics.

As it was, the Lilliputians were labouring under two mighty evils, revealed the Emperor: a violent faction at home, and the danger of an invasion by a most potent enemy from abroad.

"As to the first," said the Emperor, "you probably noticed that We have two struggling parties in Our Empire, the High and Low Heels, under the names of Tramecksan, the T-party, and Slamecksan, the S-party. We sometimes distinguish between them by their colors, red and green. This most useful state of affairs is holding for above ten moons past."

Lemuel was curious. "Pray, why is it useful?"

"My Holy Blundecral," said the Emperor. "I keep forgetting that you are but a savage and have no understanding in refined politics.

"Having struggling parties is essential for every monarch.

"True, seventy moons past we had thirty-two parties struggling for power, but our wise ancestors recognised that this was too confusing for the masses, and it even gave the dangerous impression that any Lilliputian could just start a new party.

"During the course of six and thirty moons my wise forefathers managed, with careful manoeuvres, threats, and manipulations to trim down Our court, and, as of but ten moons ago, we are blessed with the sufficient number of two parties: the S's and the T's.

"To make it even easier for the masses, we distinguish between them quite conveniently by their heels and by their colours.

"It is a double-edged solution: while a Lilliputian glances down to see what sort of dignitary he is facing, he has to bow his head, and this gives Our dignitaries a priceless satisfaction."

"But," ventured Lemuel, "why two parties? Why not just one? Surely that would be even simpler . . . ?"

The Emperor sighed and exchanged a tired glance with his wife. "Sorry, woman, this is going to take longer than I thought. Bear up!"

"It is quite alright, Darling. Pray, proceed. I do find it very exciting to see you taming the giant!"

The Emperor laughed kindly and pinched his wife's cheek.

Lemuel felt the ugly monster of jealousy raise its head. If ever he would be alone and intimate with the Empress, the woman he so desired, he would never be able to pinch her cheek without chopping her head off.

The Emperor, ignorant of Lemuel's complaint, went on. "If we were to have only one party, the masses would feel that they have no choice; that this Party is imposed on them. As it is now, the S's and the T's suffice to convince the masses that they are governed by a fair system, which expresses all of My citizens' political visions.

"Everybody is happy. The Lilliputians feel that they have a choice, the politicians of the S's and the T's have each other to squabble with, and We can go ahead, uninterrupted, to execute Our own plans, while in Our court, Our politicians are busy fighting with each other for the crumbs that fall off Our table.

"People all over Lilliput amuse themselves with political discussions. They are quarrelling with each other about what they think We should do, and this gives them a healthy illusion of Power."

Gulliver admitted that this sounded convincing, as well as convenient.

"As long as the Lilliputians are bombarded with information about which they can do nothing but gossip to their hearts' content, they feel that they are part and party to that which is going on in court and that they have political power!"

The Emperor could not help laughing. "They discuss these bits and pieces of information which We leak out, or invent, and they feel superior to Our court, thinking that they would lead Lilliput better than We do!"

The Empress sniggered behind her fan and Lemuel ventured, hoping to please the Royal Couple, "That is ridiculous. It surely takes proper breeding and much learning to be a leader!"

The Royal Couple burst out laughing.

"Of course it does not," retorted the Emperor. "You have still so much to learn!"

The Empress giggled and Lemuel felt his face was reddening with shame.

"Anyone can be a leader. The challenge is to be perceived as a potent leader because, in fact, no leader is ever needed. This is another Top Secret I share with you, seeing that you have so much to learn, and knowing that no Lilliputian will ever grasp this truth.

"If Our court and all of Our administration were to disappear tomorrow by some mysterious force, you can rest assured no Lilliputian would ever notice Our absence.

"Well, at least not in a negative sense.

"Lilliputians would continue to work their fields, make, sell and buy goods, eat, drink and be merry, fulfil their matrimonial duties to everyone's content. Why would they not? It might take a few months before they would notice that no tax collector came by, or that no new stories about scandals in court were heard lately, but soon they would get used to that, too."

"That is awful," gasped Lemuel. "Will they not feel abandoned?"

"It is most gratifying," said the Emperor, "that even you, Man-Mountain, are convinced that leaders are necessary. You renew my hope in Lilliputian-kind.

"You see, even We sometimes lay awake at night, fearful that Our Lilliputians might discover that We are not necessary at all. That is why Our forefathers wrote the Blundecral, you know."

"No . . . I do not know." Lemuel was truly finding all this hard to follow "Never heard of the origins of the Blundecral before this day."

"Dear me, I keep forgetting that you are a total ignoramus. Our Blundecral is the Holy Book which was written by one of my fore-fore-fore-fathers, Our great prophet Lustrog.

"He was very holy and had numerous ways of communicating with Our Creator and bringing back the gospel of the One and Only Truth. Lustrog was also chosen by Our Creator to discover the cannabaceae, which brings me to what We actually want to discuss with you today."

"Oh, the cannabaceae. I have noticed the abundance of cannabaceae fields in Lilliput. I gather it is one of Your Highness' main produce?"

"And for once, you are right!" exclaimed the Emperor. "The sacred knowledge of cultivating and using cannabaceae is closely guarded and is passed on in Our family from generation to generation."

"Move on, dear, please," the Empress whispered impatiently. "I need to get some fresh air."

"We are almost there, woman," snapped the Emperor. "You insisted on being at this audience, so bear up!"

"If I may," ventured Lemuel, "Her Royal Highness does seem a bit pale. Shall I take her in my palm for some fresh air?"

"We will hear of no such thing," barked the Emperor and turned to His Empress, whispering, "I[141] know you abhor this creature. So far you have demonstrated much stamina, I grant you that. So, if you wish, you may depart. I will conclude this on my own."

The Empress glanced at Lemuel, who pretended to hear nothing, and whispered back, "No, darling, let us resume this tomorrow. We can suffer to postpone The Plan one more day, can we not?"

Chapter Twenty-Four

STELLA IS HAPPY: THE AUTHOR AGREES TO MEET THE
PROSPECTIVE HUSBAND, PROVIDED SHE WILL BE ABLE TO SPEND
TIME AT THE WELLS; LEMUEL IS INTERCEPTED AND IS ORDERED
TO A SECRET RENDEZVOUS ON THE BEACH; HE IS GIVEN HIS
FIRST SPYING MISSION AS THE OFFICER OF SHINBET.
(Redriff, Monday, August 18th,1703)

My plotting seems to bear fruits! Stella was ever so thrilled that I
"agreed" to meet Mr. John Lowsley, my second husband.

I did not want her to suspect that I have other intentions, so
I only said I agreed to a non-formal meeting between this young
widow (me) and that old widower, Mr. Lowsley.

He is also a hosier, and she is bent on making our family rule the
world's socks-markets. "First we conquer Northamptonshire," she
wrote to me in her letter, "and then we take Berlin!"

What an ambitious sister I have. She must have taken it from our
father. I, like my mother, prefer to read and write.

Mr. John Lowsley lives in Northamptonshire, a twenty-hour
coach drive from Stella's home. Of course, I do not intend to take
this tiresome, two-days' journey.

I wrote to Stella that I must prepare myself for my future husband by properly enjoying the waters at Sadler's Wells first. Islington is but a short walk from Stella's home, our childhood home, and
Stella will surely assent to my last wish as a widow.

Years ago, so many years ago, when Stella and I were but little
girls, we spent many a Sunday afternoon in Islington, strolling at our
leisure among the trees and flowers, feasting our eyes on the marvellous dresses of lovely women. Locking arms with Stella, I pretended
that I was a beautiful woman, and that Stella was a strong, handsome

man.

We never set foot inside that wooden imposing house of Sadler's Wells Musick-House, where the famous ferruginous water was served to thirsty spectators of musick and dance entertainment. We were too young for that, but I always longed to be a grown-up, to put on a fancy bonnet and, hanging on a handsome man's arm, to promenade into that exciting, secrets-full Sadler's Wells Musick-House.

Now, my handsome man is lost somewhere at sea, Stella claims that he is dead, and I am to wed another.

Strange how the road of life lets us see life's events totally differently when we reach another milestone. Anticipating my first marriage felt so much different than the second . . .

But I am not going to wed this widower.

I go through the motions because I want to help Lemuel's little friends. That is the least I can do to profess my eternal love for him. I will go as far as Sadler's Wells Musick-House, hanging on James' arm (my sister's handsome boy will be glad to chaperone me there) and, once I accomplish my mission, I will find a fine excuse to waive off this ridiculous marriage and go back home to Redriff, to await the safe return of my Lemuel, or to die as a widow.

When I will be at Sadler's Wells, my plan is to somehow steal the poor Lilliputians. I will release them and hide them all on my person. They are used to fly about with Lemuel, so they will keep quiet inside my pockets till we reach Newgate Street.

I will tell Stella that I do not feel well, and I will insist on returning home . . . with my Lilliputians, hiding in my luggage!

Once we will reach Redriff, I am sure I will be able to hide them till Lemuel will be back, and then we will find a way of getting them back home to Lilliput. Johnny and Betty are big enough to keep the secret, I am sure.

But first I must convince Stella to change her plans. She is a cunning fox, my sister! Officially, I am to be chaperoned by James, her sixteen-year-old son. While her boy will be discussing the financial details with my future husband, I am expected to be beautiful and keep quiet. I am flattered that Stella thinks I can do both, and at the same time!

She is convinced that Mr. Lowsley will fall madly in love with me, and that they will merge their businesses as soon as the priest will bless our marriage.

According to her plan, we are to leave from the Black Swan Inn in Holborn by the Thursday morning stagecoach to York, which leaves punctually at five a clock in the morning. We will arrive on Friday evening at the Cock and Bull Inn, where Mr. Lowsley will come to call on us.

We are to insist on staying at the Cock and Bull, but to relent the next day to Mr. Lowsley's invitation to stay at his home. On Saturday night I should pretend to have a fever and to faint in Mr. Lowsley's arms. Etc. etc.

But, since I know that she expects me to stay with Mr. Lowsley in Northampton, to prepare the wedding, I wrote to her that I insist on taking the waters before we take to the road.

I have my plans, too!

Of course, I do not intend to marry Mr. John Lowsley, no matter how rich or how old he might be. I am loyal to my Lemuel and will always be.

And I am bent on trying to rescue the poor Lilliputian refugees who are forced to perform at Sadler's Wells. Yes, I know that some of the Lilliputians were quite abusive towards my Lemuel three years back but, still, I pity these refugees and feel no vengeance.

Here is what happened to Lemuel after his secret audience with the Emperor and the Empress:

* * *

He was walking back to his Liberty-Temple, deep in thought, scanning the ground without paying much attention.

By then Lemuel had gotten used to automatically make sure he was not trampling on any Lilliputian human or animal. Only occasionally did he still feel the unsettling crack under his foot, when he stepped on tiny animals, such as Lilliputian mice or birds that were too small for him to notice from high above, or too slow to escape from under his boot.

He was deep in thought about the Emperor's bizarre ideas on politics and human nature, not to mention the elusive Top Secret, of which he still has had no clue.

Suddenly he was shocked out of his reveries by shrill voices:

"Halt! Man-Mountain! Halt!"

"What . . . where?"

Lemuel looked down and saw a few yards ahead of him several Lilliputians waving frantically, pointing at an old Lilliputian lady slowly crossing the road. She was wearing the traditional blue sac, which only allowed her a front vision through the eye-slit.

Crossing the road ever so slowly, she was not able to see the approach of the Man-Mountain and, being so old, she was probably also hard of hearing and did not hear the people's cries.

Lemuel froze where he was and watched the old lady making her ever so slow progress to the other side of the road.

Lemuel bent down.

"May I help?"

"Oh!" the old lady raised her head, in shock. "It is you, the Man-Mountain! I heard about your strong hand and soft heart. Yes, please!" she croaked on. "I wish to go to the beach, for fresh air. Could you please transport me there?"

"By all means," said Lemuel and scooped her up carefully in his palm. But as he straightened up the old lady removed her blue sac, and Lemuel was shocked to discover that he was holding none other than the feared Skyresh Bolgolam in disguise!

Lemuel had to make a frantic effort not to drop the mighty Lilliputian.

Bolgolam seemed to be just as averse to the close proximity with Lemuel.

"Man-Mountain, take hold of yourself, you beast," he grumped as he folded the blue sac, which covered his fancy uniform. "This is a secret meeting. It never happened. Now pretend to take the old lady to the beach and do it quick!"

As carefully as he only could, Lemuel stepped over the field to the nearest beach. It was but a couple of steps away, but Lemuel tried to make the journey last for as long as he could, pretending that he was walking slowly, in fear of trampling on Lilliputian creatures.

He could not fathom why Bolgolam would intercept him in this secret manner. Was this going to be his last day on earth?

Wishing he could squash his tormentor, and fearing to do so, Lemuel finally did reach the Lilliputian beach. It was still populated with late-bathing Lilliputian families who were, as always, thrilled to see Lemuel walk by. They waved and yelled greetings at him, the children shrieking, running after him, certain they could catch up with his long strides. He waved back his greetings with his free hand, a bit relieved that these eyewitnesses might prevent Bolgolam from executing him right there and then.

But Bolgolam instructed Lemuel to continue walking along the beach a few more steps until they reached a deserted stretch of sand with rocky hills all around it. It was far enough from any Lilliputian habitation, said Bolgolam, and instructed Lemuel to sit on the sand, bending so that the surrounding rocks would hide them from view.

"That is better," he said. "Now place me there, on that ledge," and he pointed to a shelf of rock where he could stand, a bit above Lemuel's eye level and still be concealed from the rest of the world.

Lemuel obeyed and discreetly wiped his sweaty palm on his pants. Glancing at the sea, he could see it extending to no end. Straining his eyes he scanned the horizon, as he always did when he was near the Lilliputian beaches, always hoping to see a British sail, or any sail, but to no avail.

What he did see was a Lilliputian warship anchored a few yards away.

"They can see us from there . . ." he ventured.

"These are my men, of course. Nothing to worry about," Bolgolam retorted curtly.

"Oh, that is good." Lemuel rather hoped to have had unbiased witnesses to the crime he feared Bolgolam was intending to commit upon him.

But he did not have much time for such gloomy thoughts.

"Man-Mountain, this meeting never took place."

"Of course," asserted Lemuel, and immediately went on to swear in the Lilliputian complicated way, while Bolgolam did the same.

With this ceremony over, Bolgolam announced dramatically, "Man-Mountain, the moment of truth has arrived!"

Lemuel wished he could run someplace and hide.

Silly wish, of course, but Bolgolam seemed to have the power of bringing out the little child in Gulliver, the child that could never satisfy his ambitious, portentous father. Well, by now Lemuel knew better than to speak back to Bolgolam, so he just nodded politely, trying to seem nonplussed as he knew a real giant should.

"I am pleased to welcome you among us Slamecksans." A trace of a benevolent smile could be seen on Bolgolam's lips, but that did not reassure my Lemuel at all. "You made a wise choice to be an S-man, which you will never regret."

"I did? Oh, of course I did," Lemuel hastened to say.

"As I already told you, Man-Mountain, I know everything."

"You do." Lemuel could not help deriving some hope from Bolgolam's being so clearly misinformed.

"As a loyal S-man, you should now report to me on your meeting today with Our Emperor. Yes, I know everything, and I want to hear it from you!"

That was quite worrying, and Lemuel was pressed for words. "I just reported to him on my survey of the Lilliputian Empire. You know, that was in my contract, Article Number Eight."

"I know that," retorted Bolgolam. "But I think you should do the survey all over again. I have severe doubts about your findings."

Lemuel's professional pride was hurt again. "I am a certified surveyor, Skyresh Bolgolam. I had much occasion to study this in my travels to remote countries all over the world!"

"So you say," said Bolgolam haughtily, "so you say. But did you see anything suspicious while you were inspecting our shores?"

Lemuel had a strange sense that all this has already happened to him before. "No," he said, somewhat irritated. "It is the usual landscape, only smaller than what I am used to."

"These are your pitiful delusions, Man-Mountain! Lilliput is the mightiest nation in the universe. Never forget this!"

"Of course," Lemuel assented in haste.

"But did you see people hiding? Anyone crossing by boat to Blefuscu at night, for example?"

Now Lemuel was sure these were the exact same questions the Emperor has posed to him but a while ago. What could be behind these interrogations? Are they together in this plot against him, or did each one of them have his own reasons for this examination?

Carefully, he answered, "No, I did not see anything. If they were hiding, how could I have seen them? And I conducted my survey during the day, of course."

"Of course!" Bolgolam was furious. "That was your mistake! How can you catch them during the day when they only operate at night?!"

"Catch? Catch who?"

"Never you mind. I want a full report on the nightly activities on the Blefuscuian Channel. Be very careful, those beastly Blefuscudians can be very dangerous! I need you for the impending war. Tell your Chamberlain, Little Lalcon, to inform the women that you will be back next week, that you are sent on a mission of the SHINBET."

The SHINBET!

Lemuel was suddenly reminded that he was holding this high office. Gingerly, he posed the assumption that, as the head of the SHINBET, he was not obliged to get orders from Bolgolam . . .

"You are wrong there, too, Man-Mountain. Do not try my patience," snapped Bolgolam. "The office of the SHINBET is under the jurisdiction of the Admiralty of the Realm, and that is me. Ask the Emperor, if you dare to doubt me. He will tell you."

Lemuel felt lost and kept silent.

"War is imminent, and we have chatted enough. Your mission is clear, I presume? Do not make me repeat it, I defy you!"

So Lemuel nodded feebly his assent.

Next, Bolgolam instructed Lemuel to transport him to the war-ship and, as soon as Lemuel planted Bolgolam on the deck, the war-ship raised anchor and set sail. Obeying Bolgolam's commands, Lemuel blew on the sails as hard as he could and the war-ship disappeared around the rock.

As he scanned, crestfallen, the horizon, not seeing any human ship, Bolgolam's final words echoed in Lemuel's ears: "We will meet next week, Man-Mountain, and I want a full report! You can expect our meeting when you least expect it!"

Chapter Twenty-Five

THE AUTHOR ALMOST MANAGES TO SAVE THE CAPTURED
LILLIPUTIANS, IF IT WASN'T FOR THE DEBAUCHERY AT SADLER'S
WELLS; LEMUEL'S DAILY REPORT TURNS INTO ANOTHER TOP
SECRET REVEALED, THAT OF THE LOLS; ALONG WITH THE SHOCK
AND AWE COME FRIENDSHIP AND FRATERNAL LOVE.
(Newgate Street, Wednesday, September 5th 1703)

Back at Stella's home. Here, at my childhood home in Newgate Street, I feel I can purify myself from the filth of Sadler's Wells.

If the waters were ever ferruginous, they were nowhere to be found. The only available liquid was beer and liquor, with lamentable evidence of their effects all over the gardens. And I remember so vividly how, back in my youth, the water was recommended as useful in removing obstructions in the system and purifying the blood!

No, I am not sorry I went there. I am not even sorry to have spent the six pence entry fee for James, my chaperone nephew, and myself, even though I was shocked by the folk, and even though I missed the poor Lilliputians by a day.

Poor James. I dragged him all over the gardens (which are still lovely, that is true), inventing reasons for my eagerness to see every corner of Islington. Finally, when he told me that his breeches had a motion, and he retired to the Jakes,[142] I used this opportunity to quickly rush into that imposing building, Sadler's Wells. By luck, I directly encountered Mr. James Miles, the new manager.

Was Mr. Miles ever so disappointed I was not in need of work, and therefore would not make love to him!

When I asked him, ever so urgently, where could I see the "Iliputians," he told me curtly that Captain Biddel left that same morning. Mr. Miles added that Captain Biddel's show is that much better than the one Mr. Gulliver was peddling over a year ago, seeing all the tricks the Lilliputian humans could perform.

I almost felt insulted for my Lemuel! But my spirits rose when Mr. Miles told me that Biddel took his show in haste, to make it in time for the Thursday fair in Northampton.

Northampton!

Where my second husband awaits me! Is life not stranger than any fiction?

Well, now I am ready to take the long road to meet my new master, if it means I might be able to save Lemuel's little friends.

James will chaperone me there tomorrow morning. (Stella was so surprised I was suddenly so eager to go . . .!)

I cannot sleep.

I am so thrilled and excited. I better continue writing what happened to Lemuel in Lilliput, three years ago:

* * *

That evening, when General Reldresal came to get his daily report, Lemuel was very careful not to mention the "Top Secret" (of which he knew nothing yet, anyway) or the new mission he was ordered to complete for Bolgolam.

Lemuel sensed that the General was behaving somewhat apprehensively, but he could not ascertain if it was because he, Gulliver, was behaving strangely by trying to behave normally, or did the General really suspect something? Was the palm of his hand, on which the General was standing eye to eye with Lemuel, sweating? Was it shaking, perhaps?

Lemuel noticed that Reldresal was a bit anxious, shuffling his legs on Lemuel's palm. He seemed a bit pale. Concerned, Lemuel asked Reldresal if he felt unwell, or if he had a sudden bout of vertigo. Would he prefer that Lemuel placed him back on the ground?

Reldresal declined the offer, and coughed as he stated, "Well, Man-Mountain, you had a private audience with Our Emperor today."

Was he jealous? Lemuel could not tell. But, of course, it was impossible to deny the fact that Lemuel did visit the Palace today and that nobody was allowed nearby. Still, Lemuel could not help suspecting that something else here was at stake, especially when he remembered so vividly that Bolgolam was just as anxious to hear all about the meeting with the Emperor.

"Could you follow Our Emperor's Lilliputian well? Were there many new words you did not understand?"

Was that an innocent question, or a trap?

Lemuel was very careful. "It was quite basic. I reported to him on my survey of the Lilliputian Empire. You know, according to the contract . . ."

"Oh," said the General. "This is very good. But are you sure of your findings? Perhaps you should check them again?"

Why did they all doubt his professionalism? "I am a qualified surveyor, you know, General Reldresal. I had occasion to practice this in my numerous travels!"

"No offence," said the General, "but pray, tell me. In the course of your survey, did you see anything suspicious?"

Lemuel was sure that all this has already happened to him before, and more than once. "No," he said, somewhat irritated. "It is the usual landscape, only smaller than what I am used to."

"Of course," the General reassured him amiably. "But did you see people hiding? Crossing by boats to Blefuscu at night, suchlike?"

Now Lemuel was truly alarmed. These were the exact questions the Emperor and Bolgolam had posed to him. What could be behind these interrogations?

Cautiously, he answered, "No, I did not see anything. If they were hiding, how could I have seen them? And I conducted my survey during the day, of course."

"Of course." The General was indeed behaving strangely. "You see," he went on to explain to Lemuel, "we have many enemies, and it is hard to tell who they are."

"Are you referring to the Slamecksan . . .?"

"Those too, but the Blefuscudians are even worse."

"Why? What did they do?"

"Oh, Man-Mountain, you still have much to learn about us. It all began upon the grave controversy of breaking eggs—"

"Oh, that," said Lemuel, relieved. "I heard all about that, from Admiral Bolgolam, and—"

"Oh, him." Lemuel could not help feeling that Reldresal was mocking him. "If you have heard all about that from Admiral Bolgolam, you have not heard anything yet. Our Admiral tends to confuse facts with truth.

"He might have told you about the opposing sides of the egg, and about the Holy Wars that plagued us, but I do not think he is ever aware of the dangers that the monarch of Blefuscu is posing for us. I myself have my private doubts, if the monarch of Blefuscu is our enemy, or if our enemy is within.

"What we do know for sure is that there is much activity on the other side of the channel, and we all share the fear of imminent invasion. Rumours are that they have now equipped a numerous fleet and are just preparing to make a descent upon us; and his Imperial Majesty, placing great confidence in your valour and strength, has commanded me to lay this account of affairs before you, and to command you to your duty, to defend our Lilliput with your body and soul."

Reldresal took a deep breath and Lemuel desired him to present his humble duty to the Emperor, and to let the Emperor know that he was ready to defend His person and state against all invaders.

On a second thought, Lemuel added, "That should not be too dangerous, or would it . . .?"

"For you, Man-Mountain, defending Lilliput would not only be easy, but also holy. After all, we gave you shelter, we gave you food, we gave you the Lovers! Surely, you are now one of us. You share our values, our high morals, our life, and our death."

That was a fine little speech, but Lemuel did not feel he was willing to share his death with anyone, not just yet.

"Are you sure, Reldresal, that all this is strictly necessary?"

"The mere existence of Lilliput is at stake! You cannot desert us at this heroic hour! Not after all I did for you! And anyway, it is good to die for our country!"

"Sure, sure. What is it you want me to do?"

"Nothing," was the surprising response of Reldresal. "I only want to recruit you to our army, under my command. You will get brand new uniforms, though it will take some months before the outfit will be ready. You will get your weapons back after Shumclum, our High Priest, will sanctify them, and you will get free board and food."

"But . . ."

"I know, I know, you already get these. But you will not have to perform matrimonial duties for other men anymore."

"I will not?" Lemuel was not sure it was a fair deal.

"You will not have to," hastened Reldresal to explain, "but you could continue, if you wished, and you will be paid for it. Only that the money will be forwarded to the Emperor, who is, after all, the owner of the Army and as such, the owner of you."

Lemuel could not care less who will get the money, as long as he could get his nightly Lilliputian bliss.

"That is alright," he assented and was soon to regret his words.

"Splendid!" exclaimed Reldresal. "So I now pronounce you a Soldier of The Lilliputian Holy Army!"

"You do? But . . .?"

"You are a hero, my dear Man-Mountain. You are a brave soldier and the most loyal person I ever encountered. You can and you should be proud of yourself, and of your new position!"

Despite himself, Lemuel did feel a tiny swell of pride rising in his breast.

"But what . . . what about the SHINBET?"

"I will now confide in you the Top Secret," said Reldresal, and Lemuel's ears pricked up. Was he about to hear, at long last, what the Emperor was trying to convey? He was only disappointed that, since the Top Secret was about to be revealed then and there, he would not have another opportunity tomorrow to see the Empress again.

"As the head of the SHINBET, you are to become the Emperor's Weapon of Mass Distraction!" announced Reldresal proudly.

"Oh, that sounds . . . massive."

"It is! It is awesome!"

"And . . . is it very dangerous? I mean, for me?"

"For you, not at all!" Reldresal seemed to understand Lemuel's fears. "Your task, as the Emperor's Weapon of Mass Distraction will be to swim all the way to Blefuscu, rise out of the water with a terrifying scream, and trot through the streets of Blefuscu, the capital of Blefuscu, stampeding all Blefuscudian creatures, though trying to avoid cattle and other valuable properties."

Lemuel could only grimace his disgust.

"Oh, do not worry, Man-Mountain, we will all be behind you, following you in our warships, and we will slaughter every living soul that would survive the Weapon of Mass Distraction! You, brave Man-Mountain, will lead the invasion and together we will conquer and annihilate Blefuscu!"

And Reldresal proceeded to entreat Lemuel to prove his vigour and bravery by annihilating the Blefuscudian nation. "You are our greatest ally," said Reldresal. "The Emperor saw fit to give you the SHINBET, to enlist you to his glorious army. Now you could defend Lilliput to the heroic end!"

Reldresal drew his small frame and declared that, had he been bestowed with the size of the Man-Mountain, he would willingly risk his life for the glory of his Emperor and the Holy Lilliputian Blundrecal, which clearly instructs all believers to believe, and therefore, to obey.

He quickly added that, obviously, Lemuel was also bound by the Lilliputian Blundrecal, as he was a Lilliputian resident, holding an official stay-permit.

All these arguments being indisputable, Lemuel solemnly promised to obey his Emperor's commands, and to annihilate the Blefuscudians as soon as possible.

I can well imagine the emotional turmoil that my Lemuel experienced then. Away from home, not knowing when—and if at all —he would ever see again any human being of a proper size and stature; having spent almost two years under the influence of the Lilliputian perceptions of the world, my poor husband's mind was turned and tossed, was infused with ideas he had never thought of before, excreting out of his mind notions of which he has always been so sure.[143]

So, my poor husband became a Lilliputian soldier and conceded to annihilate the Blefuscudian nation.

"May I have another word with you, Man-Mountain?"

"But of course," said my good man.

"I do not want you to think I am a bad Lilliputian, or a Blundrecal heretic."

"Of course, you are not!" exclaimed Lemuel, bewildered.

"Hear me out," beseeched Reldresal, "and when you have heard my full, tragic story, perhaps you will find it in your heart to understand me and perchance to accommodate my desires."

And thus, Reldresal began the sad tale of the LOL, the "Lilliputian Outlawed Lust."

As far back in time as the Lilliputian memory could go, there had always been Lilliputian men who could not possibly satisfy any Lilliputian woman.

In the dark ages of time, tells the Holy Blundrecal, such men were grouping together, forming colonies of men only, and thus cursed to extinction. Nowadays, Lilliputian schools teach the children that the LOLs were lost in the folds of history.

But every so often a Lilliputian man grows up to discover that he cannot help it; he, too, is an LOL. Such men are bound to lead a very tragic existence should they be discovered. They do not marry, they have no children, they are a shame to their Emperor.

"Are you a LOL?" asked Lemuel, curious.

"Not so loud, if you please!" cried Reldresal.

"And . . .?" ventured Lemuel, hesitantly.

"And I am the only LOL in the village since my dear, dear Deputy Principal Secretary Of Private Affairs, Laserdler, was lost at sea, fighting the cursed Blefuscudians."

And at that Reldresal fell to his knees on Lemuel's palm and burst out in bitter tears.

My Lemuel stretched his left arm and closed all the curtains of all the windows.

Darkness fell in the room.

Lemuel brought Reldresal closer to his face and, whispering as softly as he could, he said, "Do not worry, dear Reldresal, your secret is safe with me. I know how it feels to be a man among men only, and to relish men's desires."

(Yes, I knew of the sailors' love, but I personally thought it unwise of my Lemuel to tell it to Reldresal. After all, buggery[144] is a crime here in England!)

Reldresal sniffled still, dabbed his eyes with his tiny handkerchief, and asked, "Do you desire me too, oh Man-Mountain?"

"Please, call me Man," said my generous Lemuel.

"Oh, Man," gasped Reldresal.

"Of course," said Lemuel reassuringly. "I desired men before, but never did I desire a man of your grandeur. "

"May I get a good look at you, Man?" asked Reldresal.

"Of course," said Lemuel," but only if I can have a good look at you, too."

"Oh, gladly, so gladly!" said Reldresal and undressed himself right away, still standing on Lemuel's palm. Upon which Lemuel beheld the finest male creature he had ever seen. For Reldresal's skin was as fine and smooth as ever he saw, his tiny yard already proudly swollen, with a hint of soft curls surrounding it. A roundish tiny bag was delicately hanging between his strong, little legs.

Lemuel was greatly impressed with the relative hugeness of Reldresal's yard, compared to his diminutive size. While Europeans' yards are between one tenth to one sixth of a male's body (in very extreme instances), it turned out that the Lilliputians' ratio was one sixth to one third of their body! (which accounted, Lemuel thought, for the eager state of Lilliputian women).

Tenderly, Lemuel proceeded to caress Reldresal's skin with the tip of his left hand's index finger. As Reldresal's eyes rolled, Lemuel stuck out his tongue and gently rolled it from the bottom of the General's quivering yard to its top, rolling his tongue around it, and amazed to see it growing even more.

"Stop it, please!" cried Reldresal all of a sudden. "I want to ravish you, too!"

And while Reldresal was catching his breath, after Lemuel placed him gently on the floor, he watched in awe as Lemuel removed his breeches.

"Ah," gasped Reldresal. "Are you not so savagely ugly. You make a truly beautiful picture. I care not, I mind not. Having seen you, being about to penetrate you, I can soon die as the happiest of LOLs".

Having fully undressed himself, Lemuel set on the floor with his legs parted.

Smiling tenderly, he watched how Reldresal ran under his knee and how he halted, with his hands on his hips, in front of Lemuel's yard (which was only just beginning to grow).

"Dear, dear," said the General. "Your skin appears much fairer and smoother when I look at you from afar than it does upon a nearer view such as now. But oh, these great holes in your skin are ever so attractive! The stumps of your cruel bush are ten times stronger than the bristles of a boar. I resolve to name you 'My Little Huggy Haggy Boar' if you do not mind."

With this announcement he proceeded towards Lemuel's bollocks, which rested limply on the ground, and, caressing and hugging them, the General hid his face among the folds, sniffing and sighing all the while, in a manner very pleasing for Lemuel, too. He soon felt little feet climb on top of his bollocks, and little hands pulling at his full bush, as Reldresal continued his ascent up towards Lemuel's proud yard.

"This is too much," heaved Reldresal. "Let me ram you now, my Little Huggy Haggy Boar!" and he slid diligently down Lemuel's groin, while Lemuel, indulgingly, leaned further back on his elbows.

Spreading his legs as much as the space in the Temple allowed him, he felt his Bollocks being shoved, pushed, and heaved up for some time and then he heard the muffled voice:

"Will you help me, my Little Huggy Haggy Boar? I have no access . . . !"

Lemuel brought his right hand forward, scooped up his bollocks and felt Reldresal's little hardened yard sharply tickling his arse, while Reldresal's little hands clung to Lemuel's anal bush, with all his might.

Reldresal was lost to his lust and unable to control himself anymore. He pushed his whole leg up Lemuel's rear, while ramming his sting at the soft, slightly wet skin of Lemuel's arse.

Lemuel spit into his hand and was caressing his own machine vigorously, while trying not to crush his new little lover, when he suddenly felt a warm liquid pouring over his arse in several gushes.

Apparently, as tiny as the Lilliputian was, his love juice came in huge quantities.

Sighing deeply, Reldresal appeared from behind Lemuel's soft sac and, shuddering with pleasure he announced, "This was the happiest day of my life." He dressed up swiftly and asked that Lemuel would lie on his belly, so Lemuel's chin would be on the ground.

Reldresal then walked towards Lemuel's face, and clasping Lemuel's cheeks with his hands, planted a long, wet kiss on Lemuel's lips. "You will not tell anyone about us, of course? I suspect the Emperor is an LOL too, and I want to keep you all to myself!"

He then opened the gate carefully, mounted his white horse, and galloped away.

Chapter Twenty-Six

THE AUTHOR INTERCEPTS CAPTAIN BIDDEL AND HIS ILLIPUTIAN
SHOW AND PLOTS THEIR IMPENDING RESCUE; SHE MEETS HER
FUTURE HUSBAND AND IS SMITTEN; LEMUEL REALIZES THAT HIS
SALVATION FROM THE LOL IS IN WAR, BUT HE DEVISED A NEW,
HUMANE STRATAGEM TO PUT AN END TO IT ALL.
(Northampton, Cock and Bull Inn, Friday, September 7th 1703)

It is somewhat bizarre, but I do feel attracted to my future husband.

I expected to loathe Mr. Lowsley. I was determined (as soon as I would have saved the poor Lilliputians) to find the first excuse to hasten back home to Redriff. But here I am, craving this man I only just met.

Maybe it was his eyes, smiling at me so warmly, that melted me thus. Or his large, soft palm, holding my hand for the softest of kisses? Most likely it was his bidding me good night and so gently asking for a kiss which, at first, I grudgingly refused, as expected, and then readily granted.

The effect was instantaneous. It has been a long time since I had the occasion to notice the physical effects of lips meeting each other: there is one nerve of the fifth pair, which goes from the mouth to the heart, and thence lower down. With such delicate industry has nature prepared everything! The little glands of the lips, their spongy tissue, their velvety paps, the fine skin, ticklish, gives them an exquisite and voluptuous sensation, identical and analogical to the lips below the belly . . .[145] I felt them both and melted within.

But as soon as our lips parted, I remembered the poor Lilliputians and, as I was determined to set them free, before starting the second chapter of my life with dear Mr. John Lowsley, I refused to spend the rest of the night with him in his home. He whispered in my ear that he would send his carriage for me so that, as soon as James would fall asleep, I could sneak into his carriage and off to his home. Even though he reassured me that Balegule, his black Moor driver,[146] was totally trustworthy, and even though seeing Mr. Lowsley's collection of etchings was most tempting, I refused.

Mr. Lowsley looked as disappointed as I felt, but promised to send Balegule with the carriage tomorrow morning to get us to his home, where he also conducts his business.

I was determined to stay tonight at the Cock and Bull, because I did get to see them, Captain Biddel and his notorious box, when I alighted from the carriage at the inn.

He was probably returning from exhibiting the poor creatures at the market of Northampton. Though I was quite spent from those two days rocking on mud roads, I instructed James to unload our boxes and wait for me inside, and as soon as he turned his back, I went and tapped on the shoulder of that dreadful Biddel, just as he was unloading that prison box with its innocent occupants off his horse.

I did notice that the box was not locked.

I breathed deeply. "Captain Biddel, I presume?"

But to my surprise, he did not seem to be surprised.

"My deaw Mws. Gullivew! My deaw, deaw pawtnew!"

It was also clear that Biddel was drunk. That might explain why he did not lock the box.

"Sir, this is deplorable," I said, shaking with indignation.

"Do not wowy, my faiw lady." Biddel was trying to mock me. "You will get youw fawe shawe. I am as good as my wowd." He leaned nearer to me. "And I expect to get a good shawe of you, once we conclude ouw business?"

I nearly choked from the stench of his breath. But I collected myself bravely and told him, "Captain Biddel, I am here with my cousin, Mr. James Lavender, and I must be short."

He just laughed. "I must be showt too, for we awe expected tonight at the Palace of Malplaquet! If you will be so kind to come to my wooms at the Cock and Bull tomowow mowning, we could shawe the money, and the bed!"

Before I knew what I was saying, I said, "Captain Biddel, I have never been to a palace before. May I come with you to the Palace of Malplaquet?"

He seemed to like this idea even better and he said, "Of couwse my deaw. But, you know, no need to bwing youw chapewone. I will take the utmost cawe of you."

As if I would involve James in all this!

We set to leave a couple of hours later, at six o'clock, and luckily, as soon as he disappeared inside the inn, my Mr. John Lowsley arrived, smiling broadly. And because of my plans for the Palace of Malplaquet, I had to postpone the consummation of my impending matrimonial contract with Mr. John Lowsley to tomorrow night.

I am so nervous now. I have but a couple of hours before the rescue will commence!

The only way I know of passing the time and keeping sane is to continue writing Lemuel's story. Now that I have met Mr. John Lowsley, I find it easier to accept the fact that Lemuel is lost at sea.

* * *

When Reldresal left, Lemuel was quite confused. He liked Reldresal, yet he was hoping that Reldresal was indeed the only LOL in Lilliput.

Though Lemuel did relieve his manly needs with other men, as opportunities presented themselves on various sea voyages, he preferred the physical company of women. He also knew that sodomy is punishable by law, also in Lilliput, and therefore concluded that it was a bad thing.

He had enough reasons to fear the wrath of the Lilliputian Emperor and Empress, each for their own (and contradictory) motives. He did not want to allow a Lilliputian Anti-LOL law to be hanging over him. He realised that, as much as he liked Reldresal and was happy he could render the poor little man some moments of bliss, still, for the sake of the safety of them both, he must put an end to their liaison.

His only salvation, he resolved, was to go to war.

But the thought of his impending death was not agreeable to him at all.[147]

As much as Lemuel was excited to join the Lilliputian army (he felt young again, bold, and brave!) still he was old enough[148] to grasp that war could be dangerous, even to someone as big as he was.

Indeed, two years before, when he first laid eyes on the Lilliputians, he had no second thoughts about killing them, as he would kill any insect. But, in the meantime, Lemuel got to know almost all the Lilliputians, and at times even forgot that he was that much bigger than they were.

Though Bolgolam and Reldresal tried to imbue Lemuel with hatred of the Blefuscudians, still, Lemuel could not help feeling that they were human beings, too. Annihilating a whole nation, as challenging an endeavour as it was, did not appeal to Lemuel at all.

My wise man devised a plan, which he thought would appeal to the Emperor as much as mass murder would, since it involved lasting financial gains.

The next day, when Lemuel put it to him this way, the Emperor was convinced and agreed to Lemuel's plan of action, to seize the enemy's whole fleet and bring it over to Lilliput.

This would double the Emperor's navy and would humiliate for good the hated Blefuscudians. Not least, it would render them incapable of exporting goods and thus dependent on the Lilliputian economy, and in turn on the goodwill of the Lilliputian emperor, who would control the prices of EVERYTHING.[149]

And, of course, anyone who is not annihilated needs to buy food and other goods.

This would be a win-win-win situation, well, for the Emperor.

And also for Lemuel. Now he would not have to put his life on the line.

As soon as he managed to convince the Emperor of the wisdom

of his plan, Lemuel insisted to get his possessions back, which were confiscated from him upon his imprisonment.

In due ceremony the items were fetched from the Royal Coffers and handed back to Lemuel, who had to sign for each item: his handkerchief, snuff box, journal-book, comb, pistols, bullets and gunpowder (still in good condition!), coins, knives, purse, scimitar and scabbard, and even his timepiece, though Shumclum, the High Priest, strongly objected to the releasing of this blasphemous object.[150]

The Emperor, Bolgolam and even Reldresal were pressing Lemuel to go ahead with this new plan, which was presented to them as the Emperor's, as soon as possible, repeatedly asserting that the Blefuscudians were ready to attack, that they would set sail with the first fair wind and invade innocent, peace-loving Lilliput.

And my Gulliver was the only one who could save them.

For the sake of peace Lilliputians he had to be the first to wage war.

Chapter Twenty-Seven

The empire of Blefuscu is an island situated to the north-northeast side of Lilliput, from whence it is parted only by a channel eight hundred yards wide.

Keen on his mission of ship-confiscation, Lemuel consulted the most experienced seamen upon the depth of the channel, which they had often plumbed, and they told him that in the middle at high-water it was seventy Glumgluffs deep (about six foot[152] of European measure). They said that the rest of the channel was fifty Glumgluffs deep at most.

Armed with this intelligence, and with that intelligence only, Lemuel embarked upon the northeast coast over against Blefuscu. Lying down behind a hillock, he took out his pocket perspective-glass, and viewed the enemy's fleet at anchor.

It consisted of about fifty men-of-war[153] and a great number of transports.

But he had a plan!

Lemuel returned to his Temple, and established there a command post, from which he gave order (for which he had a warrant from the Emperor) for a great quantity of the strongest cable and bars of iron. The cable was about as thick as packthread, and the bars of the length and size of a knitting needle. Lemuel trebled the cable to make it stronger, and for the same reason twisted three of the iron bars together, binding the extremities into a hook.

He was quite gratified by the admiration of the many Lilliputians who came to follow this massive operation, waving Lilliputian flags and singing the national anthem whenever any of Gulliver's feats overwhelmed them. Lemuel had a terrible ear, so he could not really repeat this song properly, but the lyrics were thus:

So long as there is the earth and the heavens,
So long as the world endures,
So long as there is life in the world,
So long as a single Lilliputian breathes,
There will be this Lilliput.

And the arrows' red glare, the spears bursting in air,
Gave proof thro' the night that Lilliput's flag was still there.

O say, does that Lilliput banner yet wave
O'er the land of the free and the home of the brave?

Strongly fought for, fiercely contested,
You are in the center of the Seas
Like a strong heart,
You have borne since the earliest days
The burden of a high mission,
Much tried Lilliput.

Our hearts will defy death itself!

O adored Fatherland,
Cherished and revered,
All hail! All Hail!

God save our gracious Emperor,
Long live our noble Emperor,
God save the Emperor!

Send him victorious,
Happy and glorious,

Long to reign over us,
God save the Emperor!

It took a whole week, during which time Bolgolam was constantly nagging Lemuel to be quicker, while achieving the opposite effect. Lemuel was ever so confused and terrorised by Bolgolam, that he botched his task miserably when he heard Bologna's screams.

Finally, having thus fixed fifty hooks to as many cables, Lemuel went back to the northeast coast and, putting off his coat, shoes, and stockings, walked into the sea in his leathern jerkin, about half an hour before high water. He waded with what haste he could and swam in the middle about thirty yards[154] till he felt ground. He arrived at the fleet in less than half an hour.

When he swam near enough to the Blefuscudian bay, careful to keep his head in the water, only his eyes peeping to prevent being detected too soon, he was surprised to see that all the ships were deserted.

Fearing a trap, he raised his head a bit and scanned the shore and city walls.

His jaw dropped in utter surprise, and he nearly choked. All the roofs of the city, for as far as he could see, were populated with little naked women bidding him to come nearer!

In amazement, he rose out of the water to get a better view.

As they saw this gigantic figure emerging from the sea, dripping water, algae and fish, those thousands of naked women fell on their backs in fear and surprise.

It was then that Lemuel saw the thousands of men who were standing behind the women, holding fans of all sizes and waving them vigorously.

He could not but appreciate the stratagem. Obviously his existence in Lilliput was no secret, and all citizens of Blefuscu had heard of his prowess. Realising that they could not fight him, they resolved to conquer him by temptation. And when Lemuel waded, dazed, toward this inviting mob, he understood the purpose of the fans: he was soon engulfed with the most enchanting scent of women's love-juices.

"Come! Come!" they were all bidding him, pointing to the right. His eyes followed their direction, and he saw a large field on the edge of which thousands more women and men were standing, naked, waving, inviting.

Stumbling in that direction, as if under a spell, Lemuel just collapsed to the ground, looking in amazement at the swarm of people running towards him.

Was this a trap?

That was his last thought before he felt the touch of the first Blefuscudian on his body. Despite his curiosity to see more, he could not help but surrender to these sweet, new sensations of thousands of tiny hands, legs, bodies, breasts, mouths, tongues, asses, pricks, rubbing, pressing, hugging, licking every part of his submitting body.

Lying on his back, afraid to move lest he would crush his new lovers, he heard soft, enchanting music and dived even deeper into this bliss. Lemuel opened lazily one eye and saw the Blefuscudians taking turns at admiring his love toy, like ants, forming a line going up and down. Other Blefuscudians, who were not making love to him, were vigorously engaged with one another in all possible combinations.

The unceasing hugs, pressures, tiny kisses and squeezes on his shaft and testicles finally took their toll and Lemuel reached the peak of his pleasure, groaning and laughing at the same time. The awe that struck the Blefuscudians fed their frenzied lust and almost as one, they all came, content and consumed, and collapsed where they were, on top of him, beside him, inside each other.

A few moments later they recovered, and as they got dressed, Lemuel was expecting to discern their social positions according to the quality of their dress, but he could not detect any major fashion differences.

"Welcome to Blefuscu," said one Blefuscudian.

"It is our pleasure to have you here," said another woman. "And to pleasure you!" said many others, clapping and cheering.

"Thank you, indeed," said Lemuel. "It is a pleasure to be welcomed by you, kind folk."

"And you are welcome to stay, of course," many called out.

At that moment Lemuel remembered his mission and the oath he made on the Lullupiter Lapis. He was considering what would be the most polite way to leave the festivities and steal the ships. While he was pondering this etiquette, sitting in that field of love, Lemuel was briefed about the views on politics as seen from the Blefuscudian shore.

Being so remote from the influence of other societies, and recognising the failings of the Lilliputians, the Blefuscudians developed quite a unique and seemingly (to the European mind) perverted society, which turned human morals upside-down.

Possessing healthy instincts for the good life, and a nihilistic approach to fears and worries, the Blefuscudians conceded that by collaborating and accommodating each other, they would all flourish to enjoy the good life.

The Blefuscudians were able farmers and grew enough food to sustain them all. Despite the Lilliputian embargo, there were still lively contacts between the two nations, not only in the form of Lilliputian refugees, but also in the form of Lilliputian smugglers.

The Blefuscudians were in want of nothing, except for cannabaceae, which they did not succeed to grow in Blefuscudian soil.

As they described their life and habits of commerce, suddenly Lemuel grasped what were the reasons for the strange behaviour and insistent questioning of the Emperor, Bolgolam and Reldresal. It came to him like lightning the reason why they were all so adamant that he should find out what was going on at nights on the shores of Lilliput.

The Emperor, Bolgolam and Reldresal were each running his own smuggling band!

The Blefuscudians were rolling in laughter when they told Lemuel how, when the bands would bring the merchandise to Blefuscu, a cannabaceae party would be announced and the smugglers would join the fun, smoke and sex.

Back in Lilliput, the smugglers would claim that the other band robbed them of the revenues. It worked for a while but, after a number of years, the suspicions of the Emperor, Bolgolam and Reldresal were aroused.

They had no way of finding out what was going on, since they could not reveal to each other, to the court and to the Lilliputian population, that they were involved in breaking the embargo and trafficking drugs.

Life was good in Blefuscu, the Blefuscudians contentedly conceded to Lemuel. Word of the Blefuscudian good life did leak to Lilliput, and that accounted for the constant flow of Lilliputian refugees.

"But who is taking care of you? Who is ruling you?" Lemuel was totally baffled.

A roar of laughter rose when they heard that question.

"We take perfectly good care of ourselves. We are free people. We surely need no ruler!"

The Blefuscudians' naïveté quite touched Lemuel's heart, he told me, and he could not find it in him to explain to them the grave political mistake which they were making. He also did not find it in his heart to steal their ships. By the way, those were not men-of-war. No, they were simple fishing vessels. What Lemuel mistook as canons were but thick rods, to catch sardines.

Though he solemnly swore to the Lilliputian Emperor just the other day to return with the Blefuscudian fleet, he was suddenly overwhelmed by surging emotions towards those naïve, little, friendly people.

Their peacefulness and utter trust in him simply demilitarised his spirits.

Instead of feeling shame at the loss of his valour, he was filled with vigour, as he plotted his next move. He suggested to the Blefuscudians that he would fake their defeat, and transport their fleet to Lilliput, and then convince the Emperor to issue peace with the "defeated" island.

The Blefuscudians could not care less, as long as he would help them build new vessels so that they could go on fishing. Before Lemuel set back to Lilliput, he chopped down a good quantity of trees and transported them to the Blefuscudian shipyard where, he was reassured, within a fortnight they would be able to replenish their fleet and eat fish again.

Chapter Twenty-Eight

THE AUTHOR, BY AN EXTRAORDINARY STRATAGEM,
ACCOMPLISHES AT LEAST ONE OF HER MISSIONS; LEMUEL RETURNS
TO LILLIPUT TO MANY APPLAUSES AND A HIGH TITLE OF HONOR;
THE EMPRESS'S APARTMENT IS SET ON FIRE BY AN ACCIDENT;
PROUDLY, LEMUEL PISSES THE ROYAL FIRE OFF.
*(Northampton, Cock and Bull Inn,
the early hours of Saturday, September 8th 1703)*

The excitement I feel does not let me fall asleep. I am so full of my glorious success, so full of love to mankind and Lilliputiankind.

No, I cannot sleep.

The sun will rise in a couple of hours, on the day I will properly meet, speak and finally, hopefully, make love to my future second husband.

What better reward could I ask for, for the feat I accomplished but an hour ago?

And to top it all, I am confident that my name will live forever with future generations of Lilliputians to come. The Lilliputians I just rescued will forever be grateful to me and will tell of this glorious night to their children, and grandchildren, and grand, grand, grandchildren!

I do feel pride when I remember the resilience I demonstrated tonight, when I saw Captain Biddel at the Inn's court, as good as his word, at eight a Clock, with the Lilliputians prison-box strapped to his horse, and one more horse side-saddled[155] for me.

He suggested that I join him when he exhibits the Lilliputians at the Palace of Malplaquet, and promised to share with me the revenues. I even relented to promise him that I will share his bed afterwards.

The fool!

James was pleased to stay in the inn, eyeing the innkeeper's fair daughter. I told James that I would be back as soon as I can, but that he should not bother waiting up for me. He smiled broadly and promised not to tell his mother. Though I was piqued, I preferred not to put him straight then, but to hurry on my mission.

The road outside our inn was still populated with late night passersby, and through the windows I could see homely activities, which made me miss my family back in Newgate. I thought how much more miserable the captive Lilliputians must be feeling, and that filled my heart with vigour and resolution.

I took a couple of wine bottles with me and, as soon as we left the village, I proposed to Biddel the first toast.

He was already quite intoxicated, and I could tell that I made the right decision wearing a deep décolleté. It was getting dark, and my fair breasts were glowing in the moonlight. He could not and would not miss the sight. When we reached the South Bridge on River Nenn, I noticed an island in the river, and an upturned little boat. My course was clear to me.

By then Biddel gulped one whole bottle and was quite pleased with himself.

I begged him to stop, smiled modestly to him and pointed out the wonderful, romantic moon, which hung right above us. Biddel understood my meaning right away and proposed, though slur-ringly, that we should get off our horses and enjoy the moon for a while.

Of course, I assented, knowing full well that he would collapse to the ground the moment he would dismount his horse. He did take a few steps in my direction, gallantly offering to help me off my horse, but as he was simultaneously trying to unbutton his front flap and grab me, he soon lost his balance and fell flat on his nose.

I must admit, I was shaking with fear and apprehension when I jumped off my horse and rushed to Biddel's horse, to the Lilliputian's prison-box. I was afraid Biddel might recover; I was afraid someone would pass by; I was afraid some highwayman would seize the opportunity of robbing a woman alone . . .

None of that happened, lucky me.

I planted the other wine bottle next to Biddel's hand, to make sure he would drink himself into another oblivion before he would realise what had happened.

Next, I was ever so relieved to see that Biddel, in his drunken arrogance, had neglected to lock the box again. I only had to lift the lid and gently call to the Lilliputians, who were fast asleep, to tell them that they were free. I told them that I would help them escape by boat to the uninhabited island down the river.

Flimnap, who was the first to wake up (being the least tired, since the other Lilliputians were serving as his servants, once their chores to Biddel were done), grumbled when he saw me. "I thought you would never come!"

That was a different tune than his hated proclamation that he didn't want to have anything to do with me, being Mrs. Gulliver.

I lifted him out the prison box and carried him into the boat. He was complaining all the while, and it took a few seconds before it dawned on me that he was speaking English! In a heavy Lilliputian accent, but still!

The rest of them were ever so grateful to me, but fearful. They climbed eagerly on to my palms, and I transported them, one by one, to the boat. I decided to leave the prison box straddled to Biddel's horse, to remove any suspicion that a human hand—my hand—was involved. I did pack all of the Lilliputians' belongings in my head kerchief, joined them in the boat, and set out rowing upstream the River Nenn.

Those little people are amazing, indeed. I have good reason to believe they will prosper on that safe little island. They were ever so appreciative of my deeds, and even Flimnap nodded when they were promising enthusiastically to cherish my memory and tell their young, for generations to come, about their exodus.

As I rowed back I heard Flimnap's voice fading away, announcing to them that they will celebrate this day yearly, with a feast and stories the whole night through, of how much they suffered under the hands of Captain Biddel and the rest of the Mountain People, and how with the grace of the Lord and the Lilliputians' constant belief in Him and in His Blundecral, and Flimnap's own resilience, they had made it from slavery to freedom.

I think, though I am not sure, my name was mentioned, too.[156]

Rowing back was easier downstream, and I was grateful for that. I landed back on terra firma just as Biddel finished gulping the wine. He probably saw a blurred vision of me, walking in his direction, for I could distinctly decipher what he was trying to say: "Come, lass, let us make lo . . ." and he was off again.

Now that I am safely back in my room at the Cock and Bull, I cannot sleep anymore. The sun will soon rise, my new love will soon come, so what a better way to spend these glorious hours but in writing about Lemuel's glorious return from Blefuscu to Lilliput?

* * *

Lemuel's return to Lilliput was glorious. The Emperor, the Empress and the whole court stood on the shore, expecting the issue of this great adventure. Many Lilliputians were standing at a respectful distance behind them, and they all saw the ships move forward in a large half-moon, but could not discern Lemuel, who was up to his breast in water.

When he advanced to the middle of the channel, they were yet more in pain, because he was under water to his neck. The Emperor concluded that Lemuel drowned, and that the enemy's fleet was approaching in a hostile manner.

Bolgolam was already issuing orders to set the archers on the attack, and to send all women and children back home, but he was soon eased of his fears, for the channel growing shallower every step Lemuel made, he came in a short time within hearing, and holding up the end of the cable by which the fleet was fastened, he cried in a loud voice, "Long live the most puissant Emperor of Lilliput, his Empress and his Court!"

The Emperor received Lemuel at his landing with all possible encomiums, and proclaimed this a NARDAC (Not A Regular Day At Court) in his honour, which was the highest homage to one's honour among them. It was a ceremony which Lemuel cherished, since it involved the Kissing of the Hands of the Royal House.

The day after Gulliver's heroic victory, court was convened to discuss the next steps. Lemuel was the guest of honour and was ever so gratified that the assembly hall was re-arranged thus, that he could poke in his head, right between the Emperor and the Empress's seats.

His majesty desired Lemuel to take some other opportunity of bringing the rest of His enemy's ships into His ports. He was egged on by Bolgolam, whose ambition was so immeasurable, that he could think of nothing less than reducing the whole empire of Blefuscu into a province.

"Now that they are on their knees," proclaimed Bolgolam, "I am ready to sacrifice myself for the honour of Our Great Emperor, and go govern Blefuscu as its Viceroy."

Some dared voice their doubts about selecting Bolgolam to be the Viceroy of Blefuscu.

Reldresal, for one, was also eager to get the job, since Lemuel already hinted to him that there were numerous LOLs in Blefuscu.

"I am best equipped to destroy the Big-Endian exiles!" he announced.

"But would you have enough courage to exert confessions and compel the heretics to break the smaller end of their eggs?" demanded Shumclum. "This Viceroy is a holy post, by which our beloved Emperor would remain the sole monarch of the whole world!"

"We will decide about this post later," concluded the Emperor benevolently. "I know that each one of you is in possession of a vigorous and fearless heart. None of you will flinch from the sight of Blefuscudian blood, which you are rightfully eager to shed. But first, let Our Man-Mountain finish off the work he has begun. When all the vessels are here, along with the King of Blefuscu and his court as Our prisoners, We will decide which of you, good people, will be most suitable for the lucrative job of Viceroy of My Blefuscu.

"Let us eat the egg after we have broken its shell—," he concluded with the famous proverb, and the assembly answered in a chorus the traditional line: "—at its one and only right and holy end!!!"

It was not easy, but, as much as Lemuel was craving to visit Blefuscu again, he was not ready to do that under such expectations, and he resolved to divert the Emperor from his design of kidnapping the rest of His enemy's ships, king and court.

Anyway, the Blefuscudians had no king nor court.

When the traditional clamour following the saying of the proverb subsided, he said softly, "I would never be an instrument of bringing a free and brave people into slavery."

Everyone gasped, and Lemuel sensed that the Empress was much disappointed with him.

He hastened to explain. "Your Majesty, and enchanting Empress, mighty Court and dear friends, I humbly put it to you that I have learned much from your Lilliputian wisdom and courage. Just as you have granted me freedom with your unending sense of justice and commerce, I put it to you: do grant the Blefuscudians freedom too.

"If you do not, if you invade and occupy Blefuscu, Your Hugeness, You could expect that they would form guerrilla units to fight the Lilliputian occupation and terrorise Lilliputian citizens!

"On the other hand, if your Highness would not be engaged in constant wars, You would be able to direct all the war money into peace-time projects, for the benefit of Lilliput and for You and Your Court's eternal glory!"

A deep and long silence ensued.

Lemuel thought it was because his surprising words and their wisdom were slowly penetrating the Lilliputian's minds. But he was soon put right.

"I beg to differ," Bolgolam said at last, hardly able to hide his scorn. "Anyone here knows that there is no better way to keep the Lilliputians at bay but by terrorising them with an enemy. Your Highness, my Emperor, this Man-Mountain of Yours is but a savage, as I told You from the start. Let me be the Viceroy of Blefuscu, and I grant you constant war and revenues."

Lemuel was shamed and hurt, but insistent. "Your Highnesses," he turned to both the Emperor and his Empress, "innocent Lilliputians will die in unnecessary wars! And in terror attacks!" He turned to Shumclum. "I turn to your religious feelings, as the High Priest of the Holy Blundecral. Do you not feel pity for the impending sufferings of your believers?!"

Shumclum was clearly ill at ease, but not so much because he was convinced by Lemuel's arguments, as he felt it beneath him to relate to that heretic. So, instead, Shumclum directed his words to the Emperor. "Your Grace, it is true that some Lilliputians might die in terror attacks of the Blefuscudian's terror units, but the numbers will always be negligible. Especially when the news about the victims will not spread. At any rate, these victims will be mostly the helpless women and children. In short, those who anyway do not pay taxes. Another side effect of terror attacks would be a terrified and thus a submissive nation, eager to procreate in order to fill in the ranks. War has always been good for making new babies.

"In short, give me the Viceroy of Blefuscu, and I will make sure to avenge in Your name those deplorable yet useful terror attacks. Your popularity among the Lilliputians will surge with each cycle of violence. As the future Viceroy of Blefuscu, I can guarantee this, for Your Prosperity and that of both our parties."

As one, they all turned to Lemuel, who felt totally dejected, and could not find any argument to counter those overwhelmingly convincing views.

"So sorry," said Lemuel, sneaking a glance at the Empress and her cleavage. "I am too tired now. I need to recuperate before I can go on another war mission."

Lemuel made to retire, but the Empress held him by his earlobe.

"Not just yet, Man-Mountain." She leaned forward and addressed her husband over Lemuel's nose, "Let us now celebrate Our Glorious triumph. My dear, give orders to bring out the Glimigrim!"

"Oh, yes," assented the Emperor. "Good of you to remind me, my dear."

And as the Empress blew a kiss to her husband over Lemuel's nose, the Lilliputian special wine, Glimigrim, was brought up in gargantuan quantities (by Lilliputian standards).

Lemuel was so gratified by the fact that the Empress spoke up to prolong his stay by her side, and she was ordering barrel after barrel of delicious Glimigrim to be served to him, that he gulped the drink without measure. When the party was over, he was quite tipsy, but managed to get back to his Freedom Temple without trampling on any Lilliputian, and he was so tired that he just fell on his bed and snored away.

Till he was woken up in horror by loud cries.

He heard the word "Burglum" repeated incessantly. Hasting out, he saw a large crowd and several of the Emperor's court making their way through the crowd, entreating him to come immediately to the palace, where Her Imperial Majesty's apartment was on fire, by the carelessness of a maid of honour who fell asleep while she was reading a romance.

Lemuel glanced in the direction of the palace and saw it lit up by the vicious flames. Immediately he took to the road and, it being likewise a moonshine night, he made a shift to get to the palace without trampling on any of the people.

He found they had already applied ladders to the walls of the apartment, and were well provided with buckets, but the water was at some distance.

As he was handed buckets of water and pouring them as quickly as he could on the furious flames, he was scanning the palace, desperately looking for signs of the Empress, but could not get any information on Her whereabouts.

Those buckets were about the size of large thimbles, and the poor people supplied him with them as fast as they could, but the flame was so violent that they did little good. Lemuel might easily have stifled it with his coat, which he unfortunately left behind him for haste, and came away only in his leathern jerkin. The case seemed wholly desperate and deplorable, and this magnificent palace would have infallibly been burnt down to the ground and the Empress gone up in flames if, by a presence of mind unusual to him, Lemuel had not suddenly thought of an expedient.

It was but a few hours before that he drunk plentifully of the most delicious and seductive Glimigrim, which was very diuretic to boot!

By the luckiest chance in the world, he had not discharged himself of any part of that liquid. The heat he had contracted by coming very near the flames, and by labouring to quench them, made the wine begin to operate by urine which he voided in such a quantity, and applied so well to the proper places, that in three minutes the fire was wholly extinguished, and the rest of that noble pile, which had cost so many ages in erecting, preserved from destruction.

To his greatest relief, as he was shaking his hose to get rid of the last drops, he distinctly saw the Empress, soaked to the bone and in some haze, sitting with her legs asunder in her burnt-out bedroom.

An awed silence fell on the Lilliputians who witnessed his feat, and Lemuel bade them good night, and retired back to his Freedom Temple, ever so proud of himself and his life-saving resilience.[157]

Chapter Twenty-Nine

The indignation! I feel so upset, I cannot sleep, though I am spent and exhausted from the latest events in Northampton and the wearying, two-days' coach ride back home. I must pour my heart on these sheets of paper. Perhaps it will ease the injuries of my lost pride.

Where to start?

I feel my whole being aching to scream against the injustices which befell me. How dared he believe the gossip and not even once ask me, ME, what has happened?!

The outrage!

Somehow he heard that I left at night with a stranger, riding a horse next to the stranger's and returning to the Cock and Bull Inn alone late that night. Is that a reason to suddenly be so cold and haughty? To call the whole thing off?

I am also sorry for Stella. My sister was so eager to strike a deal with a partner in Northamptonshire. And to think that I blundered it.

With my "infidelity"!

I could cry if I had any tears left.

About Mr. Lowsley, I feel I could not care less. I already had one jealous husband. I do not need another. If he would only have asked for my explanation! Not that I would have supplied any, of course. I could not betray the trust of the Lilliputians, but if he had only asked, I would have come up with a convincing story that would prove to him that he could trust me blindly.

Oh, was I full of pride and happiness, riding back to the Cock and Bull Inn! Little did I think of what might happen should my little escapade be known!

In my worst fears I could not imagine that Mr. Lowsley would be the one to hear about it!

Since I lost Lemuel at sea, I have never been so near to marital bliss, and now I have lost it.

Forever.

My loyalty to one species proved to be the ruin of my good reputation with another.

My only consolation is that I did the right thing by the standards of my eternal true love, my Lemuel. He is lost at sea, but alive in my heart, and memory.

Forever.

* * *

Having extinguished the fire so diligently, Lemuel retired to his home, to his Freedom-Temple, well satisfied. He interpreted the silence that accompanied his departure as marks of awe and respect, and he nodded magnanimously to the multitude of awe-struck Lilliputians that followed his retreat.

He was so excited by his feat, so sure he would find a way to save his Blefuscudian friends from his Lilliputian friends—so much so that he felt that sleep would definitely elude him that night.

He decided to take a walk and savour that precious moment.

The Lilliputian nights have always been very inviting for Lemuel. Free of the fear of trampling on people, he could roam the fields and roads, lay fully stretched on his back wherever and whenever he pleased. Lilliputian wild beasts, which forced all Lilliputians to seek shelter in their homes at night, were too small to pose any danger to him.

Indeed, in Lilliput he felt invincible.

As he lay on the field near his temple, gazing at the stars (somehow they seemed larger and nearer in that part of the world), he suddenly heard a whisper at his left ear.

"Do not stir, Gulliver." He heard a familiar female voice. "I am right at your left side. And I am alone."

"The Empress," Lemuel gasped. "Your Highness. Is there new trouble? Can I assist you? How come you are outside your safe palace, tonight of all nights?"

"Ssh," she whispered fiercely. "Safe? After you have treated it so generously? Ha! The hubbub that followed your despicable act at least enabled me to get out unnoticed. But I forbid you to speak. We must not be discovered. And I am naked."

Lemuel could not breathe.

He heard his heartbeats so loud in his ears, he was sure the whole of Lilliput could hear them too. He felt the blood rushing through his veins, yet his body was frozen.

"Do not dare to move." He heard the Empress's sharp whisper and felt her warm breath on his left earlobe. It was pleasant.

Lemuel felt the Empress's tiny hands caress the folds of his ears and felt her warm body clinging to it, climbing on its folds. She clasped his beard and, pulling herself onto his face, she sat with her legs spread on the tip of his nose and, in the dim light of the stars above, he could clearly see her smiling.

"Now is my last chance," she said, "and I am going to take it."

Lemuel did not dare move, fearing she would drop off his nose. Crossed-eyes, he watched the Empress caressing her full breasts and playing with her nipples. He felt his yard growing and he slowly, delicately, moved his arm to open his front flap.

"Do not touch yourself," she whispered furiously. I want to see your hands. Now." So Lemuel raised his hands carefully and placed them next to his cheeks.

"That is much better," she said. "I hear you are very good with your tongue." And she bent forward, clasping his nose, prostrating her behind above his mouth. "I am going to pee on it."

Lemuel felt a shudder running down his spine. This was beyond his happiest dreams. He was lying on the field and felt that he never loved this land, this little Lilliput, more than at that very instance, when he distinctly felt the warm, salty drops of Her Highness, the Empress, trickle on his tongue. The Empress breathed in deep satisfaction.

"Delicious," she said.

"Ahh," groaned Gulliver softly, lovingly.

"Quiet, you!" said the Empress harshly and then commanded in a livid whisper. "Now, lick me with this famous tongue of yours!"

Thanking mutely all the gods he could think of, Lemuel stuck out his tongue and felt the wetness of the Empress at its tip.

"Oh, they were right," gasped the Empress. "Move on, move on."

While Lemuel traveled with his tongue softly and dedicatedly over the Empress's behind, he felt her breasts, for which he longed for so long, pressing on both sides of his nose, her nipples brushing his eyelashes. She stretched her hands and clung to his eyebrows, breathing quickly.

Lemuel felt his yard swelling distressingly inside his pants and pained to touch and caress it, but, loving the Empress, craving, yet fearing her wrath, he only moved his tongue, faster and faster, while the Empress heaved and breathed, writhing her body, pressing and rubbing her soft breasts on the bridge of his nose, letting her nipples be caressed by his eyelashes. She was full of lust, her desires overwhelming her, moving so fast, pressing her wet Royal seat harder and harder onto Lemuel's tongue, and she suddenly lost her balance, slipped and fell into his open mouth.

Lemuel jerked up, terrified lest he might swallow the Empress. He felt her body wriggling inside his wide-open mouth and he was afraid she might drown in his spit. As he brought his hands to his mouth he felt her clinging on to his teeth and finally, when he let her slide out of his mouth, all covered with his saliva, he was relieved to hear her laugh:

"Oh, Gulliver," she said. "Now let me sample your prick."

Lemuel could not believe his good fortune. He leaned back on his left arm and brought the Empress down to his crotch, safely scooped in the palm of his right hand. Caressing her wet long hair, he let her stay there, standing firm among the dark curls of his bush, watching amazedly Gulliver's prick as it was rising proudly again.

The Empress did not wait for it to rise fully. She clung with her body, wet and slimy due to Lemuel's saliva, and clasped his raising shaft with both her hands, spreading her legs and rubbing her slit, adding her own wetness to his. Lemuel felt the Empress's breasts on his prick, her body pressed and dancing all over it. She reached with her hands to the crown of his fully erect love-toy and pressed her fingers hard down the hole. The sensation of those tiny, sharp squeezes was overwhelming. Lemuel wanted to prolong the moment forever and ever but could not control it anymore. He felt his testicles squeezing, his prick heaving and the utter sweet joy when shooting his heavily scented life-liquid into the Lilliputian night air.

The Empress was beyond herself. She collapsed on his bush, her legs still clasped around the base of his shrinking penis, rubbing her slit at it insatiably. Lemuel realized she had not reached her own peak, and was terrified of her wrath, but then he saw, amazedly, how the love juice just ejaculated out of his shaft, slowly descending, and then—poof—splashing right on top of the Empress's breasts and belly. Rolling her eyes in delight, biting her lips, the Empress tossed and turned in Lemuel's flowing life-juice, rubbing her hungry slit onto his bush, and, finally, squealing softly her own ultimate pleasure.

When she recovered, she ordered Lemuel to take her to the stream that flowed from the volcano, where she prepared her clothes beforehand. She washed herself, dressed up and was gone, as mysteriously as she had appeared.

Chapter Thirty

THE AUTHOR IS FACED WITH CRUCIAL DECISIONS CONCERNING
HER FUTURE, NOW THAT SHE HAS RESIGNED TO HER HUSBAND'S
DEATH; STILL, SHE DECIDES TO COMPLETE THE NARRATIVE OF HER
BRAVE HUSBAND'S STORY OF TWO YEARS PAST, BEFORE SHE DROPS
THE QUILL FOR GOOD; GULLIVER IS FACED WITH MORTAL DANGERS
AND MANAGES TO ESCAPE FROM LILLIPUT; HE ARRIVES SAFELY IN
LONDON, BUT LEAVES HIS LOVING FAMILY AFTER A FEW MONTHS,
NEVER TO RETURN; PROBABLY LOST AT SEA; WELL, SURELY LOST.
(Redriff, Tuesday, December 28, 1703)

This will be the last time I write my memories, and Lemuel's.

I have matured.

I understand that my hopes of ever seeing my Lemuel again are but a folly. Stella is right. I must accept the reality of my life and resolve to dedicate it to the happiness of my surviving children.

These are days of making resolutions, and this one is mine: I will always love my Lemuel, but I will also abandon the foolish hope of his ever returning safely from his last voyage. I thank the fates for having brought him back to me from Lilliput, and I accept that the voyage he took next was indeed his last.

I will never see him again.

I have to stop crying. Tears will help me not. Stella is right. I should sell this house, our Redriff love-nest, and repair to my childhood home with Johnny and Betty. It is a big house, and since the hosiery business is expanding, Mr. Owen Lavender Jr. resolved to take on a workshop nearby. Stella will furnish it to accommodate my little family. Johnny is big enough to work and he will join the family's business. Betty will take care of me in my last years. I fear I will not live now much longer, with this broken heart of mine.

The story of Lemuel in Lilliput is also drawing to a close. These will be the last ink marks I will ever apply to paper:

* * *

If Lemuel thought that his relationship with the Empress had taken a new turn after their nightly encounter in the fields, and that now he would be favored in court, he was miserably mistaken.

If anything, it seemed as if she now openly detested him to no extent and never lost an opportunity to express it.

Reldresal was eagerly confiding in Lemuel all that which had transpired in court, and with each new token of hatred of Her Majesty, Lemuel felt that another Lilliputian poisoned arrow stung his heart.

In the days that followed, Lemuel was using any excuse to postpone accomplishing the mission he was given, to steal the rest of the Blefuscudian ships, kidnap their non-existent king and court, to enable the Lilliputian monarch to conquer and occupy Blefuscu and its people.

As all dignitaries but Reldresal were too dignified to be seen with him, following his infamous fire extinguishing, it was not that difficult to avoid complying with the draft he was given, and Lemuel was hoping that, given time, this indignation of his would pass away.

His only consolation was that he was nightly requested to accomplish far more Lilliputian matrimonial obligations than ever before.

A fortnight after that fateful meeting with the Empress, Lemuel was woken up in his Freedom-Temple, and when he opened the gate, he saw but a close chair, carried by two chairmen. They did not wear any uniforms, so Lemuel could not detect who was the noble person inside the close chair.

His heart missed a beat when he saw the chairmen retreating respectfully to wait outside.

With shaking hands Lemuel picked up the chair and brought it inside his temple, but was he ever disappointed when it was not the Empress who stepped out. He was still hoping that she would come to her senses for another night of passionate lovemaking.

But it was Reldresal who emerged from the close chair. He came to see Lemuel clandestinely. After the common salutations were over, Reldresal desired that Lemuel would hear him with patience in a matter that highly concerned Gulliver's honour and his life.

"You are to know," said Reldresal, "that several committees of council have been lately called, in the most private manner, on your account, and it is but two days since his Majesty and his Empress came to a full resolution.

"You are very sensible that Skyresh Bolgolam has been your mortal enemy almost ever since your arrival. His original reasons I know not, but his hatred is increased since your great success against Blefuscu, by which his glory as admiral is much obscured.

"This lord, in conjunction with Flimnap the high-treasurer (whose enmity against you is notorious on account of his lady), Limtoc the general, Lalcon the chamberlain, and Balmuff the grand justiciary, have prepared articles of impeachment against you for treason, future treason and other capital crimes. I procured information of the whole proceedings and a copy of the articles wherein I ventured my head for your service."

"I am ever at your debt," said Lemuel, extremely worried.

"No need to thank me," said Reldresal, very earnestly. "Our relationship is sacred to me, and I will risk my life to save yours. Our fates are intertwined."

And he handed the document to Lemuel but, of course, Lemuel could not read that little print, so Reldresal went on to read the "Articles of Impeachment against QUINBUS FLESTRIN (the Man-Mountain)":

ARTICLE I.
"Whereas, by a statute made in the reign of his Imperial Majesty Calin Deffar Plune, it is enacted that whoever shall

make water within the precincts of the Royal Palace, shall be liable to the pains and penalties of high-treason; notwithstanding, the said Man-Mountain, in open breach of the said law, under colour of extinguishing the fire kindled in the apartment of His Majesty's most dear Imperial Wife, did maliciously, traitorously, and devilishly, by discharge of his urine, put out the said fire kindled in the said apartment, lying and being within the precincts of the said Royal Palace, against the statute in that case provided, etc., against the duty, etc.

ARTICLE II.
"That the said Man-Mountain, having brought the imperial fleet of Blefuscu into the royal port, and being afterwards commanded by his Imperial Majesty to seize all the other ships of the said empire of Blefuscu, and reduce that empire to a province to be governed by a viceroy from hence, and to destroy and put to death, not only all the Big-endian exiles, but likewise all the people of that empire who would not immediately forsake the Big-endian heresy, he, the said Man-Mountain, like a false traitor against his most auspicious, serene Imperial Majesty, did petition to be excused from the said service, upon pretense of unwillingness to force his consciences to destroy the liberties and lives of an 'innocent' people. Even though the Man-Mountain relented to do his duty to his Emperor, he seems to be avoiding it and there is ground to suspect that he will be bold enough to betray the Emperor's benevolence and there is even ground to suspect that the Man-Mountain will defect and will join our mortal enemies, the Blefuscudians."

Reldresal rolled up the parchment.
"My oh my . . ." Indeed, Lemuel was gravely concerned. This did not bode well.

"There is one more point," continued Reldresal, very earnestly, "which seems to underlay all these manoeuvres, and this is that our cannibacea fields are ready to be harvested, and there are rumours that a number of secret, powerful players are pressing to smuggle and sell all of the crop to Blefuscu before you annihilate them all, or else we rob ourselves of that market."

"Is that it?" Lemuel was lost for words. "Is it all about the income from smuggling, which, I am privy to the knowledge, is always deficient?"

"How do you know that?" Reldresal's ears perked.

"They told me all," Lemuel said. "The Blefuscudians collaborate with your smuggling bands that collaborate with each other. If you, the lords of this country, would trust each other and tend to your own people rather than to your own pockets, you would not be so easily fooled by the ingenuity of your hired criminals."

"My dear Little Huggy Haggy Boar." Reldresal could not hide his sarcasm. "You have a most unfortunate misunderstanding of politics, and I cannot fathom how to begin educating you. In any case, it is too late now. I spared some other articles from you, but these are the most important, of which I have read you an abstract. And your fate is not rosy."

"So, what will become of me?" Lemuel's voice quivered.

"In the several debates upon this impeachment," Reldresal was choosing his words carefully, "it must be confessed that His Majesty gave many marks of his great lenity, often urging the services you had done him and endeavouring to extenuate your crimes."

"And the Empress, what did she say?"

"Nothing. But the treasurer and the admiral insisted that you should be put to the most painful and ignominious death, by putting you on a strict non-Glimigrim diet for a few days and then setting fire to your house at night, and the general was to attend with twenty thousand men, armed with poisoned arrows, to shoot you on the face and hands upon your emergence from within."

"Oh," was all Lemuel could utter.

"Some of your servants were to have private orders to strew a poisonous juice on your shirts and sheets, which would soon make you tear your own flesh, and die in the utmost torture."

"Oh."

"The general came into the same opinion, so that for a long time there was a majority against you, but His Majesty resolving, if possible, to spare your life, was unfortunately outflanked by the chamberlain."

"Oh."

"Upon this incident, I, Reldresal, principal secretary for private affairs, who always proved himself your true friend, was commanded by the Emperor to deliver my opinion, which I accordingly did."

"And what did you say?" Lemuel was desperate. "What could you possibly say?"

"I did justify the good thoughts you have of me, my dear Huggy Haggy Boar." Reldresal blew a kiss at Lemuel's direction, which did not cheer Lemuel up at all. "I allowed your crimes to be great, but that still there was room for mercy, the most commendable virtue in a prince, and for which His Majesty was so justly celebrated."

"Well done, old chap!" For the first time Lemuel thought he had reason for hope.

"I said that the friendship between you and me was so well known to the world, that perhaps the most honourable board might think me partial. However, in obedience to the command I had received, I would freely offer my sentiments."

"Which were . . .?" Lemuel was getting excited, sensing rescue on the horizon.

"That if His Majesty, in consideration of your services, and pursuant to His own merciful disposition, would please to spare your life, and only give orders to put out both your eyes, I would humbly conceive that, by this expedient, justice might in some measure be satisfied, and all the world would applaud the lenity of the Emperor, as well as the fair and generous proceedings of those who have the honour to be his counsellors."

"Oh . . . ?"

"That the loss of your eyes would be no impediment to your bodily strength, by which you might still be useful to His Majesty (and may I add now, between you and me, dear Boar, your bodily virtues would still be useful for us)."

"I dare say . . ." mumbled Lemuel, aghast.

"And you are right, my dear! I knew you would see eye to eye with me! Blindness is an addition to courage, by concealing dangers from us. Poking out but your two eyes would be sufficient in the eyes of the ministers, since the greatest princes do no more."

"I hope this idea was not too popular," whispered Lemuel.

"Oh, this proposal was received with the utmost disapprobation by the whole board," said Reldresal to Lemuel's relief. "Bolgolam, the admiral, could not preserve his temper, but, rising up in fury, said he wondered how I durst presume to give my opinion for preserving the life of a traitor; that the services you had performed were, by all true reasons of state, the great aggravation of your crimes; that you, who were able to extinguish the fire by discharge of urine in Her Majesty's apartment (which he mentioned with horror) might, at another time, raise an inundation by the same means to drown the whole palace."

"Only if it will go up in flames . . . !" ventured Lemuel, helplessly.

"Bolgolam shrewdly suspected that the same strength which enabled you to bring over the enemy's fleet might serve, upon the first discontent, to carry it back; that he had good reasons to think you were a Big-endian in your heart; and, as treason begins in the heart, before it appears in overt acts, so he accused you as a traitor on that account, and therefore insisted you should be put to death."

"He never liked me too much," said Lemuel. "But, were there no sane voices speaking up for me beside yourself? What did Her Royal Highness, the Empress, say?"

Reldresal ignored the question. He just went on to count Lemuel's enemies. "The treasurer was of the same opinion. He showed to what straits His Majesty's revenue was reduced, by the charge of maintaining you, which would soon grow insupportable; that the secretary's expedient of putting out your eyes, was so far from being a remedy against this evil, that it would probably increase it."

"Thank heavens," sighed Lemuel. "I always knew that Flimnap had more sense in him than to suspect me of having an affair with his wife! Jolly good fellow, Flimnap the Treasurer! And what did the Empress, Her Highness, say?"

"Well," Reldresal was trying to avoid Lemuel's eyes. "Flimnap said that His Sacred Majesty and the council, who are your judges, were, in their own consciences, fully convinced of your guilt, which was a sufficient argument to condemn you to death, even without the formal proofs required by the strict letter of the law."

"What shall I do . . .? What shall I do? What did the Empress say? Pray, tell me, Reldresal, you are my friend, after all. Are you not?"

"Of course I am," said Reldresal, "and will always be. His Imperial Majesty, fully determined against capital punishment, was graciously pleased to say that, since the council thought the loss of your eyes too easy a censure, some other way might be inflicted hereafter."

"I dare not imagine what that would be." Lemuel was beginning to sweat.

"And then I, your friend, the secretary, humbly desiring to be heard again, in answer to what the treasurer had objected concerning the great charge his majesty was at in maintaining you, said that His Excellency, who had the sole disposal of the emperor's revenue, might easily provide against that evil by gradually lessening your establishment; by which, for want of sufficient food, you would grow weak and faint and lose your appetite, and consequently, decay, and consume in a few months; neither would the stench of your carcass be then so dangerous, when it should become more than half diminished; and immediately upon your death five or six thousand of His Majesty's subjects might, in two or three days, cut your flesh from your bones, take it away by cart-loads, and bury it in distant parts to prevent infection, leaving the skeleton as a monument of admiration to posterity, against a visit-fee, of course."

"Of course . . ." Lemuel was thinking hard.

"Thus," triumphed Reldresal, "by the great friendship of your friend, I, the secretary, the whole affair was compromised. It was strictly enjoined that the project of starving you by degrees should be kept a secret, but the sentence of putting out your eyes was entered on the books none dissenting except Bolgolam the admiral who, being a creature of the Empress—"

"Yes," Lemuel cut Reldresal short. "What did the Empress say?"

"Well, Bolgolam was perpetually instigated by Her Majesty to insist upon your death, she having borne perpetual malice against you, on account of that infamous and illegal method you took to extinguish the fire in Her apartment."

"I thought she forgave me." Lemuel was crestfallen. "I thought she even liked it . . ." he mumbled to himself, but Reldresal heard him.

"Have you lost your mind with fear? Are you not a man? How could you even think that Her Royal Highness liked . . . well, it . . .?!"

"Sorry," said Lemuel, realising that he disclosed too much. "You are right. I am despicable. Perhaps I should have all my organs pulled out. It would be a quicker death, if not less painful."

"Courage, my friend!" exclaimed Reldresal. "Not all is yet lost!"

"It is not?" Lemuel could not hide his skepticism.

"Of course not." Reldresal was jumping with joy, having apparently reached the best part of his narrative. "In three days, I, your friend the secretary, will be directed to come to your house and read before you these articles of impeachment; and then to signify the great lenity and favour of his majesty and council, whereby you are only condemned to the loss of your eyes, which his majesty does not question you will gratefully and humbly submit to; and twenty of his majesty's surgeons will attend, in order to see the operation well performed, by discharging very sharp-pointed arrows into the balls of your eyes as you lie on the ground."

"And this is a good thing, because . . .?" ventured Lemuel, desperately trying to understand.

"We will elope, my dear friend, my true love, my dear Huggy Haggy Boar!" exclaimed Reldresal enthusiastically.

"Elope?! Where to?!"

"Oh, my dear, you have no notion of your powers, that is so clear and so endearing! I will sit on your head and you will swim back to your country, to Ingland, about which you told me so many wonders! We will live together, happy for ever after!"

"What a preposterous idea," said Lemuel, knowing that his days were numbered if this was Reldresal's solution. "Do understand me right, my dear little fellow. I love and cherish you as ever a man cherished an LOL, but I could never swim back home. It is too far away."

"We have a three-days' window of opportunity," pressed Reldresal on. "I was directed to come to your house in three days time and read before you the articles of impeachment. Then very sharp-pointed arrows would be discharged into the balls of your eyes and then the general idea was to starve you to death."

"In three days time . . ." mumbled Lemuel, deep in thought.

"If you will not elope with me to Ingland, I will bear this as an LOL. I will survive. But for our love's sake, I will stick my neck out to delay the execution as long as possible," Reldresal said resolutely. "So this is probably the last time I will see you, dear Huggy Haggy, and we do not have time for one last lovemaking. Your life is at stake. So, I leave to your prudence what measures you will take but, pray, take them right away." And he sniffled.

"Yes. Yes. Of course." But Lemuel had no idea what to do. Not just yet.

"Oh. One last thing. I made sure to nip from the palace archives the box marked "Quinbus Flestrin." Get rid of it as soon as you can, in any manner you see fit. It is full of incriminating evidences against you." Reldresal sniffled again. "To avoid suspicion, I must immediately return in as private a manner as I came."

Reldresal did so, and Lemuel remained alone, under many doubts and perplexities of mind.

But by and by he fixed upon a resolution, and having his Imperial Majesty's license to rob the rest of Blefuscu's fleet, Lemuel took this opportunity, that very night, to send an official letter to his friend the secretary, Reldresal, signifying his plan to set out that very morning for Blefuscu, pursuant to the leave he had got; and without waiting for an answer, he went to that side of the island where the Lilliputian fleet lay.

There was no one in sight. The Lilliputian Navy was under the impression that there were no enemies left to mighty Lilliput, and the ships were not manned anymore.

Under the blanket of a starless sky, Lemuel raised the anchors of six of the eight men-of-war which lay in the bay and stealthily slid them out of the harbour. He resolved not to take all the Lilliputian fleet, for fear that Blogolam would immediately understand that Lemuel decided to escape, and in the process to rob all of the Lilliputian men-of-war, to prevent Blogolam from chasing him.

No one noticed how he circled to the shores of Lilliput where the fields of cannabaceae stretched wide in full bloom. Proud of his ingenious plan, Lemuel hastened to harvest as many plants as he could and stuff the handfuls into the ship holds, pressing down to squeeze more and more in.

Remembering that the Blefuscudian soil was not fit to grow cannabaceae, Lemuel dug dirt from the fields and loaded a few ships with soil only.

At high tide, nearing exhaustion, Lemuel swam back to Blefuscu.

That was his finest moment, he told me, when the sun rose and the grateful Blefuscudians realised what an immense service he had done them.

While they hastened to unload the ships, spread the soil and plant the seeds they found, Lemuel sauntered off to relieve himself of his own fertile soil mix in a not too distant valley.

Upon his return he suggested that the Blefuscudian cannabaceae fields will be refreshed from time to time with samples from the deposit he left in the valley.

The free-from-this-moment-on people of Blefuscu vowed eternal gratitude to Lemuel, but they were soon disappointed to hear that Lemuel was not intending to stay. He told them about the forces plotting his immediate demise at the Lilliputian court, and stressed that he only had a few days' time, perhaps a week, before his enemies would grasp that he deserted them. Lemuel calculated that it would take a few months for the Lilliputians to build enough men-of-war to ship all of their army over to Blefuscu, to hunt Lemuel down and execute him. Lemuel could not help thinking that some at the Lilliputian Court would be relieved to have his carcass rot on Blefuscudian soil rather than on Lilliputian soil.

"Your survival, and my only salvation," Lemuel told the horrified Blefuscudians, "is that I will be gone, so that the Lilliputians will not be able to kill me here."

Some voiced the idea that Lemuel's presence in Blefuscu might be a deterrent for the Lilliputians to ever set foot in Blefuscu, but others said, more judiciously, that the Lilliputian Emperor is not known to think straight, and he might resort to venomous vengeance, just for spite. Thus settled, Lemuel begged them to help him scout for any form of vessel they might spot on the ocean, north of Blefuscu, so he could escape.

They all went scouting and, lo and behold, that same day they spotted about half a league off in the sea something that looked like a boat overturned!

Lemuel pulled off his shoes and stockings, and, wading two or three hundred yards, he found the object to approach nearer by force of the tide, and then plainly saw it to be a real boat, which he supposed might by some tempest have been driven from a ship.

With the help of the Blefuscudian fishermen, the wind, the tide, and his own manly force, Lemuel got the boat to shore, and by the assistance of two thousand men with ropes and engines, he made a shift to turn it on its bottom and found it was but little damaged.

It did not take long to get it ready to sail again. The next two days were declared days of emergency. No cannabaceae was consumed and no love was for the making. Everybody worked hard, to save Lemuel and themselves.

Five hundred workmen were employed to make two sails for the boat, by quilting thirteen folds of their strongest linen together. A great stone that Lemuel happened to find after a long search by the seashore served him for an anchor. He had the tallow of three hundred cows for greasing the boat and other uses. He was at incredible pains in cutting down some of the largest timber-trees for oars and masts, wherein he was, however, much assisted by the Blefuscudian ship-carpenters, who helped him in smoothing them after he had done the rough work.

They all worked day and night, and Lemuel was nearly ready to sail when word came—via the cannabaceae smugglers—that the Lilliputian Emperor and His Court were suspecting something.

The cannabaceae smugglers brought the latest gossip from court, that Reldresal was insisting that Lemuel would soon be back with the rest of the captured Blefuscudian fleet and, when that took too long to transpire, he himself was suspected of treason. Then Bolgolam, Shumclum and even the Empress insisted that Reldresal should get the punishment which eluded Lemuel. To prove his innocence as well as his loyalty, brave Reldresal volunteered to cross the channel by boat, all by himself, to avenge Lemuel singlehandedly.

But Bolgolam insisted that he was the one to lead the whole of Lilliputian fleet to attack and annihilate Blefuscu, including the Man-Mountain. The upside of the plan, they said, as Lemuel wisely deducted, was that the Man-Mountain's carcass would then be left to rot on Blefuscudian soil, sparing the Lilliputians from stench and plague.

Having heard all that, Lemuel advised the Blefuscudians to leak the information via the smugglers that Gulliver had resolved to stay in Blefuscu and defend it till his last drop of blood. "Tell them that my last drop of blood will be shed only after the last Lilliputian invaders' drops of blood would be shed, so there."

My wise man trusted that the Lilliputians would never dare

attack Blefuscu once they realised that Lemuel was resolute in taking the Blefuscudian side. He hoped that the Lilliputians would never learn of his departure and, in fear of confronting him on the battlefield, would resort to keeping the lucrative state of affairs with Blefuscu.

And, thus, he quickly stored the boat with the carcasses of a hundred oxen and three hundred sheep, with bread and drink proportionable, and as much meat ready-dressed as four hundred cooks could provide within a few hours. He took with him six cows and two bulls alive, with as many ewes and rams, intending to carry them back home and propagate the breed. And to feed them on board, he had a good bundle of hay and a bag of corn.

A number of the Blefuscudians begged to join him, to entwine their fate with his, but this was a thing he would by no means permit, fearing they would be ill-treated in England, or anywhere else in the known world, for that matter.

In tears of sorrow and gratitude, the Blefuscudians waved Lemuel good-bye as he pushed his vessel onto the sea, jumped into it, and sailed away. Lemuel's eyesight was bleary, too, from his own tears of gratitude, love and fear of what was to become of him.

He resolved to die as far away from Blefuscu as possible, hoping that with this heroic action he would preserve their lifestyle of love and peace.

But fates decided otherwise, both for Lemuel and the poor Blefuscudians (as I heard from the refugees Biddle smuggled into England).

When he had by his computation made twenty-four leagues from Blefuscu, he descried a sail steering to the southeast. He hailed her but could get no answer, yet he found he gained upon her, for the wind slackened. Lemuel made all the sail he could, and in half an hour she spied him, then hung out her ancient, and discharged a gun.

It is not easy to express the joy he was in upon the unexpected hope of once more seeing his beloved country, and the dear pledges he left in it.

The ship slackened her sails and he came up with her between five and six in the evening, two years ago, on September 26th, the year 1701. But his heart leaped within him to see her English colours. Lemuel put his cows and sheep into his coat-pockets and got on board with all his little cargo of provisions.

Well, the rest is history. The captain, Mr. John Biddel, seemed at first to be a very civil man. He treated Lemuel with kindness and desired he would let him know what place he came from last.

Lemuel obliged him in a few words, but Biddel thought Lemuel was raving, and that the dangers Lemuel underwent had disturbed his head, whereupon my unsuspecting Lemuel took his cattle and sheep out of his pocket, and these, after great astonishment, clearly convinced Biddel of Lemuel's veracity and gullibility.

Six months later they arrived in England, and two months later Lemuel went back to sea, for the very last time.

* * *

And now, a year and a half since I last saw my love, I have resigned to the fact that, yes, it was the last time I was ever to see him.

And so,
I conclude this book, the stories of our lives,
With a deep sigh.

THE END

Epilogue

THE AUTHOR HEARS FROM CAPTAIN JOHN NICHOLAS OF
THE *ADVENTURE* THAT LEMUEL WAS STRANDED IN THE
GIANTS' LAND; HE REFUSES TO GO AND SAVE HIM;
SHE DECIDES TO DO IT BY HERSELF AND, IF SHE WILL SURVIVE,
WILL TELL HOW IT HAPPENED WHEN SHE WILL BE BACK.
(Redriff, Friday, April 18th, 1704)

This is impossible—but it must be true. It must be true, or I will go mad!

Captain John Nicholas of the *Adventure*, the man and ship I cursed for the last year for having taken my love from me and hurling his body somewhere at sea—they, at least, are back!

I was busy finishing packing to join my children who were already at my sister's home in Newgate Street, when the Captain knocked on my door.

His tale was incredible and scary. He told me that my love, my Lemuel, Mr. Gulliver, might still be alive!

What a mind-boggling story he told me!

My Lemuel was last seen, ten months past, on Sunday, June 17th, 1703, on a great unknown island or continent (for they knew not whether, they lost their position due to a storm).

They cast anchor there in search of fresh water, and a dozen men, well armed, were sent by Captain Nicholas in the long-boat, with vessels for water, if any could be found.

I was spellbound when Captain Nicholas told me that Mr. Gulliver desired his leave to go with them, that he might see the country and make what discoveries he could.

A few hours later, told me the Captain, the boy on the topmast cried in horror, and the Captain saw a huge creature walking in the sea as fast as he could. He was dressed as a human and, in fact, was a prodigious human, chasing the long-boat, which was making haste to get back to the ship!

That huge monster, which seemed to be twelve times as big as a normal God-abiding Christian, waded not much deeper than his knees and took prodigious strides, but the men had the start of him half a league, and the sea thereabouts being apparently full of sharp-pointed rocks, the monster was not able to overtake the boat.

"And?" I asked, breathless.

"They all returned safely, except for Mr. Gulliver, I am afraid. We raised anchor right away, resumed our route to Surat where we concluded our business satisfactorily, and came back to England safely last week. I came to see you, dear Mrs. Gulliver, as soon as I could."

"And my husband?"

"He might still be alive if the monster hasn't found him till now. Or he might be dead, M'am, I am afraid."

"You are afraid?!" I screamed, forgetting myself completely. "You are afraid? I am desolate! This is impossible! Why did you not return at night to bring him back? Why did the fool have to go explore the land? Why did you let him? He is but a ship-surgeon. He is not supposed to be eaten alive by giant monsters!"

I sobbed.

"Will you take back to sea, to rescue him?" I asked.

"No, M'am, I cannot undertake such a dangerous voyage. No one, no king and no merchant, will see a commercial prospect in such an undertaking. I am afraid you must accept my condolences, Mrs. Gulliver, along with your husband's salary and shares."

I accepted them, and he left.

But I am resolved to use the money he gave me, the rewards of my Lemuel's hard work, loyalty, and gullibility, to do whatever I can to find my man and rescue him.

Time is short. But the plan is already hatching in my mind.

I know exactly what I should do, and I intend to do it.

If it costs me my life, I shall rescue my man.[158]

To be continued!

Keep your eyes open for the next titles in the series:

Go, Gulliver!
Mrs. Gulliver and the Mystery of Men

No, Gulliver!
Mrs. Gulliver and the Riddle of Reason

Giddyup, Gulliver!
Mrs. Gulliver and the Hoax of Horses

And the bonus autobiographical novel:

Goodbye, Gulliver!
Mrs. Gulliver and I

Notes

1. For example, Lady Mary Wortley Montagu (1689–1762), an English aristocrat and writer, was instrumental in the writing of many works of John Gay (1688–1732), an English poet, and Alexander Pope (1688–1744), considered the greatest English poet of his time. Lady Mary was never mentioned in any of their publications.

Likewise, Richard Sympson, Lemuel Gulliver's cousin and publisher, neglected to mention Mary Burton-Gulliver's contribution to the editing of her husband's memoirs, in his "The Publisher to the Reader" introduction to *Gulliver's Travels* (1727).

Another example: as of 1859, Mary Anne Evans published her books using the pen name of George Eliot. Charlotte Brontë used the name of Currer Bell, Julia Bécour used the name of Paul Grendel, etc., etc. All names long forgotten and their books no longer read. But nobody reads books today, anyway. Except for the Harry Potter series, of course, written by J.K. Rowling.

2. Lara Croft is presumably a fictional character that came to the public's attention in 1996. Though she was a celebrity at the time and a household name, by now people under 50 would probably not have heard of her. Croft was famed for her wild adventures, which were depicted in computer games and movies.

Toby Gard (b. 1972, UK) is an English computer game designer who got the credit for creating Lara Croft as a fictional female British archaeologist.

Lara Croft is mentioned in the *Guinness Book of World Records* for being the "most successful human video game heroine." Legend is that due to a programming mistake she is well endowed.

3. In these notes you'll be enlightened not only about life in the 17th and 18th centuries, but you will also understand better our messed-up lives in the 21st century.

4. Thank you, Izzy Abrahami, Ledig House, Upstate NY; Faber Residency, Olot, Catalunya; Robbie and Ilana Stel, Belgium; Orly Ginossar, the Netherland; Mikella and Kent Carter, France; Yoel Netz, Israel; Hasoferrett Corina, Israel; Rolanda and Julian Chagrin, Israel; Samuel de Leeuw, the Netherlands; Volodia, Israel; Francis Greenburger, USA; Josien Schreuder, the Netherlands; Yaakov Bader, the Netherlands, and the wonderful colleagues I met along the way!

5. Now you all know what you missed out on! But don't despair. The movie rights are still available!

6. Lemuel's candidness might have been the key to their happy marriage. He treated his wife as a friend, and not as a foe. He believed that she would be happy for him, and he was right.

Amazingly, Mary continued to love her husband, even when the relationship was not reciprocal. (See Chapter Eight.)

7. Like the theory that William Shakespeare was not the real author of many plays in his body of work, but rather another contemporary of his, also named Shakespeare, I believe there's a similar misconception regarding the true authorship of *Gulliver's Travels*.

Indeed, there was a man called Jonathan Swift (1667–1745), Irish satirist, essayist, poet and the Dean of St Patrick's Cathedral, Dublin, but it is unclear if Lemuel and Mary Gulliver ever knew of him, and why they chose that particular pseudonym, though I expand on my theory in Note 36, in Chapter Four.

Swift himself used the pseudonym of Isaac Bickerstaff. Confused? You ought to be.

8. Yes, there were times when people would come by to visit each other unannounced. In our post-Corona-Days, in which we can meet each other digitally, such physical, surprise visits would be unthinkable. Indeed, "Divide and Rule" took on a new, much more effective and sinister form. Or did it? It looks like the pressure to Divide is mounting too much, and the Ruled begin to find it in themselves to revolt. At the least, we can always hope.

9. Here I took the liberty of translating Mary's "scite" into "shit," since the Old English "scite" would not be understood anymore by the modern reader.

10. It is common knowledge that Feminism started in the 19th century, and the date for its first achievement is set for 1839, when the Custody of Infants Act was established. Few people realise that this act was another tool of oppression, handing over the tasks of taking care of children as the sole responsibility of women.

But even fewer people know that the movement started back in the 17th century, with Marry Gulliver's incitements. Sadly it took a couple of centuries to catch on, and the struggle isn't over yet.

11. Lemuel Gulliver returned from Houyhnhnms in 1715. He couldn't stand the sight, sound and touch of his loyal wife, and retired to live with a couple of horses.

In the last book of this series, you will read about her clever ways of coaxing him to tell her what has happened to him in his last voyage. Mary wrote the full story for him, so as to get the *Travels* book into publication. The rest is history.

12. See Note 1.

13. Mary refers here to the dangers which faced earlier authors of erotic nature, such as *L'École des Filles* (Girls' School), which was written in 1660 by Madame de Maintenon, Louis XIV's mistress, and Nicholas Fouquet, his finance minister, using the names (and persons) of Michel Millot and Jean L'Ange. The book is a conversation about sex between Fanny, a sixteen-year-old girl, and her slightly older cousin, Suzanne.

The successful publication of *L'École des Filles* resulted in a court case and a short imprisonment of the two "front guys." The real authors couldn't save them from prison, but did save them from hanging.

We can assume that Madame de Maintenon wrote her little book to amuse and arouse her lover, Louis XIV, while Nicholas Fouquet did it to enrich Louis XIV's treasury. I guess they were both successful.

14. The book that gave Mary hope of safely publishing her own story was *Memoirs of a Woman of Pleasure (Fanny Hill)*, written by John Cleland in 1748.

The story of an innocent fifteen-year-old country girl who's forced into prostitution when she arrives in London, this novel was banned for obscenity as recently as 1963, when it was still forbidden in the USA!

In 1748, when Mary Burton-Gulliver wrote this letter, John Cleland was not—yet—prosecuted for his novel. But just one year later he was arrested, along with his publisher, and forced to renounce the book.

This didn't stop the book from being secretly printed, circulated and widely read (till today), but the fear of arrest and persecution probably prevented Mary from publishing her own manuscript. I imagine that the news of Cleland's arrest came to Mary as a shock, and she probably then decided to keep her manuscript in hiding.

15. Torn between the urge to express themselves and the need to survive, authors have always been at the bottom of the "literary food chain."

Debates about copyright and the early copyright laws did not even mention authors as parties in the discussion. The result was self-publishing, or authors participating in the costs of publishing.

The "Statute of Anne" (1710) was the first legal attempt to regularise the rights to copy books. Recognising (mistakenly) that the free reprinting of books would discourage authors from writing, it granted publishers of books the right to reprint them for 14 years only.

The right of renewal of the copyright was given to the author, but only for 21 years, provided the author was still alive.

Mary demonstrates here a marked innovative nature, when she's actually asking for an advance!

16. James II (1685–88) was a Catholic, a fact that caused much concern among the Protestant power brokers of his time. Both factions claiming to have the better understanding of God's will, they tried to settle their disagreements by killing as many of their opponent's people as possible, without reaching any theological conclusion.

So the English Protestants called the Dutch Protestants for help, and this changed the power balance and convinced James II to flee to France, where God was Catholic and thence he had great time in the court of Louis XIV (paying for it by what he managed to plunder before his hasty departure from England).

His successor, William III (1650–1702), was a Protestant. Born "Prince of Orange," he was Stadtholder, from 1672, over a number of Dutch provinces. (When negotiating with Louis XIV and rejecting defeat, William III promised to "die, defending the Netherlands in the last ditch," expecting his soldiers to do the dying bit, of course.)

In 1689, when William III was invited by the English Protestant power brokers to chase away James II, he insisted that, in return, he would replace him as the King of England, Ireland and Scotland, using different numbers in each place: William II and III, probably to confuse the opposition. In Northern Ireland and Scotland he was rather disrespectfully called "King Billy" (which makes Billy Connolly the II).

17. "Yahoo" is how the noble horses called the inferior animals in their kingdom that eerily resembled humans as we know them.

You will read all the secrets about the trip to Houyhnhnms, in the fourth installment of this series.

18. A linguistic note: I find it interesting to note how human selfishness is reflected in our languages: the words for Mama and Papa derive from the sequences of sounds ma/, mama/, pa/, papa/, which are the first word-like sounds made by babbling babies. Proud parents tend to associate these sounds with themselves.

The exception, curiously, is the Japanese "mamma", which is altruistically interpreted to mean "food."

Come to think of it, die-hard Feminists could use this example to demonstrate again how women are being used and abused.

19. By the 17th century children no longer shared beds with their parents. There were laws against it, and they were the results of incidents of poor parents confessing to their priests that one of them had accidentally rolled over on their infants while sleeping.

Suspecting that those poor, desperate parents actually strangled their children in this way because they couldn't afford to feed them was the cause of these laws, which were enacted to stop this infanticide.

20. A hosier was a tradesman who manufactured and sold socks.

The history of hosiery is laced with manipulations and intrigues, which are plainly evident in the 1663 Charter, in which King Charles II granted some 25 people the power over the business—for life—in return for a share of their revenues. One of these people was Mary Burton-Gulliver's uncle-in-law, the father of her sister's husband.

It was hard, masculine work. Using machines, as well as knitting by hand, hosiery was a respected profession, especially when one made a lot of money doing it. Not unlike today.

But, unlike today, at that time machine-made silk stockings were more expensive than hand-knitted ones since machines were not considered as reliable as they are today.

21. Despite all the evidence that women are better equipped for life, baby boys have always been preferred to baby girls, and still are. It's a phenomenon that perpetuates itself. Ever since ancient times, women, being physically weaker, were oppressed and considered to be men's property, to be sold by their fathers to other men as soon as they were old enough to produce children. As such, it was the male child who took over his father's enterprise and the one who carried his father's name down history lane.

22. Researchers discovered that women have always had a higher life expectancy than men, ever since such data could be collected. Except among the child-bearing age group.

Even today, bearing a child is the sixth most common cause of death among women ages 20 to 34 in the United States.

23. Elizabeth I (1533–1603) was sometimes called The Virgin Queen because she had no children.

The daughter of Henry VIII and his second wife, Anne Boleyn, Elizabeth was orphaned at the age of two and a half when her father executed her mother. This, and the bloody wars with her half-siblings that preceded her ascent to the throne, might have convinced her never to get married.

She should rightfully be accredited with the invention of "Realpolitics": Her motto had always been *"video et taceo"* ("I see, and say nothing"). It enabled her to rule for 44 years.

24. Song of Songs 5:5.

25. Prudent religious leaders chose to read The Song of Songs of Solomon as an allegory on the relationship between God and Israel as husband and wife, while Christians later ruled it to be all about Christ. Go figure.

Yet it was quite a controversial book, and was almost left out of the

Bible altogether, had it not been for one sage, Rabbi Akiva (50–135 AD), who learned to read and write at the rather late age of forty. Being an analphabet for so many years might have shielded Rabbi Akiva from the brainwash of his time. Apparently, he also had a keen sense of humor and knew how to have fun. He liked the Song of Songs, and that was that!

(On a personal note: I never thought this text could have such an arousing effect, as Mary reports. *EN*)

26. The origin of the name "Lemuel" is in the Book of Proverbs, which is attributed to King Solomon. Rabbinic tradition identifies King Solomon with King Lemuel, who is mentioned in the first verse of chapter 31: "The words of King Lemuel, the prophecy that his mother taught him," etc. In that chapter, King Lemuel is described as sometimes acting foolishly.

Mary was already in love with King Solomon, having read his erotic Song of Songs, and this could explain her naïve enthusiasm towards marrying Lemuel Gulliver.

Come to think of it, it's remarkable how often parents give their children names which turn out to be uncanny descriptions of their character. One might ask which is the cause and which is the effect. "Lemuel Gulliver" is one such example.

The surname "Gulliver" has Old French origins. The French word "goulafre" means "glutton." Variants of this surname are Gulliford and Galliford, and are first recorded in the Domesday Book of 1086.

Some scholars, mistakenly assuming that Gulliver is a fictitious character, thought that the author—again, mistakenly identified as Jonathan Swift—chose the name Gulliver because it sounded like Gullible. Now that we have the proof that Lemuel Gulliver did exist, we can sneer at those far-fetched assumptions.

27. In 1686, Stella Burton married Owen Lavender Jr., the son of Owen Lavender Sr., who was nominated as an Assistant for Life to the "Society of the Art and Mystery of Frame-Work-Knitters" in the 1663 Charter.

Mary Burton-Gulliver was fourteen years old when her sister got married, so she couldn't grasp that the real reason for her father's choice of a son-in-law was the guaranteed future of his own business, under the protection of the Guild.

28. In the published book of Gulliver, he mentions the amount of four hundred pounds for a portion, which is about 4,500 pounds today. Not that

much. A cleaning lady today would cost a bachelor over a period of 50 years much more, and that's only part of the "services" of a wife.

It's interesting to note how hard it is for scholars, even now, to acknowledge the facts behind this custom. If you search the Internet you'll find the widest scope of justifications for the fact that women were considered the property of men and, as such, brides were traded between fathers and husbands.

The fact that no money changes hands over the bridegroom serves as the final proof that this is a deeply-rooted discrimination.

29. Mary refers here to the Plague that affected England in 1665, from June until November, peaking in September when in London 12,000 people died in one week. Before the plague, London had a population of around 500,000 and after, about 400,000.

This was the last major outbreak of the Black Death that ravished Europe since 1347 and surged back in waves every ten years or so. At the time of the Plague, Gulliver was four years old.

As the world today is still plagued with plagues, one must lament the short memory or lack of knowledge of history in today's generation, that gullibly abides by the contradictory rules which our leaders dictate to us, while they, themselves, ignore them.

30. In Mary's time, marriageable age was 14 for boys and 12 for girls. (At that time, they didn't call 12- and 14-year-olds "boys and girls," but "men and women." People had shorter life expectancies, and had to start early.)

Nowadays, in most countries the legal age of marriage varies from 16 to 21.

Strangely, in most countries men are required to wait longer before they may marry. Only a handful of countries, states and Authorities pose the same age barrier for both sexes. These are Egypt (18), Kenya (16), Libya (20), Morocco (18), Senegal (20), Kyrgyzstan (18), Yemen (17), Cyprus (16), France (18), Iceland (18), Sweden (18), Switzerland (18), Scotland (16), Kansas (18) and the Palestinian National Authority (18), while in Brunei there's no minimum age for marrying, boy or girl. Does that make you shiver, or not?

31. This page was as empty in the original manuscript of Mary Burton-Gulliver's as it is here. She was intending to tell about those years in detail later on, but never got around to it. (See Chapter Fifteen.)

32. Though there's evidence of matches being used in China as early as the 13th century, this invention arrived in Europe only in 1669, when the German alchemist Henning Brandt discovered the flammable nature of phosphorus. But only as of the beginning of the 19th century were Lucifer Matches available in markets in England.

Yet, the first evidence of man-controlled fire comes from China (where controlling people has since been refined with awe-striking results). Dating back 780,000 and 400,000 years ago, evidence of cooking was found in the Chinese site of Zhoukoudian.

Up until the mid 19th century, if you didn't keep the fire burning day and night, you'd have to clash flint on steel to make a spark, as Mary evidently just did, using her "Tinderbox."

33. The Old Jewry is the current name of the Jewry street, which was the main street at the London Ghetto, established in 1070.

William I, who led the Normans to conquer England for him in 1066 and, in the process, devastated London and its economic infrastructure, didn't want to invest the riches he plundered back into the economy (a tradition which is kept by politicians till today) so he found an original solution: He invited rich Jews from France to come and settle in London, on condition that they lend him money (under his conditions). The Jews were lured to England with the promise that, as opposed to their (non) rights in Europe, here they would have the liberty of movement throughout the country, exemption from tolls, protection from misuse, free recourse to royal justice and, most extraordinarily, permission to retain land pledged as security.

It was all spelled out in "De Judaismo" law, which listed also numerous severe and arbitrary penalties to the Jews, and even the ever-since-popular Yellow Badge.

Still, the Jews who could afford it preferred to move to England, since all over Europe, Jews were not allowed to own land, and were forced to work as labourers, or as petty traders. In France, they were practically treated as slaves.

Keeping the Jews in Ghettos, away from the rest of the population, was one more expression of Divide and Rule, with the expected result that Jews were periodically massacred. In 1290, the remaining Jews were expelled from England. Apparently, their financial services were no longer needed.

But in 1656 Jews were needed again, this time by Oliver Cromwell, who lifted the ban on Jewish settlement in England and Wales. Through the centuries, Jews fared well in England, so much so that a Jew named Benjamin Disraeli (1804–1881) joined the Church of England and consequently rose to prime ministership.

It's curious to note that the area of Old Jewry is still today London's financial center, home to the Bank of England, Lloyds of London, and the Reserve Bank of Australia.

34. "God's pennies" was the term used for advance payment made when work had begun.

As a ship-surgeon, Gulliver would earn 24 shillings a month. For the estimated voyage of three years, that would be the equivalent of £3,844.31 (€4.480,43 or $4.464,59) today. But, of course, you could buy larger quantities of the fewer merchandice that was available back then with this amount. Mary and her children could have survived handsomely on the advance until Gulliver's return—if he would return.

35. Helping the poor has always posed a challenge to the wealthy. To this day, keeping the balance between losing money and risking revolt is still hard to maintain. Fearing that the poor will stop slaving if they get financial peanuts, many solutions have been sought.

The English Poor Law Act of 1697 forced paupers who received parish relief to wear a badge of blue or red cloth on the shoulder of the right sleeve, as a form of humiliation, with the declared hope of deterring them from emptying the parish's coffers.

Another motive might be traced to the fact that the person responsible for the act was Henry Blaake (1659–1731), a Whig who sat for the Wiltshire textile borough. We can assume that the demand for textile had risen in the years following the Poor Law Act, when the poor were forced to buy badges of blue or red cloth.

To ensure the sales, it was decreed that if a parish officer gave money to a poor person not wearing a badge he could be fined 20 shillings per disbursement. A pauper who refused to wear the badge (or simply couldn't afford it) was denied help, or was whipped and committed to Bridewell Prison for three weeks' hard labour. In Europe, beggars were forced to "wear a sign" as early as 1370.

It is unlikely that people like Mary Burton-Gulliver, who had no other choice, were deterred from seeking help by the shame inherent in wearing a badge. After all, in small communities, everyone knew just about everything about everybody else. And when we note that according to the 1696 Board of Trade estimation, expenditures on poor relief totalled £400,000, which was slightly less than one percent of national income, we are left to wonder to what depth can the greed of the rich sink.

36. I was pondering about these nicknames, which Mary uses in her tale. They might give us a hint to the choice of "Jonathan Swift" as the pseudonym Gulliver chose for his book.

"Swifty" might hint to the speed in which Mary would reach her climax, which must have pleased Gulliver enormously, and "Jonathan" might come from BigJon, in attribute to the size of Gulliver's genitals.

37. It is very touching to read this passage. Anyone who's a bit familiar with life in 17th-century England would know that divorce simply didn't exist. Marriages ended with the death of one of the spouses. Well, that's almost true. The rich could pay for the expensive process of nullifying the marriages by Parliament.

By her answer, it was clear that Lemuel was beseeching Mary to love him forever.

38. By now the list of Ends of the World is much longer than the one which was known in the times of Mary Gulliver. This phenomenon, of blind belief in that which has been proven time and time again to be false, testifies to the talent of man to learn nothing. It's bizarrely comforting to ignore accumulated knowledge while giving in to induced fear.

Mary would have been a witness, or would have remembered stories about the world's due endings in:

1666 — 1000 = millennium + 666 = number of the Beast. The Great Fire of London in 1666 was for many a token of the validity of this prediction.

1688 — Doomsday calculation #1 of John Napier, a mathematician who was better at discovering logarithms than at predicting the end of the world. Many a pupil struggling with logarithms would rather he was right about the end of the world. Me, too.

1700 — Doomsday calculation #2 of John Napier, based on the Book of Daniel.

John (Henry) Archer, a Fifth Monarchy Man claimed that the world as we know it would end on January 1st, 1700, in his 1642 book *The Personal Reign of Christ Upon Earth*.

And now:

2000 — The world was expected to end because of a computer glitch that didn't happen.

2020 — Politicians and pharmaceutical industrialists all over the world predicted its end, due to the Covid-19 pandemic. So far, it did not transpire, though there are signs that the pandemic will spell the end of their world-dominance.

2022 — Putin's threats of nuclear war go to show you that one end of the world could spell the end of a previous end of the world. Miraculously, as soon as the bombardment of Ukraine started, the Covid-19 pandemic was forgotten.

39. Cardinal Roberto Bellarmino (1542–1622) was an Italian Bishop, Confessor and Doctor of the Church. Among his notable writings is the sentence: ". . . to affirm that the sun really is fixed in the centre of the heavens and only revolves around itself without travelling from east to west, and that the earth is situated in the third sphere and revolves with great speed around the sun, is a very dangerous thing, not only by irritating all the philosophers and scholastic theologians, but also by injuring our holy faith and rendering the Holy Scriptures false."

In 1600, these words represented eternal wisdom. Still, it took the church 400 years to acknowledge the Cardinal's genius. It's a mark of great faith that the Vatican canonized Roberto Bellarmino in 1930, when convincing evidence to the sun's habits were already known to children in (secular) kindergartens.

40. In June 2009, Dr. Alan Massey, a former chemist and honorary fellow of Loughborough University analysed the contents of a Witch Bottle which was found buried in a garden in Greenwich. It must have contained Mary's urine and Lemuel's fingernails, because the *British Archaeology Magazine* (July/Aug 2009) goes on to list: "some bent nails and pins, a nail-pierced leather 'heart,' navel fluff and hair. The presence of iron sulphide in the mixture also suggests that sulphur or brimstone had been added."

Dr. Alan Massey also detected nicotine in the urine, suggesting the one who produced the urine was a smoker. Of course, he didn't read Mary's diary, so he didn't know that smoking was part of that particular witchcraft ritual.

41. Seamen are very superstitious to this day. (Actually, aren't we all?)

This "Sunday sail, never fail" superstition arises from Christ's resurrection on a Sunday. The worst day to go out sailing was believed to be Friday. Even though there's a hair-splitting theological debate on whether Christ was crucified on a Thursday or on a Friday, most sea-farers declined to debate it any further and decided to stick with the Friday choice.

The reason, I think, was that it gave them an extra free weekend on shore before embarking on a seven-day work week, for months and years on end.

42. This is not a printing mistake. As you'll read in the next chapter, dramatic events suddenly forced Mary to stop writing at this point.

43. The history of condoms is said to be traced to ancient societies, and engraved for posterity on cave walls. But the word "condom" first appeared in 1665. Invented by two men: Dr. Conton, a physician, and Colonel Condum, a soldier under King Charles II.

Before they came with their improved version, contraceptives were made of sheep intestines. Conton-Condum's device was made from dried lamb intestines and was oiled to make it flexible. And, when needed, it was also oiled for easier penetration.

44. This is a citation from the Bible, Book of Judges 14:14. Samson killed a lion. When he came back later ". . . behold, there was a swarm of bees in the body of the lion, and honey."

Samson penned this expression, "Out of the strong came forth sweetness" to annoy the Philistines, and eventually to kill as many of them as possible. Just a regular day in the Bible.

45. Thomas More (1478–1535) published *Utopia* in 1516. In this book More tells how King Henry VIII sent him to Flanders on a diplomatic mission, where More met Raphael Hythloday. This traveller tells More about the island country of Utopia, where an orderly and reasonable society flourishes. With no private property, and with equality between women and men, and tolerance of all religions, Utopia sounds even today like a real good place (except that secular people were not welcomed there).

Ironically (and sadly) Thomas More was executed by Henry VIII, when More refused to accept Henry's newest religion.

More was canonised in 1935 by Pope Pius XI and, in 1980, he was declared Patron Saint of politicians and statesmen by Pope John Paul II, though I doubt if any politician ever made any use of Saint More. Politicians don't believe anyone, and for good reason. A liar knows better than to believe other liars.

46. Francis Bacon (1561–1626) was an English philosopher, statesman, scientist, lawyer, jurist, and author. In *The New Atlantis* he describes the discovery of an ideal land, were people were chaste, honest and loyal.

Written in 1623, it was only published a year after Bacon's death. Quite understandably: In 1621, having reached the high office of Lord Chancellor, Bacon was found guilty and admitted to having taken bribes and was charged with twenty-three separate counts of corruption. So much for statesmen's honesty.

This was not the first time, nor the last, that a politician is caught abusing his position. Yet each time it is revealed, it still comes to us as a shock. And this is shocking.

47. I searched in many libraries and all over the Internet for this title and this author, but couldn't find anything. I think it must have been a poorly written story, lost in obscurity.

48. Mary refers here to the liaisons which Gulliver had in Lilliput during the two and a half years he was stranded there.

Though Mary forbade her husband to commit those scenes to paper, she herself wrote about them, candidly and juicily, in Chapters Fourteen, Twenty-Five and Twenty-Nine of this book. Something to look forward to!

49. Anne, Queen of Great Britain, was a tragic figure, if you disregard her royalty and look at her as a woman.

Suffering from gout and other maladies whose names were not yet known at the time, gradually she became lame and consequently obese.

She was pregnant seventeen times in seventeen years and had miscarried or given birth to stillborn children at least twelve times. Her only son who survived his first year died at the age of eleven. Clearly, she betrayed her role as a monarch to deliver an heir.

Obviously, the ruling powers of her day found a solution, as royalty still exists.

50. Mr. John Biddle was the Captain of the *Explorer*, the ship that happened to find Gulliver on its return from Japan by the North and South Seas. Of course, they were all very curious to know how Gulliver's ship was wrecked, how he managed to save himself, and how he spent those years away from civilisation.

When Gulliver told them candidly all that had happened to him, they took him for a lunatic, of course, and attributed his madness to the long years of solitude. In order to prove his sanity, Gulliver produced his herd and the rest of his Lilliputian souvenirs.

Apparently, Captain Biddle saw the commercial possibilities of conquering Lilliput, and wasted no time in tracing Gulliver and inviting him to join this business venture.

51. Slave trade is as ancient as humankind (though the word "kind" doesn't seem to be appropriate here).

The African slave trade was made possible by the collaboration between white traders and African "elites," those who had the power to capture and enslave others.

The white population in Europe and America regarded the Black slaves as inferior beings, hardly human, and as such considered their transportation in inhumane conditions to be quite acceptable though lamentable, seeing that so many (15%) perished en route.

The African traders, too, exhibited an unfathomable contempt towards their brethren.

(If you think that slaves are no longer traded today, Google it, and think again.)

52. Mary was screaming at Lemuel, "He's a nothing! Away with him! Beware of him!" (Using the notes at the end of Mary's memoir, it was possible for me to decipher Lilliputian.)

Irving Rothman, a Professor of English at the University of Houston, claims that the Lilliputian language stems from Hebrew and, researching this even further, I can confirm that the Lilliputians are possibly descendants of earliest "mythical" creature in all of Jewish lore: Lilith.

Lilith was rumoured to have been Adam's first mate, before Eve. Lilith is said to have abandoned Adam to return to the wilds and live among the animals and night beings.

"Put Yan" literally means a small genital (or "little fucker"), so it is plausible that given the ancient Hebrew nuances that pervade their language, "Lilith Put Yans" ("Lillith's Vagina") slowly evolved into "Lilliputian" over the aeons.

53. Indeed, that secret pocket wasn't discovered by the two officers who searched Gulliver in Lilliputt (three years before this chapter was written) and his condom was undetected.

I guess Gulliver was hesitant to let the Lilliputian officers see his condom, as they would've quite surely confiscated it. They were likely to suspect that Gulliver would use it to kidnap the Emperor for ransom. Mary writes all about it in Chapter Twelve.

54. This, amazingly enough, is just a part of the list of chores that Mary Burton-Gulliver, as well as all women of that time, faced daily.

55. The distance between Wapping and Redriff (Rotherhithe) is just 5 miles (8 km), with the Thames running in between.

But in the 17th Century, Mary would have to be a rich woman to pay for a seat in a stagecoach, and travel in this heavy and cumbersome carriage, often without any form of springs, squeezed next to seven more passengers, for hours. The speed, if one can call it so, was 4 miles per hour, and there were plenty of risks of highwaymen.

Second-class travellers would sit in a large open basket attached to the back, and cheaper seats were also available on the roof with the luggage, where you'd have to hang on to a hand rail to prevent from slithering off.

And, yes, in the city of London there were traffic jams back then, too.

56. "Li lon ina i hekdebul" = "We're not the same;" "Li Quinbus. Ina Ranfu" = "I'm a Man. You're a woman;" "Li i Hurgo" = "I'm superior."

It seems that men have always thought alike, all over the world, in all languages.

57. The value of £600 in 1702, would be £76,600 (€89,275.14 or $88,959.33) today, using the retail price index, or £1,090,000.00 (€127,036,424.89 or $126,587,041.00) based on average earnings. I didn't get such an advance on my *Oh, Gulliver!*

It's also interesting to note that Gulliver got this huge advance in 1702 while the book was ready for publication only in 1726. I doubt if there was ever a more patient publisher in history.

58. "Yard" was the word used for "penis" as of 1379, and Steven Blankaart's definition of "penis" in his *Physical Dictionary of 1684* is: "the Yard, made up of two nervous Bodies, the Channel, Nut, Skin, and Fore-skin, etc."

I decided to keep the various terms Mary used for the various private parts in her memoir because, otherwise, this publication might seem too vulgar for the modern, educated and self-respecting reader.

59. Bollocks = Testicles.

60. "Hekinah Degul" means something like "His flag is erect" in colloquial Lilliputian. Clearly, Mary didn't need to translate this into English in her memoir, since she had mastered Lilliputian.

Luckily, Lemuel Gulliver, in his Voyage to Lilliput (1726) was careful to translate into English all the Lilliputian words he inserted into his story, so that I was able to learn Lilliputian myself, and to translate Mary's Lilliputian into English.

61. "Tolgo Phonac" means in Lilliputian "Let go" or "Release the arrows" meaning, in this context, "Shoot him!"

62. A buff jerkin is a man's sleeveless leather jacket, usually short and tight. In the 16th and 17th centuries it was worn over the doublet. (A doublet is another jacket, ok?)

63. "Hurgo" is the Lilliputian equivalent of "Celebrity," a person known by everyone, but nobody knows why.

64. Peplom selan!" = "Obey orders!" "Bosan gue empos!" = "He's going to release his water on the empire!"

65. Asimov (see Bibliography) calculated that in Lilliputian scale, Gulliver urinated about a ton of liquid, which could explain their haste to get out of the way, but which left Asimov wondering about the environmental impact of that urinous flood.

On the other hand, urine is used by some people as a medicinal (see Note 124), and there are people who cite Jesus as saying, "He that believeth in me, as the scripture hath said, out of his belly shall flow rivers of living water." (John 7:38)

That's how religious authorities can get away with anything, by shifting the responsibility onto the believer.

66. It seems that Gulliver wasn't too bothered about washing his hands between urinating and eating, though hygiene health principles were already known at his time.

Well, they have been known for more than 500 years and still you read in every restaurant's restroom the worrying sign: "Employees must wash their hands before returning to work." The fact that they need to be reminded is what I find worrying.

67. Larks are small- to medium-sized birds, 5 to 8 inches in length and 0.5 to 2.6 ounces in weight.

During Gulliver's time, people couldn't afford to be vegetarian, and were not bothered by animal rights. They had enough on their plates concerning their own human rights.

Come to think of it, seeing that nowadays human rights are not less abused, is it possible that the animal rights flag is waved as a distraction from the abuses of human rights?

68. Corn, wheat and marijuana. Apparently, it was legal in Lilliput.

69. The report mentions William of Orange and Mary II as "unknown Lilliputians," because the word "Lilliputian" means in Lilliputian "human being."

William of Orange (1650–1702) and Mary II (1662–1694) were cousins and Protestants. Their marriage was intended to keep England, Scotland, and Ireland under the clutches of the family.

Mary II cried for almost two days when she heard she was to marry William. The reason might be that he was twelve years her senior, but it's also likely, judging by the passionate letters she sent to one Frances Apsley, that she might have preferred the company of women.

William, on the other hand, was faithful to his mistress, Elizabeth Villiers. On the farthing, though, William and Mary are depicted as quite content with each other.

70. It's interesting to note that the concepts of time and its financial value were celebrated 300 years ago as avidly as today.

Various time-measuring devices are known to have been in use since ancient times such as the sundial, candle, water and sand clock. But it's the invention of the balance spring (1657) that made early pocket watches useful, affordable (for the more affluent), and handy timekeepers. Gulliver, being a sea-surgeon, needed one, and evidently could have afforded it.

71. A scimitar is a backsword or sabre with a curved blade. Scabbard = sheath.

72. A small telescope

73. "Blundecral" is what Lilliputians called their Bible. Some later readers of Gulliver's Travels have translated "Blundecral" as "Alcoran" or "Blunder-All." But in this day and age, I dare say, this is an outright, deadly blasphemy. A safer, and more accurate translation would be in resorting to the original Hebrew "Doesn't promise anything." (In Hebrew: Bli Neder Clal.)

74. The resemblance between this speech and the one Gen. Patton made to his troops prior to D-Day (June 5th, 1944) is quite eerie.

I know for sure that no one before me has ever seen Mary's manuscript, so I suspect that the General, perhaps as a child, discovered the descendants of those Lilliputians who were kidnapped by Captain Biddle and rescued by Mary. (Mary tells of these events in Chapters Twenty and on.)

Little Patton must have heard from the Lilliputians about the famous speech of Blogolam, and it made such an impression on him that he repeated it almost word for word when the opportunity presented itself to him.

75. Another misconception that resulted from Mary Burton-Gulliver's reluctance to publish her diary is the common mistake that the word "chaperone," in the sense of "protector," dates from 1720 (and later in Jane Austin's "Elinor and Marianne", 1811.)

Originating from the French word *chaperone*, which means "the hood of a hawk," the word lent its protective usage to describe the person who accompanies a helpless person out in the world.

Women are still considered helpless in many parts of the world.

76. The London Penny Post was established in 1680 by William Dockwra to supplement the service of the Royal General Post Office, which only operated between cities and towns.

It started as a courier service for royal purposes only, but soon the royal purpose of making money inspired the Duke of York to make the services of the Royal Courier available for anyone who's willing to pay for it. Trouble was that the London Penny Post, charging one penny (from the receiver of the post) for a same-day delivery within the cities of Westminster, London and Southwark, only enriched Dockwra.

So, in 1683 the English Monarchy claimed the business to itself, on the grounds that Dockwra was circulating newsletters that were criticising the Duke of York. (William Dockwra, by the way, died a pauper.)

Successive governments started raising the prices, saying that the money was needed to finance the wars with France. The tradition of raising prices under the pretext of war is still successfully practiced to this day worldwide.

77. A short note on contraceptives in the 17th Century:

First historic evidence of women understanding their fertility cycles well enough to plan their families is of African and Native American women in the 17th and 18th centuries. Mary Burton-Gulliver's manuscript is a groundbreaking document, proving that English women were also privy to this knowledge.

We can assume from this one line in Mary's memoir that Stella was monitoring the quality of her cervical mucus, to make a judicious decision on the best time of the month to take a few days' trip. Other methods known at that time were coitus interruptus, breastfeeding, vinegar and of course, condoms.

78. Mary writes freely in her diary about all sorts of bodily activities, but she never mentions bathing. So, Gulliver's scent must have been quite strong, and Lilliputian women were attracted to this.

This attraction to smell might have to do with natural selection. Females tend to mate with males who exhibit signs of being stronger, of working harder than other males.

With the impending success of Women's Lib, though, the natural selection starts shifting, and men start wearing perfumes, desperate to attract successful, hard-working women.

79. The close chair was invented in London in the early 1630s, and later was called "sedan chair."

Sed from the Latin *Sella:* carried chair, though Henry Peacham, author of *Coach & Sedan* (1636) claims that the name comes from the Principality of Sedan, on the North European mainland. Hardly probable, since that place was a Protestant enclave, and the first person to have his chair being carried for him was the Pope, as early as the 16th century.

The idea that VIPs should be carried in special wagons, preferably by toiling humans, never wore off, and by the 21st century we see stretch limousines fulfilling the same purpose.

Impression-making vehicles were to be rented as early as 1634. By the late 18th century, more than 2,000 sedan chairs were available to hire in over 37 cities and towns across Great Britain and Ireland.

Talking about the Pope, a recent one bravely declined to use his bullet-proof Pope-mobile, claiming that God would protect him.

80. The Colossus took twelve years to build, in the 3rd Century BC, in the harbour of Rhodes. It was said to be constructed by the architect Chares from scrap metal of abandoned war ships of Antigonus.

Despite having an army larger than the entire population of Rhodes, the Greeks gave up on the idea of conquering it, when the Egyptian navy came to the rescue of Rhodes. And, thus, the Rhodesians made a clever and creative use of all that metal and wood, erecting a 110-foot-high sculpture, standing on a 50-foot pedestal. Ships could sail in and out, between Colossus' spread legs for 56 years, until it was struck down by an earthquake.

81. Asimov explains that, given the difference in size between Gulliver and the Lilliputians, items such as a needle and a thread, that would be plainly visible to any Lilliputian, might well be invisible to Gulliver's grosser vision.

In our own world, loss of sharp eyesight serves as a great aphrodisiac for ageing lovers, who can't see anymore the blemishes on their lovers' bodies. In this respect, cataract operations are a grave mistake.

82. Mead is a fermented alcoholic drink. It is known to have been around for the last 9,000 years, according to archaeological findings.

There's a recipe from 1669 stating: "Whereby is Discovered Several ways for making of Metheglin, Sider, Cherry-Wine, &c. together with Excellent Directions for Cookery: As also for Preserving, Conserving, Candying, &c. First edition, London, 1669."

83. We must remember that the political system in Lilliput, at that time at least, was not like ours today. The reference to "parties" should be compared to the concept of "parties" in English politics as it was until the mid-19th century.

At that time, ordinary people were ruled by the Royalty, which was aided by two groups of people calling themselves the Whig Party and the Tory Party. Indeed, the one thing over which they were unanimous was the fact that they could party, while the ordinary people had to work, and work hard.

The aristocratic dynasties formed the Whigs (and later were forced to accept into their folds the emerging industrial interests and wealthy merchants).

The Tories were the landed gentry. They also had their religious affiliations since the Church was essential in keeping the ignorant population ignorant and obedient.

Women were of course at the bottom of this political power food chain.

84. Another point of note to consider is the crucial importance of eggs. We can see it also in the rest of the known world. As far back as human memory goes, aided by archaeological evidence all over the globe, the egg has always been a symbol of fertility and life.

So much so that, already in the 9th century, the heads of church recognised its symbolic importance and therefore banned the eating of eggs during the 46 days of Lent. The result was asserting even greater power over the populace and increasing the sales of eggs in Easter.

85. It seems that Lilliputians' life span was as short in years as they were short in stature. If we calculate the Lilliputian life span to be one-twelfth of humans, and knowing that in the 17th century the average life span was 36 for the poor and 60 for the rich and famous, we can assume that poor Lilliputians lived 4 years and the rich 12. Of course, they lived faster.

Anyway, this can explain their Lunar Time-Measure System and their botching it so well.

By the way, according to a UN report published in June 2000, contemporary human life span was 37.9 for the poor and 100 for the rich.

Noting in alarm that the top 200 billionaires had the combined wealth of $1,135 bn (up by $100 bn from the previous year), while the total income of the 582 million people in all the developing countries, barely exceeded

10% of that ($146 bn), the UN declared that these inequalities should be classified as human rights violations. So it was declared.

That was in 2000. Since then things have changed, but not for the better.

One solution, which seems to be very popular among the 200 billionaires, is called The New World Order, in which this inequality will be fixed by reducing the number of the rest of humanity.

86. See Note 73.

87. Even though the saying goes: "Taxes and death are the two certain things in life," in fact, the first ever tax to be introduced in England was in 1572, the Poor Law Tax, which was the best solution Queen Elizabeth could find for the sudden increase in the number of the poor. The blame could be squarely placed on her predecessor, Henry VIII, whose lust drove him to establish a new religion. This resulted in hundreds of thousands of unemployed monks and nuns, the nouveau-poor.

While Henry VIII confiscated the Church's riches for himself, the religious rug was pulled from under the feet of the English population. Whereas till then religious values and social pressure dictated that alms should be given to the poor, Henry's flip-flop resulted in the disillusionment of the people. Up until then, everyone felt noble when parting with a penny to help the poor, but now they took example from their monarch, and couldn't care less about others.

The rest is history. Taxes of all sorts and justifications were introduced ever since, and by now they seem as essential as the sun which circles the earth, and as unavoidable as Death.

88. In England, the job of treasurer was the most important one in court. Seeing that control was no longer gained by fists and armoury but by purchase powers, the man who held the key to the treasury was the man who held the key to the Ruler's whims.

Not all treasurers were equally apt, and Elizabeth I (1533–1603) inherited a royal debt. But thanks to Lord Treasurer Winchester and his successor, Burghley, by 1584, when the debt was gone and the royal coffers were stuffed with the spoils of one year's revenue, Elizabeth called Burghley fondly, "Both Our Treasurer and Our principal treasure."

Lord High Treasurer Burghley's death in 1598 and the incapability of his successor, Thomas Sackville, led to the Stuarts spending more money than they could amass. Charles II (1630–1685) was so broke that he couldn't pay his navy enough for proper maintenance, resulting in the humiliating defeat at sea by the Dutch in 1667. Recognising that his navy was not at fault, Charles II replaced his treasurer, appointing George Downing (who was also into real-estate, building Downing Street) as Secretary to the Commission whose wise pondering led to the treasury no longer being responsible for keeping AND spending the royal's money.

The concept of divide and rule that worked so well for the Roman emperors, was now adopted also for internal affairs, and as soon as a committee was set on an issue, the last word was back again with the ruler.

Interestingly, Downing was also the man who invented what is now known as government bonds. He also abolished the business of private tax collectors, recognising that cutting out the middleman would leave the treasury with more income. For a while people were happy, thinking that with the demise of the cruel private tax collectors, their tax miseries would be over.

In the context of the treasury, I'd like to tell you about Lady Damaris Cudworth Masham (1659–1708.) Too little is known about how instrumental she was in shaping the thought of the philosopher John Locke (1632–1704), who also acted as an unofficial economic adviser to the treasury. The concept of a person's ownership of his or her body is one of many that John Locke would have grasped from his intercourse with Lady Masham.

89. Not surprisingly, it was a Germanic tribe, the Saxons, that introduced the policing system to England in the 5th century.

The Saxon rulers divided their people into groups of ten, named "tythings." One of the ten was representing the group; each ten tythings had its "hundred-man" who was responsible to the Shire-reeve, or Sheriff, of the county. This system took deep roots by the 17th and 18th centuries when each parish appointed or elected annually a suitable person to serve for a year as the parish constable.

Already then, the job was underpaid and, in fact the first constables were not paid at all.

In the towns, it was the guilds' responsibility to keep the public peace, and they hired men to guard the city gates and enforce the nightly curfew. Their name, "The Watch" derives from the mission of keeping the streets empty as a measure to prevent crimes from being committed—on the streets.

90. The institution of army has evolved smoothly and naturally from the feudal times, when the lords were obliged to deliver to the king a certain number of soldiers (knights, men-at-arms and yeomanry) to fight for him upon request.

The number of soldiers to be delivered depended on the size of land the lord got from the king, and the number of people populating it. The people were counted as the lord's property, along with the flora and fauna. Those accidental bands were forged into the first professional army, called the New Model Army, as a result of the Civil Wars of 1642–1651.

Even though it was called a civil war, it was quite savage. It cost a total of 868,000 combined casualties on the English, Scottish and Irish sides (about 11.5% of the population). The opposing parties were numerous and hard to distinguish between: Royalists against Parliamentarians; dissenting nonconformist religious sects; English against Scots and against Irish; Catholics against Protestants, and many shades in between, as allegiances were shifting along with the outcome of various battles and the everchanging anticipation of who would ultimately win.

War has always had manifold advantages for its initiators: it was, and still is, good for the business of arms trade, it is a great excuse to raise taxes, a good camouflage for channelling national funds for personal needs of the one doing the channelling, and an excellent way to keep the numbers of the populace low enough for the rulers to control.

When that war was exhausted in 1651, it drifted to the seemingly cleaner fields of politics, with new opportunities presenting themselves to send young people to kill each other, first in 1648, with the Second English Civil War and then, in 1649, with the Third Civil War.

Eventually the army itself became the target of the conflict between the parliamentarians and the monarch. The Bill of Rights, which the English Parliament passed in 1689, defined the new power balance, preventing the monarch from keeping an army in peacetime, without the consent of Parliament, a tradition that is kept to this day, when Parliament must convene at least once a year to renew the Army Act, as it is now called.

The rest is a bloody history of wars all over the rest of the world, all legalised in parliaments, blessed and glorified by religious authorities.

91. Mary scribbled here a note on the edge of the page: "Shall I omit this, before the book is published?" I guess Mary was worried lest men would read this line and start suspecting their wives.

I decided to leave this remark, thinking that we've reached a stage in history in which men started recognising women's talents, and cunning is no longer needed in man-woman relations. Well, at least in some quarters of the western world. And at least so long as America doesn't attempt to be "great again."

92. To the keen reader, this is not a spelling mistake. Apparently "teat" was the word used already since the 1540s relating to small things and, when relating to women, in a deprecatory sense.

93. Some might find it bizarre that Mary refers to Saturday as the Sabbath. No, she was not a Jew.

The controversy whether the day off should be celebrated on Saturday (as many believed was decreed by no other than God) or Sunday (as many others believed was decreed by no other than God) became an issue in the years that followed Henry VIII's break with the Catholic Church, when he forced the Act of Supremacy (1534) on his populace.

When the Pope wouldn't bend God's known laws to fit Henry's marital wishes, Henry forced the whole of England to change their religious allegiances and follow his new take on religion.

One of the changes he instituted was the keeping of the Sabbath on Saturday. It took a few centuries and many debates before England synchronised its week with the rest of the Christian world.

94. Evidently, Mrs. Poppins was a midwife.

Midwifery was a respected profession ever since God "dealt well with the midwives" (Exodus, Chap. 1, verse 20) back in Pharaoh's Egypt.

Since those days, midwifery was practiced by men, too, and in the 17th and 18th centuries, their tools were butter, to help ease the baby's passage, and scissors, needle, and thread, to cut and tie the umbilical cord.

By the way, the fashion dictated a tight tie for baby girls, to ensure that when they became women, their wombs would hold their babies tight. Baby boys, on the other hand, would require a dangling umbilical cord, to ensure that their reproductive organs would be well endowed.

95. A few readers pointed out to me that this word is cut abruptly. Indeed, that's exactly what seems to have happened. Mary dropped her quill, due to the sharp and sudden pains of labour contractions, and when she recovered

and resumed writing, she overlooked the fact that her previous sentence was not complete.

96. Though not on par with physicians, midwives were requested by the Church to get a certificate, give an oath and pay a fee, as far back as the 16th century.

The midwife's oath ensured her loyalty to the Church and in fact, made her a Church-informer, regarding the parish's morals. Besides helping in childbirth, the midwife was also expected to perform Baptism in emergency cases, when a baby would not survive.

Interestingly, the midwife's oath also included the promise that she would "not use any kind of sorcery or incantation in the time of the travail of any woman." (One must conclude that in earlier periods of history the midwife was also a witch.)

97. Apparently, Mary came across a copy of *Observations in Midwifery* by Percival Willoughby (1596–1685).

We can assume from Mary's writing that she kept her ability to read a secret from her women friends, and also from her midwife, but it's safe to assume that she did read this pioneering book.

In *Observations in Midwifery*, Willoughby tried to convince midwives to let nature take its course in birthing. It seems that already in the 16th century the medical world treated the body of a birthing woman as a tool that couldn't function without medical intervention. The needs and well-being of the mother-to-be did not concern most birthing practitioners already then.

98. The invention of the forceps is incredulously credited to Pierre (Peter) Chamberlen (1560–1631). The official version is that Peter Chamberlen invented this method of pulling the baby out of the womb.

His children and grandchildren, who were also obstetricians, managed to keep this instrument a family secret for three generations. Their scheme of keeping the secret was to get everyone out of the room and to blindfold the mother. The forceps would be brought into the house in a large box and only opened once the coast was clear.

These forceps were finally discovered in 1813 under a trap door in the loft of Woodham Mortimer Hall, the family's home, and so the secret was revealed. This is the official version.

Mary's memoir presents us with alternative facts, and this time it clearly exposes another incident of denial of women's ingenuity. Either the forceps were stolen from Mrs. Poppins, or, to give the Chamberlens the benefit of the doubt, the family's secret was not that well-kept.

Today's enlightened readers might assume that the forceps were kept a secret for commercial reasons. Wrong. The real reason was that the Midwifery Oath, which was taken when getting the license from the local Bishop, stated that the midwife will not use any instrument.

99. Some readers might be startled by the fact that Mrs. Poppins didn't slap the baby to get him to start breathing. This manner of resuscitation enjoyed but a short vogue in medical history in the beginning of the 20th century and today is no longer practiced.

100. The Gypsy was probably right. The third child was Lemuel, whom Mary tended to as a child for many years.

101. Besides keeping the room warm and welcoming for the newborn, the fire was also believed to keep evil spirits outside. The shut windows had a similar function, but probably the true reason was to muffle the screams of the mother-to-be.

102. Mugwort is a herb known to induce labour, assist in birth and after-birth, and ease labour pains. When Mary mentions saffron, we can assume that she's referring to the common pain-killer which was popular in those days, made of 2 ounces of opium, 1 ounce of saffron, a drachm of cinnamon and cloves—all dissolved in a pint of Canary wine.

It is likely that Mary also read *The English Physician* (1652) by Nicholas Culpeper (1616–1654), who spent most of his life collecting and cataloguing hundreds of medicinal herbs. As we become acquainted with Mary, we can again assume that she liked Culpeper for his attitude.

Besides believing that no authority was beyond questioning, he was also critical of the unnatural methods of his contemporaries, and he worded that in such poetic, unscientific ways:

"This not being pleasing, and less profitable to me, I consulted with my two brothers, DR. REASON and DR. EXPERIENCE, and took a voyage to visit my mother NATURE, by whose advice, together with the help of DR. DILIGENCE, I at last obtained my desire; and, being warned by MR. HONESTY, a stranger in our days, to publish it to the world, I have done it!"

103. It seems that Mary had a healthy instinct protecting her from becoming addicted to opium. This is remarkable, noting that Thomas Syedenham (1624–1689), who was considered the "English Hippocrates" recommended opium to treat pain, sleeplessness, and diarrhea, asserting that:

"Among the remedies which it has pleased Almighty God to give to man to relieve his sufferings, none is so universal and so efficacious as opium."

Being a medical observation, this positive view on opium was maintained and manipulated by rulers in China to control their population up until the 16th century, and from the 18th century the British traded and smuggled opium into China, to make money and to control the Chinese rulers by trying to reduce them all to helpless opium addicts.

Interestingly, George Orwell (who once likened Britain to a wealthy family that maintains a guilty silence about the sources of its wealth) is closely linked by family ties to this history. Born as Eric Blair, George's father, Richard W. Blair, managed the production of opium on plantations near the Indian-Nepalese border as a civil servant, and also supervised the export to China.

Unfortunately for Orwell, the Blair family fortune had been largely squandered by the time he was born. That might explain why he switched sides, and tried in his novel *1984* to alert his fellow humans to the conspiracy of the rich and powerful. Unsuccessfully.

104. Five thousand Blustrugs is the equivalent of twelve miles. In Lilliputian terms it seemed to be the end of the world.

105. Luckily, nowadays important people settle for shorter, often abbreviated titles, such as HSH—His Serene Highness (as in Prince Albert of Monaco) or simply The Honorable (as in Al Gore) or Her Majesty (as in the Queen of England) or The Rt. Hon (The Right Honorable) So and So. And so on, and so forth.

106. There must be a reason for the evolution of such an elaborate ceremony, which only says, "I promise." It is likely that having gone through such complicated maneuvers, one cannot forget that he made a certain commitment.

It is probably similar to the proverbial making a knot in a handkerchief, which some older readers might remember. (It became extinct by the end of the 20th century, with the invention of paper towels and mobile phones.)

There's evidence that already in ancient Greece, it was agreed that "it is the oath which holds democracy together" (Lycurgus of Athens, 390–324 BC). Indeed, only when people make agreements and keep them can people survive as a group, with individuals depending on each other and helping each other.

This common knowledge is shared from time immemorial, with the Biblical first recorded oath which God gave humankind, of never again "smiting every living thing." With some minor exceptions, He did keep his oath and never produced a colossal, global flood again.

Mankind has imitated God, but has resorted to elaborate ceremonies to impress and imprint the agreements that were made. In ancient Judaism, one held the testicles of the person to whom he gave oath while pledging to do something. This historical fact is also to be assessed in the Latin *testiculus*, diminutive of *testis*, meaning "witness;" the Romans worshiped a stone, curiously naming it *Iuppiter Lapis*, on which pigs were slaughtered and the oath taker begging, "Strike the Roman people as I strike this pig here to-day, and strike them the more, as thou art greater and stronger." (I find it strange that the Roman people never questioned why they were the ones to suffer the consequences of the oath-taker breaking his own oath.)

Then came Jesus, the anarchist, who expressed his displeasure with the authorities of his time by calling on his fellow man not to be part of their system, not to feel obliged to the oaths, which authorities expected people to respect and abide by. Jesus' protest was soon embraced by newly emerging authorities, to be used and abused. To confuse people even more, words were joggled: "oath" was replaced with "affirmation" and later with "affidavit."

Secular and religious authorities of all shades and creeds, who have always recognised the validity of Lycurgus of Athens "it is the oath which holds democracy together," replaced as they pleased "democracy" with "republic," "communism," "fascism," "nationalism," etc. Adding the symbolic holding of the testicles (in the form of taxes, enemies, etc.), sprinkled the dish with the required amount of fear to make it easier for people to swallow, to this day.

107. See Note 68.

108. Glimigrim = Lilliputian potent alcohol. On top of its intoxicating properties, it was also diuretic, which proved to be Lemuel's doom.

109. Of course, once Lemuel was set free the name of his dwelling was no longer the Prison-Temple, but the Liberty-Temple.

110. Godsibb is an old English word, made of "God" and "sibb" (which comes from the German *Sippe* = close family).
  Originally used for what we now call Godparent, in the 16th century it took the meaning of describing a person (usually a woman) who cherishes idle talk, spreading news, rumours and shallow insights. (With the evolution of civilisation, these women are nowadays replaced by Yellow Journalism.)
  Women, as we saw in Chapter Eight, Note 54, were labouring to maintain their homes and families most hours of the day and night, so the only time they could sit, relax and exchange Godsibb, was while attending birthings.

111. See Chapter Eighteen.

112. In Mary Gulliver's time, the average life expectancy was just under 40 years. This statistic reflects the high rate of infant and child mortality.
  Documents of that period indicate that 2% of live babies would die in their first day of life. 5% would not survive a week. 4% would die within the month. 13% would not celebrate a birthday. 36% died before the age of six, 24% between the ages of seven and sixteen. Of 100 live babies who'd arrive in this world in the 17th century, 60 would die before the marriageable age of 16.
  Causes of death would start with birth trauma, such as tetanus (due to the use of an unsterilised knives or scissors to cut the umbilical cord), diarrhoea, infection and gangrene.
  Childhood diseases would include fungal infection, worms, whooping cough, diphtheria, dysentery, tuberculosis, typhus, typhoid fever, rickets, chicken pox, measles, scarlet fever and smallpox. Accidents were also featured in the annals of the day, such as drowning, either in laundry tubs, ditches, ponds, wells or the sea. Less frequent was burning, and ending this gruesome list is death by being run over by a cart or horse, or hit by a falling object.

113. The debate about baptising babies (pedobaptism, as opposed to credo-baptism) seems to have started, according to the *Didache, The Teaching of the Twelve Apostles*, somewhere in AD 40–60.

Credobaptists argue that people should be able to believe and to declare their faith when they join the church, while pedobaptists cite the new testament (Colossians 2:11–12) where baptism is described as a circumcision performed by Jesus, which relieves the newly baptised from further ruling of the flesh.

Since this is essential for eternal life in Heaven, pedobaptism was considered a crucial service for the newly born, lest he or she should die before being able to prove their good Christianity all by themselves.

If the Internet is any indication, the argument is as alive today as it has ever been, indicating that many people have nothing better to do.

I would like to add my humble addition to this debate, by noting that whenever and wherever Christianity was introduced into the world, most people who joined it were adults, and required credobaptism to mark their transition from one group of people to the other. During the ages, as this source of new recruits was exhausted, Church authorities, urged by secular rulers, were required to perform pedobaptism as a foolproof way of getting the believers to register their children and letting the rulers know how many people they ruled.

114. See Chapter Eight.

115. Menstruation has always been a mystery to mankind.

In ancient times, Hippocrates (460–370 BC) and Galen (AD 129–c. 216) explained that because women led a more sedentary lifestyle, their bodies were less efficient than men's at utilising the blood that they produced. The resultant buildup of blood and other waste in the female body had to be eliminated through menstruation for the sake of their health.

By the 17th century not much had changed. And while normal menstruation was still considered a manifestation of female illness, failure to menstruate monthly was also considered a disease.

Lazare Riviere (1589–1655) wrote a whole anatomy guide about women's health in which he counted that the womb was the source of "six hundred miseries and innumerable calamities."

He was not the first, and not the last. In the 1st century, Pliny (23–79 AD) proclaimed menstrual blood to be poisonous, turning wine to vinegar, causing trees and crops to die, clouding mirrors, blunting swords, and causing dogs to go mad should they chance to taste it.

In the 20th century similar opinions were rife, with one, Freud, suggesting that menstruation is the "bloody sign of a woman's loss of penis;" and it is a reminder of a woman's "uncleanliness and inferiority." Freud was undoubtedly influenced by the fact that menstruation was considered a bad thing far and wide, and throughout history. For example, menstruating women were refused communion by Christian churches, while in Judaism, Hinduism, and Islam, sex is outright out of the question during menstruation.

Feminists would claim that this is another manifestation of male domination, but, as much as they might be right, I think they too would agree that menstruating is not much fun.

116. Some readers (mostly female) might find the idea that a man has a right to "claim" his wife a bit bizarre. But throughout history, and certainly at the time of Mary Gulliver, owning people was the rule of the day. A husband's ownership of his wife, children and servants was commonly accepted as part of life, as was the King's ownership of them all, justified and glorified by God's ownership of kings and their dominions.

It probably evolved way back in prehistory, when the stronger specimen accumulated so many subordinates that sheer power was no longer sufficient to keep them enslaved. At that point (probably) higher powers were called into action, sowing the fear of the Gods into the hearts of the enslaved, assuring them that the King was appointed by those very Gods, who would make sure that the enslaved would be rewarded for their further obedience, surely, in the world to come. Since no slave has ever come back to contest the validity of that promise, rulers felt safe to bestow these promises right and left.

In Mary Gulliver's time, women were pretty much at the bottom of this power chain (God-King-Man.) As such, they were the property of their fathers and later, the property of their husbands.

117. Ever since biblical times, only male children were counted when telling the chronology of who begat whom. Therefore Lemuel Gulliver, in telling about himself, fails to mention that besides having five brothers he also had two sisters.

118. This is quite confusing. Mary seems to be quoting here from a play that was written more than hundred years after her death.

Edmond Rostand (1868–1918) wrote his smash-hit play *Cyrano de Bergerac* in 1897. It is based on the true story of Cyrano de Bergerac (1619–1655) written in beautiful French verse.

Cyrano, both the real and the fictionalised, had a mega-nose, which was admired and ridiculed far and wide. Due to his low self-esteem, he didn't dare express his love to Roxane, his beautiful cousin. She, in turn, was in love with Christian, a handsome, though slow-witted, musketeer.

Being the officer and gentleman that he was, Cyrano did everything he could to ensure Roxane's happiness. He whispered sweet verses in Christian's ear, and Christian repeated them in Roxane's ear. When Christian died in battle and heartbroken Roxane retreated to the monastery, Cyrano paid her weekly visits, in which he continued to entertain her with his wise verses.

Only when he was about to die in her arms did she realise that Christian's verses were Cyrano's and she laments, "I loved one man, and now I've lost him twice!"

It's impossible that Rostand was acquainted with Mary's diary, of course (since I am the first to ever set eyes on it), so I think we can conclude that this is a case of subconscious plagiarism. That is, if we believe in the existence of subconscious.

119. Just as any expression of the individual's free will has to be crushed in order to maintain social structure in which the few dominate the rest of us, so were sexual drives channeled into the institution of marriage.

At times labeled holy, and still appreciated as a great achievement for both parts of the union, marriage was the only legal framework for sexual activity.

Bearing in mind that sexual activity resulted in the production of new subordinates (of the father, King, God), it is easy to understand how sex and marriage were considered inseparable throughout history. In this context, any sexual activity that would not result in procreation was punishable by law, being deemed "unnatural."

This twisting of concepts got a major boost from Paul the Apostle nearly 2,000 years ago. In a breathtaking contortion of concepts and words, Paul the Apostle, in his Letter to Romans, managed to blind and confuse his readers for generations to come.

Paul cunningly uses the accepted role of women as property of their husbands to demonstrate that just as a woman can become another man's property upon the death of her previous owner, so does the death of Christ release the Jews from their chains to "that God" and thus they may have no scruples accepting the rule of the new one, Christ.

Paul's letter was religiously cited to define which sexual acts were acceptable and which were not. It is consistent with the patriarchal trend that he blames it all on women, even bestiality and homosexuality. (1:26: "For this reason God gave them up to vile passions. For even their females changed the natural use into one contrary to nature.")

In this respect it is somewhat comical to note that lesbianism wasn't recognised as a crime in many countries for many centuries. Only after 1550 do we find sexual acts between women listed among other unnatural acts in legal statutes, with death as the appropriate measure. But not all statutes include female-female acts in the list of no-no's. It was more the cross-dressing and women getting married with each other that threatened the delicate fibre of society than the fact that women were having some harmless fun.

Still, there were cases of women brought to trial and perishing all over Europe, with Holland somewhat lagging. The Sodomy Bill was only introduced there in 1730, and women were not even mentioned in it. This might explain the current-day Dutch tolerance to sexual diversions.

Another point of interest is that Queen Victoria removed any references to women in the Labouchere Amendment (Clause 11) of the Criminal Law Amendment Act of 1885, which outlawed oral sex between men. Common knowledge is that Queen Victoria could not believe that women "would do such things." Buggery, or anal sex between men, was already illegal, and the punishment was death. Only in 1967, with the Sexual Offences Act, was homosexual behaviour partially decriminalised. Partially.

120. There was an instance in modern history of practicing Lilliputian's child-rearing methodology, in the form of the Israeli Kibbutzim's Communal Child Rearing. It prevailed in those collective communities in Israel until about the end of the 1980s. The downfall of Communist Russia, due to bankruptcy, marked the end of communal life of the Israeli Kibbutzim.

Some say that Utopia will work well only when it will be all over the world. There is one village in Spain that proves the contrary, but I will not disclose its name.

121. Mary doesn't explain this point, and only mentions once more in her diary the subject of Gulliver's daily defecating. But putting together the various hints in her manuscript, we can deduce that Gulliver, in his ingenuity, realised that the volcano, with its flowing water, would serve as a perfect "water closet," or "Ajax," as it was known in the time of Mary and Lemuel.

The "Ajax" was invented in 1596 by Sir John Harington (1561–1612), godson of Queen Elizabeth I (1533–1603).

The first-ever flush toilet in England was built and installed at the Queen's chambers at Richmond Palace. At first everybody wanted to have one in their homes, of course, but as soon as it was known that the Queen refused to use it because it made too much noise, the "Ajax" fell into disrepute and even talking about it became taboo. The fact that Mary writes about this shows that some wise people did go about using the "Ajax," though more discretely.

122. See Chapter Eight.

123. Swaddling is a form of full-body diapering that was practiced throughout history, all over the world, till the 17th Century.

The theory was that, besides the benefit of easy transportation of the infant, keeping the immediate surrounding free of the baby's bodily rejects and restraining his free movement so he wouldn't wiggle away, the young creature would also learn at an early age that stronger powers than his or her own are controlling him or her at all times.

When the medical theory in favour of swaddles was disproved, it went out of fashion. Church attendance fell sharply and the rest is history.

124. *Lōtium* is the basic Latin noun for urine, relating to *lavāre:* to wash.

In the pre-soap Roman era, people preserved urine in cisterns, using the ammonia to wash their clothes. Some even washed their teeth with urine, which resulted in very white teeth and even a poem by Catullus (Verona, 82–54B C) about a man called Egnatius, who was prone to do just that:

> Egnatius, because he has white teeth,
> Is everlastingly smiling.
> If people come to the prisoner's bench,
> The counsel for the defence is making everyone cry,

He smiles.
If they are mourning
At the funeral of a dear son,
When the bereaved mother
Is weeping for her only boy,
He smiles.
Whatever it is, wherever he is,
Whatever he is doing, he smiles.
It is a malady he has,
Neither an elegant one as I think,
Nor in good taste . . .
There is nothing more silly
Than a silly laugh.
As it is, you are a Celtiberian.
Now in the Celtiberian country
The natives rub their teeth and red gums,
Every morning with what they have urinated,
So that the cleaner your teeth are,
The more urine you are shown to have drunk.

This of course is an allegory, and nowadays we wouldn't say that Egnatius was drinking urine and therefore smiling, but that he's been "licking asses" and therefore successful.

125. Indeed, deciphering the first paragraphs of this chapter was quite a challenge, since the handwriting was so shaky. It was obvious that Mary had suffered much, and it is amazing to realise how calming an effect it had to share one's experiences, even if only with oneself, as Mary did, writing down what had happened in such brave honesty.

126. Anyone who ever had to wear a surgical mask under the pretext of protecting others from catching a disease, would know that covering mouth and nose is a sure way of forcing submission.

127. Mary's range of knowledge is staggering. It seems she could also handle arms, or at least the flintlock pistol variety, which used a flint to strike sparks against a steel plate, in order to ignite a powder charge that would fire a bullet.

128. Sabbath comes from the Hebrew word *Shavat* which means "to stop," and it first appears in Genesis as the day in which God completed the creation of Earth and rested.

Following this example, the Jews were instructed to do nothing on the seventh day but to worship God. The male Jews, of course. The females were expected to prepare the meals and clean up just the same.

Those males who did work on the Sabbath were facing excommunication and even execution (which, of course, was carried out on a week day). Such harsh punishments were used throughout history and, to this day, to force people to do things they otherwise would not willingly do, such as pay taxes, desert the battlefield, etc.

So it is curious to note that not keeping the Sabbath was considered to be a mortal sin. It would be the equivalent of nowadays imprisoning someone for not going abroad for the summer holiday.

The only feasible explanation seems to be that people were then forced to spend much of their "free" day worshipping God. Other religions were quick to adapt this concept, though choosing different days as their Holy Sabbath, to demonstrate the righteousness of their respective Gods.

During those weekly forced visits to that variety of houses of worship, people were numbed with psalms and then exposed to brainwash, via sermons.

129. Lilliputian for "It's a nasty woman."

130. "Beware of us, Big Mountain Nasty Woman! Set us free!"

131. A corrody was the earliest form of pension practiced in England.

When Biddel gives this promise, he's referring to the "Chatham Chest." Established in 1590 by Sir John Hawkins and Sir Francis Drake, it helped convince young men to enlist to the navy, despite the grim fate of former sailors.

What tolled the Chatham Chest was nine months of sea war against the Spanish Armada, and nine months of active service in small ships. Many of those who didn't perish in battle came back to England suffering from ship fever, probably typhus. The death toll was such that young men were looking elsewhere for work.

Sir John Hawkins and Sir Francis Drake, fearing that there would be no new recruits to the navy, established the Chatham Chest, promising that it would provide pensions to disabled seamen.

If you wonder where the money came from, well, it was deducted from the salaries of the seaman. You didn't expect Sir John Hawkins, Sir Francis Drake or Queen Elizabeth to pay for it, or did you?!

132. Spangle: a shining tiny metallic piece, usually circular, that is sewn to clothing for decoration.

133. The debate on perpetual motion, that seems to have been perpetually debated, first appeared in writing in the *Philosophical Transactions of the Royal Society* by Denis Papin (1647–1712) in 1685. The quest for a machine that would operate forever echoes the humans' longing for eternal life.

134. See Note 35.

135. "Spike" was the colloquial name for the workhouse, a place where destitute London dwellers were, in fact, enslaved.

The origins of this practice can be traced as far back as to the Poor Law Act of 1388, which aimed at restraining the free migration of people. In the aftermath of the Black Death, which killed nine-tenths of England's population, whole villages and fields were abandoned. People were fleeing their homesteads, hoping that elsewhere conditions would be better. Work forces on the fields were dwindling, and those who fled were looking for higher wages. In between jobs, they were simply begging.

To curb this, new laws (which, by the way, had their revival in the 21st century, with the establishment of the European Union) prohibited migration and prohibited giving money to able-bodied beggars.

Unsurprisingly, consequent parliamentary acts, which obliged people to donate to the poor (but only via tax collectors), didn't diminish the number of the poor and, surely, didn't alleviate their suffering. And so, to keep the problem tucked away and, in the process, get cheap labor, workhouses were erected all over England, offering roof and food in return for hard labour.

The term "spike" refers to the tool used in the laborious task of picking oakum.

136. By now you probably have noticed how insistent ruling powers have always been in intervening in all aspects of people's lives, so it won't come

to you as a surprise that the most private feelings two people have for each other were also heavily regulated.

At the time of Mary Burton-Gulliver, rules obliged couples to register their impending union in the church archive. During the following three Sundays, the upcoming marriage would be announced at the service to enable contestants of this marriage to come forth and protest.

The Marriage Act was modified by Parliament a number of times throughout the ages, with the latest taking effect on October 1, 2012. It repealed the prohibition that forbade marriages to take place between 18:00 and 08:00. It took seven years of debating to establish this change.

The idea first struck lawmakers at the wedding ceremony of Charles, Prince of Wales, and Camilla Parker Bowles (April 9, 2005 at 12:30) when they realised that this was not a broadcast prime time, and revenues from commercials suffered accordingly.

137. *The London Gazette* started as *The Oxford Gazette* on November 7, 1665.

When the Royal House tried to escape the Plague by moving to Oxford, and anything "London" was deemed contagious, Henry Muddiman (1629–1692), a well-connected journalist, continued the publication of his news-books under the healthier name *The Oxford Gazette*. These publications were not sold to the wide public but were sent to subscribers, nobility and merchants.

138. Amazingly, this piece of paper has survived these 300 years, almost perfectly preserved among the pages of May Burton-Gulliver's manu-script.

139. Richard Sadler was running a Musick House when, in 1683, during a renovation of the gardens, discovered the mineral spring.

To increase clientele of his establishment, he claimed that the waters could cure "dropsy, jaundice, scurvy, green sickness and other distempers to which females are liable—ulcers, fits of the mother, virgin's fever and hypochondriacal distemper."

As even this was not enough to draw the crowds, live entertainment was also offered, not of the highest level, either. The Inquisitor of 1711 char-acterised Sadler's Wells as "a nursery of debauchery," most likely having seen the Lilliputians' performances.

140. See Chapter Eighteen.

141. This might be a good occasion to note that nobility communicates within its circles differently than it does with commoners. A person of nobility would be approached by a commoner as, for example, "Von" (in Germany) or "de" (in France), but when addressing each other, the nobiliary particle would be omitted.

I once saw a "Von" handing out his visit card to another "Von" and striking out the "Von" from his visit card.

We can see in this exchange between the Emperor and his Empress that the same etiquette was also practiced in Lilliput 300 years ago.

142. Since the "Ajax" went into disrepute (see Note 121) the Jake became the common word for the recently invented flush toilet. Since then, the Jake has changed many names: water closet, latrine, lavatory, loo, potty, privy, John, pothole, and crapper, to name but a few.

One wonders how the repulsion felt by humans towards their excrement made them look up names that would also keep the stench away.

143. What a lovely way to describe "brainwash"!

144. Laws against homosexual people who were considered to commit the crime of sodomy (called in England and Wales "buggery," referring to anal intercourse between two males) were first defined in the Buggery Act of 1533, during the reign of Henry VIII. Up until 1861, convicted criminals faced the death penalty.

In 1957 the Wolfenden report pointed out that the function of government's laws is not to intervene in the private life of its citizens. Still, it took another 10 years for sexual acts between two adult males to be made legal in England and Wales, while it was only made legal in Scotland in 1980 and in Northern Ireland in 1982.

The USA is trailing behind, seeing that only in 2003 anti-homosexual sodomy laws were invalidated by the U.S. Supreme Court decision Lawrence v. Texas.

Curiously, lesbian relationships were never deemed illegal. We can see here again the heavy mark of chauvinism: Heterosexual men were always aroused by the sight of women loving each other.

145. This might be another uncanny example of the phenomena of different people creating similar, sometimes identical, texts.

This is what Voltaire (1694–1778), a French Enlightenment writer, historian, and philosopher, wrote in his essay "Kissing."

146. No, Balegule was not a slave. Africans were never slaves in England, ever since 1569, when the English court resolved that England had "too pure an air for slaves to breathe in." This did not prevent English men and women to own slaves elsewhere in the world.

By 1833, when the Slavery Abolition Act made it illegal for English citizens to own other people, some 46,000 English citizens owned about 800,000 slaves.

The Act, which freed the slaves, also compensated financially the owners for the loss of their property. The government paid a total of £20m, 40% of the total expenditure for 1834 and the equivalent of £16 bn to £17 bn of today's money.

That was money raised by taxes levied on the people, not on the slave owners. The freed slaves received their freedom and nothing more, of course. More than that, in the next four years after they had been "liberated," they were forced to work for their former masters, unpaid, 45 hours a week.

The staggering sum of £16 bn to £17 bn is only surpassed by another bailout, that of the British banks in 2009.

147. It is for a good reason that the official age of recruitment is usually very young: sixteen for the British army, and seventeen for the United States, Bahrain, Iran, Kazakhstan, Mexico, Pakistan, and Tajikistan. And Turkmenistan will make soldiers of fifteen-year-old children.

The reason being, most likely, that at this tender age the concept of death is unfathomable, and the poor youngsters feel invincible. Till they're killed, and then it's too late.

148. Gulliver was 39 years old at that time. Nowadays we would attribute his behaviour to mid-life crisis, which could explain his strange reactions.

149. So, Monsanto was not the first to try and own all food available. Some might see the history of Monsanto as giving hope to humanity.

This publicly-traded American multinational agrochemical and agricultural biotechnology corporation was founded in 1901 by one 30-year-old John Francis Queeny.

Figuring that using his own name might sound presumptuous, he used his wife's maiden name instead. By now, Monsanto is a monarchy de facto that tries to rule the world's supply of all foods and, in the process, poisons many.

150. See the debate about the Time Deity in Chapter Twelve.

151. We can assume that it was for the sake of the rhythm of her book, and in order to build up the tension, that Mary created here a new chapter. As we can see by the date, she wrote this chapter the same evening she wrote the previous chapter. (And this she did without attending a single creative writing course!)

152. 6 feet is 1.8288 meters.

Imitating the act of separation which is told in the Biblical story of the tower of Babel, powers that rose ever since adapted the simple trick of divide and rule wherever it was possible: languages, measures, currencies, etc.

153. Man-of-war in this context is not the painfully aggressive jellyfish. Mary uses man-of-war here to describe a powerful warship or frigate.

154. 30 yards is 27.432 meters.

155. Women were expected to ride horses sitting aside rather than astride the horse, as far back as can be remembered. There is evidence of this on ancient Greek vases, sculptures, and Celtic stones.

Since it is only possible to control a horse by riding it astride, it was decreed that side-riding was the right, modest way for a woman to be transported from place to place.

Early sidesaddles were but a seat mounted behind the man's saddle, enabling the woman to be relatively comfortable hugging the rider's back, or while a male person would walk leading her horse. Common knowledge had it that the woman who would ride a horse astride would lose her virginity. Yet, married women were also expected to ride using sidesaddles.

Unsurprisingly, there were two women who invented the sidesaddle that enabled them to actually control their horses, by adding "horns" that allowed them, modestly, under the cover of the long skirts, to grip the saddle with their thighs. These were Anne of Bohemia (1366–1394) and, later, Catherine de' Medici (1547–1559).

We owe much to nonconformist, brave women such as Diane de Poitiers (1499–1566), mistress to Henry II of France, Marie Antoinette (1755–1793), and Catherine the Great of Russia (1729–1796), who defied conventions and rode astride, most likely because they were riding other powerful horses: their male lovers/husbands.

156. Sadly, Mary's crucial contribution to the rescue of the Lilliputians was totally forgotten.

According to the chronicles revealed in *Mistress Masham's Repose* (White, T.H., G.P. Putman's Sons, New York, 1946), future generations of Lilliputians never heard of the woman-mountain named Mary Burton-Gulliver, and didn't know how much they were indebted to her.

We cannot attribute this to female oppression (unfortunately), since a similar denial of a similar history is also to be found in the Jewish Hagadah. Celebrating annually for the last 3,000 years their escape from slavery in Egypt, the Jewish descendants of the enslaved read the Hagadah, which glorifies the role of God in their release, and only once mentions Moses, who took many risks and did much work.

157. "A Lilliputian Ode on the ENGINE with which Captain Gulliver extinguish'd the Flames in the Royal Palace," published anonymously May/June 1727):

I.

Engine strong,

Thick and long!

With Surprize,

Have our Eyes,

View'd its Size;

And its Nose,

Like a Rose;

And its Beard,

Much rever'd!

How it stood,

When the Flood,
Pouring down,
Sav'd the Town!
Ev'n the Queen,
Who has seen
How it plays,
In Amaze
Fury quits;
And has Fits
Of Delight,
Since the Sight.
'Tis a Thing
Makes the King
Sometimes glad,
Sometimes sad;
Pray Heav'n he run not mad

II.
O how strange
Is the Change
In the Crowd!
Wives are loud
In its Praise;
And with Bays
Want to spread
Its high Head!
Maids, with Joys,
Hear the Boys
Talk it o'er,
And adore!
Husbands now
Jealous grow;
And a-Nights
Are in Frights!
All Day long,
Every Tongue
Says or sings
Wondrous Things.

Titty Tit,*

Master Wit,

Tries in vain,

Lofty Strain,

To set forth

Its Magnitude and Worth!

*This is a name under which Pope published poems on Gulliver.

III.

Mountain-Man,

He who can

Reach thy Fame,

And proclaim

Stature odd,

Is a GOD.

O descend,

As a Friend,

To our State;

And beget

Such a Race

In this Place.

Female blest,

By thee prest;

Whose fierce Fire

Of Desire

Thy great Tool

Can but cool!

But 'tis such,

That too much

We intreat!

Ah! hard Fate.

One Flame out,

'Tis past doubt,

That thy Parts

Have rais'd one in our Hearts.

158. By now we know that Mary Burton-Gulliver did manage to come back and to write down what REALLY happened to Lemuel in Brobdingnag, and

how she saved him—and herself—from the giants.

It will all be told in the next book, *Mrs. Gulliver and the Mystery of Men*, that will be published as soon as circumstances will allow it.

Bibliography

Apple, Rabbi Dr. Raymond. "The Two Wise Women of Proverbs Chapter 31." *The Jewish Bible Quarterly*, Vol. 39, No. 3, July–September 2011.

Asimov, Isaac (editor), and Jonathan Swift. *The Annotated Gulliver's Travels*. Clarkson N. Potter, Inc., 1980.

Brabcová, Alice. "Marriage in Seventeenth-Century England: The Woman's Story." *Theory and Practice in English Studies, Volume 2*. Masaryk University Press, 2004

Brown, Richard. *Society and Economy in Modern Britain 1700–1850*. Routledge & Sons Ltd., 1991.

Canfield Willis, Marjorie. *Medical Terminology: The Language of Health Care*. Lippincott Williams & Wilkins, 2005.

Defoe, Daniel. *An Essay Upon Projects*. Project Gutenberg, May 2003, https://www.gutenberg.org/files/4087/4087-h/4087-h.htm.

Fairchilds, Cissie C. *Women in Early Modern Europe, 1500–1700*. Pearson Education Ltd., 2007.

Felkin, William. *A History of the Machine-Wrought Hosiery and Lace Manufacturers*. Longmans, Green, & Co., 1867.

Fell, Alison. *The Mistress of Lilliput*. Anchor Books, 1999.

Greenberg, Robert A. (editor) and Jonathan Swift. *Gulliver's Travels: An Annotated Text with Critical Essays*. W. W. Norton & Company, 1961.

Hindle, Steve. *Dependency, Shame and Belonging: Badging the Deserving Poor, c. 1550–1750*. University of Warwick Institutional Repository, 2004.

Hunt, Lynn Avery (editor). *The Invention of Pornography, 1500–1800: Obscenity and the Origins of Modernity*. Zone Books, 1996.

Marcus, Sharon. *Between Women: Friendship, Desire, and Marriage in Victorian England*. Princeton University Press, 2007.

More, Thomas. *Utopia*. Sterling Publishing, 2005.

Paley, Maggie and Ruzzier, Sergio. *The Book of the Penis*. Grove Press, 2000.

Slade, Joseph W. *Pornography and Sexual Eepresentation: A Reference Guide*. Greenwood Publishing Group, 2001.

Smith, Captain Alexander. *Key Writings on Subcultures, 1535–1727, Vol. 3*. Routledge & Sons Ltd., 1926.

Toulalan, Sarah. *Imagining Sex: Pornography and Bodies in Seventeenth-Century England*. Oxford University Press, 2007.

Voltaire, François. *The Philosophical Dictionary*, selected and translated by H. I. Woolf. Alfred A. Knopf, 1924.

Ward, Ned. *The Second Volume of the Writings of the London-Spy*. J. How, 1706.

About the Author

Now a Dutch citizen, Erga Netz was born in Israel. She moved to the Netherlands in 1988 for her work as a TV and film producer-director and editor. Since 2012, she has focused on cultural entrepreneurship, production and theatre acting. And writing.

Oh, Gulliver! is her debut novel, to be followed by four more novels in the series.

Visit www.antv-amsterdam.com to find out more about her past work, and you can get much more information about Mrs. Gulliver at www.mrsgulliversecret.com

Acknowledgments

The author and publisher would like to thank the following individuals for their generous financial support, which helped to make this publication of *Oh, Gulliver!* a reality:

Ofir De Groote Abe, Kevin Adams, Yochanan Afek, Annette Anderson, Ohad Arama, Irit Asher, Piete Avrahami, Shabtay Bonfeel, Rev. Justin Baldwin-Bonney, Thomas Young Barmore Jr, Nick Barry, Yael Ben-Shalom, Sam Bertram, Batya Ten Brink, Marisa Broitman, David Brownless, Bruno!, Michala Carter, Elaine M. Cassell, Mordechai Chachamu, Rolanda and Julian Chagrin, Edwin Chappell, Scott Chiddister, Joel Coblentz, Trude Cone, John Coombs, S Costa, Uri Cotani, Jason Crane, Malcolm & Parker Curtis, David, Flip de Liema, Edward De Vere, Joshua Doughty, Ira Dvir, Matthew Egerton, Isaac Ehrlich, Livat Eschar-Netz, Colleen M. Fagan, Fawn of the Woods, Fred Filios, Richard France, Justin Gallant, Gershon Gershon, Nir Geva, GMarkC, Damian Gordon, David Greenberg, Francis Greenburger, Lesley Hall, Ole Steen Hansen, Gwendolyn Hartung, Chloe Ana Haskins, Loes Hegger, Erik Hemming, Aric Herzog, Dave Holets, J. Holmes, Elijah House, France Hyman, Steve Irwin, Volodia Itskovich, Fred W Johnson, Jacob H Joseph, Sergey Kochergan, Nurit ter Kuile-Herschowich, Kyle, Stephane Lacoste, Michelle LaCrosse, The Ladinskys, Brian Lallatin, J.J. Larrea, Cari Liebenberg, Gardner Linn, Nick Long, Bert Maas, Orly Mani, Donald McGowan, Jack Mearns, Spencer F Montgomery, Savvy Moore, Steven Moore, Gregory Moses, Scott Murphy, David Natale, B Newton, Joseph Nicely, Richard Novak, Michael O'Shaughnessy, Iftach Ophir, Mirav Ozeri, Drew Palacio, Natalie Paz, Andrew Pearson, Lilach Peled, Orian Peled, Pedro Ponce, David K Pryor, Orly Noa Rabinyan, Rachel Rashal, Judith Redding, Michal Reichman, Blair Roberts, Dubi Roman, Saxo and Chubbles, Martin Stein & Scott Saxon, Florian Schiffmann, Jozien Schreuder, Boaz Shulruf, Spike Schwab, Peter Skolnik, Yvonne Solomon, Ilana Stel,

K. L. Stokes, Michelle and Perry Swenson, Brian T, Shirley T.,
Jacob Tashoff, Threemoons, Jennifer Trethewey, Ariel Tsovel,
Sydney Umaña, Ronald Veldman, Audrey Gran Weinberg,
Charles Wilkins, Marcel Wolf, T.R. Wolfe, Beth Worley,
WovenPixel (Danie Evans), The Zemenides Family, and Anonymous